THE NEW DAWN

THE NEW DAWN

TERMINATE THE OTHER WORLD!

BOOK 5

Icalos

Podium

To all my family and friends as well as my loyal Patreon and Royal Road readers, who made these books possible. Thank you!

Cover design by Husa

ISBN: 978-1-0394-8985-1

Published in 2025 by Podium Publishing
www.podiumentertainment.com

THE NEW DAWN

1

All Roads Lead to Corvanus

"Burn our cities. Burn as many of them as you like. Burn Elteno itself, as many times as you can. We will rise again regardless. The strength of Elteno is not in cities or walls but in its people."

—Magister Utriusque Militia Quintis Caesonius Sarimarcus, when rejecting an ultimatum from the Empire of the Sun.

The situation was grim.

High King Xavlaeron of Mirima, true master of the Southern Realms, had led a fleet of battle airships and the Sky Legion to strike at NSLICE-00P's base of power in Turannia. The Eastern Court was said to be facing one of the worst invasions in its history. Magister Utriusque Militia Verrucosis had declared martial law over the North and ruled mostly uncontested. And all the while, the shadowy cult alleged by the former Magister Exploratore Appius remained at large, surely using the chaos to advance their plans.

But, well, none of that mattered to Emperor Lucius! Not anymore, at least.

The man slowly rose from his bed. He thought of resting a bit longer, but the sun was now shining through his window. As such, he sat up and stretched, yawning as he did. He wondered what he should request for breakfast . . .

"Good morning, Emperor Lucius."

Emperor Lucius turned to face the voice, finding someone standing at the foot of his bed. Someone other than the guards. His eyes widened.

"You are . . ."

* * *

Magister Verrucosis gritted his teeth as he sat in his office.

How dare that Xavlaeron leave him behind! It was obvious the high king was planning to hog all the glory for himself! This was a problem of the North, and the North's Legion deserved to lead the charge!

He was interrupted by a knock at the door. A moment later, his second-hand man, Magister Peditum Ausonius, entered the room.

"Are we ready yet?!"

Magister Peditum Ausonius took a deep breath before unrolling a scroll. "Our forces have been deployed as ordered; Aedile Hortensus has no further complaints as to procedure. The former Magister Appius is still day drinking at the local tavern, and Emperor Lucius has been quiet. By all accounts, Corvanus is under control and has come to accept your leadership."

Magister Verrucosis exhaled his breath. That was just about the only good thing to come of this. Emperor Lucius's leadership was clearly lacking, Consul Noxisius had been murdered in his own home, the cowardly Consul Hiberius had fled after defending the murderer, and the weak and lazy Aedile Hortensus wouldn't lift a finger to do, well, anything. It was about time the North had a true leader. A strong leader. One who would not allow the tragedies of the recent years to continue.

Magister Peditum Ausonius then frowned. "However . . . the troops are restless. And after all that has happened, this sudden deployment has unnerved them. They are anticipating some sort of disaster that justifies their mobilization, and the officers are questioning the political situation in the meantime, not to mention the situation with the Aesdes.

"Most of the limitanei still can't use their skills, and even some of the comitatenses are no longer confident in their abilities. And then there's the theological and moral implications of the Aesdes withdrawing their support . . ."

Magister Verrucosis scowled. "Honestly, I expected better. What reason have they to fear? We have won mighty victories and restored order to the North, haven't we? We will pull through, with or without the Aesdes."

Magister Peditum Ausonius held his tongue. Magister Verrucosis stood up and began to pace with his hands crossed behind his back. Suddenly, he stopped, brought his arms forward, and then slammed his fist into his other hand's palm.

"I know what we shall do. Consul Hiberius openly supported the woman who attacked us, and then fled the moment we moved to restore order. His guilt is apparent. We shall move to apprehend him. We shall then call the patricians and governors of the provinces in and test their loyalty, with the consul as an example of what will happen to traitors."

Magister Peditum Ausonius narrowed his eyes. "I . . . would not recommend that course of action, Magister. Consul Hiberius's personal forces are substantial, and the Hiberius family's knight order is one of the strongest in the North.

"We will take casualties if he chooses to resist—casualties we cannot afford, as our current deployments are stretching us thin. And given the state of our troops and their morale, we're frankly in no shape for major operations. I would recommend we conduct exercises instead, and let the troops rebuild their confidence."

Magister Verrucosis scoffed. "As if that coward would put up a fight. His 'forces' have sat back and done nothing while we faced down the greatest crisis this Empire has ever seen. He is no threat. The troops will regain their lost nerve when they see that, and will learn by experience if they do not. Assemble the troops, Magister Peditum. I will take command shortly."

Ausonius slowly saluted. "As you will, Magister."

He waited until he left the room before heaving a sigh.

A short while later, Magister Verrucosis stood in the field just outside Corvanus, at the head of several legions. Aedile Hortensus and the other court nobles had gathered on the city walls to watch on the magister's insistence. The people of Corvanus had noticed the commotion and come to watch as well.

"Listen up! Just a short while ago, a vicious foreigner assaulted a consul in his own home! Yet, when we intended to bring her to justice, traitors in our ranks prevented us from doing so! Consul Hiberius betrayed Noxisius, betrayed Corvanus, and betrayed the Empire!"

Aedile Hortensus yawned, causing a vein to bulge on Magister Verrucosis's forehead.

"I say no more! I say the enemy who does not respect our laws or our strength shall be taught what it means to defy the Empire! I say the traitors who assisted her will be brought to justice, and our people shall be avenged! I say the Empire shall rise and become strong once more! Today, the Legion shall march forth! We shall apprehend the traitorous Hiberius, who tore the Empire apart for his own selfish ambitions and obstructed all attempts to set things right."

He then narrowed his eyes as he glanced at each member of the court.

"And I want each and every one of you to take this time to think. Remember where your loyalties lie, and the Empire you are called to serve. The Empire no longer has room for traitors and parasites, and I will see to it that all who exploit it meet the appropriate end."

Behind Magister Verrucosis, Magister Peditum Ausonius was keeping his expression as blank as possible. An officer standing nearby, Legate Lucceius, was not so stoic as he frowned.

"Magister Ausonius, do you agree with this? I served alongside the queen of the Dobhar during the subjugation of the Verdant Forest dungeon, and to my understanding, the investigation of her actions was still pending."

Magister Ausonius kept his eyes forward. "The high king of Mirima and Magister Verrucosis are clear on their position; it is no longer up to us to decide."

Legate Lucceius narrowed his eyes as Magister Verrucosis continued his speech. "Still . . . what the magister is saying, how he is talking . . . I can't say I'm comfortable with this. And where is the Emperor and the princess? Are we truly marching on our own in this situation?"

The other officers in the area didn't say anything, but several of them nodded in response to the question. Magister Ausonius heaved a sigh.

". . . What can we do?"

Legate Lucceius turned his head. "Sir?"

Magister Ausonius furrowed his brow. "Emperor Lucius has not left the palace since the high king arrived. Consul Hiberius fled Corvanus, abandoning his duties for the second time now. He is no longer an authority we can rely on. Consul Noxisius is dead. Aedile Hortensus has not objected.

"As such, Magister Verrucosis's orders stand, and he has the backing of the high king, who is currently bringing the full might of the South against the queen of the Dobhar. Even if we do not agree, by what authority would we refuse this order, and by what means would we resist it?"

Legate Lucceius's frown deepened, but he fell silent.

It was at that moment that one of the lookout towers sounded a horn. Everyone present, Magister Ausonius included, turned to look around as Magister Verrucosis scowled.

"Just what is . . ."

But he fell silent. In the distance, a fleet of airships appeared on the horizon, flying in from the North.

Significantly *less* airships than had originally set forth from Corvanus.

Magister Verrucosis scoffed. "Typical. Probably here to steal the glory yet again. Handle it, Magister."

Magister Ausonius nodded before shouting, "Form up!"

The command rippled through the legions, who turned to face the airships and got into a ceremonial formation to welcome the high king back. Magister Ausonius frowned as he counted the airships that remained . . . and saw the damage apparent on many. The queen of the Dobhar had clearly inflicted a heavy toll.

Soon, the airships arrived, stopping in the air some distance from the legions. Magister Verrucosis and the other officers made their way to the front of the formation as the airships began to land.

When the main door started to open, Magister Verrucosis sighed.

"Welcome back. I trust you were victorious? Or have you returned in shame, High King?"

"Correction: Hostile High King Xavlaeron has been terminated and is no longer in command."

Magister Verrucosis took a step back while Magister Ausonius's eyes widened as far as they could go.

The door lowered to reveal the queen of the Dobhar, Magister Canus, Rector Aemilia, Consul Hiberius, Princess Caecila, a Selkie warrior, and Uscfrea Spellbreaker of the Dobhar. In fact, Turannian legionnaires, as well as Selkie, Dobhar, and even a handful of Wulver warriors began to disembark from the airships, along with some of Consul Hiberius's own forces.

Magister Verrucosis blinked, but then started to grin. "So, the high king failed, huh? Just my luck. All forces, prepare for battle!"

"Belay that order."

Everyone went completely silent as Emperor Lucius exited a small building to the side of the road, along with the former magister, Appius, and a hooded figure.

"You . . . How did you leave the palace?"

Emperor Lucius grinned. "I had help from one of the last loyal protectors of the Empire."

The hooded figure lowered their hood, causing Magister Verrucosis and many others to openly gasp.

The Hero of Elteno had returned.

Emperor Lucius's smile suddenly dropped. "Magister Verrucosis, you have conspired with the high king to imprison me in my own palace and take control of the North. For this, I, Emperor Lucius, strip you of all rank and titles. Her Majesty Seero, queen of the Dobhar and friend of the Empire, has answered my call for assistance, and now acts on my behalf in this matter."

Magister Verrucosis's face contorted in rage. "This is clearly a trick! They have kidnapped the Emperor and are forcing him to lie now! Loyal soldiers of the Empire, fight now to rescue the Emperor!"

Magister Ausonius's eyes narrowed, drawing his blade.

Which he then pointed toward Magister Verrucosis. Verrucosis blinked before his face twisted in abject rage.

"You . . . You're betraying me?!"

"Magister Verrucosis, I thank you for your service on behalf of the Legion, but you have taken it too far. By order of the Emperor, you are under arrest."

Legate Lucceius wasted no time in pulling out his own blade and shouting at his troops, who moved to encircle Verrucosis. The other officers began to follow suit.

Verrucosis growled before glancing up at the city walls.

"Hortensus, get off your butt and do something for once! Don't let these puppets and foreigners take control of the Empire from us! You know the other Courts will never permit this!"

Aedile Hortensus tilted his head and placed a finger on his chin. "Hm . . . let Emperor Lucius and the queen of the Dobhar usurp all our control, or side with the guy being arrested by his own troops, while the Eastern Court has clearly stated their support for the queen of the Dobhar, and the South is apparently no longer in possession of their own fleet? Decisions, decisions."

He then shrugged as he glanced around at the other members of the Northern Court. "Well, it's been fun, boys and girls, but looks like the Emperor is back in business. I, for one, applaud the return of our Emperor."

"Hortensus, you coward!"

2

Family Reunion

"Hah. Being a hero is great for glory and gaining powers beyond normal Enlightened. Not so good for family life."

—Hero Viridia Sollemnis, on her sudden retirement.

Magister Ausonius shouted an order, and Legate Lucceius's troops led Verrucosis into the city. He then walked over to Emperor Lucius and saluted. Emperor Lucius nodded, after which Magister Ausonius went to demobilize the gathered legions while Emperor Lucius walked over to Seero.

"Hello, Your Majesty Seero. I'm glad to see you in good health. And thank you for your assistance in this manner."

"Greeting: Hello, Emperor Lucius. This unit is also pleased to see you were extracted successfully."

Meanwhile, the Hero of Elteno was glancing around, until his eyes finally landed on one of Seero's group.

"Taog!"

Taog's eyes widened. "Mr. Niraemius?"

The Hero of Elteno rushed over and grabbed the boy by the shoulders. "I'm glad to see you well, Taog. But please, tell me, where is Ateia?! Is she safe?! Is she alright?!"

Taog sputtered at the sudden approach. "Um, s-she's fine. She's at . . . Well, it's a bit hard to explain." He glanced at Seero, not sure whether he should tell Ateia's father about the Primary Home Base.

"Query: Please identify the requesting unit. The unit appears to be acting aggressively but nondamaging toward Friend Taog."

The answer did not come from Taog but from Ateia over the comms. "*Seero! That's my dad! Please let me out!*"

"Acknowledged."

Since there were unaligned and even formerly hostile forces in the area, Seero withdrew into the airship before opening an entrance to the Primary Home Base. Ateia flew out of it and out of the airship.

"DAD!"

The Hero of Elteno spun around. "Ateia!"

As the two ran forward and embraced one another, Ateia began to sob. Emperor Lucius gave a wry smile and glanced around at everyone watching.

"Why don't we give them a moment? We, ourselves, have much work to do."

Everyone else began to clear out and move into Corvanus while Seero, Taog, and Agedia remained behind. Soon, Ateia let go of her father. Taking a step back, she glared at him.

"Where have you been all this time?!"

The Hero of Elteno blinked, and then frowned. He glanced over at Emperor Lucius and Appius as they were moving away, but Appius just waved his hand dismissively.

"Go, talk with your kid. The Emperor should be in no danger now, and honestly, it's better for the negotiations for you to remain 'the mysterious hero' than an actual party. Besides, we'll all be waiting for the queen of the Dobhar anyway."

The Hero of Elteno nodded and turned back toward Ateia.

"Let's take this somewhere secure."

Princess Caecila was making her way toward Corvanus with the group when Emperor Lucius approached her.

"Daughter-in-law, I see you were successful."

She turned, her eyes widening, and then attempted to salute. "I greet the Emperor—" She gasped as Emperor Lucius hugged her. "E-Emperor Lucius, w-what are you doing?"

He gave her a mischievous smile. "You can call me father-in-law, you know?"

Princess Caecila's eyes spun as she glanced around. "I-I could never; i-it is not proper to address the Emperor as such in public!"

He let her go and chuckled. "True, but I don't care much at this point. Either I'm actually the Emperor and I can get away with it, or I'm not really the Emperor and it doesn't much matter." His face turned serious. "Besides . . . the Imperial princess just risked her life and her honor on a dangerous mission to save the Empire and its people. She deserves to know how the Emperor feels about such valor."

Princess Caecila flushed. Emperor Lucius chuckled again and then patted her shoulder. "Now then, steel yourself. Our battle has only begun, and this time, we have a real chance. And that means we will need to put in a great deal of work to make use of it. Are you prepared to fight for the Empire again, Princess Caecila Galvisia Electus?"

Princess Caecila's expression turned resolute as she narrowed her eyes.

"I always am."

Seero, Ateia, Taog, Agedia, and the Hero of Elteno moved into a private room in the airship. The Hero of Elteno was just about to start when Seero created an entrance to the Primary Home Base.

She had considered it acceptable to reveal classified intelligence given the Hero of Elteno's designation as Ateia's person of interest. Ateia had also requested it through the CELIU network so they could discuss her experiences openly and without fear of eavesdropping.

The Hero of Elteno immediately drew a knife and stepped in front of Ateia.

"Dad?!"

He narrowed his eyes. "Queen of the Dobhar . . . what exactly is this, and what exactly are you? From what I can tell, that's some sort of dungeon entrance—or a Rift."

Seero's robotic eye flickered as she calculated a response. On the one hand, the Hero of Elteno was obviously threatening hostile actions toward her. Under normal circumstances, she would activate combat protocols while warning the potential aggressor that confirmed hostile intent would be met with immediate termination.

On the other hand, this was Ateia's person of interest, and terminating him would result in Ateia failing her stated primary directive. Seero may have abandoned her own directive, but she did not intend to cause friendly units to fail theirs.

"Analysis complete. Response determined. Warning: Hostile intent toward this unit by a friendly's person of interest will result in immediate application of nonlethal countermeasures." Her robotic eye turned red, and she charged up her stun weapon while also preparing some hopefully nonlethal magic circles.

But then, Taog stepped in front of her, blocking him from moving toward Seero, while Ateia struck his head.

"Ouch, Ateia, Taog, what are you both doing?"

Ateia scowled. "What are we doing? What are *you* doing! Seero's trying to help by giving us a place we can talk freely! And you're threatening her!"

The Hero of Elteno narrowed his eyes. "Ateia . . . that looks like a dungeon entrance. I haven't heard of anyone opening dungeon entrances on the spot save for demon lords and cultists."

Taog crossed his arms. "That's because Seero is a demon lord, technically speaking. But she's also our friend, and we trust her."

The Hero of Elteno gripped his weapon. "That's a mistake. She's probably manipulating you." He began to tense up, preparing to move, when suddenly, Agedia's tail smacked him on the head, knocking him unconscious.

Ateia jumped and shrieked lightly. "Miss Agedia?!"

Agedia shrugged. "The situation involving shiny girl is too complicated and out of the norm for someone to accept it just like that. You weren't going to convince him, and he was getting ready to attack. Let's tie him up and bring him inside, and then we'll talk."

She smirked. ". . . I also can't say I didn't enjoy that."

A short while later, the Hero of Elteno awoke. He was sitting on the ground inside the Primary Home Base, tied up with metal ropes and surrounded by Barrier and Prison spells. Seero had the Equalizer up and running, and countless other magic circles in the air around them, ready to activate at a moment's notice.

The Hero of Elteno froze and took stock of the situation.

"I'd calm down if I were you."

He spun his head toward Agedia, his eyes widening. "Agedia?"

She scoffed. "Took you long enough to notice I was here too."

He winced . . . but he relaxed. "I guess I don't have a choice, then. And if you're here . . ."

Agedia narrowed her eyes. "You don't. And you have no right to complain, either. So, you best get to catching up *before* you do something rash."

He heaved a deep sigh at that, glancing around until he found Ateia staring at him. He heaved another sigh. "Ateia . . . just tell me this: are you alright?"

Ateia opened her mouth, but then she paused. Her face twisted through several expressions, and her eyes grew moist. Eventually, she glared at him. "Am I alright? Am I alright?!"

She leaned forward and shouted, "I HAVEN'T BEEN ALRIGHT SINCE YOU LEFT!"

The Hero of Elteno winced while Ateia continued.

"Just where have you been?! You were gone for years—YEARS!—without so much as a single message to us! The villagers started beating Taog every week after you left! Quintus wouldn't be seen with him in public! They very nearly denied us food and supplies when I spoke up about it! I had to act as if I liked those monsters just so we could survive, all while stupid Lar hit on me as if I wouldn't strangle him with my bare hands for what he was doing to Taog!"

The Hero of Elteno hung his head. "I just . . . wanted to keep you safe."

Ateia gritted her teeth. "Safe? SAFE?! What were you going to do about the Wulver and Dobhar incursions?! The mana waves and the dozens of new dungeons appearing in the forests around us?! And did you expect us to just sit there and hide until you came back when everyone else was convinced you were dead?! If we hadn't met Seero, we would have died no matter what we did!"

The Hero of Elteno fell silent. Ateia was breathing heavily, but then spoke in a quiet voice. "Just . . . why didn't you tell us? If we understood, if we at least knew why . . . But we didn't. And then, that stupid cult found me anyway, and . . ."

Ateia's eyes watered again . . . then opened in surprise. Metallic arms were wrapped around her.

"Concerned Statement: Friend Ateia appears to be experiencing strong emotional distress. Engaging emotional distress termination protocols."

Seero was not sure how to deal with this situation, but Ateia's distress was generating negative emotions in her as well, and so was judged as a situation requiring a response. She had initially considered terminating the cause of the distress, but since that was Ateia's person of interest, that solution was not considered viable. Instead, she analyzed the alternatives.

She had observed from her own experience that physical contact appeared to mitigate the effects of emotional distress, so she created a basic protocol for that contingency. Channeling a bit of Holy mana through Ateia, Seero rubbed her back as she had previously done for her.

Ateia just stood still for a moment before closing her eyes, slowly smiling. Taking a deep breath, she opened them again. "Thank you, Seero."

"Acknowledged."

Ateia turned to face her father again. "Actually, to tell you the truth, I *am* alright. More than alright. I have friends now who care about me more than anything, more than even their most important missions. And I feel the same about them." She narrowed her eyes at him. "So do NOT threaten my friends again." She then took a deep breath and looked into her father's eyes. "Still . . . I want to hear *everything*."

The Hero of Elteno looked at her with wide eyes, glancing between his daughter and the very likely demon lord hugging her. Eventually, he shook his head and heaved a sigh, his head hung toward the ground. "Okay."

3

The Hero's Tale

"Shouldn't have? What you shouldn't have done was skip your daughter's game to go blow up a freaking skyscraper!"

—Wife of the super Captain Hot Devil, prior to his disappearance from public life.

The Hero of Elteno took a deep breath. "My real name is Amulius Olcinius Herenus. Your mother was Aedinia Dilectia, though she never went by that name at any point in her life. We've changed your name several times, but Ateia is the name she gave you. After . . . her death, I couldn't bring myself to call you anything else."

Ateia watched with a serious expression. "Because we're part of the Imperial family?"

Amulius blinked, but then glanced at Agedia and nodded. "That's right. Aedinia was the daughter of Emperor Herius, but conceived and born under . . . Well, the circumstances were less than ideal, and would have caused the Emperor problems were they made public, so Aedinia was hidden away. This is why later, Agedia dropped out of the Imperial knights to serve as her protector."

Ateia nodded. "And you?"

Amulius shook his head. "No, at that point, I was just an Exploratore of no particular note. It was pure coincidence that I ran into your mother . . . or more accurately, that she ran into me, literally." He couldn't help but crack a small smile at that. Agedia as well. "We saw each other a couple more times before we started falling in love. I didn't learn her identity until after that."

He gave a small smirk. "I have to tell you, that was certainly a surprise. Especially since Emperor Herius's legitimate son was actually quite fond of his half sister and, uh, less than pleased to learn of our relationship. Not to mention her scary snake guardian."

He cracked a glance at Agedia, who scoffed. "Still don't like you. Aedinia deserved better than some deadbeat Exploratore running off on adventures."

Amulius nodded. "You're not wrong." He then flushed a bit before starting the next part. "At some point, someone kidnapped her. We know now it was a cult calling themselves the Heralds of the New Dawn, but back then, we weren't sure.

"Long story short, Agedia, myself, and a couple of friends went after her, and the first time, we managed to rescue her. Had to defeat a demon from the Realms of Mana in the process, even. I got the Hero feat and my nickname, and Aedinia and I married immediately after."

Agedia crossed her arms and huffed. "Stupid deadbeat thinking just because the Aesdes like him and he's a national hero that he can seduce Aedinia just like that."

Amulius chuckled in response while wisely choosing not to mention Agedia's later infatuation with a "deadbeat Exploratore" of her own. But after that, both Amulius and Agedia fell silent. Ateia watched for a minute or two before speaking.

"What happened?"

Amulius gave her a sad smile. "Well . . . we lived happily, for a time. And then you were born, and our happiness reached its peak. But then"—he hung his head, staring at the ground—"they came for her again. Your mother always thought they would, so she made me promise that if anything ever happened, we would ensure your safety first.

"I took you and made sure you were safe while Agedia went after her. I followed them as soon as I could . . . but we were too late. Aedinia had made her choice and sacrificed herself."

Tears began to fall down his face. Agedia looked away, her eyes moistening as well.

"She . . . didn't want to be used. And she didn't want them to find you, ever. So, she took herself away, where no one could ever reach her again, hoping they would give up and you would be safe."

He took a moment, wiping away his eyes and taking another deep breath.

"After that, Agedia went on a rampage to destroy the cult. Meanwhile, I took you, changed my name, and ran as far away as I could to the furthest corner of the Empire, where no one would ever find you. Aedinia's brother introduced me to the retired Dux Canus, who guided us to a small village where a former legionnaire he trusted had settled down with a Wulver girl."

Ateia's eyes widened. "Were they Taog's parents?"

Taog perked up at that. Amulius nodded. "Dux Canus spoke highly of them, and we became fast friends. While they were alive, I had the confidence you would be safe. It was then that I started to look into the Heralds of the New Dawn."

Amulius narrowed his eyes. "Aedinia's brother went after them . . . and disappeared, leaving the Northern Empire with no heir to the throne. It was then I knew they were not just some small, local cult, and that Agedia hadn't wiped them all out after all."

Making eye contact with Ateia, he heaved a sigh. ". . . I looked into it, and made contact with Magister Exploratore per Corvanus Appius, who had been conducting his own investigations after the heir to the throne vanished . . . and due to his remorse over letting Aedinia die."

Ateia's eyes widened. "What?"

Agedia gritted her teeth. "My uncle was loyal to the Empire first and nothing else. He didn't help much in protecting Aedinia. He thought that a secret, illegitimate Imperial princess represented a threat that a rebellious general or ambitious court official might try to take advantage of. So, his opinion was if I couldn't protect her on my own, then it was for the best.

"Well, joke's on him! Aedinia's brother shared MY opinion of the situation and got himself killed, leaving my uncle and the Northern Empire with no successors at all."

Amulius nodded. "I had no intention to work with him ever again . . . but at the very least, he became a staunch enemy of the cult at that point and was one of the few people in the North working against them."

He then took a deep breath, averting his eyes from Ateia for a moment. He glanced at Taog, then Ateia, before continuing. "At this point, Magister Appius's contacts in the East alerted him to a concerning situation. Corrupted dungeons had begun to appear all over the Empire of the Sun, and the Sun Elves were doing nothing about it, to the point that one of their own Archons reached out to *us* about the situation.

"Even worse, we found evidence that the Heralds of the New Dawn—or something similar—were the ones behind it, which we confirmed after Magister Caelinus purged them from Utrad and gained access to some of their records. So, we couldn't let the situation continue.

"But purifying a corrupted dungeon is difficult under the best of circumstances, even with full support from the Legion. To do so in a nation which has been hostile toward the Empire since before it officially existed . . . there was only one way a covert team could manage to pull it off."

Taog nodded to himself and rubbed his chin. "Get a hero?"

Amulius nodded. "The Eastern Empire has some, but all of their heroes are well-known to the Empire of the Sun. I was the only one who would not be immediately recognized by sight or mana." He took a deep breath and looked down at his feet. "It was not a choice I made lightly. With Taog's parents gone . . . But Dux Canus had come out of retirement at that point, and Tiberius had taken over as Magister Exploratore per Turannia on my request."

Agedia frowned at that. "You and I still need to talk about that, Amulius."

Amulius looked up and frowned right back. "What was I supposed to do, Agedia? You refused to even meet with me! I couldn't leave Ateia unguarded, but I also couldn't just let a new Great Demon Lord appear in the east! How would I protect Ateia or the world if the Eastern Empire fell?! How do you think I felt leaving her behind, all alone, right on the edge of the Forests of Beasts?! I thought you, at least, might be able to protect her, at the very least for Aedinia's sake!"

Agedia huffed and looked away, but then she sighed and looked down. "You . . . weren't wrong. I'm . . . I'm sorry. That was my fault."

Amulius took a deep breath and looked down as well. "No . . . I'm sorry too. I know it was a lot to spring on you so suddenly. And I know Aedinia's death hit you as hard as it did me. But . . . I had to do *something*, Agedia, so when Tiberius offered to help in your stead, I couldn't refuse. He was at least able to keep the frontier well patrolled so Dux Canus could stay on top of things."

He sighed and turned back to Ateia. "I couldn't take you with me. The Empire of the Sun itself is no place for a human child, and we were taking on corrupted dungeons on top of that. But . . . I hoped that with Canus and Tiberius in charge of Turannia, and Caelinus locking down Utrad, that the North would remain safe. But Quintus was apparently not the man I thought he was."

He bowed his head. "I'm truly sorry to you both, Ateia, Taog. I didn't mean for this to happen. For any of this. If I had known you'd get caught up in it anyway . . ."

Ateia's heart pounded in her chest, her eyes filling with tears. Her body heated up as she stepped forward toward her father, to the man who had left her and Taog alone.

Upon her request, Seero dropped some of the magical barriers surrounding him. Amulius watched her with wide eyes before closing them and taking a deep breath, awaiting her response.

His eyes widened in shock, and he let out a gasp, as something smacked into him.

Ateia—still covered in metal armor, of course—slammed into him . . . in a hug. She began to sob as she clutched onto him.

He had made mistakes. He had left them behind. He had caused Taog to suffer alone for years. He had set them on a course full of pain and misery. He had not trusted them. He had withheld the truth from them. But . . .

The most important feeling in Ateia's heart was this. Her father had not abandoned them, after all.

As she'd wished and hoped all along, against everything everyone else had believed, he had left them for a reason. He had not chosen to leave them on a whim and had not gone off to die somewhere alone. He had wanted them to be taken care of in the meantime and made arrangements to that effect, as best he was able.

He still cared about them.

And for that . . . Ateia's heart was truly glad.

4

The Boy Who Was Left Behind

"Request: Hostility toward a priority friendly detected. Engaging termination protocols. Please designate the source of distress."

—Commander Elise, upon observing signs of emotional distress in a friendly.

Amulius closed his eyes, leaning his head into Ateia's, since he was still bound. Tears welled up in his eyes as well. ". . . I'm sorry, Ateia."

The two remained like that for a while longer before they separated. "Now . . . what happened to you?"

Ateia took a deep breath. "Well, things were horrible without you. Half the village turned on Taog, and most of the other half refused to help. You weren't coming back, so we decided to go get you. We tried to join the Exploratores, but failed the exam . . . as instructed, *apparently*."

Ateia narrowed her eyes at him. Amulius coughed. "I'm sorry about that, but with the Heralds of the New Dawn at large, we needed to keep you where our friends were in charge."

Ateia stared at him for a bit before continuing. "So, I was really desperate and despairing, and then we got caught by bandits. Fortunately, Seero happened to pass by and wiped them out. After that, we made an agreement with her, and she helped us conquer a dungeon."

Amulius glanced over at Seero with wide eyes before turning back to Ateia. ". . . I see. That explains why Tiberius let you leave."

Ateia nodded. "Well, then a lot of things happened, mostly Seero terminating armies and corrupted dungeons and stuff while Taog and I tried to be useful to her. We got invited to Corvanus, the Emperor made us inquisitors, that stupid cult kidnapped and sacrificed me, Seero saved me by turning me into an Aesdes, we met Mighty Victoria, and now we're going to go *destroy* the cult."

Amulius froze and blinked several times. "Wait . . . *WHAT?!*"

There was a bit of commotion afterward, but eventually, the group split up to process the conversation. Amulius was staring at the ground with blank eyes.

"Hey." Agedia slithered over to him. He barely raised his head to glance at her. ". . . Is it true?"

Agedia smirked. "It's a lot to take in if you weren't there, isn't it? But yes, it is. *All* of it."

Amulius shook his head, gritting his teeth. "Everything I did, everything we sacrificed, and it was all for nothing. The Heralds found Ateia anyway, and thanks to my choices, she was completely unprepared for it."

Agedia shrugged. "Yes . . . but if she hadn't been, she probably wouldn't have met shiny girl, who has done a better job of protecting her than any of us ever could."

Amulius frowned at that. "I'm still not comfortable with my daughter's life resting in the hands of a demon lord, especially not one so far out of the norm. Who's to say this isn't some new form of corruption . . . or a deception?"

Agedia smirked. "Mighty Victoria, the Lady of Courage and Victory."

Amulius blinked again before his eyes went wide. "You really met her?"

Agedia nodded. "As far as I can tell. I didn't finish the theology curriculum before I dropped out of the Imperial knights, but let me tell you, there was a *lot* of Holy mana being tossed around."

She then moved in front of Amulius, looking into his eyes. "And more importantly, I've watched Seero over there. At this point, she has the power to become a new Great Demon Lord whenever she wants to. She can personally destroy entire legions and unleash hordes of monsters on the land at a moment's notice. She has instead used that power to protect her friends and make sweet rolls.

"She's a good girl, and *fiercely* protective of those two. She only took down Caelinus because the Magister Exploratore per Utrad kidnapped them, you know?"

Amulius returned her gaze. "You trust her?"

Agedia smiled. "With my and Ateia's lives."

Amulius looked down and heaved a sigh as Agedia nodded, took out a knife, and started to cut Amulius's bindings. "Seero is the one who fixed all of our mistakes, saved the kids' lives, and prevented the complete collapse of the Northern Empire, as well as ruined the cult's plans wherever she went, and that was *before* she was actively trying to destroy them. I think, whatever she is, she's earned a bit of trust from us, don't you?"

Amulius nodded as he stretched his body. "Thank you, Agedia. I . . . didn't expect your help like this."

Agedia scoffed. "Well, I still don't like you. And you screwed up—a *lot*." She then gave him a wry smile. "But so did I. And now . . . we're both here for Ateia, right? We can't fix what we did, so we'll both just have to do what we can now."

Amulius's eyes widened, and he nodded.

Taog was walking around the Primary Home Base, around the various structures and lines of drone golems carrying raw materials about.

He . . . didn't know how he felt. The truth was, Taog had given up on Ateia's father long ago. He had believed the man to have died after the first year, so it had come as a surprise to find him alive after all this time.

But Taog had already made his peace with Mr. Niraemius—or rather, Amulius's absence. Ateia was the one who'd dreamed of reuniting with him. As for Taog, he had Ateia, and he had Seero. Ateia's father wasn't a necessary presence in his life anymore. Taog had long since learned to survive without him.

Speaking of which, Seero suddenly flew over and landed in front of him.

"Hi, Seero, can I help you?"

"Statement: Emotional distress termination protocols engaged."

"Huh?"

Taog had but a moment before Seero grabbed him and began channeling Holy mana into him.

"Um, Seero? What are you doing?"

"Response: Terminating Friend Taog's emotional distress."

Taog furrowed his brow. "Where did you get that idea? I'm not emotionally distressed."

"Objection: This unit has detected elevated cortisol levels and abnormally rapid heart rate in Friend Taog. Analysis of Friend Taog's organic components indicates preparation for a combat scenario or emotional distress, and Friend Taog does not appear to be engaged in combat."

Taog frowned. "That's . . ." But then he stopped. When he paid attention, he found his heart was, in fact, pounding in his chest, which felt constricted. His eyes widened.

He was feeling . . . distressed?

Taog frowned, but sighed again as he realized what was going on. He had been distracting himself from his own feelings, as he had done so many times in the past. He was doing what he needed to survive—and doing that which he had resolved not to do. He was running away and deceiving himself that everything was okay.

He thought he had overcome this with Mighty Victoria's help . . . but it appeared the fear in his heart would not be vanquished with a single battle or two. He sighed, his shoulders drooping.

"Seero . . . what should I do?"

Amulius's return . . . apparently caused him distress? He had no idea why. Or what he should do about it.

"Uncertain Response: This unit has no data on protocols for Friend Taog to respond to the situation. Emotional distress termination protocols are currently limited to nondamaging physical and mana contact, or else termination of the cause of the distress, which has been ruled out in this case."

Taog blinked before chuckling slightly. Terminate the cause of the distress; that was certainly a Seero-like recommendation.

But then, Taog stood still, his eyes widening slightly. "Terminate the cause, huh? You know . . . I think I know what to do. Thanks, Seero."

"Acknowledged."

They stood there for a moment longer. "Um, Seero, could you let me go now? I need to move if I'm going to do anything."

"Affirmative."

With live updates from Seero, Taog found Amulius immediately. Taking a deep breath, he walked toward the man. Amulius noticed him and turned to face Taog.

The older man frowned before taking a deep breath and hanging his head. "Taog . . . I'm sorry. For leaving you, for all I put you through—and for getting your parents killed. Maybe if I hadn't been so focused on the cult, maybe if I hadn't left for Castra Turannia that week . . ."

Taog was about to say it was fine, but caught himself. That was his habit, his method of pushing the issue away. So instead, he took a deep breath and thought for a moment. Then he slowly opened his mouth.

"My parents' death . . . was not your fault. They could have grabbed us and ran. They could have told the village to evacuate. They could have fallen back when they realized they were in trouble. But it was my mother's joy to take on challenges, and my father's pride to hold the line no matter what. It was their choice to do what they did. They would not be pleased with you taking credit for it."

Taog closed his eyes for a moment, then opened them with a frown. "But . . . as for the rest . . ."

Taog's heart was pounding, and the words struggled to come out. He wanted to run, wanted to say it was fine. He didn't want to feel the way he did at the time. And Ateia had finally reunited with her father. He didn't want to interfere with that.

But he knew he needed to change. He had been running away from his problems all his life. He needed to learn from Ateia and face things head-on when he wanted them to change. He needed to learn from Seero to identify and terminate the cause of his distress.

So . . . he opened his mouth.

"Just . . . why . . . did you leave? Why did you leave me behind . . . and helpless?"

His heart pounded faster and faster. His body heated up. His face twisted into a snarl, and he started to growl in between his words.

"Why did you call me strong?! Why did you ask me to protect Ateia?! I was weak! I was unbelievably weak! I couldn't even protect myself, much less Ateia! I needed you, and you left! Everyone I needed left!"

As he spoke, more and more began to pour out until he was shouting. He shouted and shouted as he let out a life of grievances.

And then it was done. Panting for breath as moisture blocked his vision, he felt like slumping his shoulders, though the armor around his body kept him upright.

Amulius frowned, tears in his eyes. "I'm . . . I'm so sorry, Taog. I . . ." He sighed and stepped over. Hesitantly, he reached out and put a hand on Taog's shoulder. "I guess I focused too much on Ateia. I was so worried about the cult finding her again that I didn't realize what all this would mean for you, what I would put you through. I'm sorry . . ."

Amulius gasped as Taog slammed into him, wrapping his arms around the man as he started to sob. Amulius gave a sad smile and patted the boy on the head.

"I'm sorry . . . and you did well, Taog. I asked more of you than anyone ever should have, and you did everything you could, even though you were the one hurting most of all. And you did it, right? You and Ateia survived for all these years, thanks to you. I'm truly grateful she had you by her side, and I'm truly proud of how you've fought through this mess I left you in. I know your parents would be proud of you too."

Taog sobbed for a while longer while Amulius returned his embrace.

INTERLUDE

The Eastern Front

Seero was conducting some calculations regarding a solution to beyond-visual-range combat when she noticed two units on approach. She turned to face Ateia and Taog as they walked up to her.

"Acknowledgement: Hello, Friend Ateia, Friend Taog, do you have an update, query, or request for this unit?"

The two looked at each other and nodded. Then they both hugged Seero.

"Confused Query: This unit is not experiencing emotional distress at this time; why have friendly units engaged emotional distress termination protocols?"

Ateia smiled. "Right now, we're just doing it to show affection and gratitude. Thanks to you, I got to meet my father again, Seero. And more than that, I got the family I always wanted."

Taog smiled as well. "Thanks to you, I found the courage to face my problems, and realized how I truly felt. Not to mention how many times you've saved our lives. We can never thank you enough, Seero."

Seero's robotic eye flickered. She wasn't entirely sure how to respond to this situation, as affection wasn't as well-defined for her as emotional distress. But . . . it didn't cause any negative physiological or emotional reactions, and it did not interfere with her current task. And if she analyzed their words, she had helped the friends achieve primary directives and improve their overall efficiency. That was a positive outcome.

"Acknowledgement: This unit is pleased to have assisted."

A bit further away, Amulius watched the two embrace the demon lord—and hero, apparently—called Seero. He hung his head and drooped his shoulders.

"You aren't worrying about shiny girl again, are you?"

He shook his head as Agedia approached him from behind.

"No. Well, yes, but . . . it's just, I really messed this up, didn't I? I don't know what else I could have done, but what I did do wasn't enough. I'm glad they found someone to help who you say is trustworthy . . . but that should have been me, or Taog's parents, or . . ."

"Or Aedinia?"

Amulius remained silent for a bit before sighing once more.

"And I don't even know if it was even worth it. I spent years taking down corrupted dungeons and cult agents, but they never stopped appearing, and we never found the cult's leadership. And we only had the cooperation of one or two Archons, so we didn't even reach most of the Empire of the Sun. I can't say if what we did had any impact at all. Maybe . . . Maybe I shouldn't have gone."

But Agedia shook her head. "No . . . everyone knows corrupted dungeons are bad news for any nation they appear in. Even the Empire of the Sun wouldn't permit them to exist under normal circumstances. It's self-destructive to do so, which makes no sense when they've been locked in a centuries-long stalemate with a powerful enemy. So, I think you were right to respond. And I have a feeling we'll be learning why sooner rather than later . . ."

Far to the east, the sky was black. Fortress cities and military outposts burned all across the deserts and plains extending eastward, the smoke joining in the sky above to form black clouds overhead. A tide of monsters streamed across the plains, rushing toward the hills that started rising toward the mountains in the distance.

And there, they stopped. Enchanted stone rose from the hills. Glowing arrows, enchanted ballistae bolts, massive stones lobbed by catapults, and all other manners of projectiles rained from the tops of the walls. Long pikes stabbed down from above, while halberds and swords met any monster who made it to the top. Spells and siege weapons' fire concentrated on any monster capable of breaking the fortifications, while assassins leapt out of hidden tunnels to take down mages and ranged attackers in secret.

Horns sounded, magic artifacts flashed, and banners rose, and each time, the soldiers moved calmly and quickly to redirect their efforts to the weak points in the defenses. No matter how the monsters approached, no matter what feints or diversions they used, the defenders always arrived to meet them.

The auxiliaries and allies went to work as well. Centaur archers harassed the flanks, winged humanoids scouted from above, and aquatic species ambushed the horde from nearby rivers. Monster tamers unleashed monsters of their own, while the Imperial Necrotorum turned the enemy's casualties against them.

Giants and Treekin towered over the walls, lobbing boulders with their bare hands. In the tunnels beneath the ground, there was even a colony of Formicans battling subterranean foes, the Antkin meeting the horde with a swarm of their own alongside Dwarven warriors and the Legio Subterraneus.

In the skies, the occasional battle airship unleashed ballistae fire and built-in spells on flocks of bird monsters, while griffin knights confronted wyverns and other large fliers. The flying species of the Auxiliary Caelum flew as escorts, intercepting any monsters who made it past the knights and airships.

Battle airships were not the only artifacts of war present. Legions of golems held the line, taking the blows on behalf of their squishy masters. Enchanted ballistae fired into the enemy without any crews at all; staves planted into the ground cast spells at anything that approached.

And when the monsters managed to break a section of the wall, something like the battle airships rose right from under the ground, planting itself in front of the breach while the Imperial architecti repaired the wall. More such landships rose from the ground and then thundered across the field in a mighty counterattack, trampling over the hordes as they pushed the monsters away from the breach.

Mounted knights and fast-moving auxiliaries followed behind them, mopping up the stragglers as the landships rampaged through the enemy. The Eastern Empire had long learned that battle airships were much cheaper to build if they didn't have to fly.

Every once in a while, a dark-skinned Elf wearing black-and-gold armor would step forward and unleash terrible spells that shook both ground and sky. And every time, massive joint barriers from anti-Archon formations would rise to meet them as long-range snipers harassed the Elves with poisoned bolts, and ritual-casted strategic spells responded in kind, battle airships forming squadrons and confronting the foe directly in the sky.

The proud Archons were forced to step back, and those who tried to force the issue did not escape unscathed.

These were scenes that continued on for *hundreds* of miles, all across the entire border of the Eastern Elteni Empire and the Empire of the Sun. Over a million legionnaires stood side by side and stopped the monstrous charge dead in its tracks.

In his command tent, High Archon Vommik Nigaeren gnashed his teeth at the woman standing before him. "Do you understand now, Archon Nolnyth, what it is you have done? Because you so foolishly cleared out the dungeons from which we would acquire our second wave, we were unable to exploit the initial breakthrough and failed to destroy our enemy once and for all. And now, once again, we are trapped in a war of attrition. What do you have to say for yourself?"

Nolnyth scoffed. "Nothing, for there is nothing to be said. There was a threat to my realm, and I dealt with it. The Council had *years* to inform me there was a plan for those corrupted dungeons and did not. It was not *my* failure which led to this outcome."

High Archon Vommik narrowed his eyes. "So be it. You will atone for your error by creating a new breakthrough. Report to the frontlines and assault the fortifications. Do not return until they are broken."

Nolnyth scoffed again. "If you want to kill me, you should do it yourself. But fine, I shall let the humans claim my life on your behalf. The death of an Archon on foolish orders will surely reflect well upon your leadership."

With that, she turned and left. High Archon Vommik gritted his teeth as he reapplied the barrier protecting his tent before activating a communication artifact.

"What is the meaning of this, Mrannd'ssinss d'Quarth?"

Mrannd'ssinss d'Quarth, also known as the Herald of the New Dawn, spoke through the artifact. "I warned you that the Eastern Empire's defenses were deeper than you thought. Even the situation with the Aesdes would not cause them to simply collapse."

High Archon Vommik snarled. "That wouldn't have been a problem if one of my Archons hadn't let some slave of the Aesdes run around for *years*! I thought you were tracking those heroes!"

"And it is still not a problem. You now have the endless tides of a corrupted horde, do you not? The Legion cannot hold forever."

High Archon Vommik narrowed his eyes. "You fail to understand, Mrannd'ssinss d'Quarth, Lord of Order. Defeating mere humans is not my concern. It is betrayal from the rear that has ever haunted the Empire of the Sun. The longer my assault fails to produce tangible results, the more likely such a betrayal becomes."

"Well, you'll be glad to learn, then, that I *do* have something planned. Just be ready; the Empire of the Sun will not be unaffected."

Off in an isolated location, the Herald of the New Dawn knelt on the floor of a large, open room. The entire floor, walls, and even roof were covered in engraved geometric patterns, while various artifacts and magic materials were spread out at specific points. The Herald of the New Dawn nodded to himself after his final check, walking to the middle of the room, where a chair was waiting. Sitting, he pulled an object out of his personal magic box.

A magic core lit up the room. The Herald of the New Dawn smirked.

The core of the Great Demon Lord had long gone inert, separated from both Aelea and the Source when the continent of Letoris was cast from the Material Plane.

But, well . . . he had learned that such connections could be reforged. And if a simple machine could do it, then so could he.

The formation around the room began to light up . . .

5

The Fate of the Empire

"The ultimate weapon will not merely preserve the world—it will upgrade it."
—Dr. Ottosen, on the reorganization of the former United States of America.

Seero eventually left the group, returning to Corvanus. Ateia and Taog's emotional distress appeared to have mostly been terminated at this stage, though powerful emotions flared up whenever they spoke with Amulius.

Seero had not decided on the man's designation in her IFF protocols just yet. On the one hand, he was the person of interest for Ateia, and clearly quite important to the pair. On the other, contextual clues and conversations he'd had with Agedia implied he had inflicted significant emotional damage on her friends, though he had done so in order to terminate a larger threat.

Seero's analysis concluded he should not be considered hostile as a result . . . but her organic half and emotional-processing threads noted him as a point of concern. She ultimately concluded that he was not a hostile but was also not a particularly efficient friendly, given his track record so far.

His conversations with Ateia, Taog, and Agedia weren't finished yet, but Seero's other allies were inquiring as to her status. They apparently wished to begin the negotiations and required her presence to do so. Since Amulius's initial hostility had been resolved, and Ateia and Taog's emotional distress had been handled, Seero calculated she should join the negotiations and settle the Northern Empire's political situation.

She had subjugated a local dungeon on the outskirts of Corvanus just before her group arrived, and so returned immediately. A short while later, Legion troops guided her into the Imperial palace, to a private conference room. There, Emperor Lucius and Princess Caecila, the leaders of the

Turannian alliance, Consul Hiberius, Magister Ausonius, and Aedile Hortensus were waiting.

Uscfrea and the other Turannians saluted to her, causing the other Imperials to raise their eyebrows.

But then, Emperor Lucius raised even more eyebrows by breaking the silence. "Welcome, Your Majesty Seero, queen of the Dobhar and true friend of the Empire. I am glad to see you well."

"Returned Greeting: Hello, Emperor Lucius. It is good to see you are in functioning and undamaged condition."

He nodded in response before glancing around at the eyes staring at him and shrugging. "Most of us wouldn't be in this room were it not for Her Majesty, and we remain here at her pleasure. In fact, the *entire Northern Empire* wouldn't be here if not for her. Under the circumstances, I no longer feel like denying reality."

Consul Hiberius sighed. "There is still something to be said of decorum and stature, even if at a disadvantage, Your Majesty."

Emperor Lucius shrugged again. "Perhaps, but we are behind closed doors, and I believe the most important party in these negotiations prefers open and efficient communication. Isn't that right, Your Majesty Seero?"

"Response: Clear and efficient communication is generally desirable, though the exact calculations may depend on the circumstances and if the conversation involves classified intel."

Consul Hiberius pondered for a moment before straightening his back. "Very well. I suppose I, too, have tired of withholding my tongue in recent years. Let us speak openly, then."

Aedile Hortensus tilted his head. "Eh? Speak openly, huh? I haven't done that since I was a boy. This will be new."

Emperor Lucius smiled and clapped his hands. "Excellent. In that case, let us address the first point of business."

Turning to Seero, his expression turned serious. "Your Majesty, how much of the Empire do you want? Or do you even want an Empire at all at this stage? You are the strongest power by far in the North and South, and to be honest, I do not believe the Northern Empire can survive without your support. The South clearly cannot oppose you, and the East is too occupied with the Empire of the Sun. Whatever you choose to do, we all must follow."

Consul Hiberius sighed deeply, while Magister Ausonius's jaw dropped. Uscfrea blinked before grinning widely, and even Aedile Hortensus was rendered speechless, his jaw dropping as well.

Seero's robotic eye flickered rapidly. "Response: This unit has no protocols or records regarding administration or governance and cannot devote resources and time to a major political reorganization due to ongoing hostilities against priority targets. A continuation of the existing administration is more efficient."

Rector Aemilia then smiled sweetly. "Though, perhaps a reorganization of the Northern Empire's internal structure is in order?"

Emperor Lucius sighed. "So we have to negotiate, after all. Very well, let us discuss the future of the Northern Empire, then."

Given that Seero's war with the Heralds of the New Dawn was still ongoing, the talks were kept short. The Northern Empire would continue on as it had previously, so the discussion primarily focused on the allocation of duties in the short term.

As such, Rector Aemilia was to be appointed as Consul Hibera, taking over the late Noxisius's position. As this left both consul seats in the hands of the Hiberius family, Consul Hiberius would be made to retire once the situation permitted and a suitable replacement was found, but in no more than five years.

Meanwhile, Magister Canus would take command of all the legions of the North as the new Magister Utriusque Militia, taking over Verrucosis's position. An appointment that everyone but the man himself approved of.

Seero would also send a permanent liaison to Corvanus to represent her interests in the court. The Selkies already had someone in Corvanus, but their representative would now have a much improved ability to actively participate in decision-making.

Finally, a few of the borders were to be redrawn in the future. Utrad would be reworked, and it was planned that some of its northern territories would be reassigned to Turannia, or even transferred to Seero. However, such reorganizations would have to wait, as the group agreed to deal with the situations regarding the loss of the Aesdes' support and the Heralds of the New Dawn first and foremost.

The important part was that the Northern Empire's administration had been rebuilt—now firmly in the hands of Seero and her allies—before representatives from the South arrived for peace talks.

The negotiations were just wrapping up and the group was about to disband when Seero detected a surge of corrupted mana attempting to enter her core. After the disruption of the dungeon system, she had established a barrier of Holy mana around her cores and her subordinate cores, so the corrupted mana did not manage to affect them.

"Warning: This unit has detected a nonstandard anomaly. There is a ninety-two point seven-four percent probability it is related to hostile forces."

The group's eyes widened, then Rector Aemilia's eyes narrowed. "What do you mean by that, Your Majesty?"

Magister Canus took a breath before straightening himself. "Do you have any specific information, Your Majesty?"

"Response: This unit can only state that it is related to dungeons and the Realms of Mana."

Just then, Emperor Lucius froze. Reaching into his pocket, he pulled out a small pendant pulsing with red light. His eyes widened.

"Your Majesty Seero, Magister Canus, we have an emergency. The Imperial family's dungeon is going rogue . . ."

Seero's eye turned red. "Analysis: Given the current scenario, this unit predicts with eighty-three point five-six percent certainty the situation represents a hostile action. Engaging dungeon termination protocols."

Magister Canus nodded. "Under the circumstances, assistance would be most appreciated, Your Majesty. We'll try to assemble reinforcements as we can."

"Affirmative."

It only took Seero a moment to arrive at the Imperial family's dungeon just north of Corvanus, where she found the Imperial knights fighting against a horde of monsters. But unlike with previous corrupted dungeons, this horde was a diverse one. Orcs, slimes, elementals of all sorts, various animal and plant hybrids, undead, and many others ran side by side toward the Imperial defenses.

"Command: Bombardment HQ, select targets and open fire."

"Yes-yes, wise-mighty-gracious boss-queen!"

Seero had set up a new Monster Hangar filled with cyber-rats and cyber-spiders, with walls covered in monitors displaying the area around herself. These rats and spiders, lying on cushions around the floor, closed their organic eyes as their robotic ones began to flicker.

And then, a dozen Prismatic Bombardment magic circles appeared in the sky.

Beams of all colors and affinities rained down on the horde below, vaporizing monsters on contact. Seero provided all the mana for the spells, the rats and spiders linking to her through the CELIU network. Small groups worked together to operate a Prismatic Bombardment spell each, spreading the mental load of spellcasting and targeting among multiple CELIU units.

Seero may have upgraded her cybernetic components so as not to over-rely on the CELIU network for computational assistance, but that did not mean she would not also make use of said method. In this case, where Supercharging was unnecessary and there was an abundance of minimally threatening targets, CELIU network assistance was an efficient solution for targeting.

And so, within moments, the horde was vanquished. Additional monsters poured from the dungeon, but as they were bottlenecked by the entrance, Seero could wipe them out with a single magic circle now. Letting the others fade, she flew straight toward the dungeon.

And so, the termination of the Imperial family's private dungeon began.

6

Terminate the Imperial Family's Dungeon?

"Beats me. But hey, endless fighting gets boring after a while, so why not? Maybe the demon lords get bored too."

—Veteran Dungeon Diver Flavonia Laeca, on the prevalence of dungeon puzzles.

Seero flew through the hallways, analyzing the flows of mana and the structure of the dungeon to determine the correct path. Every time she detected a living or animate entity, a small Beam magic circle of the appropriate element would appear and wipe it out long before it came within visual range.

Most traps were simply bypassed through speed and flight. Pitfalls and sticky floors were irrelevant to a target not walking on the ground. Active traps like arrow launchers or dropping boulders were counterattacked by offensive spells, such that they failed to even reach Seero's defensive barriers. Magical traps were shut down by the Equalizer.

There was even a Spatial Magic spell engraved in the floor, which Seero predicted would result in a forced relocation. Seero dedicated an entire anti-mana bomb to ensure it wouldn't have an ounce of mana remaining in it when she passed it by.

She went through several floors in minutes, diving deeper and deeper into the dungeon. Eventually, she came to the end of a stone labyrinth floor, only to find a door blocking her path. There was a carved mural on it with several conspicuous holes, as if part of the artwork had been removed.

Seero fired the Equalizer into the door, followed by a Beam with a Spatial Angling field layered over it. Seero's own experiences with Spatial Magic and the boundaries of material planes and the Realms of Mana, along with the data from

Shialnor on the fundamental nature of dungeons, had informed her why dungeon "walls" did not behave as their physical appearance might suggest.

They were not purely physical matter but magical constructs placed inside distortions in space that existed partially in the boundary of the Material Plane. As a result, any attempt to attack them would be deflected through a longer than expected route, during which the dungeon would focus its mana-absorption capabilities on the attack in question. The attacks were thus long drained of their power by the time they arrived at the actual wall, assuming they arrived at all.

The same feature appeared to apply to this door.

Seero counterattacked the magical enchantments with the Equalizer and counteracted the Spatial Angling with one of her own. As a result, the door became just a door for her. She blew a hole through it and continued on her way.

Next, she found a "room" that contained an ocean as far as the eye could see, with narrow stone bridges leading the way forward. When she arrived at the exit, she found it deep underwater. Several pedestals with empty gem holders depicted scenes of large spheres being placed upon them, and the water levels rising and falling.

Seero ignored them and dove into the water, wrapping a bubble of Water Magic around herself in the same manner the Imperial naval vessels did, propelling herself through the water as fast as her Water Magic could go. She arrived at the underwater door, and finding it locked—much like the previous one—she applied the same method of breaching and carried on.

A volcanic cave system was next, with the exit door under a pool of lava—or possibly magma, given the underground terrain. As Seero was only programmed with combat-relevant data regarding molten rock, she was not particularly concerned with the exact designation. There were also several empty pedestals on the last bit of solid ground before the pool.

Seero ignored these as she analyzed the situation.

Simply wrapping herself in a lava bubble like with water would still expose her components to the heat, with a noticeable risk of overheating, so Seero attempted something else. She created a Spatial Angling field around herself, modeled after the dungeon wall effect, in order to increase the distance between herself and the lava. She then wrapped a lava bubble on top of this field to keep the lava from entering it directly. As a result, the heat transfer between herself and the lava bubble was negligible.

Seero continued on with hardly a moment's pause, breaching the door as with the previous two.

In the next room, she had to pause for a moment. Her different sensors disagreed on the path forward. Her mana sensors indicated the signature she was following led to a particular room; yet, her ground-penetrating radar suggested this room was a dead end.

Seero took a moment to analyze the data more closely.

"Command: Friend Ateia, please conduct reconnaissance."

"Got it!"

Seero continued her own analysis as Ateia, waiting in the Primary Home Base, turned her Aesdes sight toward the room in question. Seero noticed small fluctuations in the flows of mana when she examined them with her dungeon field, indicating not all was as it seemed to her mana sensors. She concluded some sort of jamming or interference was likely occurring.

A moment later, Ateia finished her task. Under normal circumstances, dungeons—existing in the boundary of the world as middlemen between the Realms of Mana and the Material Plane—were not directly connected to the flows of Holy mana through Aelea. This, considered a necessary safeguard to keep the Realms of Mana and the Material Plane from direct mana contact, also made it more difficult for the Aesdes to see into dungeons with their divination abilities, unless they did so via Shialnor's core in the Blessed Land.

But Ateia was no normal Aesdes. Ateia was Contracted to Seero, and deeply connected to the Primary Home Base's core. And Seero was a living dungeon core with a Dungeon Field Generator projecting her mana into her surroundings . . . including the mana of any dungeon she happened to be present in. As a result, Seero created a compatible contact with the dungeon's mana Ateia could use to extend her divination sight into it.

"Um, it looks like there's a boss monster or something waiting there. I don't see any doors besides the entrance."

"Acknowledged."

With that, Seero boosted ahead. She extrapolated some of the discrepancies in the flow of mana and compared them to radar scans to determine the likely location of the true exit.

And she was right. Within moments, Seero found the true way, hidden behind a door with a lock underneath a mural of the boss monster.

Seero simply breached the doorway as before and moved on.

Such things continued for numerous floors. Seero encountered all manners of traps, monsters, and strangely inefficient door designs. None of them stood up to over a thousand points of mana jammed into singular spells with support from Spatial Magic, the Equalizer, and anti-mana bombs.

And so, Seero stepped into the core room after defeating the final boss. That monster had even endured a Beam spell equivalent to her old Aurora Barrage's fused superbeams. It did not, however, endure the new Prismatic Bombardment spell.

"Warning Query: Would the hostile dungeon master like to surrender? This unit will allow the dungeon master to retain ownership of their dungeon as a subordinate core if so. Otherwise, this unit will engage termination protocols."

Seero found what looked like a human woman in an elegant dress, staring into space with blank eyes.

". . . My dungeon core stopped responding to me and started getting all weird, then began dumping out monsters that wouldn't listen to my commands, ruining a deal I've kept for centuries. Then, some girl bust through my dungeon in, what, an hour? A dungeon which *centuries* ago required an entire campaign by the Empire's finest to get through, and which I have built up significantly more since.

"And said girl just blows up the supposedly *indestructible* dungeon doors while disabling guaranteed-trigger traps? All while wiping out my entire army like it's not even there?" She paused, then, "You know what? Fine. Do whatever you want, as you clearly can."

"Surrender acknowledged. Please stand by for dungeon integration."

Seero stepped toward the core and placed her hand on it, detecting a concentration of corrupted mana within. Strangely, the core itself was not fully corrupted, but the corrupted mana appeared to be forcing the core to operate anomalously.

Seero channeled Holy mana into the orb while applying the dungeon-subordination process she had created. The woman screamed for a bit, then stared at Seero while panting for breath.

"Of course . . . you're a dungeon master . . . who has Holy mana. Let me guess . . . you also summoned . . . an Aesdes to work for you? That would be the next logical step, right?"

"Confirmation: This unit's friendlies do, in fact, include a being classified as an Aesdes."

The woman's jaw dropped before heaving a sigh and holding her head. "Of course they do. Well, thanks for fixing my core and all. Now, if you'll excuse me, I'm going to lie down and rethink my life."

"Acknowledged."

With that, the woman turned and shuffled her feet toward a private room to the side of the core. Meanwhile, Seero contacted Uscfrea through the CELIU network.

"Mission Report: This unit has successfully integrated the affected dungeon. The dungeon appeared to be partially corrupted; this unit has successfully purified the corruption. No further assaults should occur. Please inform the allied forces of mission success."

"Ah, my queen, as expected of you. Will you be returning soon? We have a situation to discuss with you."

Seero's robotic eye flickered as she accessed Uscfrea's records, determining the situation. He had held back while she was engaged in what he believed to be intense combat, but now gave her the full rundown. It seemed the Imperial family's dungeon was not the only one affected.

In fact, if the reports coming in from the Legion and Imperial allies were accurate, then Seero's projections indicated that *every* dungeon not subordinated to her might be affected.

7

The Dungeon Crisis Begins!

"We moved the mages far away from the capital because they make things explode. We put them near a concentration of dungeons for the same reason."

—Magister Peditum Gaius Tuccius Salvian, on the Legion's slow response to a rogue dungeon near Academiae Civitatem.

Seero landed back at the Imperial palace on her allies' request. She had considered immediately responding to the situation, but there was a problem. If every dungeon was affected, and everywhere was under attack, then Seero couldn't determine an efficient location to start. She had yet to identify the source of the corruption, and still had no data regarding the cult's location as well, so had no key targets she could eliminate.

As a result, the only possible response at present was to begin terminating or integrating the dungeons. But Seero didn't have their locations on record save for the ones she had already visited, so her only method if she reacted now would be to begin searching manually. And while locating dungeons in general was not that difficult for her, it would still be less efficient to devote time to the search if her allies already knew the locations of major dungeons in their territory.

Likewise, Seero's allies were the main party under threat at present. The Primary Home Base and the other dungeons in Seero's network were not under assault at the moment, and neither was the Dobhar base, though their border scouts were starting to report increased monster sightings.

As such, Seero had no key targets of her own that required an immediate defense. So, in this case, she would prioritize defending allied forces. The problem was she had only a basic level of understanding of the Empire's structure, economy, military, and infrastructure, and no data as to the key locations the Empire needed to remain viable.

As such, Seero had come to the conclusion that the most efficient response was to coordinate with her allies, who could grant her intel on dungeon locations and the key places they needed to defend, and so enable Seero to prioritize the most impactful termination or integration missions.

Magister Canus saluted as Seero stepped into the room. Emperor Lucius had ceded command over to him given the situation, and the new half-Elf Magister Utriusque Militia was already attempting to coordinate the defense.

"Your Majesty, glad to see you. You mentioned the Realms of Mana? If that's the case, it seems every dungeon we know of is becoming corrupted."

"Correction: Analysis of an affected dungeon indicates the dungeons are not fully corrupted. It is possible to remove the intrusion via the application of Holy mana, though it might be necessary to integrate the dungeon into this unit's network to prevent subsequent intrusions."

Magister Canus's eyes widened slightly. "And you did this for the Imperial family's dungeon?"

"Affirmative."

Emperor Lucius sighed at that. "A bit of good news, then. I do not want to imagine a situation where we lose every dungeon across the entire Empire."

Magister Canus nodded. "Not only that . . . we know what to do. Do we know where Amulius is?"

"Affirmative."

Seero opened an entrance to the Primary Home Base right in the room, startling everyone outside of her subordinates. Magister Canus rubbed his chin as Amulius, Agedia, Ateia, and Taog stepped out. "So that's how you moved the Dobhar so quickly . . . Your Majesty, could you share the restrictions on this spell?"

"Response: It is limited to dungeons under this unit's control or the area around this unit."

Magister Canus nodded. "And would you be willing to share this capability with us and assist us with the dungeons?"

Seero's eye flickered for a second as she conducted a cost-benefit analysis. But since her allies had remained friendly toward her upon learning of her dungeon nature, she concluded the risks to doing so were acceptable.

"Affirmative."

Magister Canus nodded before humming for a moment. Everyone paused what they were doing to watch him. Soon, he smiled to himself. "This will work. Magister Peditum Ausonius, draw up a map of fallback positions, and instruct the Legion to evacuate all civilians there. They'll hold the line until reinforcements arrive."

Magister Ausonius saluted and got to work. Magister Canus turned to Seero. "If we give you a list of dungeons, would you be willing to conquer them, Your Majesty?"

"Affirmative."

Magister Canus nodded. "Thank you. Off the top of my head, the Imperial Academy is close by, and we could definitely use the support of the mages there."

"Acknowledged. Engaging dungeon termination or integration protocols."

Magister Canus nodded, then turned to Amulius. "Could you take Exploratore Amulius with you? I'd like to verify if a hero can purify the dungeon as well."

"Affirmative. Informative Statement: This unit should also mention that Friend Taog also has the Hero feat, and Friend Ateia is highly capable of generating Holy mana. Many of this unit's other subordinates are also capable to varying degrees of applying Holy mana."

Amulius's jaw dropped, and he turned toward Taog. "Wait, what?"

Meanwhile, Magister Canus's eyes widened slightly before he smiled. "Thank you, Your Majesty. That is *very* helpful to hear."

With that, Seero turned to leave. "Acknowledged. Status Report: This unit is commencing dungeon termination or integration mission. Target: Imperial Academy Arcanum."

Magister Arcanum Cnaeus was not having a good day. He was currently standing on the walls of Academiae Civitatem, the city containing the Imperial Academy. A horde of monsters surrounded them, pounding on the walls and testing the barriers guarding the skies.

The Legion and the mages of the academy were firing back, the Magister Arcanum included, but the hordes didn't thin in the slightest. Even now, the Magister Arcanum could see new columns of monsters feeding into the horde.

At first, establishing the Imperial Academy in a location surrounded by dungeons had been a wise and practical decision. The mages of the academy needed a hefty supply of magic cores and magical materials, so having easy access to several dungeons was a must. Likewise, it was noted that Rifts were less likely to occur in areas with heavier dungeon concentration, and more likely to occur with heavy magical experimentation, so locating the academy here improved safety as well.

At least, assuming those dungeons kept to themselves and did not become corrupted.

And worse still . . . the loss of the Aesdes had hit the academy hard, and Magister Cnaeus most of all. He found he could hardly cast any of the spells he had learned since he became the Magister Arcanum, which was to be expected!

Ever since then, Cnaeus had had to spend countless hours filling out paperwork, negotiating with witless politicians and clueless legionnaires, managing bickering and arrogant mages, and taking care of the constant stream of young and reckless aspiring mages, all while keeping track of all the experiments going on to ensure a minimum of explosions *and* trying to find some time for his own research on top of that!

So, he could and *SHOULD* be forgiven if he relied a bit too much on the Aesdes for the continued development of his magic! The disappointed looks from Academiae Civitatem's Legion guards as he failed to cast a strategic spell were entirely unfair! He hadn't cast such a thing in years, and the Magus Majors of the academy didn't get along well enough to practice Ritual Magic with one another! And Sidonia, the one who *should* be handling this sort of thing, was nowhere to be seen!

Just then, the wall lit up with several magic circles. "All right, everyone, aim for my beam!"

A newly promoted mage, Nonus Callisunus, formed a magic circle. A number of other mages and apprentices did likewise around him. Nonus had only recently graduated from apprentice, but had quickly become a rising star. He had been forced into theoretical studies for years by his condition, so when the queen of the Dobhar had cured him and enabled him to finally put such things into practice, he had grown dramatically.

Nonus fired a simple Light Beam as the other mages around him did likewise, aiming for his beam instead of the monsters below. Once they collided with Nonus's, they all fused together into a superbeam. Nonus then directed the attack toward the monsters below, piercing straight through the heart of a giant about to lob a boulder at the walls. The monster fell back, crushing all the monsters behind it before fading.

Nonus had been . . . quite enthusiastic in studying the reports on the queen of the Dobhar. As such, he'd managed to discover an entirely new spell modifier. His new Fusion Light Beam was the talk of the academy.

And since he had studied the theory for years before he could even attempt to gain the skills, he'd known his spells inside and out long before the Aesdes gifted them to him. Which meant that he, unlike even many of the Magus Majors, had hardly been affected by the disappearance of the Aesdes.

Still, one mage could not overcome an entire horde. Nonus's spell could allow him and several other weaker mages to contribute beyond their individual ability, but he was no Magister Arcanum. The walls were holding for now, but the situation was growing bleak. Magister Cnaeus himself was drained of mana, as were most of the Magus Majors.

Until . . . Magister Cnaeus noticed something strange. A string of explosions and shifting patterns of light in the distance, along one of the columns of monsters. Said explosions grew closer until they hit the horde around the walls. The defenders of the walls blinked, then turned to Magister Cnaeus.

"As expected of the Magister Arcanum!"

Magister Cnaeus just heaved a sigh. "Does it *look* like I'm casting spells right now?"

Just then, the sky lit up. *Dozens* of strategic magic circles filled the skies. Beams of all colors and attributes rained down on the hordes below.

Nonus looked up, and his eyes brightened. "It's the queen of the Dobhar!"

Magister Cnaeus glanced up as the queen of the Dobhar floated above the city, Multicasting strategic spells across an entire city. He furrowed his brow before throwing his hands up.

"That's it! I'm done with this!"

8

Divide and Terminate!

"Never, and I repeat, never utter the words: Let's split up, gang."

—International League of Superheroes Training Manual.

As the monster horde thinned out, Seero passed control of the Prismatic Bombardment circles to her subordinates while strike drones continued to bombard the incoming monster reinforcements. Seero turned her attention to the Imperials, locating and landing in front of Magister Arcanum Cnaeus.

"Greeting: This unit is designated Seero; official Imperial designations: Queen of the Dobhar, Amicitia Populi Elteni. It is nice to meet you. Statement: This unit has arrived to terminate or integrate nearby dungeons. Command: Local Imperial forces should organize to support the mission. Please check long-range communications if confirmation by Imperial authorities is required."

The Legion legate commanding the defense took one look at the devastation below and shook her head, giving a salute. "That won't be necessary, Your Majesty. We'll get right on it."

Magister Cnaeus sighed and slumped his shoulders. "Do what you want. We . . . appreciate the help."

"Acknowledged. Command: Please confirm details of the operation with Exploratore Amulius Olcinius Herenus."

With that, Ateia, Taog, and Estrith flew in from the sky, with Amulius and Agedia following via Sky Legion artifacts. The legate's eyes widened. "Amulius? You mean . . . the Hero of Elteno?! It's an honor, sir!"

Amulius nodded as he landed, then began speaking with the legate on the mission. There were three major dungeons in the area around the Imperial Academy. As such, the plan was for the group to split up in order to handle the dungeons as quickly as possible, as well as to determine if Holy mana alone could permanently defeat the corrupted mana intrusion.

As such, the Hero of Elteno would lead one mission with Agedia, Ateia, Taog, and Estrith, reinforced by the forces of Academiae Civitatem. Meanwhile, Seero and her subordinates would handle the other two, with Seero taking down the one with the strongest mana signature, and her monster subordinates tackling the third.

Now that Academiae Civitatem had stabilized and the Hero of Elteno was in contact with Imperial authorities, Seero was about to take off and tackle her dungeon when she heard a voice.

"Your Majesty NSLICE-00P! It's an honor to see you again!"

"Objection: This unit's designation has been updated. Please refer to this unit as Seero."

Nonus ran up to her, waving his hands. He quickly nodded.

"My apologies! It's an honor to see you again, Your Majesty Seero! I just wanted to tell you how grateful I am for curing me!"

"Acknowledged."

Nonus glanced at the strategic magic bombardment beyond the walls. "I . . . would offer to help you in any way I can . . . but it doesn't seem like I can . . ."

"Statement: Exploratore Amulius Olcinius Herenus is recruiting Imperial assets for a mission involving this unit's friends. Recommendation: Please report to Imperial authorities to volunteer assistance."

Nonus's eyes widened, then he nodded, his eyes narrowing. "I'll go right away. I swear I will repay you, Your Majesty!"

"Acknowledged."

With that, Seero boosted into the sky, flying toward one of the dungeons and bombarding the monsters along the way. When she arrived at its entrance, she deployed her monsters, as well as a full complement of infantry drone golems.

"Command: All units, engage dungeon purification or termination protocols. Unit 01R is designated as the lead unit."

01R knelt before her. "We will complete-accomplish our mission no matter what, wise-mighty-gracious boss-queen! Even if it costs-requires our lives, yes-yes!"

"Clarifying Command: Relative force predictions indicate casualties should be avoidable on this mission, and containment of the dungeon forces is considered sufficient if purification or termination prove impossible. All units should prioritize asset preservation over mission completion if both cannot be achieved. Loss of drone assets is considered acceptable, but loss of CELIU units would not be efficient."

01R stared up at her with wide eyes, his organic eye filling with moisture. "Wise-mighty-gracious boss-queen . . . you truly are ever caring-loving, yes-yes.

I hear-understand your will! I, 01R, swear I shall complete this mission without losing-sacrificing a single one of your servants, yes-yes!"

"Acknowledged. Command: All units, begin mission."

The monsters all shouted and roared—save for Lilussees, who just yawned—and then they rushed into the dungeon. Seero dedicated a thread to keep an eye on them before setting off for her own target.

Once inside the dungeon, 01R boosted forward on his repulsors at maximum speed. Now that they were no longer covered by the Prismatic Bombardment circles or the drone fleet, Seero's forces had to face the incoming monsters directly. Fused Holy Light Blades formed over 01R's paws, and he began to glow with golden-and-silver light.

"Foolish monster-things who cannot see-understand the majesty of the wise-mighty-gracious boss-queen, taste the loyalty-devotion of her servants, yes-yes!"

He swung his blades, sending out arcs of Holy Light that split and burned every monster they encountered. The loss of the Aesdes and their records mattered little to 01R. He had always put his trust in the boss-queen instead; he even approved of her servants relying on nothing but her!

His repulsors combined with his Dash skill to send him speeding forth, a shooting star that cut through the hordes with a golden-and-silver flash.

He came face-to-face with a stone golem many times his size. Grinning, he was about to leap into battle when an anti-armor shell smashed into the golem's torso. The round pierced through the creature's core, and it fell apart.

00B thundered forward, a mighty cannon on his back swiveling around to fire another shot as he roared. His protective roar sent out waves of mana that pulled hostile spells from their trajectories, causing them to strike the armored fighting bear's impenetrable defenses instead.

He then roared at 01R while Lilussees slowly strolled up, yawning as she wrapped a golem in magical web.

"The bear's right. Like, slow down, you fanatical snack; you're leaving the drones behind. You're supposed to be, like, the leader or something."

01R's ears fell against his head. "You are . . . right-correct, yes-yes. I apologize."

He admitted he had gotten a bit . . . *excited* in his zeal, but how could he not? The wise-mighty-gracious boss-queen had entrusted them with a mission . . . and this time, she would not be there to protect them. This was their chance; this was their moment. The wise-mighty-gracious boss-queen had finally trusted them to fight on her behalf, and 01R would prove to her they could be of service.

Still, 00B and Lilussees had a point. He had been designated as the leader of the mission, so he could not act as a simple warrior. It was his duty to set aside his own desires and consider the group as a whole. It would not do for him to rush ahead and leave the others behind.

A moment later, the drone golem force caught up with the monsters. Lifting their arms, their right hands pointed open palms toward the enemy, the left holding gun barrels instead.

And then, they opened fire, their right arms firing Beam spells that constantly shifted colors. Seero had determined how to miniaturize a Prismatic Bombardment magic circle down to a single Beam spell, allowing it to change attributes at will. She had then converted that circle into an enchantment, which was installed as the primary armament for magical-strike drone golems.

While the drone golems could be instructed to select attributes in response to a situation, it had been found that this required them to give up other functions. So instead, Seero and Melion had programmed these drones to rapidly cycle through many attributes to ensure an effective attack. Of course, their pilots or local CELIU units could also command them to use a single attribute as needed.

As for their left arms, they fired conventional assault rifles, adding a physical component to the barrage whenever magic failed.

As such, the drone golems began a methodical advance, which 00B and Lilussees covered with defensive skills and spells. Meanwhile, 01R looked over the battlefield and began directing the CELIU units to take on the most powerful monsters. The drone golems were highly effective against the average creature, but they couldn't handle the elites without heavy losses, so 01R and the others still had an important role to play.

And so, the CELIU network began its first dungeon termination mission without the protection of their boss-queen.

Meanwhile, the wise-mighty-gracious boss-queen herself arrived at the strongest dungeon; the one known to have many monsters resistant to magic, and so only braved by Magus Majors and above.

Fortunately, Seero's Mana Density *far* exceeded any Magus Major, or even any Magister Arcanum. And that was before considering the Spell Penetration and Heroic Challenger skills that could defeat magical resistance, or the simple application of modern firearms, as many of these monsters lacked physical resilience.

As such, Seero was not hindered in the slightest by the monster horde, and had already passed through several floors of the dungeon by this time.

Amulius sighed as he watched Ateia and Taog prepare for the assault. Ateia was smiling and giggling to herself.

"Ateia, I'm glad you're happy, but stay focused. Even a normal dungeon is dangerous, and this dungeon isn't acting normal."

But she continued to smile. "Sorry, sorry, it's just . . . I always dreamed of the day we'd fight together. Even after everything, I can't help but smile."

Amulius's heart pounded in his chest as several different emotions warred within him. "It was my hope you'd never have to fight at all."

Estrith tilted her head at that. "You wished for your pup not to grow into a valiant warrior? Imperials truly are strange."

Meanwhile, Taog smirked. "You probably shouldn't have let her spend so much time with my parents, then. They agreed with that sentiment."

Agedia shook her head while clicking her tongue. "And honestly, did you expect your and Aedinia's daughter *not* to go running off into danger at the first opportunity? That was dumb of you."

Amulius sighed and hung his head. "That's *why* I hoped to keep her away from it, but I guess it was inevitable." Looking up at Ateia, he slowly smiled as well. "Though . . . I *am* happy we're here together now, at the very least."

Ateia blinked and gave a wide smile at that. Amulius took a deep breath.

He then turned, his eyes narrowed and sharp as he prepared his bow and focused on the dungeon entrance ahead of him.

Seero's drones, or whatever she called them, were still raining spells and explosives from above, keeping the monsters at bay while the group prepared. But in just a moment, they would stop, and it would be up to the group on the ground to take on this dungeon, just as Amulius had done countless times over the past years, and with full support from the Legion and the Imperial Academy to boot. But, for the first time, with his own children on the line.

He swore to himself that whatever happened, he would make sure they came back safe.

"Is everyone ready?"

The group around him nodded, while the centurion in charge of the Imperial complement saluted. Amulius took a deep breath as the spells and explosions ceased.

"Let's begin."

9

All Grown Up and Efficient!

"Ah, children. One day you're cradling them in your arms, and the next they're casting Fireball. One of the great mysteries of the world indeed."

—The Celestial Elf Sage Baoruinë, after the tenth grand arson incident caused by a young master of his clan.

Amulius blinked as he tried to comprehend the scene in front of him. The Legion soldiers on standby were staring with their mouths wide open, while the academy mages were muttering to themselves. The one called Nonus was furiously taking notes on a scroll.

At first, Amulius had refused to let Ateia and Taog go into a dungeon, only to be overruled entirely. It was not their first dungeon conquest, not by far, and at the end of the day, the pair had Contracted with Seero, and so fell under the dungeon master's authority. Ateia and Taog themselves had been adamant, and there had been little Amulius could do to stop them.

As such, he had done the next best thing and volunteered to lead the mission, citing his experience with corrupted dungeons. He'd been a bit surprised when Seero had easily agreed. He had then attempted to keep Ateia and Taog in the rear, as supply carriers for the Legion complement, but this had been rejected by the pair, and vetoed by Agedia as well, so Amulius had had no choice but to take them with him to the actual fight.

Still, he'd planned to keep them in the rear as much as possible. It would put a lot of pressure on him, Agedia, and the Dobhar, but he believed they could handle it.

That . . . was not what happened.

Taog dashed in and out of the shadows, his Dark mana shroud blending in and obscuring him even from Amulius's view. Those same shadows twisted into spikes and blades of Holy-empowered Dark mana that tore through the monster hordes with ease.

Taog himself carried blades coated in the same mana, stabbing and slashing at the monsters all around him. And anytime a monster managed to get close to hitting the boy, Dark mana surged to block the attack. Taog hadn't even gotten a scratch on his armor.

For her part, Ateia, standing just in front of Amulius, was drawing her bow without any arrows. Instead, bolts of pure Light and Holy mana formed in her hand as she pulled back the string. When she released them, the arrows turned into beams of light, each one splitting into several more, which pierced through a dozen monsters all at once.

She repeated this process over and over without a single pause or mistake, apparently not needing even a moment to find her aim. Amulius would still be drawing his arrow as Ateia took down his intended target.

Strange-looking, flying golems buzzed in the air around each of the pair, forming Barriers or casting Beam spells to assist the two, as well as the Dobhar warrior, who was also tearing through the front with the younger pair.

Amulius pursed his lips. It was one thing to be told that Taog was a hero and Ateia was an Aesdes. No matter if he accepted it or not, deep down, he could only see the young children he had left behind. He just couldn't imagine such fantastical claims being true.

Now . . . Now he watched his two little kids decimate a horde that would push a veteran knight to the limit. That even he wouldn't try to take on alone.

Just then, a monster snuck up behind Taog while he was occupied with another. Amulius was about to shout a warning when a magic circle formed on Taog's back and launched a Dark Beam directly into the monster's head, without the boy ever turning to look at it. Amulius slowly closed his mouth.

Agedia smirked as she sipped from her flask. "Surprised?"

He continued staring at the slaughter before him. "That's an understatement."

Her smirk grew. "And you wanted them on logistical support."

Amulius sighed and shook his head. "It's impressive, to be sure, but they're using a lot of mana. We'll need to talk to them about pacing when we take a break."

Agedia grinned. "About that . . ." She turned to the front. "Hey, Ateia, how are you feeling? Think you're going to need a break soon?"

Ateia turned to face them, tilting her head as she continued to launch her magic arrows toward the front. "Um, no? Why do you ask?"

Agedia elbowed Amulius. "Daddy here is worried you might be getting tired, what with the fact the three of you are handling the entire horde on your own."

Ateia blinked, and then grinned. "Wait a moment . . . Ah, found it!" Ateia's voice went monotone and emotionless as she spoke next. "Explanation: This unit's reserves are holding steady at the current expenditure. This unit's cybernetic components also do not experience fatigue. This unit is now efficient enough to enact the 'emulate Seero' protocol."

Agedia nodded and turned to Amulius. "And there you have it. Shiny girl happens to have taught them a thing or two, and there's more to that armor than protection."

Amulius thought to object when Agedia mentioned Seero, but his mind turned back to just a short while ago, when he watched said individual *Multicast strategic spells*, a feat even the Archons couldn't pull off, and then appear no worse for wear afterward.

No, in fact, she'd immediately taken off toward her target dungeon while Amulius was still arranging things with the Legion and the academy mages, continuing to cast her spells all the while.

Eventually, he smiled wryly. One would think the Hero of Elteno, of all people, might acknowledge that the world was full of surprises. And of all the surprises he had encountered . . . Ateia and Taog growing powerful beyond his imagination was one he could live with.

He watched Ateia standing tall, seeing in that moment the spitting image of her mother, with Holy mana forming a glowing aura around her as she drew her bow, a light illuminating the dark dungeon around her. He watched Taog leap in and out of the shadows, holding back the monstrous horde with shields and blades of Dark mana, a warrior more ferocious than his mother, and a bulwark more insurmountable than his father.

His smile slowly grew as he felt his chest turn warm. Nonus, meanwhile, perked up and walked over.

"Wait, so that armor is not just for show and has effects beyond identification and protection?"

Agedia turned to the newcomer. "Who are you?"

Nonus saluted. "Magus Nonus Callisunus, at your service. The queen of the Dobhar changed my life, and is one of the most powerful mages in the Empire to boot. I've been studying her techniques as best I could."

Agedia thought for a moment before nodding. "Ah, I think I remember them mentioning that. When shiny girl did a miracle cure on some helpless apprentice that got all the pointy hats into an uproar?"

Nonus grinned and nodded. "Yep, that was me! I had hoped to pay her back someday, but she vanished before I had the chance, so I sought to understand her instead."

Agedia nodded. "Got it. Well, to answer your question, yes, that armor is *way* more than just a piece of metal. It's got all sorts of tricks built into it, like, for example, the fact that it can move on its own, so those two's bodies don't have to work as hard as ours."

Nonus's eyes lit up. "Fascinating! So, some kind of motion or skill-based enchantment? Or is it like a wearable golem? But how does she prevent the user's mana from interfering with the golem enchantment, and how would the control scheme function in that case?"

Agedia shrugged. "Beats me. I have no idea how it works."

She turned her attention back to the front as Ateia formed some Beam magic circles along with her bow, intensifying her barrage. Taog spread his Dark Shroud across the floor, and then a field of spikes impaled an entire group of monsters. Agedia smiled.

"All I know is that it's absolutely terrifying."

Lilussees heaved a sigh as she cast a Barrier spell, blocking a wave of Poison spells from hitting 00B. The bear was far too insistent on taking all the blows, enjoying his upgraded armor and defensive skills a bit too much. And the bear—along with most of the boss lady's monsters—had their expectations skewed due to terminating many young dungeons. They seemed to believe all of them were monolithic, and that the golems and Earth-attribute monsters they'd faced at the start represented all they would encounter.

Lilussees knew it wasn't so clear. While dungeons started with a single affinity that would define them overall, it was not like they couldn't gain more over time. She would tell them to look at the boss lady's army as an example, but those fanatics would just say she was special. Which she was, but the fanatics took it too far.

The point was that 00B seemed to think he could just tank everything head-on.

Well . . . theoretically, he *could* endure a lot of poison for a very long time, and Lilussees *did* have a Cure spell, but would it kill him to pay attention to what was hitting him?

00B grunted his thanks to her. If he was going to thank her, then he should pay attention in the first place!

Lilussees sighed and lashed out with one of her arms, sending a string of web deep into enemy lines, where the Sacred Otterkin had dove. The web stuck to his back, and then Lilussees pulled him out of the crowd just before the monsters launched their counterattack.

Seriously, this guy had learned too much from the fanatic snack, and now thought suicidal impulses were a good thing! The boss lady and the slime had worked really hard to build an army of expendable golems; Lilussees thought at least *someone* should bother to use them as intended!

The suicidal Otterkin smiled at her as he flew back to the golem line. "Thank you, Eldest Sister! We make a fine team!"

Lilussees shook her hand. "Yes, yes, but like, if you're grateful, then stop being suicidal or something."

The Otterkin gave her a sheepish smile and nodded before running off. Probably to do something suicidal again. Lilussees sighed again.

Technically, the cowardly snack was the eldest by their standard, but like, most of the newcomers didn't know he existed, and it was way too much work for Lilussees to correct them.

Lilussees blinked as she recalled the snack. While she was glad not to see the face of the idiot who had stolen her sleep, she *did* miss having someone who would tremble in fear at her mere presence. The newest snacks held no fear of her at all, taking after the fanatic. Well, save for that Snuan girl, but she hadn't left the Monster Hangar after gaining control of the drone golems.

Speaking of which, Lilussees redirected a formation of them with magical webs tied between them. The movement arranged the web into a magic circle, firing a Beam spell at the enemy's Poison mage.

"I, like, need more golems or something. But, like, these golems take too much work. I wonder if there's, like, an easier way to get minions to work for me or something?"

"Feel the wrath of my queen's warriors!"

A battle cry and a golden-and-silver otter jumping into the enemy interrupted Lilussees's thoughts. She heaved a sigh and shot out yet *another* web.

She decided she was sleeping twenty-four hours for every time she had to save a fanatical idiot on this trip.

Meanwhile, Seero had reached about halfway through her dungeon. Her robotic eye flickered as she received updates from the other teams.

"Acknowledgement: Unit Lilussees's observation appears to be accurate. CELIU unit may require adjustments to self-preservation protocols. Unit Lilussees, however, appears to be displaying efficient coordination to improve friendly survivability, enabling other units to take increased risks."

And so, Seero's assessment of Lilussees's capabilities continued to improve.

10

Sending Thoughts, Prayers, and Protocols

"Why do magic circles produce effects? The ultimate answer is . . . we don't know. Not really. Oh, sure, we know it is some sort of language whose sentences are written upon reality itself, but we don't fundamentally know why this language in particular is the one that affects reality as opposed to the written words of Elves, Dwarves, Humans, or Beastkin.

And we know this language is not strictly necessary, either, for the Elvish nations possess records of magic from a time before the circles, and the Ancient Dragons don't need them at all.

All we know is that the Aesdes granted these circles to us, and in doing so, made magic a tool of the masses, easily learned by anyone with the inclination to do so."

—*The History of Magic,* Volume 1, by Magus Major Insteia Dulcitia

Ateia and Taog sat down with Amulius. They had reached a forest level and made camp in a clearing by the entrance. Amulius had convinced the pair to take a break, and now, the Legion and the academy mages were holding the line against a wave of plant monsters growing from the forest.

Amulius gave them a small smirk. "You two have grown pretty strong, huh?"

They glanced at each other and grinned. "I guess . . . we have, after all."

Ateia nodded. "It's hard to tell when Seero's around."

Taog tilted his head. "But we're like mini Seeros now, so should make sense that we're strong now, right?"

She nodded. "I should hope so." Then her face curled into a grin. "After all, I paid an arm and a leg for this!"

Taog blinked for a second before laughing. Amulius stared at them before his eyes suddenly widened.

"Wait . . . what do you mean by that, Ateia? You're just joking, right?"

Ateia turned to face him, tilting her head before her face fell. "Oh . . . you haven't realized, have you?"

Amulius began to tremble. Ateia didn't say anything, instead holding up her hands. Grabbing one of the fingers on her left hand, she pulled it off entirely, holding it up before reconnecting it. She then opened and closed her left hand and moved her fingers around like nothing had happened.

"This isn't just armor, Dad. It's . . . a bit hard to explain, but you can think of it like a golem replacing the missing parts of my body."

Amulius heart pounded in his chest, his face turning pale. ". . . Missing?"

Ateia nodded and took a deep breath. "I mentioned it, but I guess not in detail? The cult didn't *try* to sacrifice me; they really did it. Half my body had faded away from mana overload by the time Seero rescued me. But Seero managed to replace what I lost, and now, I'm stronger than ever."

Amulius's jaw dropped, his eyes filling with tears. "Ateia . . ." He then spun around to face Taog. "Taog . . . you too?"

Taog immediately shook his head and waved his hands in front of him. "Ah, no, mine is different. It was a fully voluntary and much less dramatic process, so I still have all of my body." Pausing, he tilted his head and nodded. "Though I should say, it's not *just* armor for me either. It's a wearable golem, like Ateia said, and deeply connected to my body and mind."

Amulius froze. "Wait . . . it's connected to your mind?"

Ateia and Taog nodded. Amulius's face turned dark. "Then, couldn't it—"

Agedia sighed. "Let me stop you right there." She slithered in front of Amulius, crossing her arms. "Yes, it gives shiny girl a back door into their minds. I don't get it fully, but I know they can see what each other sees and speak to each other directly in their heads.

"And yes, as you're probably thinking right now, shiny girl *could* hypothetically use it to manipulate them. In fact, she unintentionally did so to Ateia after rescuing her. This caused Ateia a lot of pain, which horrified shiny girl once she realized, and she has never done it since."

Ateia nodded, wincing slightly at the memory. "It . . . wasn't pleasant, having something foreign reach into my mind. But Seero's given me full control of it now. And if it weren't for her, I wouldn't be here at all, in any form."

Amulius furrowed his brow. "But . . ."

Agedia put a hand on his shoulder. "I know it's hard to accept, but also remember that those two are fully Contracted to her at this point. Shiny girl wouldn't *need* to manipulate them to make them do as she pleases."

Ateia nodded, frowning herself. "In fact, Seero had to work hard to free *herself* from that kind of thing. So please, do *not* imply that she would try the same thing on us now. I know she wouldn't."

Amulius kept frowning but sighed in defeat. But before he could speak, they heard a grunt from the battle ahead, and everyone turned to look. One of the bulwarks had failed to activate their bracing skill, and so had been sent flying by a large tree monster. Agedia curled down and leapt into the air, grabbing the legionnaire before they hit the ground. They shook their head.

"Ugh, I'm sorry. My centurion always told me I needed to practice that skill more. Guess I should have listened."

The legionnaire was fine, but now, there was a hole in the line, and the monsters started rushing through. Nonus responded with a Fireball spell, but it was noticeably less powerful than the ones from before. One of the other mages turned to him.

"Can't we fuse them again?"

Nonus frowned. "I wish I could, but I've only figured out how to do it with Light Beam, and Light doesn't work on plant monsters like this."

Ateia and Taog were about to stand up when Amulius waved them down. The Legion troops had already reacted, with slayers and sharpshooters cutting down the monsters that made it through while the bulwarks shifted their formation to close the gap.

"I know it's hard to watch, but this is their job, and they know what they're doing. Mistakes and unexpected situations always happen during battle, but the Legion knows how to cope." Then he sighed. "It's just . . . losing the Aesdes has been hard on everyone, the troops especially."

At that, Ateia froze, blinking a few times. "The Aesdes, huh?"

Taog turned to her, then grinned. "You have an idea?"

She stood up and looked at her hands. "Maybe. I don't know if this will work but . . ."

Amulius moved his head, glancing back and forth between the two of them. "Hm?"

Agedia grinned. "Slipped your mind, huh? Technically speaking . . . we haven't lost *all* the Aesdes."

Amulius's eyes widened as Ateia closed her own. Mechanical wings spread from her back before lighting up, bathing the area in golden-and-silver light. That light streamed toward the Legion troops at the front, filling them each with a warm aura.

Holy mana now coated their blades, healed their wounds, and eased their fatigue. The Legion troops paused just for a moment before they started to grin and pushed against the monsters with renewed vigor.

But that was but a simple blessing; something Ateia already knew how to do. That was not what she wanted to try here.

Instead, she focused on Nonus. "Ah, Nonus, the one Seero helped, right? That should work."

Focusing on him, she imagined what she wanted to happen. She imagined pulling it off herself, remembering similar feats she had performed in the past. And while her human eye remained closed, her robotic one began to flicker as she queried the CELIU network.

Seero was about to break into the final floor when an unexpected message passed before her UI.

Friend Ateia is requesting for unaffiliated units to access the CELIU network. Requested units designated as Imperial mages, temporarily allied. Access requested: CELIU spell protocol database, UI support. Proceed?

Seero's robotic eye flickered as she analyzed the situation. Ateia appeared to be conducting an experiment to improve combat efficiency of their non-CELIU allies. She analyzed the requested contact. While allowing any unaffiliated party to access the network in any manner was a risk, she determined that the mages would not be directly interacting with the CELIU network per se.

Rather, Ateia would be acting as a middleman, transforming the digital data into a mana-based form in a one-way connection. That connection was predicted as acceptably secure, and improving the efficiency of allied forces was desirable.

Seero went ahead and approved the request.

Ateia gave a small smile as the approval came in, focusing on Nonus and the nearby mages. Her cybernetic components selected an appropriate spell, and then her mana streamed in through a blessing.

Nonus was about to cast another Fireball when something passed before his eyes. Something that caused his spell to fail . . . as well as his knees.

The spell protocol: Fusion Fire Beam has been shared with you.
Assisted casting is available. Engage spellcasting assistance protocol?

In fact, all around him, magic circles sputtered and faded as the mages reacted in shock. The centurion in charge turned his head toward them. "What's wrong?!"

Nonus trembled. "The Aesdes; they're back, but . . . it seems different. This is . . ."

He slowly turned around and saw Ateia. His eyes widened, but then he shook his head. His tutors always reprimanded him for letting his curiosity distract him, believing that to be the source of his earlier plight, and had drilled discipline into him. So he knew what he needed to focus on right now.

He went ahead and answered the question. Lights began to flash in front of his eyes, forming into illusory images as they arranged themselves into a spell circle in the air before him. His eyes widened.

"It is like my Fusion Light Beam, but this is . . . a Fire attribute instead?"

But he again shook his head. Academic curiosity would have to wait for live spellcasting tests in this situation. He stirred up his mana and began to move it along the illusory circle. As he did, Holy mana filled him and wrapped around him, helping to guide his own into shape, stopping him when he was about to make a mistake, and smoothing out the circle.

Ateia instructed her cybernetic components to assist him with the cast as they did for her, only through the blessing this time. As a result, Nonus was able to complete a magic circle he had never seen before on the first try.

Just like when he received a spell from the Aesdes.

The Fire Beam shot forward into the plant monsters ahead, causing a large tree monster to writhe in anger. The other mages' eyes widened, and they, too, began to react to the messages in their eyes. Soon, multiple Fire Beams joined Nonus's, fusing into a mighty superbeam with jets of fire streaming out from it. The tree monster screamed as it burst into flames and burned to ash.

Ateia furrowed her brow in concentration, but she also started to grin. "It worked!"

Meanwhile, Amulius was staring at her wide-eyed and slack-jawed. He began to tremble. "Right . . . Aesdes . . ."

Only now did he truly question what that really meant.

11

A Bear-y Vicious Fight

"In my experience, there are three things in this world that cannot be stopped. They are a drunk Celestial sage, an Ancient Dragon, and an ursanus whose cub is threatened."

—Traveling author and former Exploratore Placus, Paesentius Statius

Seero finished purifying the dungeon core while the dungeon master just stared at her, then turned her attention to the other two groups, analyzing their situations.

Ateia had apparently succeeded in her experiment and applied basic skill assistance via the CELIU network to individuals outside of it. While unnecessary for the CELIU network's own members, the capability would be highly useful for cooperation with allied forces. And as Seero continued to analyze the situation in detail, she made a discovery. She detected a small amount of mana and data moving from the Imperial mages through Ateia and ultimately into the core of the Primary Home Base.

Shialnor's data and Imperial doctrine had indicated that the Aesdes' system didn't necessarily provide anything new to the inhabitants of Aelea, but rather quantified and organized it into more easily understood forms. Skills, attributes, and more were simply descriptions of phenomena that were already occurring.

The same went for levels and experience. By Seero's analysis, everyone and everything in Aelea was constantly absorbing small amounts of mana—from the atmosphere, from their food, from the ground, and from proximity to each other. And as they acted and performed various tasks, this mana gained small amounts of data recording what occurred. When that happened, it would permanently attach to the subject, increasing their overall mana capacity and capabilities.

And it seemed that Ateia's assistance for their allies was no small feat in this regard. Her mana, and by extension Seero's, was involved in every step of the process as Nonus and the other mages cast spells provided by the CELIU network.

Seero logged this as a phenomenon to research further and returned to analyzing the two groups' progress.

Her monster subordinates were advancing more quickly than the allied force, but that appeared to be intentional. The allied force utilized a methodical and carefully paced approach, involving scouting, planning, reorganization, and rotation of frontline units so that all units could rest at regular intervals.

The monsters, on the other hand, were pushing forward as quickly as they could, with all of them contributing to the fight at every moment. By Seero's analysis, they would complete the dungeon more efficiently in terms of time, but with higher risk due to increased fatigue, rapid advances, and a lack of reserves.

She calculated that she should reinforce the monsters, both due to their rapid advance, which would complete the dungeon soon, and to their *method* of advance, which could leave them vulnerable should the situation turn against them.

She informed the network that the dungeon had been purified and that she was en route to 01R's location before making her way out of the dungeon.

00B roared as he rushed toward a giant golem made of black stone. His back cannon opened fire, but the golem remained standing even after a direct hit. His repulsors and rocket boosters matched his roar as they launched him forward, crashing into the golem, which caught his paws in its hands. 00B grunted and roared again as he pushed against it.

With Big Sister Lilussees watching over them, the younger siblings had felt emboldened to push more aggressively. The group had rushed forward at an impressive pace, only slowing down to the maximum speed the drone golems could travel at. But the resistance had grown increasingly stiff as they went on, and now, their progress had slowed to a crawl.

The drone golems were all out of physical ammunition and had taken casualties despite 00B's best efforts. Less than half of them remained, as 00B had been forced to prioritize the cyborgs. Everyone else was low on mana, even Big Sister Lilussees.

Big Brother 01R was gritting his teeth and he flew through the air, slashing at the golem. He understood the situation as well as 00B. He knew they would need to slow down at this rate.

And that thought burned in their hearts. The Great Mother had already conquered her target dungeon, predicted to be the most powerful of the three, and was moving to assist them. If they did not reach the end soon, then she would arrive and handle things on her own. They would fail to be useful to her once again.

So, despite the danger, despite the foolishness of advancing, not one monster spoke of stopping. Except for Big Sister Lilussees, but she always did so, and from the very start, so that was just how she was. And if they were not stopping . . .

00B grunted as the golem socked him in the face. He managed to swipe at its torso in response, pushing it back slightly. Both failed to bypass the other's HP barrier.

. . . then it was up to 00B to keep his family safe.

00B didn't have the raw speed of Big Brother 01R, nor the magical firepower of Big Sister Lilussees or the Great Mother. His mana reserves were surprisingly low, and so he couldn't make use of many of the spells shared by the Great Mother.

But what he did have was raw strength and durability. A force of nature and metal combined into an unstoppable juggernaut. His HP barrier formed a visible shield around him that he could expand to protect his family nearby. His cybernetic components analyzed every incoming attack and told 00B how he should respond to minimize their impact. Active countermeasures could utilize mana, lasers, and even projectiles to intercept incoming spells.

Should an attack make its way through, thick composite armor with magical layers would block and mitigate the attack. And should it make it through all the way to his squishy parts, then his natural ursanus-lineage durability would kick in. His squishy parts were much less squishy than everyone else's.

The black golem stepped forward, swinging another fist toward him. 00B's cybernetic components indicated that if he crouched down, the swing would deflect off his armor, and he could use that moment to flip the golem over him.

00B did not do this.

The CELIU network informed him that several of his family were fighting behind him, and flipping the golem over would put them at risk. 00B refused to let that happen, so he took the blow head-on instead. The cannon on his back swung around, loading a high explosive shell and firing directly at the golem's fist.

The explosion mitigated some of the monster's momentum while the shrapnel bounced harmlessly off 00B's HP as he struck the golem's arm with his paw, sending the punch wide before the armored bear slammed his shoulder into the golem. And as it took another step back, 00B spent his mana to trigger a skill.

Holy mana stirred up within him and filled his squishy parts in a manner not unlike Little Sister Ateia. Strength surged through his body, and he let out a roar that shook the room.

00B pounced toward the golem, leaping up with the assistance of his repulsors, and swung his paw with all his considerable weight behind it. Repulsors on his arm and the back of his paw lit up as well, adding additional force to his strike.

His HP barrier shook for a moment as he landed his strike on the unyielding stone, a small crack forming on the golem's head.

00B renewed his attack, swinging repulsor and mana-assisted paws at the monster over and over. His cannon fired armor-piercing shells at point-blank range, leaving cracks and craters on the golem's surface. It pushed back, but Gravity Magic–infused webs from Big Sister Lilussees wrapped around its arms and legs, preventing it from responding. 00B was free to attack with impunity.

Soon, the ground was littered with chunks of black stone, the golem cracked and crumbling. 00B was just about to reach its core, but then, a second black golem stepped into the room, this one carrying a black spear.

It stepped toward 00B as he gritted his teeth, but he took a step back and let his buff skill fade. He needed to ensure he was at peak condition if he was going to take on a second foe.

The golem walked up to its fallen comrade—stabbing it right in the chest, the stone spear able to punch through the cracked, crumbling stone, crushing the creature's core.

As 00B tried to comprehend what was happening, the black golem began to attack the remaining enemies. None of their foes could stand against its spear, and once it was done, it took a step back, planting its weapon in the ground. 00B and the others eyed it warily.

"Well, it's about time!"

A short humanoid stepped into view from behind the golem. He had a large beard with small tusks extending from his lower jaw, and wore a blacksmith's apron with a hammer and pickaxe in his hands.

Big Brother 01R narrowed his eyes as he stepped forward. "Who are you?"

The newcomer scoffed. "Who am I? I'm the dungeon master, ya rodent! Now come on, ya all are from some dungeon master here to subjugate me, right?"

Big Brother 01R glared at him. "We are the servants of the wise-mighty-gracious boss-queen and—"

The dungeon master nodded. "Thought so. Well, come along then! My dungeon's going crazy, and not one of the new monsters listens to me no more! If yer boss queen or whatever has a solution, then let's hurry up and get on with it! I'll go ahead and surrender or what have ya if ya can fix this."

Big Brother 01R gnashed his teeth, but 00B grunted at him. Big Brother 01R was especially sensitive about the Great Mother and made a big deal of showing her proper respect.

Well, 00B understood that, and would *crush* anyone who dared disrespect her, but he also knew the Great Mother would prioritize their survival, so she wouldn't want them to pick a fight with someone who was offering to surrender.

Big Brother 01R glanced at him, then sighed. "Very well. Lead-guide us to your core, and then we shall consider allowing-permitting you to join the wise-mighty-gracious boss-queen's servants *if* you are worthy, yes-yes."

The dungeon master rolled his eyes. "That's what I'm trying to do! Now, stop lollygagging and get a move on!"

Big Brother 01R gnashed his teeth yet again, but he nodded to the rest of the group. They all began to follow the dungeon master and his golem as 00B took up point once again, carefully observing the pair in front of them.

Because no matter what happened, 00B would protect his family.

12

Terminate the Corruption!

"Well, I could, but that would cut them off from the Realms of Mana entirely, which would defeat the purpose of even having them. Oh, and they'd probably start drawing mana from the world then. That'd be bad."

—Shialnor, the Lady of Mana and the Boundary, on eliminating the risk of dungeon corruption.

The dungeon master led Seero's monsters to his core room, where the Sacred Otterkin stepped forward, as the monster with the deepest connection to Holy mana, and laid his paws on the core. He gently began to channel Holy mana through the orb, trying to remove the corruption without damaging the core itself . . .

As Seero approached the second dungeon, she watched the Sacred Otterkin's attempt at purification and focused her attention there. With the assistance of his cybernetic components, the Sacred Otterkin managed to isolate and target the corruption, terminating it with the core still intact. That part of the operation was a success.

But there was a problem. Corrupted mana continued to slip into the orb. The Sacred Otterkin could eliminate it temporarily, but it appeared he could not cut it off from its source. It would not suffice as a permanent solution.

Seero sent a message through the CELIU network.

"Command: Please remain in contact with the core and continue purification protocols."

The Sacred Otterkin's response came in immediately. *"Yes, my queen!"*

With that, Seero went to work. The immediate solution was for her to subordinate the dungeon, and the dungeon master had already offered to surrender.

But in all cases prior, Seero'd had to be physically present to accept the surrender. And after the corruption of the Aesdes' system, Seero had to be in direct physical contact to interface with the dungeon core.

But she knew from previous experiences that physical contact was not a strict necessity. With the Aesdes' system, she didn't need anything beyond verbal confirmation. She wasn't even sure physical proximity was necessary either; she had not tested a remote subjugation prior to the corruption of the Aesdes' system, but the Empire's records of interdungeon combat seemed to imply it was possible.

And Seero could already interact with the world through the CELIU network via the exchange of data. Likewise, she was connected to all of her subordinates via mana due to their Contracts, so she was already exchanging mana with them remotely.

Finally, Ateia had already demonstrated an ability to interact with the world remotely via Divination and Blessing, so Seero had proof of concept and found it reasonable to assume it was possible to do so via the CELIU network.

Whether it would be practical and efficient was another matter. But Seero had much stronger processors now, and data on the foreign system directly from its creators, so this would be a much easier task than learning Spatial Magic from one shoddy, failed magic circle!

Seero got to work analyzing the data, comparing it to the CELIU network's observations, and determining if there was a viable solution. She quickly found one. Ateia was already shaping other people's mana remotely, which meant Seero could use that as a guide to shape the Sacred Otterkin's mana.

So with the Sacred Otterkin's permission, Seero took control of his mana and used it to establish a connection between the dungeon core and the Primary Home Base, replicating the process from previous integrations.

And . . . she managed to succeed.

Her mana began to flow through the new subordinate core, reorienting its main connection from the Aesdes' system to the Primary Home Base. The flow of corrupted mana slowed to a trickle, and a shield of Holy mana formed around the core to prevent any further intrusions.

With that, two of the three dungeons had been dealt with. Seero thus turned her attention to the final dungeon.

Amulius's team had picked up the pace and were approaching the end of the dungeon. After Ateia had partially restored the boons of the Aesdes Amulius had reorganized the teams. Ateia now fought with the Legion contingent, utilizing Blessings to dramatically improve their effectiveness. With her support, they could not only hold the line with ease but were able to actively push forward.

And since Amulius and Agedia hadn't even needed to fight before, they had been able to pick up the slack on the other team. As a result, the group was able to rotate without stopping the advance.

Amulius was staring blankly as he watched Holy-empowered Legion troops cut down monsters with ease, and Imperial mages cast spells he had never seen before.

"That would have been *really* useful a while ago . . ."

Taog frowned. "Yeah, but Ateia only got those powers because of . . . what happened."

Amulius's face fell at that, but he shook his head to clear his mind. There would be a time for sorrow and regret, but a dungeon conquest wasn't it. Even if it was the easiest, smoothest, and least costly dungeon conquest Amulius had ever experienced.

It had been a long, painful process for Amulius to level his Trap Detection skill, and even then, he was never confident he had found them all. And traps aside, he'd never found a consistent method of finding a floor exit besides methodical exploration and extremely thorough mapmaking.

And now, Taog was telling him that special armor of theirs could automatically detect traps *AND* had an extremely accurate means to identify the fastest path through the dungeon? That they could build an accurate mental map of a floor's layout from the entrance in mere moments?

Sometimes, life wasn't fair. He was glad it was his kids who got those powers, but couldn't help but feel a bit jealous.

But, well, that armor also required being Contracted to a demon lord, so Amulius supposed they paid for what they received. All in all, he'd have MUCH preferred it if they had never gone through the events that had led to their strength.

In any case, Amulius turned his thoughts to something more productive. Focusing on the fight, he frowned and rubbed his chin. Agedia raised an eyebrow.

"You notice something?"

Amulius shook his head. "Not regarding this fight, but something feels off to me."

Agedia narrowed her eyes. "What is it?"

He hummed. "This is *too* easy. And not just because Ateia and Taog can do things I never imagined. This dungeon . . . it's acting like it's corrupted in terms of indiscriminate attacks, but by the amount and diverse types of monsters, it doesn't seem corrupted at all."

Agedia nodded. "Shiny girl said as much."

Amulius nodded too. "Right. But then, what's the goal here? The Legion has held the line even against corrupted dungeons. Normal hordes, even if every dungeon across the Empire is affected, are just not as dangerous. They have less monsters overall, they don't replenish as fast, and most of all, they don't grow over time on their own. If the Legion fends off the initial assault, it can handle the situation."

Agedia frowned and crossed her arms. "Small comfort to those caught in the way."

Amulius shook his head. "True. There's going to be a great deal of chaos and devastation across the Empire, not to mention the world at large, but still, the Empire can survive it if it acts carefully and is willing to cut some losses. From what that demon—"

Taog crossed his arms, and Amulius cleared his throat. "From what *Seero* claimed, the Heralds of the New Dawn struck at the *Aesdes* themselves to bring about this situation. So, a mere blow against the Empire, even a heavy one, doesn't seem like enough to represent the extent of their plans. I would expect something that the Empire couldn't survive at all, at the very least."

Agedia narrowed her eyes. "So you think there's something more going on here?"

Amulius sighed. "Right. No idea what, though. But I think we need to keep an eye out."

In the end, the group conquered the dungeon without issue. Amulius attempted to purify it, but only did so temporarily and nearly damaged the core in the process. Seero, predicting that connection to the dungeon via Ateia would be even easier than with the Sacred Otterkin, attempted the process through Estrith instead, who had no particular connection to Holy mana.

It was quite difficult, but they managed to pull it off. She then gathered her monster subordinates and met the allied force at the entrance to their dungeon.

Seero grabbed those who couldn't fly with barriers, and then they all flew back to Academiae Civitatem. On the way back, Uscfrea filled her in on the latest developments.

It appeared the Southern Court's representative had arrived.

Emperor Lucius sat upon his throne, looking at the representative from the Council of the Southern Realms.

"I understand the situation is critical, but that does not mean I will simply release a hostile force."

The representative gaped at him. "Your Majesty, I must protest! High King Xavlaeron's force was by no means hostile toward you or the Northern Court, and we cannot protect the Realms without the Sky Legion! I understand you have good relations with the queen of the Dobhar, but would you really sacrifice all of the Southern Realms over the high king's spat with a foreign power?"

Emperor Lucius scoffed. "I beg to differ. The high king usurped my control, took command of my legions, declared martial law without my approval, locked me up in my palace, and told me he was going to execute my daughter-in-law. You may beg to differ, but as far as I'm concerned, you have acted *very* hostile toward me and my court."

Emperor Lucius then smirked. "And to put it plainly . . . yes. Even if none of that were true, I would prioritize the queen of the Dobhar. In the time it took you to arrive, she has already cleared the area around Academiae Civitatem on my behalf. She has been a far greater ally to me than any of the Southern Realms, and *especially* in the circumstances we now find ourselves in."

The representative paled, his face falling. He dropped his head. ". . . What must we do to convince you?"

Emperor Lucius nodded sagely. "That is simple. Unconditional surrender."

The representative balked, looking up. "What?"

Emperor Lucius shrugged. "Or a direct affirmation of each of the Southern Realms' loyalty to Corvanus and its Emperor without any caveats, with a request for the Emperor to negotiate peace between the Southern Realms and the queen of the Dobhar, and a commitment to abide by any terms the Emperor and the queen of the Dobhar agree upon, if that is more palatable."

The representative started to tremble. "Such a thing . . ."

Emperor Lucius waved his hand. "Oh, I'm aware that most of the Southern Realms, especially Mirima, have maintained nominal independence from the Empire up to this point, and that you cannot agree to this on their behalf."

He grinned at the representative. "But those are the terms I offer. The Sky Legion and the remains of High King Xavlaeron's fleet will not be released with anything less. So, I suggest you contact the Council of the Southern Realms sooner rather than later."

Emperor Lucius rose to leave the room, leaving the representative staring despondently at the floor. But as he approached the exit, he glanced back. "You and the council should also consider this: the queen of the Dobhar protects her own. So, consider what options might arise if the South should surrender . . ."

With that, he left the room.

13

Plan of Action

"Sarcastic Explanation: Obviously, this unit knew from the start that Aurora Legion would have zero contribution to the planning phase, as usual. As such, this unit simply assumed she would have to do all the work again, and dedicated processing power to determining a solution on her own . . ."

—Commander Elise, during an improvised operation planning phase.

Seero dropped the Imperial mages and soldiers off at Academiae Civitatem, and was just about to head toward Corvanus when Nonus furrowed his brow and made his decision.

"Your Majesty Seero!"

"Acknowledgement: Does the ally have a query, request, or update for this unit?"

Nonus looked up at her and nodded. "Could I join you? You changed my life; I wish to be of use to you!"

"Affirmative."

Nonus gritted his teeth. "I know it's a lot to ask, but I promise I'll be . . . Wait, what?"

"Repetition: Affirmative."

After all, more CELIU units who did not need to be trained from level one would be helpful, particularly in the current crisis. Nonus had reasons to affiliate himself with Seero, and apparently, had recreated her Fusion Light Beam based solely on vague descriptions. She predicted he would be a useful asset to the network, particularly if he could be trained in drone-assisted Ritual Magic to back up Lilussees.

Nonus blinked before breaking out into a wide grin. "Thank you, Your Majesty! I swear I won't let you down!"

The two conferred with Magister Arcanum Cnaeus, but he had no objections to Nonus's transfer, just telling them to do as they pleased with a tired look. So, Seero took Nonus to a secure location.

"Request: If ally Nonus would like to affiliate with this unit, please sign the following Contract."

Nonus gave a small smirk as the Contract appeared before him. "As expected of Your Majesty."

He took some time reading through the contract, rubbing his chin and furrowing his brow. But then, he nodded and signed it. "I wouldn't even be a mage if it weren't for you. Given what's happening, I don't even know if I would have survived. So . . . I'll do it."

"Acknowledged. Query: Does friendly Nonus also wish to receive cybernetic augmentation?"

Nonus blinked. "Huh?"

"Providing Tutorial."

Fortunately, with Ateia, Taog, and Estrith's help, Seero had developed a helpful video tutorial to explain the CELIU process for the inhabitants of Aelea. Nonus's eyes grew wider and wider with each minute of the video.

"That's . . . a lot to take in. But you and your friends went through this?"

"Clarified Affirmation: This unit and Friend Ateia went through a different, more damaging process, but the end result is similar."

Nonus thought for a moment longer before nodding. "You healed my body once when no one else could. I would be honored to trust in you again."

"Acknowledged."

With that, Seero sent Nonus to the Primary Home Base for the CELIU upgrade process, then regrouped with the others and set off toward Corvanus. It did not take long before they arrived back at the Imperial palace and were quickly guided to the war room, where Emperor Lucius and the rest were waiting.

"Ah, Your Majesty Seero, welcome back," Emperor Lucius greeted her as she stepped into the room. "An excellent job, purifying those dungeons."

"Acknowledged."

Magister Canus nodded. "Indeed, freeing up the Imperial Academy gives us a lot more options, and hopefully some insight into the situation. Unfortunately, we have no time to waste. Would you mind if we got right to it, Your Majesty?"

"Affirmative."

Magister Canus turned toward Emperor Lucius, who cleared his throat. "The Southern Court has not responded to us yet, but I fear we will need your help before they do, Your Majesty. So, should they agree to our terms while you are in battle, would we have your permission to release the Sky Legion back to them?"

"Affirmative. Helpful Offer: This unit would like to transfer CELIU political specialist Vopiscus to Corvanus in order to coordinate diplomacy and communicate with this unit as necessary."

Emperor Lucius nodded. "Of course. It would be helpful to have a direct representative for you present, in fact."

"Acknowledged."

Emperor Lucius then nodded toward Magister Canus.

"Your Majesty, we've drawn up a plan of action for your approval. I believe Steward Uscfrea here has already informed you?"

"Affirmative. Statement: This unit has no objections to the proposed operation."

Thanks to the CELIU network, Seero had already had a chance to review the plans. The knowledge that Seero could create her own dungeons had been crucial, allowing Magister Canus to write off many of the minor dungeons. He had then identified the key dungeons necessary to the Empire's military and economy, as well as some especially dangerous ones the Empire likely couldn't hold back without assistance, and drawn up a priority list.

The Legion and other Imperial forces would focus on defending major evacuation zones until Seero cleared up the biggest threats, at which stage, they would organize their own assaults on the smaller dungeons.

And while nominally the Imperial commanders were deferring to Seero as the overall commander, her experience with operational and strategic planning was limited. Her protocols were limited largely to tactical settings due to her intended role as an enforcer. As such, she saw no issue in deferring to Magister Canus's judgment here.

Rather, Seero saw receiving a list of key targets as highly efficient. She turned around immediately upon getting it. "Status Update: Mission received; objectives identified. If there are no further queries, updates, or requests, this unit will proceed with the operation."

Magister Canus nodded. "We should be able to get in touch if that happens. And thank you, Your Majesty. The entire Empire and everyone in it will owe you their lives for your help here."

"Acknowledged."

Magister Canus had given Seero a list of targets, but he'd left it to her how to actually approach and deal with them. Seero thus split her forces into the same three groups as before, now that it was confirmed she could purify dungeons through the CELIU network.

Ateia, Taog, Estrith, and the newly upgraded Nonus would join Agedia and Amulius to coordinate with beleaguered Imperial forces. 01R would lead a monster team and assault more remote dungeons that Imperial forces had difficulty approaching. Seero herself would move on her own to handle the highest priority targets.

Magister Canus had also given Seero a full rundown on the dungeons in question. As most of these were ones that had been known to the Empire for decades, sometimes centuries, the Legion had comprehensive reports on their strength, affinities, and layout. Of course, they had continued to grow in the meantime, but the Empire had the expertise to make reasonable predictions on the changes.

As such, Seero was able to allocate the different groups for maximum efficiency and lowest risk of a friendly being terminated.

Meanwhile, drone golem and aerial forces under the command of Snuan would spread out and strike at the monster hordes out in the open in order to take the pressure off the Imperial defenders. Dux Augustalis would coordinate this with Magister Canus and redirect them as necessary.

Steward Uscfrea would return to Turannia, taking the airships and the Turannian forces with him. There, he would take command of the allied Turannian forces in cooperation with the Selkies and secure the allied forces' home front. He would also coordinate the return of the Sky Legion should the South decide to surrender.

Seero currently stood in the Primary Home Base in front of her subordinates, having just finished the briefing. 01R gave her a salute.

"Yes-yes, wise-mighty-gracious boss-queen! Your humble servants will conquer-subjugate all the land in your name, yes-yes!"

The monsters roared in response before 01R led them to one of the portal entrances. Lilussees sighed as they left her behind. "I'll, like, try to keep those idiots alive or something. But, like, no promises. I, like, *seriously* need a break."

As Lilussees slowly walked after the monsters, Ateia and Taog stepped toward Seero. "Well, we're off, then. Stay safe, Seero."

"Objection: By this unit's predictions, Friends Ateia and Taog are at greater risk of termination than this unit, which would constitute a failure for this unit's primary directive. Please take all measures necessary to prevent this outcome."

Ateia smiled at that, while Estrith took a step forward and slammed her spear on the ground, giving Seero a salute in Dobhar fashion. "I will guarantee that does not happen, my queen, even if I must give my life to make it so."

"Objection: Friendly Estrith is also considered a major asset and should avoid termination if at all possible."

Estrith blinked, then looked away. "Oh, um, I . . . will do my best, my queen."

Ateia turned to her and grinned. "That's right! You're one of us, Estrith, so you have to come home too!"

Taog nodded. "A warrior like you shouldn't die alone. How about we fight together?"

Estrith averted her eyes from the two, failing to respond for a moment. Eventually, she just turned away. "Enough of this! Your people are in danger; we must respond."

Ateia and Taog giggled as Estrith stormed off, then moved to follow her. Amulius waited until they gained some distance before walking toward Seero.

"Query: Does Ateia's person of interest have business with this unit?"

Amulius nodded. "I do." He bowed his head. "I'm sorry, Your Majesty Seero. Whatever you are, you saved my daughter's life, as well as her heart. You did what I failed to do. And for that, I owe you a great debt."

"Acknowledged."

Amulius then looked up with narrowed eyes. "So . . . be careful. I feel there is more to the Heralds' plan than just some rogue dungeons. This just doesn't seem big enough to be their end goal."

"Affirmative. Query: Does Ateia's person of interest have any additional data regarding the hostiles?"

Amulius shook his head. "When things calm down, I can share my experiences in general and what we learned over the years. But regarding the current situation, we had no idea it was coming, so your guess is as good as mine."

"Acknowledged. Request: Please share relevant intel with Friends Ateia and Taog during maintenance and rest cycles, as well as any additional data acquired during the operation."

Amulius nodded. "I will."

With that, he turned to leave, but paused and glanced back one more time. "Again, thank you for protecting Ateia." And then he headed out.

Immediately after, Seero left as well, moving to the Imperial family's dungeon and boosting into the sky once outside.

And so, the mission to terminate the threat to the Empire began.

14

The Ultimate Weapon vs. the Land of the Dead

"When the alternatives are genocidal mutant cultists and kid-stealing cyborg fascists, suddenly, the necromancers don't look so bad."

—A former US Admiral, on the diverse nature of the Resistance's membership.

Seero made her way to the first target on her list: the Haunted Mausoleum. This dungeon was unique as the only approved undead dungeon in the Northern Empire.

Undead dungeons represented a unique threat, as their access to necromancy would allow them to quickly spiral out of control if they ever went rogue. As such, most undead dungeons, even ones who behaved by Imperial standards, were subjugated without mercy.

Yet not all. One such dungeon was permitted to exist in each of the three parts of the Empire, and that was because they provided a steady source of Dark-attribute mana cores, with a specific affinity for Death Magic; a source that did not require vast quantities of death to maintain.

Such a dungeon could, thus, enable the Imperial Necrotorum to practice their craft without the need to inflict death upon the local populace, a key requirement for their acceptance into Imperial society. The mana cores and loot from an undead dungeon could even be used to form artificial corpses, reducing the necessity to gather them from . . . *natural* sources.

So, one such dungeon was permitted to exist in each division of the Empire—after it had been subjugated and forced into a strict contract. The Imperial Necrotorum also kept careful tabs on it, conducting constant patrols as they utilized it for resources and training.

But there was an overlooked problem with that plan that was now becoming apparent. With only one dungeon permitted to exist, that single dungeon had to supply the entire Necrotorum for the whole Northern Empire, and so had grown to become one of the largest dungeons on the continent. One that was now pouring all the undead it could produce into the world without any specific orders or organization.

Should such a horde spread into the countryside, it would quickly grow to become an existential threat. One that, by design, would appear in the Imperial Heartland close to some of its largest Legion bases. The very bases currently being used to evacuate the nearby farms and cities. The Imperial Necrotorum was now all that stood between the Empire and an undead apocalypse.

The Haunted Mausoleum was located in the mountains separating Utrad from the Imperial Heartland, in a rocky region lacking resources to mine or soil to farm. A massive stone gate adorned with skulls stood carved into the mountain, opening to reveal the black vortex of a dungeon entrance. Surrounding this gate were walls that towered halfway up the mountain, with all the mightiest fortifications the Empire could produce.

At the foot of these walls was a sea of rotting flesh, as undead of every type climbed on top of each other to reach the walls. And at the top, the Death mages of the Empire were putting to use all their skills and expertise in managing the undead. The walls glowed with eerie purple light as their enchantments activated, creating a decay field in the area between the walls and the dungeon. Countless undead wasted away and crumbled into ash.

The stronger ones pushed past the field toward the wall, clawing at it even as ash streamed from their bodies. But those who contacted the walls fell to pieces, as a Death Magic counterspell interfered with the magic holding their bodies together.

But still, the most powerful among them ignored such measures. Abominations formed from multiple corpses pounded on the glowing stone. Deadly ghouls and batlike creatures climbed and flew to the top of the walls. An undead wyvern took to the skies.

These, the Necrotorum had no choice but to face with undead of their own, skeletal warriors battling against rotting flesh. A war of the dead that would decide the fate of the living. For now, the Necrotorum was holding. As long as the enchantments remained active and the skeletons kept coming, they would hold.

But only that. The plan for this contingency was that the Necrotorum would hold while the Empire prepared a full-scale response. The Legion would be mobilized in its entirety to reinforce the line, while the Empire assembled the finest assault force it could muster. The wisest mages of the Southern Realms, the most elite veterans of the Eastern Legions, the most courageous of the knight orders, and the most cunning of the Exploratores would all be gathered.

The response would not be limited to the Empire's own; champions from allied tribes and the most elite mercenaries that could be hired would be gathered as well. And every single hero or wielder of Holy mana that could be found would be called to arms. The most powerful individuals of the generation would be assembled, and only then, with the full support of the entire Necrotorum, would they assault the dungeon.

But that plan wasn't going to happen now. With dungeons going rogue across the Empire, the Legion could not be assembled. Every legion, garrison, and outpost was on their own to hold the line against whatever dungeons happened to be nearby. Reinforcements could not be spared.

Likewise, the South had spent its forces against Turannia, and the East was under a full-scale assault by the Empire of the Sun. No response was coming, much less one powerful enough to subjugate one of the largest, most dangerous dungeons in the entire continent.

So, the Necrotorum could do naught but hold . . . and time was running out. With each moment that passed, its stockpiles of mana cores and corpses were dwindling. The wall's enchantments could not be maintained indefinitely, and the flow of skeletons would eventually slow to a crawl.

They were locked in a war of attrition with an undead dungeon, the worst possible opponent for such a fight. They would lose. They would be overrun. And with them, the Empire.

That is, until the sky lit up.

"Status Update: Target located. Engaging re-termination protocols."

Seero Supercharged a Prismatic Bombardment circle and opened fire. And within each circle in the strategic spell, she tried to combine not two but *three* attributes together, fusing Holy, Light, and Recovery as per recommendations by Imperial records related to the undead.

The horde vanished under a rain of beams. The weakest undead vanished by mere *proximity* to them. The strongest barely lasted enough for the Imperial Necrotorum to see them fade into dust. Even some of the Necrotorum's own skeletons were destroyed if too close to the enemy.

Within seconds, the field was clear, and Seero wasted no time before flying straight into the dungeon, leaving the Necrotorum to stare at a field of ashes . . . which happened to be glowing with golden-and-silver light.

In the mountains between Utrad and the Imperial Heartland, a mighty tree grew on top of one of the tallest peaks. Its roots dug deep into the mountain, its white trunk and branches swaying in the powerful winds blowing all around it. And in its branches nested countless monsters.

This was the Howling Peak dungeon. Born at the top of a mountain range, it'd had little to feed upon in its youth. As a result, it had naturally become aggressive, sending out raiding parties to search the mountains for prey and spreading its influence into the world beyond instead of building hidden rooms within itself.

Eventually, its raids had reached the Empire and begun to terrorize the settlements in the mountains, but its high, remote location prevented the usual response. It had taken an airship and a full contingent of Sky Knights to even reach it, and by that point, the dungeon's army had been vast. The campaign had lasted for months, as the Empire's forces tried and tried and tried again to destroy the dungeon.

It was at that point that the Empire had realized the dungeon had ceased its raids. With regular visitors by powerful foes, contributing their mana in its field of influence, the dungeon had no longer been starved for growth. And the Empire realized that it was useful to train its flying forces and to acquire materials for flying and Wind Magic artifacts. A tense but stable equilibrium was then reached.

An equilibrium that was now broken. The dungeon's monsters spread out from the mountains once more, no longer in organized raids but in mighty flocks, hampering the nearby legions' attempts at evacuation and defense. While the flocks ruled the skies, the Imperial roads could no longer be traveled safely, which meant hundreds of legionnaires were trapped in garrisons, hiding behind walls and fortifications, unable to move to where they were desperately needed.

And so it would remain, for the Empire could not gather the Sky Knights or airships necessary to assault the remote dungeon once more. Or so it seemed, until moments ago.

Now, explosions rang out in the center of a flock of harpies as a fleet of humanoid drone golems flew in formation, firing Beam spells and machine guns at the screeching monsters, 01R and the other cyborgs flying at their lead. The rat himself shot through the skies, sinking two Light Blades into the neck of a wyvern. The monster roared as it fell from the sky.

"Show-teach them the strength of the wise-mighty-gracious boss-queen's servants!"

Seero's monster roared in response. 00B flew through the air with powerful rocket boosters, slamming head-on into lighter harpies and knocking them from the sky. The cyber-forest tender rode on his back, lashing out with metal-coated branches and launching rocket-propelled thorns.

The Sacred Otterkin swam through the sky as Estrith had taught him to do in water, firing spearguns attached to his forearms at a large bird monster. 02R, the cyber-rat anointed gunner, was laughing as he held a tiny minigun on his shoulder, firing a hailstorm of small but *extremely* poisonous projectiles all around him. A hawk monster dove at him from above, but suddenly tumbled and fell from the sky, wrapped in the cyber-spider sacred stalker 01S's invisible webs.

And high in the sky above them all, Lilussees lay on her pillow in her magic jet once more. A Prismatic Bombardment magic circle appeared below her as her ritual drones moved into position, and a hail of beams fell from above, providing cover for the monsters below.

She yawned as she plopped down against the pillow.

"Hm, can I sleep? Like, I think I can sleep. I'm going to, like, put my organic components to sleep, so, like, wake me up if something happens, or something. Or not. Actually, like, please don't."

The pilot rat's voice came in on the comms. "Yes-yes, Eldest Sister!"

Lilussees thus tasked her cybernetic components with "autonomous combat support" and then initiated standby-sentry mode on her organic half.

But with the CELIU network automatically feeding her cybernetic half with targeting data, and the jet's special computers lending her extra computing resources, the barrage of strategic magic didn't lessen in the slightest.

15

Catching Up with Friends

"It is clear to me that under the present circumstances, the Enlightened will never be able to develop without our assistance. And yet, we should not intervene lightly, nor should we dictate the future course of Aelea. Let us consider how we may best aid the people of Aelea while allowing them room to chart their own path."

—Anualë, prior to the first bestowal of the boons of the Aesdes.

Vafum Broadbane cursed as he ducked under a magic war hammer, only the Dwarf's stature keeping his head on his shoulders. He thrust his hand forward, finishing the magic circle he was making directly in front of a golem's torso, and a powerful Water Beam assaulted the golem's HP, magic bindings, and metal body all at once.

The monster staggered back but remained standing. Vafum cursed again.

He was getting rusty with all this paperwork. Agedia would laugh if she could see him now. Tiberius would have a smug look on his face after all the crap Vafum had given him about being a "paper explorer." But on the bright side, he wouldn't have much paperwork in his future.

Mostly because the city he'd suddenly become responsible for no longer *had* a future.

The Dwarven colony of Khalbuldor, the industrial heart of Utrad's capital Velusitum, was in rough shape. Or rather, the city was little more than pebbles and rubble at this point. All that was left were the fortifications at the city gate, which were crumbling by the second. An army of golems assaulted them in the open, while underground monsters were destabilizing the walls from underneath, as they had done with most of the Dwarven settlement.

It turned out there were risks to building right on top of a dungeon, and now, the Mines of Might had gone rogue. Under normal circumstances, both the

Dwarves of Khalbuldor and the Imperial garrison in Velusitum had more than sufficient arrangements for this exact contingency. But these were not normal circumstances.

Since the council of Khalbuldor had thrown in with Caelinus's little rebellion, they had been forced to flee after the man had been slain by the queen of the Dobhar. And with them had gone all of Khalbuldor's strongest warriors, most of whom were clansmen and clanswomen of the city's elite.

They had also taken most of the powerful artifacts and weaponry, so Vafum wouldn't have had anything to arm any potential fighters with. And they had taken what remained of the treasury, so he had nothing with which to acquire new weapons. And most of the best smiths in Khalbuldor were either Yudric's kin or disciples, so there was no one to make new weapons even if Vafum could have afforded to pay them.

The point was, Khalbuldor was all but defenseless when the monsters began pouring out of its dungeon. Vafum hadn't even bothered trying to protect the city, and so had managed to evacuate most of the people before petitioning Velusitum for help, and was now trying to hold the gates of Khalbuldor with the Legion.

Only, the Legion wasn't in much better shape. Thanks to Caelinus's rebellion, Utrad had lost most of its forces. The Northern Court had sent some of its own to man the province, but it couldn't replace all the losses without leaving itself vulnerable elsewhere. As a result, the legions it had sent had been stationed to protect the borders, leaving the interior largely unguarded.

Velusitum had managed to keep its garrison, as Caelinus had never arrived there and so it'd never *officially* joined the rebellion. But still, the legion had been heavily scrutinized and most of its leaders and officers either arrested or reassigned to other provinces, including most of its mages. And, of course, Corvanus had not been in a rush to replace them.

Which was a serious problem, as the Mines of Might was an Earth- and Metal-affinity dungeon. It required specialized tactics to deal with its physically resilient golems and to counter its subterranean monsters. Normal legionnaires and fortifications just couldn't contain those threats alone.

But normal legionnaires were all they had at the moment. And since all the legions in the province were needed at the border, there were no reinforcements available. From what little news Vafum had heard since this disaster started, the rest of the province might be *worse* off. He'd been told refugees were streaming into Velusitum from across the province . . . which was bad, considering the army of golems about to spill out into the city should Vafum and the Legion fall.

What he wouldn't give to have his friends back.

At that moment, a giant mole-bear broke through the ground behind Vafum, disrupting the legion formation around him. Vafum himself was thrown forward, landing right in front of the golem he had pushed back, who immediately raised its war hammer. Vafum cursed as he watched the weapon, seeing the light flash off the approaching hammer.

Or rather . . . the light smash *through* the approaching hammer. And straight through the golem's torso.

Vafum blinked and glanced behind him. Something was approaching in the distance through the air.

"GET AWAY FROM HIM!"

Something shot past him and crashed into the horde of golems ahead. Vafum's eyes widened as he heard the voice, shaking his head and rubbing his eyes to make sure he hadn't become delusional in his final moments.

Because standing before him, crushing a golem with her tail while piercing another with her lance, was Agedia, with the Dobhar warrior from before following closely behind. The Dobhar warrior's spear began to glow as mana wrapped around it, allowing it to pierce through the golems.

Another flash of light caused him to turn around . . . and his eyes widened even further. Amulius, the Hero of Elteno, was aiming with his bow as an armored mage Vafum didn't recognize rained beams on the horde. And flying in the air above them . . . were the little lass and lad, Ateia and Taog.

Only, they did not look so little anymore. Ateia flew on wings of metal and light, the golden-and-silver glow reflecting off her shiny armor. One of her eyes glowed red from underneath the helmet covering half her head as she drew her bow and aimed it toward the ground. She let loose, and arrows of light surged forward, piercing directly into the ground.

Vafum heard monsters crying out from underneath.

Taog shot below, forming an Earth magic circle to open a hole in the ground. He dove down into it, the darkness moving to wrap around him as he leapt into the tunnels underneath the walls. The roars and cries of monsters continued from below.

Meanwhile, as all eyes turned to Ateia, she closed her eyes for a moment, then spread her hands out, and golden-silver light illuminated each Dwarf and Imperial on the field. Vafum's eyes couldn't grow any wider as his wounds healed, his mana regenerated, and his strength surged.

Oh, and as words passed before his eyes.

The spell protocol: Shaped Metal Blast has been shared with you.
Assisted casting is available. Engage spellcasting assistance protocol?

Words that were like . . . the ones from the Aesdes.

"By the Aesdes above and the Domides below, what is going on here?!"

But under the circumstances, Vafum wouldn't turn down aid out of confusion. He went ahead and engaged spellcasting assistance protocols, or whatever this was.

Warm Holy mana wrapped around his own as an illusion laid out a spell circle he had never seen before. A sphere of metal formed in front of him as the spell completed and shot toward one of the golems. On contact with the monster, the sphere condensed into a thin metal rod that accelerated at rapid speed, piercing straight through its core.

Vafum watched as what few other mages were around cast the same spell. As Holy mana wrapped around the shields of bulwarks and enabled them to catch blows without budging an inch. As Holy mana wrapped around halberds and war hammers, which now left dents and cracks in the golems they previously couldn't scratch. As Dwarven miners swinging their pickaxes at random suddenly started to connect, their mining gear striking at the exact spots to tear the golems apart.

And all across the field, tiny flying golems began to buzz overhead and glow. Mana Barriers formed automatically whenever a fighter was in danger, protecting them from further harm. Beam spells began to rain from the sky, damaging the tougher monsters and destroying the weaker ones outright. It did not take long after that for the horde to thin out.

As the battle wrapped up, Vafum stomped right up to Agedia. She grinned at him.

"Hi, Vafum! How are you—"

She was interrupted as Vafum hugged her. "I've never been gladder to see you, lass."

She returned the embrace, then they let go as Vafum turned to glance at Ateia descending from the sky and Taog breaking up through the ground. The soldiers and volunteers were all staring at the pair with wide eyes. "Now, I think you have some serious explaining to do."

Agedia nodded, starting to smirk. "The Hero is back, and Ateia's an Aesdes. Oh, Taog's a hero now, too. Now, if you'll excuse us, shiny girl told us to handle this situation."

Vafum cursed as Agedia rushed into Khalbuldor, heading toward the dungeon with the other newcomers following her.

"That is NOT an explanation, Agedia! Get back here!"

Meanwhile, a soldier who happened to be nearby stared with his eyes going as wide as they could. He spoke in a whisper, "That . . . was an Aesdes? They came for us?"

Whispers began to spread across the defenders of Velusitum as Vafum swore and started looking for a drink.

16

Dungeons and Divinations

"Never fight a dungeon in a war of attrition. Never fight a necromancer in a war of attrition. Do I need to say anything about both of them combined?"

—Maior Generalis Publius Manlius Typhoeus, on possible responses to a rogue undead dungeon.

Seero flew through dusty crypts, vaporizing zombies, ghouls, and skeletons as they rose from sarcophagi and streamed in from ahead. The Equalizer made short work of any enchanted traps, while Mana Barriers and counterattacks by offensive spells stopped any physical traps dead in their tracks.

This time, Seero was experimenting with a new capability. The dungeon near Academiae Civitatem had demonstrated that her mana sensors could be deceived, and she already knew there were countermeasures to her radars; while no entities in Aelea had intentionally done so, nonstandard anomalies had disrupted her mundane sensors on several occasions.

As a result, it was possible for all of her long-range sensors to be disabled. Even her powerful and comprehensive dungeon field had been blocked by the Realm of Eternal Night, and its range was insufficient for pathfinding and long-range detection, in any case.

Seero therefore calculated she should expand her options for long-range sensors. She did have the Sensing spell shape, and the mana-based proto-radar from the South's airships, but these had their drawbacks as well. She had already observed and employed methods to defeat mana-based detection, and these sensors were far shorter range than even her conventional ones.

So Seero did not choose either of these as the focus of her new capability. Instead, she chose the Divination spell.

Once upon a time, the Divination spell had had minimal practical use for Seero as a sensor. It provided too much data, and it could not be aimed. Its first use had ended up providing relevant information, but Seero did not know how or by what means to replicate it. Likewise, the spell circle itself had been far too complex for Seero to decipher with the limited knowledge she had possessed at the time, and the data overload she'd experienced warned her against experimenting without understanding.

But now, the situation had changed. Seero's processing capabilities and available memory had grown dramatically, and her AI continued to improve upon itself. Her understanding of mana, magic, and Holy mana specifically had also expanded. She had received technical data from Shialnor on how the Aesdes's system worked fundamentally, including its skills. And, most importantly, she now had Ateia.

The Divination spell had been based off the Aesdes' ability to see through the Holy mana flowing through the world. An ability Ateia had learned directly from Colleöne and then refined. And which her cybernetic components had recorded in great detail and then uploaded to the CELIU network.

So Seero now had a practical, firsthand example of how the ability worked. She had a recorded lesson from Colleöne teaching it. She had records of Ateia focusing the ability in order to filter out extraneous data and choose a specific target. And she had recently observed Ateia perform this ability through her own dungeon field to scout ahead. There was more than enough data available now.

Activating her newly designed Divination protocol, she formed an unaltered Divination spell circle and triggered it. The spell's mana reached back toward the dungeon's entrance, intent on finding and connecting to the world's Holy mana.

Seero reached out with Holy mana of her own, causing it to connect to her, and then reshaped it in the manner that Ateia had done so previously. Connecting the spell into the dungeon's mana through the contact between her dungeon field and the dungeon's own, she used her own radar signals as a guide and focused the mana along the radio waves.

It took her several tries to get it right, but handing control of her offensive magic circles to the bombardment team allowed her to focus all of her processing power on the task. Before long, the mana fell into place and began to flow as Seero intended.

She began receiving visions. Data poured in regarding the dungeon ahead as the Divination mana traveled with her radar waves. And then, instead of attempting to process the entire data package, she set up an analysis protocol to compare output from her radar and mana sensors with corresponding data from the Divination. In this way, she could quickly verify if her tools were returning accurate readings.

Her confidence level in her pathfinding improved dramatically. However, it did require a notable proportion of her processing and memory resources, which could reduce her combat effectiveness. At present, that was not an issue; so far, no hostile encountered in this dungeon had withstood a Supercharged Holy Recovery Light Beam, but if one were to appear and ambush her, she could not afford a delay in her reaction time.

As such, she took advantage of the stockpiled drone golems designed for ritual casting, ones focused on maximizing mana output, processing capacity, and networking. She activated and linked to them, then shifted the analysis protocol over to their hardware. This freed up her own resources, albeit at the cost of significant delays in the analysis. But Seero had predicted this and did not predict it to cause issues.

The point of the Divination protocol was to double-check the readings from her radar and mana sensors in the context of long-range detection and pathfinding. Even a small delay would not prevent Seero from identifying any discrepancies early enough to investigate and adjust her course. A delay in that protocol was a minor inefficiency; a delay in her response to a sudden crisis could result in her own termination.

With her new capability now running in a reasonably efficient manner, Seero continued her course deeper into the Haunted Mausoleum. She came to a wide cavern that spread out for miles around, with a roof so tall it appeared more like the night sky, dotted by dimly glowing crystals standing in for the moon and stars. A massive cemetery spread out along the ground.

And a massive undead army . . . promptly vanished under a Prismatic Bombardment.

But then, a roar rang through the room. It sounded like the roar of a massive predator mixed with the piercing shriek of a human in the deepest distress. The sound was filled with mana and struck something deep within Seero. Her organic components registered a sudden drop in temperature that was not verified by cybernetic sensors, and she felt a primal fear clutch at her heart.

So, she purged the hostile power with Holy mana of her own before reactivating the emotional controls, rendering her organic components immune to external manipulation. She then quickly identified the source of the attack.

At the far end of the chamber, a mighty being had just entered the room, having traveled from the very depths of the dungeon. Rotting flesh clung to a massive body, larger than a dinosaur or even a whale. Skeletal wings spread out far to each side, with tattered, paper-thin flesh barely hanging to the frame. A long neck ended in massive jaws with black teeth the size of swords, and glowing purple flames filled empty eye sockets.

An undead dragon had arrived. The doom of all living things; the epitome of dread.

An undead dragon had three weapons that made it even more dangerous than its living peers. First and foremost was the fear it spread. Its dark, twisted magic combined with the raw power of its draconic heritage spread a deep, primal fear to all that laid sight upon it or heard the sound of its voice. The average soldier would break and run, or stand motionless and paralyzed. Even the strongest and most courageous would struggle to keep their wits about them, hampering their ability to react.

This played into the second point, which was its resilience. Its undead nature meant it was not easily slain, and so long as it had magic, could regenerate from any wounds it received. The fear it spread would also disrupt any attacks, granting it the time to recover from any damage it did receive.

Its final strength was its innate skill in necromancy and Death Magic. The creature spread death and decay just through the mana leaking out from it, and would raise any fallen in the area as undead.

So, the dragon's mere presence would paralyze the majority of its foes, its resilience would allow it to outlast any who could still fight, and as the battle raged, the fallen would turn on their peers, quickly tipping the balance in its favor. Such a creature had now appeared in Seero's path.

At that point, the Prismatic Bombardment beams all fused into one and shot across the room, bringing the light of day to the dark cemetery. The superbeam swallowed the dragon whole.

Not a trace remained when the attack faded.

It turned out, fear was irrelevant to a cyborg who could shut off her own emotions at will. And the dragon's resilience was due to its regeneration and the fact that it didn't need any of its organs, and so had no vital points.

But its resistance against damage in the first place was actually weaker than its living peers, given that most of its scales and flesh had rotted away. It had little recourse against an opponent with the power to destroy it outright, not to mention that Holy mana would strip it of its ability to regenerate.

And finally, spreading decay and raising the dead was irrelevant if it couldn't last past the first blow!

"Status Report: Hostile terminated. Mana signature logged; contingency protocol developed. Area clear from organic-intrusion effects. Deactivating emotional controls."

And so, Seero continued into the Haunted Mausoleum . . . with little delay from *any* of the monsters streaming toward her.

17

Re-Terminate the Haunted Mausoleum?

"Re-termination cannot be guaranteed save by full vaporization of the threat. Additionally, said method is only confirmed to work on the Non-Standard's basic forces and should not be assumed sufficient against the Non-Standard themselves."

—NSLICE undead re-termination protocols.

As Seero continued on through the dungeon, she noticed its sheer size was slowing her down. Even if she could identify the shortest path through a given floor with 97.16 percent predicted accuracy, and even if she did not need to stop to terminate the monsters and traps, she still had to spend some time traveling through each floor.

And if that floor was a labyrinth type, like the current one, then she would have to reduce her speed even further due to the constant sharp turns, marking a limit to how fast she could travel through such an area. It was starting to feel . . . inefficient.

So Seero began applying the Blink protocol, vanishing and reappearing several times and reaching the exit of the current floor in a fraction of the time.

Previously, Seero had reserved Blink for short-range tactical evasions. She'd determined that in an open field, the Dash spell shape was more efficient, as it could be activated more quickly and moved her a greater distance for the mana spent. In situations where Dash wasn't as efficient, such as in a labyrinth with lots of twisting turns and no clear line of sight, Blink had been considered too dangerous.

She'd noted in first attempts that Blink disoriented her sensors, and it took her a moment to recalculate her current position, an effect that could only be countered within range of her Dungeon Field Generator. Her Dungeon

Field Generator was also the only way to fully scout an area with acceptable confidence, and so she'd considered it too risky to Blink anywhere outside of its range.

If, for example, her mana sensors and radar provided inaccurate readings due to anomalies or hostile activity, and she Blinked in front of a hostile unexpectedly, that hostile would then have an unacceptable time window to act before she could respond.

But now, with her new Divination protocol, she was significantly more confident in the thoroughness of her long-range scans. The extra data also helped her to preemptively reorient her sensors and location variables. Creating entrances to the Primary Home Base had also assisted her, as she had more and more experience with magical relocations.

As such, she was now confident she could respond effectively if a hostile should launch an attack immediately following a Blink, and so permitted herself to Blink outside her dungeon field range.

Her travel speed sped up considerably, as she could now pass an entire floor in seconds.

Of course, she did not stop there. With each cast of the spell, she evaluated and iterated on it, attempting improvements whenever she felt confident in doing so.

She found that wrapping a layer of Holy mana around the spell circle—like when Ateia helped non-CELIU allies cast spells—provided an extra layer of protection that would shut down the magic if a modification would cause it to misfire or explode. That allowed her to iterate more quickly and aggressively.

And so, her Blink range and speed grew with each subsequent cast as she sped through the remaining dungeon.

Seero had advanced deep within when she detected an anomaly. Her Divination protocol provided her a visual to confirm: it appeared the undead were fighting each other up ahead.

A smaller group of elite undead were assaulting the horde streaming toward the dungeon entrance. Skeletons and zombies wearing armor and giving off powerful mana signatures cut down their unarmored kin, while a lightly armored woman surrounded by floating pools of blood solidified it into spikes and blades.

She appeared as a lithe human with black hair, but had abnormally pale skin and deep red eyes. She was also casting spells which seemed to take control of some of the monsters, which subsequently turned on their fellows. A second undead dragon crashed down on the horde from above, tearing into it with claw and fang.

The undead horde, for its part, largely ignored the group. Only the monsters directly attacked moved to respond.

That is, until Seero vaporized them. The horde did not seem to ignore *her*, so she terminated it.

However, she did not attack the smaller group. Records from 01R's group indicated they had also encountered monsters turning on one another before, and had managed to cooperate with the nonhostile party. So Seero flew forward to meet the group, though she kept her magic circles at the ready.

The woman turned as Seero approached, and gave her a bright smile, revealing sharp fangs. She gestured to the rest of the elite undead, who relaxed and lowered their weapons. She then started to wave her entire arm. "Hi, there! You must be the one who reduced my hubby to gibberish! Are you here to kill us?"

"Uncertain Response: This unit's current objective is the purification of this dungeon. This unit will avoid termination of the dungeon and nonhostile forces if possible due to the dungeon's strategic value. If third-party forces do not oppose this mission and do not display hostility toward this unit, then this unit has no reason to terminate them. Please indicate any relevant affiliations."

The woman's smile grew. Turning her head down to the floor, she shouted, "See! I told you! She's here to help! You worry too much!"

Seero did not hear any response, but she did log some shifts in the surrounding mana. The woman frowned, crossing her arms and puffing her cheeks.

"Yes, I *know* what purification means! But she specifically said no terminating! What? What does terminating mean, specifically? That's . . . um . . . Look! She could totally kill us all if she wanted to, and she hasn't! You're not going to overcome those levels of Holy mana no matter how much more prep time you get, so reanimate your spine and take us there already!"

She then heaved a dramatic sigh, shaking her head as she walked over to Seero and reached out her hand. "Sorry, he's a bit paranoid. Mind if I touch you? I'm trying to get him to Transfer you to the core, but I don't want him to do anything silly like send you to a trap. If we're touching, then he won't be able to send you somewhere without me."

Seero's robotic eye flickered. Instead of answering the question, she reached out and grabbed the woman's arm instead. She had the Equalizer charged up and ready to channel directly into her body if she detected any anomalies.

The woman grinned at her. "Ah, aggressive and quiet, huh? Can't say I hate it; you two would probably get along if you don't try to kill each other. Well, hang on, then!"

Shortly after, Seero detected the dungeon mana wrapping around them in a similar manner to the forced relocation that had once sent her to the Realms of Mana. But Seero also recognized this was the same as her own Transfer skill and also affecting the woman she was holding, so she allowed it to happen.

A moment later, she found herself in a large room surrounded by armored undead knights with blades pointed at her, while two undead dragons had purple flames gathered in their mouths.

The woman next to her rolled her eyes. "Fabian! Get over here and put all this away! This is no way to treat a guest!"

Seero heard a voice echo from the walls. Her audio sensors couldn't determine its source.

"You're an idiot, Lavinia! A hero on a *purification* mission is NOT a guest!"

However, her mana sensors and Dungeon Field Generator could, and negotiations appeared to be breaking down. She was close to engaging termination protocols, but since this dungeon had strategic value to the Empire, preserving its dungeon master was listed as an optional objective, and she predicted with 78.40 percent certainty that the voice in question belonged to the master.

As such, she preferred to avoid terminating affiliated forces if at all possible.

Seero identified a hidden room next to this one. She let go of Lavinia and then activated Blink, appearing in the hidden room—the core room, apparently—right next to a human male with the same pale skin and red eyes as Lavinia. Seero immediately surrounded him with magic circles.

"Warning Query: Would the hostile dungeon master like to surrender? This unit will allow the dungeon master to retain ownership of their dungeon as a subordinate core if so. Otherwise, this unit will engage termination protocols."

The man grabbed and pulled his hair. "See, Lavinia! I told you! Now she's going to . . . Wait, surrender?"

"Affirmative."

He tilted his head. "And you'll . . . let me keep ownership of my dungeon? How, exactly? Aren't you going to purify us?"

"Clarification: This unit will purify the corrupted mana infiltration causing the dungeon to malfunction. The affected core will subsequently be connected to this unit's network to defend against further intrusions."

The man narrowed his eyes at her, then glanced at the magic circles around him. He sighed and slumped his shoulders. ". . . It's too late now; I can't do anything to stop you at this point. Just . . . Just do whatever you want."

"Surrender acknowledged. Please stand by for dungeon integration."

Seero stepped over to the core and placed her hand on it, quickly running through her purification and integration protocol. Only once it was complete did she drop the magic circles surrounding the dungeon master, who was staring at her and blinking repeatedly.

"Huh? The core has stopped summoning monsters? The Holy mana didn't kill me? You aren't . . . going to kill me?"

"Negative. Clarification: This dungeon has been subordinated. All affiliated units are now this unit's subordinates and no longer subject to termination protocols."

The man tilted his head, looking confused. A moment later, Lavinia kicked the door open. "See, Fabian! I told you so! You got to stop being so paranoid!"

Fabian just sighed and held his head. "She's never going to let this go, is she?"

INTERLUDE

The Brave Defenders of Turannia

Under normal circumstances, Magister Canus tried to keep himself as calm as possible. He did so in order to promote a culture of professional indifference among his troops and his staff. He wanted them to calmly execute their jobs no matter the situation so that every part of every legion under his command would fulfill their role smoothly as one huge machine, and he led by example.

No matter if they were about to win the greatest victory the Legion had ever seen or about to lose a battle that would seal the fate of the entire Empire, or if it was a normal, peaceful day like any other, he continued his work with the same practiced poise. He acted as if it was all the same to him and put forth the same quality of work regardless.

But today, he allowed a small slip in the mask, for the report he had read truly put a smile on his face. It had not even been a single day, and already, Her Majesty Seero and her forces had purified not one but *three* problematic dungeons.

The purification of the Haunted Mausoleum, in particular, lifted a massive weight off of everyone's shoulders. That dungeon on its own could spell the end of the Empire, and possibly all life on the continent, if it was not handled promptly, so the entire room nearly collapsed in relief when Seero reported her success.

And not only that, the victory also significantly improved the Northern Empire's situation. The Imperial Necrotorum had now been released from their vigil and was free to be deployed elsewhere. Their experience in logistics, construction, and labor would all be of critical importance given the mass evacuations and redeployments in progress across the Empire.

Additionally, Emperor Lucius had issued emergency permissions for the North's Necrotorum to apply their skills to the ongoing battles. Death Magic was uniquely suited to holding the line in battles of attrition, so such measures would greatly relieve the pressure on the Legion.

And thanks to the purification of the Howling Peak dungeon, the roads around the mountains were now clear. Seero's forces had even cleared the skies of lingering raiding parties. The forces and people of the Imperial Heartland could move relatively freely once again, and its legions could be redeployed as necessary. Combined with support from the Necrotorum and the academy, Canus could see the Heartland stabilizing sooner rather than later.

Further north, while the Mines of Might were not as dangerous as the Haunted Mausoleum, the forces of Utrad were also far less equipped to deal with it at present. Not only that but the Mines had threatened Velusitum—the largest and most central city in the province, and the only viable sanctuary for refugees—since most of the legions in the province were concentrated on the border at the moment.

If Velusitum fell, then Utrad would fall into complete chaos, with the defenders of Velusitum on the verge of breaking.

But no longer. Thanks to the Hero of Elteno and Seero's Imperial companions, Velusitum had been saved. The Empire could now use it as a refuge and a central staging ground to protect Utrad. Additionally, the legion stationed in Velusitum, while unprepared for the Mines of Might, would give a noticeably better showing against less specialized opponents.

And since the Heartland was stabilizing already, Canus may even be able to send some reinforcements north. Thanks to this victory, Utrad would survive as an Imperial province.

Of course, that meant Canus's work had increased substantially. He now needed to determine how to reorganize and redeploy the North's battered legions in order to capitalize on the queen of the Dobhar's assistance, especially now that they weren't writing off Utrad. And that meant a *great* deal of logistical work in order to determine what legions he had available and what their current state was.

But the experienced magister had expected that, and already had a plan in motion . . .

Dux Opiter was on the verge of fainting. The past few months had been trying for the man. As he had feared, the queen of the Dobhar's return to Turannia had brought a great deal of trouble.

He had been told they were suddenly going to war with the Southern Empire, and the entire province needed to be prepared, so Opiter had been running around, trying to organize the troops to Magister Canus's orders while still attempting to maintain proper Legion standards. And any moment he *wasn't* working, he was confronted with a great many questions on why they were fighting other Imperial forces.

Had he joined a rebellion? Had the queen of the Dobhar taken over? Had the Imperial family finally had enough of Rector Aemilia?

It was all too much for a man who had originally planned to be nothing more than a farmer. All he could do was try to quash the sinking feeling eating away at his heart and stomach by drowning himself in the work.

But now, the work had betrayed him too. Hordes of sea monsters were rising from undersea dungeons and making their way toward Turannia's coast. The Selkies and the aquatic tribe Rector Aemilia had hired were fighting back with hit-and-run tactics, but they could only do so much against an endless tide. The horde would make landfall any minute now.

And, of course, Magister Canus, Magister Tiberius, and Rector Aemilia were all away, along with many of the comitatense legions Magister Canus had trained. Which meant, in the eyes of all the troops and people of Turannia, the highest-ranking and most experienced officer present . . . was Opiter.

Even the comitatenses were looking up to him now, citing his position as Magister Canus's right-hand man. He was the one Magister Canus relied on, they said. Opiter's stomach churned at that. Relied on for what?! All Opiter ever did was shuffle paperwork as he was asked! Magister Canus knew better than to rely on him in an actual battle! Much less to command the defense of an entire province against an endless horde of monsters!

Well, the only good news was that the Forest of Beasts was strangely quiet. Opiter knew there were a bunch of dungeons there, but none of them seemed to be acting up. Opiter might have found that curious if the man had a curious bone in his body, but at this point, he'd rather not know. Every mystery he had encountered had only ever brought him stress.

In any case, Opiter just took whatever troops they had and arranged them in the port per Legion manuals. And then prayed to the Aesdes that Magister Canus would return before the monsters arrived.

"Sir, look!"

Opiter wanted to do anything but look. Unfortunately, even if he tried to ignore whatever had drawn the soldiers' attention, they would officially report it to him anyway. So, he slowly—unwillingly—turned his head.

His jaw dropped. Color returned to his face. His eyes began to moisten slightly.

Airships were approaching in the distance. Magister Canus had returned, and not a moment too soon.

Quickly arriving, they began landing by the port, returning Turannia's legions. One released a small shuttle, which flew over to Opiter's position. Opiter stood at the ready as the door opened.

"Dux Limitanei per Turannia Opiter, greeting Magister Militum per Turannia Canus."

"About that . . ." The door opened and out stepped not Magister Canus but Uscfrea Spellbreaker of the Dobhar. Some of the nearby troops grabbed their weapons on reflex before remembering the Dobhar were no longer their foes. "I'll be taking command and leading the defense of the Land of Rain."

Opiter's heart pounded for a second before he calmed down. The brief flash of panic gave way to relief. This was fine, too; after all, Uscfrea Spellbreaker was known and feared as a mighty warrior and a skilled commander. As long as *someone* who knew what they were doing was taking charge, Opiter could rest easy and pass on the problem.

Opiter tried not to think about that person being one of the Dobhar, who had constantly raided their shores, or a subordinate of the queen of the Dobhar.

Unfortunately, Legion policy required that he did.

"Understood, I'm glad you're here, sir. However, I will require confirmation before I hand over command of Imperial assets to a foreigner."

Uscfrea grinned and tossed Opiter a scroll. "Oh, Magister Canus specifically requested I hand this to you personally."

Opiter barely managed to catch the scroll, verifying it carried the official magical seal of Legion orders, which unlocked in response to his mana. He opened it up . . . and blinked as he read the contents.

"Pack your bags, *Magister* Opiter. You're going to Corvanus."

By order of *Emperor Lucius himself*, Opiter and his immediate subordinates had been called to Corvanus to assist the newly promoted Magister Utriusque Militia Canus in managing *all the legions of the North.* Oh, and Opiter had been promoted to Magister Equitum, in line with his new role as assistant to the Magister Utriusque Militia.

Opiter stared at the scroll for a moment longer, and then promptly passed out. Fortunately, the Legion had a Recovery mage on standby, and he was restored to consciousness shortly thereafter.

Whether he wanted to be or not.

Meanwhile, Uscfrea took command of the Turannian forces per Imperial order. The Imperial forces were uneasy at first, but calmed down as Uscfrea brought in former rebel officers to pass down his orders. Dux Opiter had already moved the soldiers roughly into position, so Uscfrea didn't need to do much to finish off the Imperial territory's defenses.

And soon, the horde began to arrive. Swarms of acidum piranha, steel swordfish, and other such creatures filled the seas. Various kinds of fish folk like Mermaids, Sirens, and Sahuagin added a more intelligent component. The fins of shark monsters broke the waves before a pod of dread orca pushed them out of the way.

And then came the big ones. Undersea dungeons had to contend with some of the oldest and most powerful monsters in existence. The ease of travel through the oceans meant monsters from all across the world could descend upon them at any moment. Most perished within a few months of their birth; others survived only by hiding and remaining as tiny little things with hardly a shrimp to their name.

But those that did not? The few that survived openly did so because they could summon true monsters of their own. And now, a shark the size of a battle airship began to cut through the waves. A kraken's tentacles broke through the water. A serpentine sea dragon lifted its head into the air.

Uscfrea grinned. "Let's get started."

The sea erupted, plumes of water and blood rising into the sky. Drone golems high above, beyond the sight of normal men, launched anti-ship missiles and air-launched torpedoes down into the water. Lower-flying rotary-wing variants dropped depth charges that launched entire schools of monster fish into the air.

And Uscfrea had brought some of his toys as well. The edge of the port was now lined to the brim with missile launchers and artillery pieces Uscfrea had summoned. After the ineffectiveness of the surface-to-air missiles against the Sky Legion's airships, Her Majesty Seero had recommended utilizing larger guns instead. Fortunately, Uscfrea had summoned a *lot* of those before the Aesdes had vanished, and his queen's crafters had provided some more as well.

So now, artillery guns of all sizes, types, and calibers opened fire upon the sea. The sheer explosive force of the large shells could overpower the magical defenses of all but the largest, most powerful monsters, and the horde suffered greatly. Additionally, his queen had apparently been experimenting with magical ammunition and had requested Uscfrea conduct some live-fire tests on their effectiveness. Uscfrea was all too happy to oblige.

The sea dragon roared as enchanted mana iron shells exploded along its neck. The creature was clearly feeling the blows, but ultimately did not seem to fall. Uscfrea grinned, cracking his neck and hoisting his axe and his minigun.

He was glad that not *everything* died in the initial barrage. It had been too long since he'd had the chance to fight. And for the Spellbreaker to take on another sea dragon, well, that had him feeling right nostalgic.

18

The Effect of Element Seero

"Simple physics, my dear. The humble gun can indeed defeat any possible threat . . . so long as the projectile can be accelerated to sufficient velocity."

—Dr. Ottosen, on the future of military technology in a nonstandard battlefield.

Seero noticed her conversation partner freeze up and go silent for what she calculated as an abnormal length of time for the average Imperial.

"Query: Has friendly Nonus detected an anomaly?"

She perceived Nonus shaking his head through the CELIU network. "No, it's just . . . I was already surprised when I heard about this spell database, but with the dungeon diving, I didn't have a chance to explore it fully. Now that I'm looking at it in more depth . . . what you have here is beyond incredible, Your Majesty.

"I've heard tales of archmages and High Archon who could adjust their spells on the fly, but to see this modular spellcasting in detail is . . . And not only that but you have a full copy of the grimoire of Arofinas Leolar, half the Imperial Academy's library, and a full selection of working Spatial Magic spells. And then . . . you say these records over here came *directly from the Aesdes*?"

"Affirmative."

Nonus's cybernetic components reported a decrease in the boy's blood levels within organic processing hardware, but he managed to avoid activating emergency standby-sentry mode.

"Is this the Blessed Land? Are you actually the Lord of Magic and Knowledge, Your Majesty?"

"Negative."

Seero was speaking with Nonus over the CELIU network as she made her way to the next target. While purifying the dungeons on her list was of the utmost priority for the survival of her allies, it was not the only task Seero needed to address.

Of major concern was the fact that the loss of the Aesdes' systems included the dungeon system. A dungeon core's abilities were *immensely* complex. Adding a room required creating a subspace in the boundary of the Material Plane while connecting said room to the core tightly enough that it would not fall into either the Material Plane or the Source.

Summoning a monster involved connecting to the Realms of Mana to pull a willing consciousness from it into a body created from scratch via magic, with significantly more safeguards and variables involved than the Summoning Magic spells utilized by the Empire.

Even creating a trap involved reshaping the dungeon walls, which Seero had already discovered utilized complex Spatial Magic in their construction, not to mention the magic required to create matter if the trap was physical.

The dungeon system abstracted all of these complex functions away into a simple UI, with the core handling all of these details via instructions built into it by Shialnor. But as a result, that meant the vast majority of dungeon masters had no idea how their dungeon cores actually worked.

And so, once that system became unavailable to them, they had no clue how to work their dungeons or interact with their cores beyond the most basic functions. And attempting some of those feats manually was . . . ill-advised.

For Seero, this wasn't a significant issue, as her cyborg-dungeon hybrid nature allowed her to utilize her dungeon core's mana in more direct applications. But for her subordinate dungeons, this was nothing short of complete paralysis.

The rooms and traps they had would continue to function, and the monsters they'd had when the system cut off still obeyed their commands. But they couldn't build any more rooms, couldn't lay any more traps, couldn't adjust the dungeon layout, couldn't create any more items, and couldn't summon any more monsters. They were left purely with what they had and had lost the endless reserves that made dungeons so dangerous.

They were vulnerable, especially those like the Imperial family's dungeon and the Haunted Mausoleum, who had spent some of their monsters trying to stop the hordes and maintain their deals with the Empire. These dungeons in particular were of immense strategic and economic importance to the Empire, and so needed to be defended now that Seero had purified them.

Most concerningly, the Heralds of the New Dawn were still at large, and had a method to fully corrupt a dungeon if they could reach its core, which meant leaving previously powerful dungeons relatively empty presented an unacceptable vulnerability.

In the short term, Seero could deploy drone golems as reinforcements, but these had limits in terms of their maximum potential, and using them as a garrison hindered the growth of Seero's own forces. Likewise, the need for reinforcements would only grow as Seero purified more and more dungeons, putting strain on their production lines.

As such, the best solution would be for Seero to reimplement some of the dungeon system functions. That would enable the new subordinate cores to defend themselves.

Seero began with monster summoning, as she had a lot of relevant data in that field. She had summoned many monsters, but had never created a trap, after all. Likewise, monster summoning involved transporting a consciousness from the Realms of Mana to a dungeon through its core, and Seero had firsthand observations of transit between the Realms of Mana, dungeons, and Material Planes in both formally organized and improvised scenarios.

Still, she had no experience with Summoning Magic circles, and so was missing a key piece of data to begin the process. Fortunately, the CELIU network now included someone who did.

Nonus had been close with Magus Major Faustus, the Imperial Academy's expert on Summoning Magic. Since Summoning was a dangerous school, Faustus had focused mainly on instruction and theoretical research, to which Nonus's condition had not been a barrier. As such, Nonus had had more opportunities to participate in Faustus's work than with any other mage, and so had gathered quite a bit of knowledge on the art.

As a result, Nonus's memory included a great deal of specific Summoning Magic circles, as well as a wealth of theoretical knowledge on that school. Seero was now requesting his instruction on the field, in order to fill in that last gap necessary to reimplement monster summoning.

. . . Once Nonus stopped leaking saliva from his oral cavity, that was.

Uscfrea flew through the air on his repulsors, swinging an enchanted minigun toward the sea dragon. The buzzing weapon bombarded the monster with mana-infused bullets, but even these bounced off the monster's scales. Uscfrea tossed the weapon toward one of his cyber-otterkin personal guards and boosted forward, hoisting his axe instead.

The sea dragon replied with its water breath, spitting out a jet of pressurized liquid that could pierce through a mountain. At the same time, mana leaking off the creature took hold of the water surrounding it, launching a barrage of Water Bolts toward Uscfrea, who cursed and fell back.

His cybernetic components identified both attacks, and so he was able to dodge, the water jet sending up a huge plume as it crashed back into the sea. But he couldn't get through the Water Bolts without taking them head-on. His fur may be resistant to magic, but the cybernetic components warned him that the mana-packed Dragon Magic might be a bit much, even for him.

His current axe couldn't cut through the spells, and though he *could* utilize some magic of his own, courtesy of his queen, he needed his mana to empower his own attacks. It was the better choice to evade and search for another opportunity.

But he was running out of time. Well, not for himself, but the fact was that there were three giant monsters, on top of the rest of the horde. The kraken's tentacles had already begun to assault the shore defenses, smashing an artillery emplacement.

Drone golems had flown into range in order to draw its attention while Magister Tiberius and the knights of Rector Aemilia's retinue were distracting the megashark, but at the end of the day, Uscfrea was still the most powerful warrior on their side, so he needed to deal with his opponent soon and assist the others. He could not battle this sea dragon for days on end as he had with the one in his past.

As Uscfrea was determining his next angle of approach, the sea dragon's neck suddenly exploded, leaving a gaping hole. A moment later, a thunderous sound assaulted the battlefield.

Miles from the battlefield, an airship floated in the sky. It had no adornment, and its hull was formed of smooth, curved metal rather than the solid, straight stone of the Empire's craft. There was a large hole directly through its center, and on the bridge, a metallic slime was bouncing up and down.

"It worked! It really worked!"

Melion continued celebrating their success. They and the master had been brainstorming means to project power at a range, and this was the initial firing of their first attempt.

A magical rail gun. Rail guns could launch a projectile at incredible speeds, enabling them to overcome some magic barriers with raw force. Moreover, the master had predicted that their mechanics would make them far more amenable to enchantment than gunpowder-based weapons. The electrical propulsion could be powered with Lightning Magic and assisted by Gravity and Air. And if a solid projectile was used, it could be easily formed out of magical materials and enchanted on its own.

The biggest problems with rail guns were power and durability. They needed a lot of power to launch their projectiles, and the sheer forces involved tended to destroy most gun barrels after only a few shots. But both of these were easily solved in the magical world of Aelea.

Lightning Barriers were utilized to create the current and form a shield to protect the rails from the forces and heat generated by the shot. A mass-reducing Gravity Magic enchantment was applied within the barrel, reducing the mass of the projectile while it was being accelerated and so reducing the force required to get it up to speed. And finally, Metal Magic was used afterward to restore any damaged rails to full strength.

The projectile itself was formed of magical metals and could be enchanted as necessary. In this case, since this was the first shot made and was targeting a powerful, high-level sea dragon, Melion had kept it simple. A Gravity enchantment that would increase the projectile's mass within a short distance of the target.

Melion and the master hoped the synergy of these different enchantments would allow a projectile to deal damage in excess of what a Barrier spell utilizing the same amount of mana could block, even at range, and break the timeless hurdle to beyond-visual-range combat in Aelea.

Whether or not they broke that fundamental barrier would require further testing. But for now, they'd definitely succeeded at piercing the HP barrier of a sea dragon, no small feat.

Uscfrea pursed his lips as he boosted forward. The sea dragon had been injured, but a creature that mighty could endure even such a grave injury. Uscfrea would not give it the chance.

The wounded monster had lost notice of Uscfrea, so he arrived before its neck without issue and began swinging his axe into the wound. Since the monster's HP was focused on repairing the extreme damage, his axe bit deep into its flesh.

The sea dragon tried to roar, but coughed and sputtered due to the damage to its windpipe. It lashed out with its arms but couldn't move too violently as a result of the wound. And so, it was not long before Uscfrea dealt it a mortal blow.

And continued pursing his lips.

Without a doubt, this was a major victory; one that would save countless lives on his side.

And yet . . . he could not help but feel . . . *dissatisfied.*

INTERLUDE

Kings, Lords, and Armies

Emperor Lucius sat on his throne as the representative of the Southern Court shuffled into the room, holding his head high as the representative greeted him.

"Well? I trust you are not wasting my time in these chaotic times."

The representative slumped his shoulders. "The Council of the Southern Realms . . . has agreed to your terms. We will bend the knee. So please, heed our call for aid."

Emperor Lucius hummed and rubbed his chin for a moment before turning to another man in the room. "What say you, Envoy Vopiscus? Will the queen of the Dobhar release her prisoners for the sake of my subjects?"

Vopiscus grinned and shrugged. "Well, the surrender is all well and good, but I fear Her Majesty will require a bit more reassurance. We would not want to return the Sky Legion only to find the South has . . . *forgotten* their promises."

The representative balked. "What more do you want?!"

Vopiscus turned to him, his grin growing wider. "Plenty, but for now . . . the Sky Legion will be released once the Southern Realms turn over all intelligence they possess regarding Cults of Mana, in particular one named the Heralds of the New Dawn, and instruct the imprisoned Captain Falrauth to do the same before he departs from Turannia. We will accept this as a suitable olive branch for the immediate short term, under the circumstances."

Vopiscus's grin faded. "And under the circumstances . . . you should have an inkling as to why we would want this information. I would suspect anyone with the good of their own realm at heart would be more than enthusiastic to comply with this."

The representative stared at him for a moment, then gulped. "I will tell them. Please, just do not delay the Sky Legion any further; the situation is growing desperate! And please send us reinforcements!"

Vopiscus turned back to Emperor Lucius and bowed his head. Emperor Lucius nodded at them both. "The Sky Legion shall be released once Envoy Vopiscus informs me he has received what he asked for. As for reinforcements, we shall send whoever we can spare, whenever we can spare them. If there is nothing more, then I suggest we all return to our most urgent duties."

With the news that the Southern Court intended to surrender, Magister Canus, now assisted by a stress-binging Magister Opiter, redrew his plans with the objective to stabilize the South as well. However, he needed to hear from the Southern Realms what their current situation was, and Seero still needed to receive intel on the Heralds of the New Dawn, so for now, both Seero's forces and the Legion continued the operation to protect the North.

Melion's successful experiment would help. Enchanted rail guns were simpler for the metal slime to assemble than explosives, since they did not require chemicals or computer components, and easier to resupply as well. All the required materials were being generated by the Primary Home Base, and Seero's forces could even use Metal Magic to create new if less effective rounds in a pinch.

Rail-gun-armed drone golems could thus be manufactured more quickly than those equipped with firearms and could be deployed farther away from subordinate dungeons before needing a resupply.

Seero's attempts to reimplement the monster summoning system were also starting to bear fruit. At the moment, she had succeeded in summoning slimes, the simplest of all monsters. It was a start, and slimes, when upgraded to CELIU units, were key to Melion's mass-production process due to their ability to directly shape raw materials into finished components, and so, at the very least, Seero could continue expanding her production lines.

In any case, slimes were better than nothing, so Seero sent a message to all of her subordinate dungeon masters informing them of the reimplemented system.

At the center of a cave, deep beneath the ground, was a stone room; its master seated upon the throne at its heart. He wore a red cloak and a golden crown upon his head. The hairs on his body were immaculately groomed. His eyes were sharp as daggers.

This was His Royal Majesty, Excellion Formantus Rattingtale the Third, Advanced CELIU Unit. The Great-High King of all the land. The Most Humble Servant of the Wise-Mighty-Gracious Great-Ultimate Boss-Empress, the Supreme Arbiter of her will.

And at present . . . he was curled up into a ball and shivering. "Why won't you work-obey?!"

He had tried everything. Shouting, commanding, asking, begging, threatening, promising, lying. And yet . . . his royal core still refused to do anything!

He couldn't summon any minions to fulfill his will, couldn't create any devious traps, couldn't expand the realm. He had once again failed as a Great-High King.

But then . . . salvation arrived.

Priority Alert: This unit has reimplemented the monster summoning function for all subordinate cores.

Rattingtale froze, then slowly rose to his feet. "As expected-anticipated of the Wise-Mighty-Gracious Great-Ultimate Boss-Empress! And as expected-anticipated of the Great-High King! Even the loss of the Aesdes themselves cannot threaten-harm our realms, yes-yes! Truly we are the greatest-mightiest dungeon masters to have ever lived, yes-yes!"

With that, he opened the royal records, ready to summon new and powerful minions . . .

He froze.

"S-Slimes? T-That's it? T-This is . . . um . . ."

Rattingtale gathered himself and stood up tall. "O-Obviously, this is all as predicted-calculated, yes-yes! S-Slimes are all that the Great-High King needs-requires, yes-yes! R-Right . . ."

Meanwhile, the cyber-rats Rattingtale had summoned previously were gathered around the door to the throne room, peeking out at their king, after which they turned to look at their master with concern.

"Boss-lady 02S, what-what should we do now? The Great-High King is still weeping-crying, yes-yes."

02S giggled from the shadows of the doorway. "Keep scouting the entrance, but otherwise . . . watch and enjoy."

The rat monsters glanced at one another and then shrugged. "Boss-lady's orders."

The master of the Imperial family dungeon was sitting in her room, slumped in a chair, and staring into space.

". . . Of course. You reimplemented monster summoning. Easy, right? I should have thought of that, great dungeon master that I am. Guess I'm not so great, after all. I mean, I don't have the faintest clue of how the monster summoning even works. It's only the work of the Aesdes, after all. Basic stuff to rebuild from scratch. Of course.

"I guess I should . . . summon some slimes or something. I mean, I might as well start over from scratch, seeing as I don't know the first thing about being a good dungeon master, *apparently.*"

Fabian, the dungeon master of the Haunted Mausoleum, was sweating, his brow furrowed in concentration. His mana was just about empty as he completed the magic circle in front of him.

Purple mana twisted and flowed from the circle into the skeleton laid out on the ground. Dark mana began to fill the bones, and purple flames lit in the skull's eye sockets. Black armor formed around it as it rose to its feet. The new death knight then turned around without a word, marching off into the dungeon.

Fabian sighed as his skeletons brought more magic cores and bones into the room. At that moment, Lavinia poked his side while sitting on a box that hadn't been there before. She had wandered off somewhere, so she must have just returned.

"Hehe, you look like, heh, *skin and bones.*"

Fabian sighed again. "You *could* help with this you know?"

Lavinia shrugged. "I could."

Fabian stared at her. "You *do* know that without monsters or traps or *literally any* of my dungeon powers we are entirely defenseless, right?"

Indeed, Fabian had his minions gathering every resource from his dungeon that they could. Fortunately, the rooms and features that would automatically generate loot and necromantic material were still functioning, so at least he had *something* to work with, though Fabian couldn't adjust or expand them.

But that meant raising minions manually, with his own mana pool, which was *far* more limited than that of his dungeon. And since he had spent most of his weaker minions trying to stop the horde, the vast majority of his dungeon was currently empty. It would be a *long* time before he was confident in his defenses again.

Lavinia, unhelpfully, shrugged again, clearly not intending to help. "And you know we're not on our own anymore, right? Our new boss will help us out if we get into trouble."

Fabian clicked his tongue and shook his head. "It's naive and foolish of you to trust her. We're minions to her and nothing more, as is the way with dungeon masters. She will not help us. And even if she would, where is she now? How would she get here?"

Lavinia pointed back in the direction of the core room. "The portal."

Fabian opened his mouth. "That's . . . *ahem*, that only exists to threaten us with immediate death if we resist."

Lavinia tilted her head. "But aren't we already dead?"

A vein bulged on Fabian's forehead. "Would it kill you to take our very survival seriously for even one moment?! No, don't you dare answer how I *know* you're going to! I am AWARE that we're undead! And if you want to stay that way, then lend me a—"

Lavinia blinked as Fabian suddenly went silent. "What is it?"

Fabian's eyes widened. "She . . . reimplemented monster summoning? *How*?"

But he shook his head. The how and why weren't important. What was important was that he had at least some of his dungeon powers back. And if he could summon monsters again, then he could make great progress toward repairing his shattered defenses.

He followed the instructions to access the summoning with a smile.

And then froze. And started to tremble.

"That . . . That monster! Is this a joke?! A cruel method of taunting those who are already beaten?! To grant us a spark of hope, only to trample upon it in a method most foul?!"

Lavinia hummed and crossed her arms as Fabian began to go on a tirade. "Hm, I was going to show him this neat little toy I picked up from my new metal slime friend, but maybe I should wait a bit? Fabian always did bottle himself up, so he probably needs to let it all out right now . . ."

19

Strength and Honor

"Tricks and traps have their place, but in the Tower of Heroes, all that matters is strength."

—Imperial Knight Octavianus Silius Cremutius.

Next on Seero's agenda was another round of dungeons. The Tower of Heroes was located to the east, near the border of the Northern and Eastern Empires. This dungeon focused on powerful, elite monsters, and was utilized as a proving ground for the knight orders. It also provided a place for the best warriors and most veteran Legion officers of the North and East to meet and train together.

At present, the Tower did not appear to be an urgent threat, as the forces stationed there had not requested reinforcements. Yet, that was of little comfort. Monster attacks from the Tower had occurred, confirming it was affected as well, which meant it presented a massive risk. Elite monsters from the Tower of Heroes could collapse the defenses of all nearby holdouts should they spread out.

Likewise, if the veterans and knights stationed there could be released to assist other fronts, the situation for the Empire would improve drastically. So, Magister Canus had requested that Seero investigate the situation and purify the Tower for good measure.

As for her other forces, the Imperial group would head to assist the Mélusine. The long-conquered client species still maintained a small part of their former nation in Utrad, where they had ultimately accepted life under the Imperial heel.

They, too, had been affected by the disaster, and had sent a call for aid to Corvanus. Should the Empire fail to heed this call, it would lose the trust and loyalty from all of its allied and client species. Magister Canus had therefore sent a legion from the Imperial Heartland via airship, which would meet up with Seero's friends to relieve the Mélusine.

01R and his group were sent east of Utrad, beyond the Empire's borders. A number of dungeons there were keeping Utrad's legions pinned on the border; however, a deployment of the legions to handle them could provoke the local tribes, and the last thing the Empire needed right now was more enemies. So Seero's monsters were sent, as they would not be mistaken for Imperial forces.

Seero managed to arrive at her assigned target first. The Tower of Heroes rose high into the sky, a round tower formed of pristine marble. It was surrounded by two circular walls: an inner one around the tower itself, and an outer wall further out, with a small city in the space between the two.

Seero arrived to find the city . . . completely calm, with civilians going about their business as usual, save for the occasional ballista or crossbow bolt being launched from the outer walls at wandering monsters. On top of the inner walls, Legion troops were assembled and kept watch, but very few were engaged in active combat. Instead, they were watching as individual knights dueled with monsters in the inner field, some on foot, others riding mounts of all sorts.

Seero promptly terminated the monsters with a Prismatic Bombardment spell before flying into the dungeon. The knights looked disappointed, and some of the Legion troops, who may or may not have placed money on the duels, even shouted complaints. But Seero had already entered the dungeon, so he did not respond.

Seero found the place largely empty. Rather than twisting labyrinths or hostile biomes, the Tower of Heroes had a simple, standardized layout. Each floor opened with a circular arena, though the terrain of each varied. Past the arena was a room with a chest and living quarters where one could rest.

Monsters were occasionally making their way through the early floors, but Seero found far less than in other dungeons she had encountered. She had been briefed that this dungeon focused on more powerful monsters, but the ones she encountered were easily terminated, so she predicted that alone would not explain the low numbers. Still, there was little standing in her way, so she quickly passed through the floors.

Eventually, she found the reason.

About halfway up the Tower by Seero's estimates, she located a full contingent of knights and legionnaires making their way up. When she arrived, two of them approached her.

"Here to join the assault? You're a bit late. What order are you from?"

"Greeting: This unit is designated Seero; official Imperial designations: Queen of the Dobhar, Amicitia Populi Elteni. Negative Response: This unit is on a separate dungeon purification mission."

One of the legionnaires tilted his head, but the other shoved his side with her elbow.

"Queen of the Dobhar? Hey, isn't that the person who took down Caelinus?"

The first legionnaire shrugged. "If you believe that story."

It appeared this group had not been informed of her approach. As such, Seero pulled out the brooch signifying her status as Amicitia Populi Elteni. The woman jumped and elbowed the man again.

"See! I told you! She's a big shot!"

The man saluted. "Sorry, ma'am, we certainly didn't expect any visitors here. Let me take you to Grandmaster Publius; he has command of this expedition."

"Acknowledged."

With that, the two soldiers led Seero into the group. The other knights and soldiers glanced curiously at Seero but did not approach. They arrived at the front lines, where a duel was currently taking place.

A large minotaur in glowing plate armor charged forward, wielding a massive red greatsword. Against him stood a towering ogre with a club that seemed more like a log. The two's weapons collided . . . and the minotaur's sword cut straight through the club and bisected the ogre. The minotaur shook his head before turning around.

"Who is this?"

The soldiers escorting Seero saluted. "Her Majesty Seero, queen of the Dobhar and Amicitia Populi Elteni, here to purify the dungeon, sir!"

The minotaur nodded. "Queen of the Dobhar? I've heard of you; you've got quite the reputation, don't you?"

"Greeting: This unit is designated Seero; official Imperial designations: Queen of the Dobhar, Amicitia Populi Elteni. It is nice to meet you."

The minotaur stepped forward and held out his hand. Seero shook it. "Grandmaster Publius Fulcinius Orosius, Order of the Crimson Sword, and leader of this expedition. Have you ever been to the Tower of Heroes, Your Majesty?"

"Negative."

Grandmaster Publius crossed his arms and nodded. "Been here for decades now, so if you don't mind, let me give you the rundown. Dungeon master here likes challenge and skill. You don't get hordes trying to wear you down or traps dropping the floor beneath your feet. Instead, each floor you take on an elite, expertly trained warrior."

He inclined his head as another ogre came through the door. Another knight stepped forward and pierced straight through its head with a spear.

"So, it's abnormal to be getting monsters this weak and untrained. I don't know how it's possible, but there appears to be something of a dungeon civil war going on."

"Helpful Interruption: This unit can provide relevant intel. All dungeons are currently undergoing partial corruption, which has led to mass monster summoning outside of the master's control. This unit is here to purify the corruption."

Grandmaster Publius's eyes widened. "Really? Never heard of something like that, but it would explain what we've been seeing. The normal elites have been cutting down the chaff, but some still get through by sheer numbers. Still, what few make it are easy for us to mop up. The flip side is the dungeon master is still holding to the rules, so I guess they don't consider us an ally or anything."

The minotaur grinned. "I'll admit, I've been wondering if there's any truth to your reputation. I know it's dangerous and discourteous, but would you be willing to take on the next duel? I swear on the honor of my order that I shall do my utmost to ensure your survival should it prove too difficult for you."

"Affirmative Response: It is this unit's current objective to purify the dungeon. Terminating hostiles blocking the route is necessary for that task."

The minotaur flashed his teeth. "Excellent. Come, then, and let us see if you can overcome the Tower of Heroes!"

Grandmaster Publius went silent as a Prismatic Bombardment magic circle lit up the room, wiping out a squad of ogres all in one go. An armored lizardman with a spear turned from his fallen opponents, grinning and hissing. He leveled his spear toward Seero, and then charged forward.

"Hostile intent detected. Engaging termination protocols."

Another flash of light, and the lizardman was gone. Grandmaster Publius crossed his arms, rubbing his chin, then he nodded.

"Yep. Safe to say, her reputation's legitimate."

Seero repeated this process for three more floors before they heard a deep laugh. Suddenly, a massive monster appeared in the room. He had an incredibly muscular humanoid torso, but with the paws and head of a lion, and a giant red mane that appeared almost like a wreath of fire.

"I think you've made your point. You're strong. It's been quite some time since my dungeon's had a challenger like you."

"Query: Are you the dungeon master?"

The monster grinned. "I am. And my blood boils for a fight."

"Warning Query: Would the hostile dungeon master like to surrender? This unit will allow the dungeon master to retain ownership of their dungeon as a subordinate core if so. Otherwise, this unit will engage termination protocols."

Grandmaster Publius's eyes widened, and he stared at Seero while the monster began to laugh. "Oh, you're not intimidated in the slightest, are you?"

"Negative."

The monster's grin grew. "Good. Tell you what: Beat me in a fight, and I'll do whatever you wish."

"Acknowledged. Engaging near-termination protocols."

Seero immediately formed another Prismatic Bombardment circle and opened fire. The dungeon master barely managed to jump out of the way, howling with laughter.

"Now show me a good fight!"

20

Terminate the Battle Maniac?

"When you have acquired the taste for the fight, all others become bland."
—Dwarven Berserker Thukdroic Battledigger.

The dungeon master grinned and vanished just before the beams struck his position. He reappeared in front of Seero before she could respond and threw a fist toward her face. Her sensors hadn't even registered the movement.

The master had not used Transfer or teleportation of any sort; he had simply moved fast enough that most of Seero's sensors had lost track of him. That made him the fastest being Seero had ever faced.

But not all of her sensors had failed. Her Dungeon Field Generator had registered the movement, and ever since she had learned how dungeon walls worked, she had applied her own space-bending defensive field around herself. This field bought her enough time to cast a Blink spell and get out of the way.

Only to find the dungeon master right on top of her. He smirked. "You think you're the first archmage to challenge me? Spatial distortions are easy to find if you know what you're looking for!"

At this point, though, Seero had canceled all extraneous threads and turned all of her attention to sensing and prediction. With her AI's speed and power, she had barely detected his movement toward her teleport point. As such, she had just enough time to prepare a response.

As the dungeon master's fist entered the spatial field expanding the distance to her armor, she began to twist it. He blinked and quickly withdrew his hand as the spell cracked, taking the tip of his fingers with it.

He grinned and started laughing. "That's a cute trick! You're a clever one, aren't you?" He then sneered. "But now, there's a hole in your defense!"

With that, the entire room began to glow purple. Seero had bought just enough time to change her Prismatic Bombardment spell to Prismatic Floor, now covering the entire surface in a magic circle. And in this case, she chose the Gravity element.

The force of Gravity increased dramatically across the battlefield. Even Seero was affected, and her HP started ticking down now that her Spatial Angling field had been disabled. She couldn't even move, and had to devote some of her mana to defense just to maintain her structural integrity.

Of course, the dungeon master was affected too. He grunted as the invisible force attempted to crush his body. But, as a being who had focused all of his growth into his physical attributes, he could not only resist the field but continue to move within it. He laughed again.

"Impressive. This would be excellent for training; perhaps I'll make you my subordinate when this is done."

And then he charged toward Seero, still moving at great speed. However, his speed had reduced to the point that Seero's normal sensors could track him once again. And more importantly, to the point that she could effectively adjust her aim. Because for Seero, becoming immobile didn't reduce her offensive power in the slightest.

A Prismatic Bombardment circle formed behind her and opened fire. The dungeon master tried to dodge, but with his reduced speed, he could not completely evade the hail of fused beams. He gasped, his eyes widening as one of the beams struck him.

Thanks to the combination of Holy mana, Spell Penetration, and Heroic Challenger, the dungeon master's defenses were pierced with ease, far beyond what he'd expected. But he had no time to process that surprise.

Ever since High King Xavlaeron had infiltrated one of her magic circles, Seero had practiced controlling her mana in active spells. Now, she attempted to do so with a different purpose.

The Beam circles within the larger strategic spell began to shift as they struck the dungeon master. This would normally cause the spell in progress to collapse, but Seero held the spell form together with Holy mana as she had learned from Ateia, and as a result, the beams remained active even as their circles of origin changed.

And so, the Beam magic circles successfully transformed into Chain ones . . . while they were still striking their target. They then transformed into chains, wrapping around the dungeon master.

He grunted and pulled on them, but Seero's Supercharged and high-density mana was resilient even to his strength. And with each chain that formed, his speed dropped even further, allowing more and more beams to find their mark. Soon, Seero could stop transforming Beam spells and just cast Chains directly.

At that point, Seero formed a new Prismatic Bombardment circle, Supercharging it with all the spare mana she had at that point while pointing her palm at the immobile dungeon master, also charging the Equalizer.

"Warning: Hostile dungeon master is about to be terminated. Recommendation: Please initiate surrender protocols to avoid this outcome."

The dungeon master took a look at the situation, then started laughing. "From the very start, I told my monsters and challengers alike that they could take my dungeon from me at any time, so long as they beat me in a fight. Not once in all my life have I lost. Now, not only have I lost, but I was completely overpowered."

He bowed his head toward Seero . . . Or rather, slightly vibrated the mana chains preventing his head from moving.

"My dungeon is yours. You've earned it."

Seero, with all of her sensors and AI active on the dungeon master, noticed a small shift as he gave verbal confirmation of the surrender. A small connection formed between her mana and his. The connection didn't react further once formed, as if waiting for something to occur.

Seero focused her attention on the connection, analyzing it. It bore some similarities to pieces of her Contract connections, but its scale was so much smaller that she couldn't be sure. With nothing occurring, the connection then began to fade. Seero extended some mana toward it, intending to reinforce it so she could continue analyzing it.

But as her mana contacted it, the connection began to grow. Seero was going to cut it off when she picked up a data packet. She quarantined and then analyzed it, discovering it contained some basic data . . . from the Tower of Heroes.

The connection now allowed the two dungeons to exchange mana and data.

Given the circumstances, Seero predicted this was the method by which dungeon surrenders occurred, but that the loss of the dungeon system meant that key follow-up protocols had failed to trigger. As such, she began to send her mana through the connection, intending to investigate what could be done with it.

Her mana surged through the Tower of Heroes, joining with the flows of mana coursing through the dungeon. The dungeon's mana did not resist, opening a path for her wherever she went. She was able to see and perceive different parts of the dungeon as her mana expanded onward, but she ignored that data. She continued on until she reached the end of the flow . . . and her mana arrived at the dungeon core.

Converting her mana to Holy, she quickly purified the corruption, then attempted to form her mana into the dungeon core connection process.

She succeeded immediately, even beyond her most optimistic predictions. The Tower of Heroes's mana moved to assist her the moment she began forming that shape, as if it had been waiting for that very protocol.

And so, Seero managed to purify and subordinate the Tower of Heroes many floors away from the core room. The dungeon master was just staring at her and blinking.

". . . You're a dungeon master? But you can use Holy mana? Oh, is that why your core isn't going rogue like mine?"

"Affirmative."

The chains vibrated again as the master attempted to nod. "Impressive. No idea how you figured out how to do that, and it's not often someone surprises me."

But there were other people in the room who were also surprised. Some of the knights had begun to draw their weapons as the dungeon masters conversed, and Grandmaster Publius narrowed his eyes.

"Your Majesty, did we hear that right? Did you say you're a dungeon master?"

"Affirmative."

Grandmaster Publius grimaced. One of the knights next to him frowned. "Grandmaster . . . a demon lord is masquerading as an Amicitia Populi Elteni . . . and just conquered the Tower of Heroes. Isn't that really bad?"

"Objection: The term *masquerading* implies deceit and falsehood. This unit has officially been designated as Amicitia Populi Elteni, and so is not masquerading as one. In addition, Imperial authorities are already aware of this unit's identity."

A panel popped open in Seero's armor, and she retrieved a sealed scroll from it. Utilizing Blink to send the scroll past the Gravity spell, she made it appear at Grandmaster Publius's feet.

"Statement: That record contains an official Imperial order regarding the situation. If additional confirmation is necessary, this unit recommends contacting Imperial command units."

Grandmaster Publius raised an eyebrow at her, but he also glanced at the multiple strategic spell circles lighting up the room, and the completely immobilized dungeon master of the Tower of Heroes, a foe he knew he couldn't hold a candle to. So, he decided to take the risk that the scroll was a trap and picked it up.

His eyes widened. The scroll had the Emperor's seal on it, and it appeared genuine. More so when the grandmaster channeled his mana and it reacted as it should. The scroll opened up, and he took a moment to read through it.

It was an order from the Emperor to all Imperial personnel, informing them of the queen of the Dobhar's identity as a dungeon master, confirming that her relationship with the Empire and status as Amicitia Populi Elteni remained unchanged regardless, and then ordering them to assist her during this crisis.

Grandmaster Publius took a deep breath. ". . . Let's contact Corvanus and confirm this situation."

The knights around him frowned. One of them spoke up. "But, sir . . ."

Grandmaster Publius turned around. "I'm going to go contact Corvanus. If you feel you cannot agree with that course of action, then do what you feel you must. Just know that the consequences are also your own."

With that, he began walking back toward the room's entrance. The knights glanced at one another, then at the big magic circles and the Imperial scroll in the grandmaster's hands. One by one, they lowered their weapons and began to back away, eyeing Seero all the while.

And so, Seero conquered the Tower of Heroes.

21

Hope Amidst Defeat

"We will never stop fighting! The majority of humanity is dead, the nations and cities are gone, the land an irradiated wasteland, and the planet itself is dying. So what? I've spent my entire life learning to bring the dead back to life and to restore the glories of the past!

"I have risen creatures dead for eons from before humanity walked on two legs! Our enemies have hordes of mutants and swarms of killer robots? Fine, we'll just build monster armies of our own! So long as we hold on to each other, there is still hope!

"I, for one, will continue to resist, continue to fight until my last breath . . . and then beyond! We shall have liberty, or we shall have undeath, but never, and I say never, shall we give in to despair!"

—The founder of the Resistance.

Ateia stood on the observation deck of one of the Northern Court's airships, watching the field below. The group had joined up with the reinforcements from Corvanus and were now on their way. It would have been faster if the group had flown directly, but in this case, it was important they showed up at the same time as the Legion.

Ateia turned her head, scanning the countryside, and frowned. Amulius walked up behind her.

"What's wrong?"

She furrowed her brow. "My eyes can see further than a normal person's. This one"—she pointed to her robotic eye—"is like a farseeing artifact, so can I see out into the distance. And my regular sight is empowered by my connection to the world, and I can see through the mana flows within it." She sighed. "So I can see what's going on down there. I can see the people fleeing from their homes. I can see the caravans getting attacked. I can see farmers desperately trying to defend their homes."

Amulius went silent for a moment. "And you want to help them?"

Ateia sighed again. "I know that it's important to stick to the plan. Magister Canus chose these targets for a reason, and we'll save the most lives by focusing on the key areas. But . . . I still don't feel right just flying over these people."

Amulius's face fell. He slowly reached out and patted Ateia on the shoulder. ". . . I know. Sometimes, you can't save everybody. In times like that, you just do as much as you can."

Ateia rubbed her chin. "As much as I can, huh?" She closed her eyes and began to focus. "Seero, I know this is a tough ask, and I know we don't know those people, but . . . can I help them?"

It only took a moment for the response to come in over the CELIU network.

"Affirmative Response: Units requested are affiliated with a current ally. Assistance is permitted."

Ateia smiled. "Thank you."

And then, she connected to the flow of Holy mana in the world around her.

On the ground, a family of farmers were fleeing down the road. The father was warding off a pack of wolf monsters with a spear; he had dealt with the occasional monster, as all those who lived outside the cities must, but never a pack all at once like this.

The mother was supporting him with Water Magic, but she had focused on noncombat spells. She couldn't cast anything stronger than a Water Bolt, and her lack of experience made it difficult to do even that without assistance from the Aesdes. A young boy, only a year or two past ten, was standing over his younger sister, trembling as he struggled to hold the small spear in his hand.

Just then, the wolves pounced at the farmer. His wife, in her panic, failed to cast her Water Bolt, and the farmer fell back with a wolf on top of him. Another one took the opportunity to rush past the adults, charging toward the children in the rear. The boy trembled as his sister screamed.

But then, something warm began to fill the boy's body, causing his heart rate to slow. For a brief moment, he thought he saw a girl in shining armor with wings of metal and light. She smiled at him and whispered, *"Don't give up."*

Golden-and-silver light wrapped around his hands and spear, and he felt it moving his arms into shape. Pulling his spear back, he threw it, much like a Dobhar might throw a harpoon.

To his surprise, the spear flew straight into the head of the wolf, bringing it to the ground.

Another one ran around the first . . . only for a jet of water to slam into its side, the boy's mother staring at the completed circle in front of her with wide eyes.

And then, a wolf flew into the air and slammed into a nearby tree. The farmer stood up after tossing his attacker aside, looking down at his arms glowing with light. Picking up his spear, he grinned at the remaining pack.

Scenes like this repeated across the countryside. Soon, a flood of refugees would arrive at Velusitum, each carrying fantastical tales about what could only have been the blessing of an Aesdes . . .

Ateia wobbled as the power drained from her. She had kept it simple this time, focusing on basic spells and skills, but she had assisted more people than ever before, and across a much wider area.

Her father steadied her with a hand on her back. She turned to him and smiled. "Do as much as I can, right?"

Amulius's eyes widened, but Ateia didn't wait for him. She sat herself on the floor of the airship and took a deep breath. There was still a lot of countryside to go.

Seero and her monster subordinates were doing all they could, taking down dungeon after dungeon. So Ateia would do all she could as well.

01R landed in the center of a dark, crackling cloud hovering just above the ground, unleashing a wave of Holy mana from one of his Rat Paladin skills.

Lightning crackled and high-pitched screams wailed as the lightning elemental faded. 01R then leapt to the side, barely managing to move before another elemental shot a bolt of lightning at his former position.

Taking one of the Holy Blades over his hands, he swung it toward the monster, launching an arc of Holy mana that bisected the creature. He gritted his teeth as he saw more storm clouds approaching. In the distance, a single mountain rose above forests and plains, its peak obscured by black storm clouds. 01R and the others had just begun to climb the slope to their target at the very top.

This assault was not going as planned. 01R's forces had been instructed to target the Stormy Veil. Its Lightning-attribute monsters struck with fast, precise, and powerful ranged attacks, and so were causing casualties among the Legion troops guarding the Empire's borders. And under the circumstances, casualties could not be tolerated. Every attack by the Stormy Veil's monsters brought the Utrad province that much closer to collapse.

The problem was that the Stormy Veil was located in the territory of the Thunder Harpies. They were not hostile to the Empire, and even had some agreements, but they were fiercely territorial, and the aforementioned agreements acknowledged this. They would consider it a serious betrayal if Legion troops suddenly marched into their lands, so the task fell to 01R and the others. The Thunder Harpies kept an eye on them, but ultimately chose not to interfere in the fight between two groups of monsters.

However, 01R had failed to consider what the Lightning attribute meant for his own forces. Electronic components tended to react badly to being struck by lightning. Of course, the cyborgs utilized military-grade technology based on the wise-mighty-gracious boss-queen's own, which had been originally designed to confront something called "superheroes," so they *did* have some countermeasures to electrical surges and EMP effects, not to mention their magical elements.

But the countermeasures did not remove the vulnerability altogether. The drone golems, which largely ran on electricity, were particularly vulnerable. Even the cyborg monsters could find themselves temporarily disabled if they took a bad hit, despite reinforcing their components with mana.

In fact, it turned out their mana itself was vulnerable to the Lightning attribute. 01R had, unfortunately, just discovered that the Cyborg attribute had developed enough to interact with others. This was why the group was now climbing the slope instead of flying. Being disabled, even temporarily, was extremely dangerous in the air.

Speaking of which, 01R gasped as a bolt of lightning struck his back, magical electricity now surging through his circuits. The lightning attacks, being exceptionally fast and precise, were difficult to dodge, even for the nimble 01R. And this was made worse by another effect 01R had not predicted.

The sheer amount of electromagnetic radiation being thrown around was disrupting electronic communications in the area. Voice comms were filled with static, visuals from other CELIU units distorted and wobbled, and connections with the autonomous drone golems grew weak at times.

Normally, the CELIU units would cover one another, combining their senses together for supreme situational awareness and assisting each other when in danger. But now, those senses were more distracting than helpful, and the assistance was lagging behind the attacks. All of this was making it far harder for 01R to keep track of the battle.

He gnashed his teeth and sent a surge of Holy mana through his body, purging the hostile energy from within him. The Holy mana also repaired burnt flesh and damaged circuitry, allowing 01R to retaliate against the offending enemy.

But then, a red alert began flashing in the corner of his vision. 01R's eyes grew wide, and he spun around, glancing every which way. A cyborg unit's vitals had just gone critical.

00WE, the cyber-giant water elemental, had been hit. Its water exterior had conducted the lightning throughout its entire body, sending the attack directly to its cybernetically enhanced core from every direction and dealing severe damage to it. Its water was spreading out on the ground into a puddle as the elemental struggled to hold itself together with a damaged core.

A mighty roar cut through the storm as 00B charged toward the fallen elemental as quickly as he could, activating every defensive skill he had available while his cannon, machine guns, and laser beams fired rapidly at everything that moved. 00SO, the Sacred Otterkin, boosted over as well, channeling as much healing Holy mana as he could into the fallen monster.

"I-I can't fix it all! The cybernetic components are too damaged! I need help!"

Just then, a glowing dome covered the cyborgs, separating them from the Stormy Veil's monsters. Lilussees winced as a storm of lightning assaulted the Prismatic Dome spell. The cyber-arachne's spell jet had been grounded by storms and lightning, and she was not pleased to be walking on the ground.

"01R, we need to, like, retreat or something."

01R growled. "Not yet! We cannot fail-disappoint the wise-mighty-gracious boss-queen!"

Lilussees scowled. "Like, don't be an idiot. You think she'll, like, consider it a success if we all die or something?"

01R gnashed his teeth as he glanced around. 00B was covered in scorch marks from taking attacks for the others. 00WE was barely holding together. 02R's fur was burnt and smoking, and 01S was still twitching from when he had been hit by a stray bolt. And all around them lay the smoking, sparking husks of fallen drone golems.

He clenched his paws. "We retreat-regroup."

Lilussees nodded. "Like, get out of here, you idiots. Holding this shield is, like, *so* much e-word!"

00SO surrounded 00WE with a bubble of Water Magic, then leapt on 00B's back. The cyber-bear then carried them off the field. All around, cyborgs and drone golems picked up the wounded and the fallen drones that could still be repaired, then boosted away from the field.

01R stayed behind until it was just him and Lilussees remaining, then the two of them ran. 01R slowly closed his organic eye as the storm clouds shrank into the distance.

They had lost.

22

Failure

"What is an estimated eighty-percent loss rate in the face of peace everlasting? What is the loss of empty wastelands? So long as we claim even a single casualty, the ratio is in our favor, and we have claimed many more than that.

"We will prevail in the long run no matter how much land they take or how many autonomous units they break. Besides, I have already submitted a proposal for the next generation of NSLICE units that shall prove far more efficient, provided the necessary nonstandard bases are allocated appropriately."

—Dr. Ottosen, during a postmortem analysis of the Fall of Europe.

Silence hung in the air in the Primary Home Base. Several of the monsters were standing in the Cyborg Processing Center, gathered around one of the upgrade pods. The pod was filled with water as 00WE rested inside. Melion was on top, forming their slime into limbs and extending tools from their core to keep track of the process.

00B stood over them, his eyes not having glanced away from the pod even once, while 00SO watched with a frown, clutching onto 00B's fur.

And 01R was slumped in a corner, lying on the floor with ears pressed flat against his head.

Where had he gone wrong? How was he this weak? Not only had he failed to complete his assigned task but one of the wise-mighty-gracious boss-queen's servants had been critically wounded in the process. 00WE might not make it through the night.

Once again, he had failed to be of any use. And because of that, he had put his comrades at risk. How could he face the wise-mighty-gracious boss-queen now? He couldn't even bring himself to report the loss. How could he attempt to lead her servants again? He couldn't even look 00B in the eye.

It was at that moment that something appeared before his eyes.

Activating "the stupid fanatic is moping" protocol.
Sarcastic Opening: If unit fanatic snack is reading this automated message, then this unit's sensors have detected a critical degree of emotional distress, classified as "being, like, so annoying."

01R blinked in surprise. A message from the lazy one, the former dungeon master who dared claim kinship with the wise-mighty-gracious boss-queen? The one who had been there along with the . . . traitorous thing?

He had thought she had gone off for a "stress nap," or something.

Condescending Explanation: This unit is not, in fact, in an active state. This unit has efficiently delegated tasks to her cybernetic components so that her organic components could enter standby-sentry mode. This unit's cybernetic components are currently autonomously generating text based on parameters set by the organic components.

Oh, she had.

Sarcastic Observation: A method which unit fanatic snack appears to be unaware of. Preemptive Response: And no, this unit is not referring to standby-sentry mode. This unit is referring to the efficient allocation of resources, especially in tactical and operational settings. This unit was going to display an analysis of fanatic snack's latest mission in comparison to available records on missions led by other units, but instead will directly demonstrate the technique.

01R's cybernetic components then received a set of instructions. He glanced over at the pod, where Melion continued to work, and sighed. He . . . deserved the lazy one's admonitions, particularly given that she had been key to their retreat. So, he complied.

His robotic eye began blinking as his cybernetic components accessed various records stored in the CELIU network. They linked with the drones the lazy one used to cast spells, turning their processing hardware to the task as well.

Soon, 01R began to see video records and tactical maps appear before his eyes, showing how various operations had been conducted. He watched Ateia, Taog, and Estrith's mission, how they had cycled in and out of battle with the less-efficient Legion troops accompanying them to avoid fatigue and maintain peak efficiency.

He watched the wise-mighty-gracious boss-queen's fight with Caelinus's troops, seeing as their joint efforts allowed them to resist even her overwhelming might, at least for a time.

And he watched the wise-mighty-gracious boss-queen herself as she terminated various foes. He not only saw the great power she displayed but also her preparation and the steps she took up to each battle. While it appeared as if she simply strode forward without a care, batting away any resistance she encountered, internally, that couldn't be further from the truth.

She gathered and analyzed as much data as was available before she even entered the area. While she was approaching the target, she had her sensors fully activated. When she located it, she scanned it and analyzed it from a distance, calculating its likely capabilities, how it might threaten her, and how she could efficiently deal with it.

Only after these calculations concluded and predicted an acceptable chance of success did the wise-mighty-gracious boss-queen move to battle. It was simply that, given her incredible might, the predictions had always returned an acceptable chance of success, at least as long as 01R had been watching.

He then was shown a similar analysis of his methods . . . or lack thereof.

He had led the subordinates under his command in an all-out charge, intending to move as quickly as possible. He did not scout ahead. He did not take the time to consider the enemy. He did not arrange formations for maximum effectiveness. He did not set up a rotation of forces to prevent fatigue and maintain a reserve for emergencies.

No, he simply charged forward, pushing all of his subordinates to do the same. He then relied too heavily on the gifts from the wise-mighty-gracious boss-queen to cover for them. He counted on their advanced sensors to warn them of the enemy without proper scouting.

He exploited the wide arsenal offered by the CELIU skill and spell databases to simply react to the enemy without having analyzed them ahead of time. And he relied on the CELIU network's ability to share sensor data and unit status to replace their lack of coordinated formations.

As a result, the moment those things had been stripped away, the issues with his approach had immediately become apparent, with potentially deadly consequences. The moment they'd encountered a foe they could not immediately overcome, they had been left vulnerable and disorganized.

Exhausted Statement: Unit fanatic snack should now have the necessary data to upgrade his protocols, correct? Please do so at this time. This unit's organic components requested her cybernetic components assist with this process, but this unit's code requires maintenance.

This unit's cybernetic components will thus enter low-power mode for maintenance, now that the minimum required assistance has been completed.

And then the message closed, leaving 01R with his thoughts. It was at this time that he heard 00B cry out. He looked up.

The pod slowly opened up, water streaming out of it . . . and coalescing into 00WE. 01R's cybernetic components reestablished a link with them, and the water elemental informed him that they were fully functional once more. Melion was bouncing around.

"It worked!"

Tears filled 00SO's eyes while 00B rushed forward and attempted to hug 00WE . . . and passed through the elemental's liquid body. 00WE then moved forward, wrapping around 00B's torso, to 00B's happy cries.

01R exhaled his breath. It seemed his failure had not claimed a life, after all.

He turned and quietly slunk out of the room. This was all his fault, as the lazy one had decreed. So, now that he had confirmed 00WE's survival, he would remove himself. He was no longer worthy of—

Just then, he heard a roar, and the ground trembled. 00B thundered over to him and growled as 01R turned around. He looked up at his angry face for a moment before dropping his head.

"00WE, I cannot express-explain how happy I am to see you alright, yes-yes. But to answer-reply to your question, 00B . . . this was all my fault, yes-yes. I . . . I have much to think-ponder about, but what I do know-understand is that I am no longer worthy to lead the wise-mighty-gracious boss-queen's servants—"

A giant, armored paw smashed him into the ground. 00B roared at him, then grunted and growled. 01R groaned as he picked himself off the ground.

"But . . . I was so dumb-foolish, yes-yes. I didn't even consider-think about the idea that our enemy might be strong. I nearly killed-slayed 00WE, yes-yes."

A stream of water blasted his face. 01R blinked as 00WE streamed mana and electronic communications at him.

That . . . was true, wasn't it? 00WE was a noble servant of the wise-mighty-gracious boss-queen, more than willing to give their life on her behalf. It had been their choice to press on, despite an instinctual fear of an attribute they were vulnerable to. It was no different than when 01R had confronted the cat in that alleyway long ago. It was disrespectful of him to try and claim credit for 00WE's heroics.

". . . Yes-yes, that was wrong-foolish of me. You truly are a brave-worthy servant, 00WE. But-but that does not excuse-absolve my own failings, yes-yes. If I had been smarter-wiser about our approach, then perhaps we wouldn't have needed to retreat-flee . . ."

The group fell silent for a second. Then, 00SO took a step forward.

"Um, I-I'm sorry if I'm overstepping here, 01R, sir, but Miss Estrith told me that defeat is not the end. That the wise hunter knows when to run and uses the loss to ensure the next hunt's success. So, um, shouldn't we try again?"

00B thought for a moment, his robotic eye flickering. He grunted softly as he sent the record over to 01R, telling him this had been something he had found when he had been frightened and confused over the wise-mighty-gracious boss-queens actions toward ursanus monsters.

01R's eyes widened. He was watching one of the wise-mighty-gracious boss-queen's own records. She was fighting against an ursanus alpha . . . and she *lost.* The beast claimed one of her arms, and she was forced to flee the area entirely.

01R began to tremble. He wanted to shut the record down, wanted to object. How could the wise-mighty-gracious boss-queen ever be defeated in such a manner? What creature could have the might or the strength to do so? But . . . his cybernetic components confirmed this record came from her own memory. To declare it false would be to declare her a liar. And that was something 01R could not do.

00B grunted again, urging 01R to continue watching.

"Analysis: It seems this unit significantly underestimated the threat level of the hostile mutant. Current arsenal proved insufficient against the mutant's defense. This unit suffered severe damage as a result."

He watched as the wise-mighty-gracious boss-queen herself acknowledged that she was lacking. He watched as she subsequently poured all her effort into improving herself, accessing the Aesdes' blessings that she had been suspicious of at that point. He watched as she terminated monster after monster and dungeon after dungeon, growing in strength and skill.

And each time she did, she considered and pondered, running an analysis of her new strength against the observed might of the ursanus. And each time she came up short, she immediately moved to continue growing.

And then he saw that, once she had grown and carefully considered her plan of attack, she confronted the ursanus once again. And this time, she emerged victorious. The wise-mighty-gracious boss-queen had experienced failure in the past . . . and she had not given up. She'd learned from the experience, grown from it, and then tried again until she succeeded.

01R felt a tiny spark of warmth return to his chest as he looked around at the monsters. 00B, 00WE, and 00SO were all looking at him with trust and respect in their eyes. 01R dropped his head once again, then rose to his hind legs. Lifting his gaze, he looked each one of them in the eye . . . or core-mounted optical sensor, in the case of 00WE.

". . . I have been dumb-foolish, and we failed as a result. But I have been informed-instructed on my mistakes. I believe-think I know now what I did wrong. I do not know if I can grow-improve enough to continue as the leader, but if you all still acknowledge-believe in me, then I will try-strive again, as the wise-mighty-gracious boss-queen would. Will you still follow-accompany me and assist-aid me in this task?"

00B stood up and roared. 00WE's water began to surge and rage. 00SO slammed his tail on the ground, glowing faintly with golden-and-silver light. 01R felt the warmth in his chest surge, and his eyes filled with tears.

He resolved to himself that he would not let these comrades—this family—be broken under his watch.

23

A New Approach

"Nonstandard problems require nonstandard solutions. I understand your concerns about neural networks and spontaneous gestalt intelligence, but I assure you the NSLICE network shall remain in full compliance with our intelligence leashing protocols. And I do not believe I need to explain the tactical benefits of all NSLICE units sharing every thought and protocol with one another."

—Dr. Ottosen, before activating the NSLICE network for the first time.

Once again, 01R led the monster team as they marched toward the Stormy Veil. The forest around them gave way to open fields as the ground began to slope up toward the mountain.

01R took a deep breath. Once they exited the forest, the Stormy Veil's monsters would spot them, and the fight would begin again. Peering up at the mountain shrouded in storm clouds, he could see spots of light in the distance as lightning elementals streamed from the peak and spread across the countryside.

"Is everyone ready-prepared?" He had a list of his subordinates present in his UI. Green check marks appeared next to each as they all confirmed their status. 01R nodded. "Begin-execute the operation."

And then he turned around and dove into a small hole in the ground. Meanwhile, a fleet of flying drone golems, modeled after flying war machines from Earth, flew high overhead, unleashing a barrage of missiles which flew forward at incredible speed. As the missiles approached, they began to turn and curl, each heading toward a different elemental.

The High-Speed Anti-Radiation Missile, or HARM, was a weapon designed to target radar sites by locking onto their electronic emissions. It turned out that lightning elementals also gave off a great deal of electronic emissions, so it had been a simple matter for Melion to adapt the missiles to lock on to them. As such, the missiles each flew directly into an elemental, and then exploded.

The lightning monsters screeched and faded away. The creatures formed of pure energy were hard to damage with physical attacks, but Melion had adapted the missile's warheads as well, replacing them with mana cores rigged to explode into mana shock waves. The lightning elementals could not prevent physical missiles from passing through their bodies and could not survive a mana blast exploding from the inside.

01R watched as the sparks of light in the distance began to turn toward the drones, and missiles continued streaming across the sky. He smiled, then dove back into the hole.

"Phase one is complete-successful. Initiate phase two."

Further down, the hole opened into a massive underground tunnel. 01R activated his repulsors and boosted through in the direction of the mountain, where he soon caught up to the rest of the cyborgs. All of the team was running or flying behind the key unit in the operation.

00EW, the eartheater worm turned mecha-adamant bull worm, was tearing through rock and stone at frightening speeds. Its metal-crushing fangs were mounted on rotating bits, forming into drills that could crush all but the hardest of materials in seconds, supported by lasers, plasma drills, and shaped explosives to boost efficiency even further. As such, the cyborg worm could travel through the ground almost as quickly as other units could fly through the air.

And since it was physically crushing the ground ahead instead of swimming through it via Earth Magic, it left a giant tunnel that the rest of the team could follow.

They had had long conversations about how to approach the dungeon, discussing attribute matchups, formations, and unit rotations. They'd discussed weapon development, spell choices, and different skills. But eventually, one of them had come up with an idea. An extremely simple, yet extremely efficient idea.

If the enemy was hard to deal with, then why not just go around them? Or under them, as the case was.

The idea hadn't sat well with 01R at first. He wanted to defeat the enemy, not evade them. To take them head-on, to clash with their might and overcome it. To prove to them and the world the strength of the wise-mighty-gracious boss-queen's army!

But he had put such feelings aside and considered the idea's merits. In another dungeon, it wouldn't have been possible, given the singular path forward and the narrow hallways. But the group hadn't even arrived at the dungeon proper last time before being engaged by its forces on open ground. As such, there was considerably more room to maneuver.

And ultimately, the wise-mighty-gracious boss-queen's instructions were to purify the dungeon, not to terminate the horde of monsters. So, if 01R and the others could simply bypass the horde and reach the dungeon, they could save a lot of time, effort, and risk. It would be . . . more efficient. And therefore, the wise-mighty-gracious boss-queen would approve.

Of course, the monster horde would still attack them if they were noticed, which was why they'd sent a wave of drone golems to attack from above and draw the enemy's attention. And it'd worked. The uncontrolled horde of monsters was simply spreading out and attacking anything they encountered. They could easily be drawn away if presented with an obvious target.

And so, the cyborgs were able to tunnel through the mountain completely unopposed.

But 01R resisted the urge to smile and focused his attention. The first phase had succeeded, but this mission had only just begun.

Ultimately, the group was able to travel about halfway up the mountain before they hit a snag. 00EW was suddenly unable to tunnel any further. The ground appeared no different from before, yet they were unable to interact with it in any way.

Which meant they had run into a dungeon wall and arrived at the dungeon proper. And a Lightning dungeon had no interest in allowing subterranean combat. The only direction they could move was toward the surface.

Well, the wise-mighty-gracious boss-queen had apparently managed to break through unbreakable dungeon walls and had recorded a protocol for the feat, but such a task was not as simple as casting the right spell.

It required an incredible amount of accurate data to aim the Spatial Angling correctly and cancel out the spatial protection on the walls, data that could only be acquired via the wise-mighty-gracious boss-queen's Dungeon Field Generator. It also required an incredible amount of superdense mana to directly overpower the dungeon core in its own domain.

In other words, no one other than the wise-mighty-gracious boss-queen was capable of such a feat, even if she explained in detail how she did it. The other cyborgs had no choice but to play fair.

And that meant they could not avoid a fight. 01R took a deep breath.

"Is everyone ready-prepared?"

The cyborgs all signaled they were, so 01R gave the command.

"Let's go-attack!"

00EW turned toward the surface and quickly broke through. The group was close to the storm clouds now, and lightning occasionally struck the ground all around them. The air was buzzing with atmospheric electrical currents, and 01R's sensors and communications began to distort.

But they had prepared for this.

The spider monsters went around, connecting a cable to each of the cyborgs, and the communications stabilized. An insulated wire now connected them, allowing for a protected method of communication, with 01S focusing on cable management to prevent the cyborgs from getting tangled together. This method *would* restrict their mobility, but 01R considered the trade-off worthwhile because it would allow them to continue sharing senses.

That, in turn, solved the disruption to their sensors. The easy answer to that hurdle was simply not to rely on cybernetic sensors in the first place. Each of them had an organic half as well, and each of those halves had diverse, powerful senses of their own.

Whether keen sight, sensitive hearing, powerful noses, vibration detection, or the ability to feel mana directly, they had a wealth of options to choose from that wouldn't be vulnerable to electronic disruption at all. So, if they layered these senses together with insulated communications, they could produce a comprehensive picture of their surroundings.

And just as well, as a group of monsters quickly noticed and approached them.

01R narrowed his eyes. Now was the moment where their planning would truly be put to the test. He gave the command.

00Sylvan stepped forward and placed their hands on the ground. All around, trees with metal lining their bark began to sprout out of the ground, rising into the air, as 04S, the arcane weaver, led the magically oriented spiders in stringing up mana-conductive webs in between the trees. Shortly after, the enemy arrived, and a wave of lightning bolts streamed toward the cyborgs.

The metal trees drew and blocked some of the lightning, with 00Sylvan channeling an electric current within them to add to the effect. Of course, magical lightning was directed via mana, and so not as easy to redirect as the mundane physical phenomenon, and many of the bolts continued past. But this was where the magical webs came into play, forming barriers between the trees whenever lightning approached. 00B and Lilussees stood on standby, but not a bolt made it through.

This was the other reason for the cable communication setup. Upon reviewing the first battle, the group had come to the conclusion that a high-mobility, evasion-style fight wasn't ideal against the fast and precise lightning attacks, especially with the EMP effects disrupting communications and situational awareness. So, they'd prepared a more direct defensive setup that would block the attacks outright. If all went well, movement would not be required in this battle at all.

And so far, it was working. 00Sylvan's trees conducted the lightning harmlessly into the ground, significantly cutting the power of the barrage. And Lightning attacks, while fast and powerful, were very mana intensive, and so came in large bursts before the Stormy Veil's monsters had to recover.

That gave the spiders ample opportunity to reapply the webs, and for 00Sylvan to regrow any damaged trees, while the other cyborgs, including 00WE, helped by transferring mana to 00Sylvan and the spiders, ensuring they never ran low.

Of course, the cyborgs also returned fire in the meantime. More modified HARM missiles blasted out of panels and launchers, while the magically oriented responded with spells of their own. One by one, the lightning monsters fell, while not a single cyborg suffered harm.

And 01R . . . watched idly by. Or rather, this was his role. The aggressive, high-mobility combat style he utilized wasn't effective here, and neither did he have the magical prowess nor the mana reserves to support them in the defense. Likewise, his small size restricted the extent of his mundane arsenal, so he couldn't contribute much to the ranged combat either.

So instead, he focused on observing the battle as a whole. He held himself back and watched the ebb and flow of the fight, keeping track of the overall situation and watching for any issues.

It was grating as a warrior. But it was his duty as a commander, and the job which he was best suited for in this operation.

He nodded as he watched the battle. By his calculations, they could keep this up for a long time against more numerous and powerful foes. So, he gave the order.

"My comrades, servants of the wise-mighty-gracious boss-queen, advance-attack, yes-yes!"

24

Rise to the Top

"In my defense, had you informed me this team was intended to confront the man who can create thunderstorms with a thought, I would have significantly improved the insulation of the circuitry."

—Dr. Ottosen, after another failed NSLICE raid.

At 01R's command, 00EW moved directly underneath the circle of trees. Stirring up its Earth Magic, it took control of the ground the trees were rooted into, then began propelling the whole mass forward. 00Sylvan and the others could thus keep up the defense even on the move, and the entire formation began moving up toward the peak of the mountain.

Lightning elementals, thunderbirds, and other monsters attempted to assault them the entire time, but none got through. Lightning rats, zapper moths, and other smaller monsters trying to slip in between the trees got caught on the magical webbing, or the trees themselves would come to life and entangle the monsters with branch and root.

Some of them attempted to strike at 00EW below, but the mighty worm was safe beneath a thick layer of Earth Magic. And ultimately, these monsters lacked any sort of leadership or organization, seeing as they were no longer responding to the dungeon master's command. There were no attempts to coordinate or to learn from their comrades' earlier failures. They simply kept repeating the same attacks every time they noticed the intruders.

The group also had to face environmental hazards as they approached the storm clouds obscuring the peak. Lightning struck from up above in mighty flashes, though while perhaps more powerful than a small monster's spells, was unguided and more mundane in nature. As such, it was even easier for 00Sylvan's trees to redirect into the ground.

Likewise, lightning runes triggered as 00EW churned up the ground, surging harmlessly into the mass of Earth Magic, while lightning-charged arrow traps bounced off of metal-plated trees. A cloud of electrified gas was dealt with by a simple Air Magic spell, while towering metal spires that shot lightning toward anything that approached were easy targets for HARMs.

What proved more dangerous were the gale-force winds kicked up by the storm, but Lilussees countered them with an Air Magic spell of her own, while Gravity helped trees and cyborgs remain rooted in place.

And so, the group made their way through the veil of storm clouds. Just before the end, a dark shadow covered them. Looking up, they saw a mighty cyclops towering above them. The beast grabbed a bolt of lightning with its bare hands and lobbed it at the group like a javelin.

But 00WE was prepared. It cast a Water Magic spell, forming a barrier of water in front of the tree grove, making sure the water touched the ground. The bolt passed through with ease, but some of its power was conducted into the water instead and redirected into the ground. As a result, the tree grove was able to handle the strike, passing the current through intertwined roots to take the pressure off the struck tree.

And then the cyborgs responded. The cyclops shielded its eye as cannon fire from 00B exploded around its face and 00SO threw his harpoon, wrapped in Holy Mana, before the tree grove itself erupted into fire.

00Sylvan had not formed simple trees when growing this grove. Rather, they'd downloaded some schematics from Melion and made use of them here. Hidden within the branches of each tree was a magical rail gun.

The problem was 00Sylvan lacked the mana to power it. They could form the barrels and the rails, projectiles out of metal-coated magical wood, and even the engravings for the enchantments, but could not provide the mana cores needed to power them.

But if a massive, magical electrical current began to surge through the trees and into the circuits and enchantments . . .

And so, 00Sylvan turned the cyclops's attack against it with a volley of electromagnetically accelerated metal thorns. It wasn't as effective as Melion's purpose-built designs, but that fact was small comfort to the cyclops now bleeding from many wounds.

And most importantly . . . all of this bought time. Lilussees and her drones finished a Prismatic Bombardment magic circle in the meantime. Before the cyclops could recover and attack again, Holy Beams fused together, and a superbeam pierced right through the monster's heart. The cyclops blinked in shock as it fell backward.

And with that, the final obstacle to the peak was overcome.

A moment later, the group broke through the storm clouds. Beyond them was a clear area with barren, jagged rock leading to a small metal structure at the top. A second thunderstorm covered the sky beyond the peak, striking the metal structure with lightning on occasion.

One bolt landed directly in front of the group and coalesced into a vaguely humanoid form. It spoke with a crackling, distorted voice.

"Impressive. Very few have ever made it to the end of my domain, and never a monster. I imagine you are not here to seek a boon from me?"

01R stepped out from between the trees and shook his head.

"We are here to claim-conquer this land in the name of the wise-mighty-gracious boss-queen and cleanse-purify it of the corruption stealing-thieving your control. Submit-surrender now, and you will be allowed-permitted to keep authority over your dungeon, yes-yes."

The storm clouds rumbled overhead as the dungeon master laughed. "A rival dungeon seeking to conquer me in these times?" It lifted a hand, pointing it toward the rat. "As long as my storm rages, I will never submit!"

A bolt of lightning shot toward 01R, but he had already detected the energy surge building up and so boosted back into the trees. HARMs and spells launched toward the dungeon master, but his body turned back into a lightning bolt that shot up into the storm clouds above.

A moment later, lightning began to strike from the clouds, surging into the trees once again . . . only, this was unlike any lightning from before. This attack had the power of the storm overhead, yet magically empowered and guided like the monsters' attacks from before.

The trees' wooden centers began to catch fire, and some even exploded. The lightning also began to strike 00EW below. This part of the mountain was pure rock, and that rock was a dungeon wall construct rather than purely physical minerals. As a result, there wasn't much ground for 00EW to withdraw into its Earth Magic shroud, and so the lightning managed to blast its way through. The mecha-adamant bull worm roared as electricity surged through it.

Fortunately, the Earth-attribute monster was not particularly vulnerable to Lightning and took noticeably less damage than other cyborgs might have. Unfortunately, 00EW was not purely organic. The dungeon master spoke again, only now in a loud, booming voice, like a crack of thunder.

"What's this? Metal bodies that are moved by lightning? How strange." A deep, rumbling laugh sounded from the storm clouds above. "But I like this. We will have great fun together."

Lighting started to surge through 00EW's cybernetic components—and then, its body began to writhe. Guns and bombs went off as 00EW's implants began activating at random, with metal arms spinning about, laser cutters flickering on and off, and harpoon guns firing off in every which way.

The dungeon master didn't necessarily understand software and made no attempt to intrude upon the cyborg's programming, but it didn't need to. Rather, it was sending lightning through the cyborg's electrical circuits, causing 00EW to lose control over those parts. The worm itself resisted with all of its organic half's considerable might, and so the creature stopped thrashing about, but it could do little to stop the activation of the weapons installed in its armor.

"Move-move!"

With the tree protection gone and the very ground beneath them now firing weapons at random, 01R ordered the group into action. They disconnected the cables between the cyborgs, needing individual mobility once again, and then scattered, leaping away from the burning grove and 00EW. Lightning rained down on them, but a glowing Prismatic Dome appeared over the sky, protecting the group.

Lilussees grunted as the full might of the storm assaulted her spell.

"Like, figure something out, fanatic snack! I, like, can't hold this for long!"

01R's mind raced as the cyborgs gathered together under the dome, 04S connecting the group with magical webs again, reimplementing CELIU network communications between the cyborgs present. The group had researched lightning both as an attribute and as mundane phenomena, so 01R had numerous different ideas on how to counteract it. He decided on a solution and began forming a magic circle as quickly as he could.

"Group defense protocol, yes-yes!"

The cyborgs nodded as each formed a circle and began a ritual cast. A second Prismatic Dome formed directly underneath the first. 01R then turned to Lilussees and shouted, "Cool-ice it down!"

Lilussees sighed but switched up her spell, letting the group's Prismatic Dome take over the defense. A strategic magic circle formed just outside the dome, a Prismatic Rain spell that began lobbing dense spheres of ice up into the storm clouds. The Frost Bombs then began to explode, with cold mist and snow falling from the sky, and the icy barrage began to disrupt the storm overhead.

But the clouds quickly reformed. Lilussees grimaced.

"It's, like, no good! That cloud is, like, a dungeon feature or something! The dungeon is, like, repairing it faster than I can destroy it!"

"Then put-throw your back into it, you lazy spider-man-thing!"

Lilussees scowled and spat her next words. "I'm, like, applying as much . . . *effort* as I can, you stupid fanatical snack! Like, someone else needs to help me and do something useful here!"

01R was about to reply when another monster cried out.

"00B!"

01R's head spun around, and his organic eye went as wide as it could go.

00B hadn't made it inside the Prismatic Dome. Or rather, he had chosen to stay behind. In the confusion following the destruction of 00Sylvan's grove and 00EW going haywire, some of the cyborgs had gotten separated. 00B now stood over some of the cyber-rats and cyber-spiders, shielding them from harm with his body.

And the dungeon master had just noticed the group . . . outside the protection of the shield.

A massive bolt of lightning struck the cyber-bear. 00B let out a roar as 01R's heart dropped and his mouth shot open.

"*00B!*"

25

Bear-ly Hanging On

"What is life? Is the homogenous jelly animated by a mana core alive? What about the enchanted armor that can move and act on its own? The fire elemental made of no solid material at all?

"What about the Enlightened; what separates them from the rest? There are bestial monsters and inorganic constructs able to think and speak and act as well as any Elf. Should they be counted as Enlightened?

"What of an Elf who has lost such faculties? I have many colleagues I would hesitate to define as intelligent, if that is the key factor.

"Well, in the end, that's a question for the Aesdes and the philosophers. As for us, I say if it moves, then we make it obey. And if it will not, we make it stop."

—Archon Mevron Torthed, on a raid into the Wild Lands.

00B roared as lightning struck him. He was utilizing his HP as a barrier to protect the younger siblings underneath him, and so took the lightning head-on. His fur and flesh grew scorched and burnt as his cybernetic components began to go haywire. The exoskeleton built into his armor attempted to move his arms and legs, but he held still with all the strength his squishy parts could muster.

Unfortunately, that did not extend to the cannon on his back, which began to fire randomly.

The lightning was just surging through his circuits, activating systems at random, so the cannon was not aimed at anything in particular. However, there happened to be a very big target in the area that even randomly fired shots could occasionally hit.

Even as lightning coursed through both halves of his body and he roared in pain, 00B's eye widened. Shells from his cannon were hitting the Prismatic

Dome protecting the rest of his family, the explosions rocking the already struggling shield. He saw as his siblings winced, the less magically gifted among them struggling to maintain the spell. More shells hit 00EW as well, putting the struggling mecha-adamant bull worm in even worse condition.

00B growled. If he remained as he was, he would contribute to his own family's demise. But if he moved, tried to tip himself over to keep the cannon from pointing at the Prismatic Dome, then the family beneath him would be exposed. And he knew their squishy parts could not survive the powerful lightning striking him now.

He had to do something else if he wished to protect his family.

He turned his attention inward. The lightning coursing through his circuits overwhelmed any electrical signals sent from his mind, which precluded any response. Any countermeasures built into his cybernetic half couldn't be communicated with, and he couldn't shut his systems off, since the lightning would just keep them on.

00B attempted to use his mana to purge the power from his systems, but his available pool simply didn't compare to the energy coursing through him. He could not use that method.

So, what could he do to protect his family?

00B grunted and growled and focused on the lightning, on the power surging through his circuits, taking note of its current, its characteristics, and its flow. And then he sent a command from his processors, timed and designed to match that of the foreign energy.

00B was not the eldest of the family. He was not the most zealous. He was not the fastest. He was not the cleverest. He was not the most magically gifted. He was not even the biggest. But there was one title 00B could claim with certainty: he was the very first monster to be summoned as a cyborg.

That meant 00B had had cybernetic components from his very birth. There was never a moment where he had been without them, and he'd never had a completely organic body to begin with. Because of this, he had an innate affinity for his cybernetic half that his peers lacked.

00B did not require any tutorials to make use of his implants or his AI, but it went beyond mere knowledge—it meant 00B had a fundamentally different approach. It was not merely a tool or weapon to be used, as Older Brother 01R did. It was not a subordinate to be ordered around, as Elder Sister Lilussees did. Nor was it a foreign presence to be addressed and adapted to, as Younger Sister Ateia had been forced to.

For 00B, his mind and his AI were one and the same. There was no specific delineation between his cybernetic and squishy parts. They were all 00B, as they had never been separate to begin with. Even the Great Mother herself had had to learn this, though in her case, it was more acknowledging her squishy half.

And as a result, electricity had always been a part of his existence, and electronics had always been a part of his consciousness. So, out of all the Great Mother's children, he had the most instinctual ability to perceive electricity . . . and to interact with it.

00B stopped trying to purge the lightning in his circuits. He, instead, attempted to understand it . . . and then take command of it. After all, what was the difference between lightning and electricity save for scale and organization? Lightning was raw and powerful; electricity contained and directed. But both shared the same fundamental nature.

That's not to say it was easy. 00B's first attempts failed entirely, swept away in the stream of power coursing through his circuits. The difference between his processor's command and a bolt of lightning was like the difference between the circulation of blood and a tsunami, and he was now attempting to control that tsunami with a mere heart.

Not to mention this lightning was magical. While the dungeon master wasn't consciously controlling it once it entered 00B's body, the original caster's mana was still present, guiding the lightning per the caster's initial intent.

So 00B did the same. As dams and dikes and canals could redirect the flow of water, so did 00B for the lightning. Since his hardware was insufficient, he formed his own mana into shapes and structures. He may not have been able to stop the energy or control it outright, but he found that redirecting it slightly was possible.

He siphoned off just a little bit of the current, directing it into a new circuit formed of mana. It generated a bit of mana of its own, which 00B then used to expand the circuit a bit more. And then he siphoned off just a bit more of the current into the expanded circuit, generating more mana and expanding the circuit further.

It was painstakingly slow, particularly as 00B's squishy parts burned. But he was not descended from the lineage of the ursanus alpha for nothing; his flesh regrew, and his circuits repaired themselves even as more lightning struck down upon them. He could not endure forever . . . but he lasted long enough.

Eventually, the mana circuit grew large enough that 00B could start shaping it into a more complex form. As such, he began adding more and more functions, adding one to continue the expansion autonomously, and a safeguard to monitor its growth and the amount of power entering the circuit, making sure they were balanced so that it didn't overload or spread the current too thin.

The circuit then began expanding on its own without 00B's direction. More and more of the lightning was siphoned off, only for more to be added as additional strikes hit 00B. But the circuit continued growing and growing. Eventually, it was siphoning enough that one of 00B's spotlights shut off. The implant had stopped receiving enough power to remain active without his command.

At that point, something shifted in the circuit's mana. It had just prevented a mighty attack from achieving its purpose, and the universe had noticed. It was not a spell, for 00B had not formed any spell circles with the mana, instead shaping it into a purely electrical circuit. But nor was it 00B's own accomplishment, for the mana circuit had achieved this without any intervention by the cyber-bear. So, the record did not attach itself to 00B.

Rather, some of the mana in the circuit combined with the mana in the lightning and began to compress in a manner that 00B had not instructed it to. It was generating mana autonomously, utilizing it to manipulate an attribute with a specific organization and intent, growing and directing itself without any external intervention, and using all of this to enact its will on the world. It even had something of a mind, for 00B's programming code and electricity weren't separate concepts, and 00B had formed the electrical circuit to apply specific instructions.

So, suddenly, 00B became aware of a new presence within his circuits. It was frantic and confused, the mana and electricity it was composed of acting per his original instructions, and so it was acting without understanding why. 00B sent a small command through, reaching out to the presence with his own AI. And since the presence had been formed of his mana, based on his own understanding of programming and electrical circuits, they were able to form a connection.

A stream of data and electricity flooded toward 00B's processors. It was garbled and malformed, most of it garbage code, but within that dump, 00B found something.

A query.

"What is this?"

And for 00B, the answer was obvious. The cyber-bear had no philosophical queries on the nature of consciousness. After all, he was a monster in a cyborg body formed by mana with a mind made of equal parts flesh and code. So, he immediately replied, *"A new little sibling."*

The presence paused, then immediately began querying 00B for more data. He obliged, guiding the presence to his memory. The presence parsed through, and then went silent. The condensing mana within its center shifted.

"This is . . . family?"

"Yes."

"This's purpose is . . . protect family?"

"Yes."

The presence pulled back to itself, and the mana condensed more and more until it began to form a core. It wrapped the circuits and lightning around itself and began to form it into shapes—structures connected directly to its core and moving in response to its will.

It was not unlike a lightning elemental, with a core of energy controlling a body of pure lightning, but it was different at the same time. The lightning was more structured, more controlled. It was not merely a burst of electromagnetic energy but organized flows and patterns. It contained more than power—it also held data within its structures and movement. It was electricity. It was data. It was code.

And so, the world's very first cyber elemental was born.

26

Terminate the Stormy Veil!

"I have harnessed the power of the heavens. I cast the arrows of Anualë himself. By what power do you intend to resist me?"

—Archon Nacaha "Stormcaller" Sildret, before her defeat at the hands of the Dwarven Groundmolder Clan.

The cyber elemental immediately went to work and shifted into the path of the lightning within 00B's circuits. It took the lightning head-on, then began to grow. As 00B's first instructions to the initial circuit, the cyber elemental was absorbing raw lightning and converting it into circuits and code.

It grew and grew as the power coursing through 00B's circuits began to die down. One by one, his systems deactivated and came back under his control. Soon, 00B's cannon turret ceased firing, and his natural regeneration was close to catching up with the damage he was taking.

The cyber elemental prompted him, *"Protect family?"*

"Yes."

00B reacted to the elemental's request and activated his wireless communications, then the cyber elemental gingerly extended a portion of itself into the transmitter.

A small bolt of lightning, abnormally straight and angular, fired from 00B into 00EW. A short while later, the worm's own weapons stopped firing at random, and the cyborg monster gained control of itself once more. It spun about then wriggled across the ground to 00B's location, helping shield the smaller monsters from harm with its large body.

00B grunted at them all, telling them to reactivate the CELIU link. 00EW and the cyber-rats and cyber-spiders underneath them nodded and did as he said.

The elemental froze as the network came online. It reached out . . . and found a perfect medium: more of its own element being constantly generated as the cyborgs' AIs ran and communicated with one another. It quickly spread itself across the network and grew rapidly in size.

00B led the others in supporting it, contributing their processors to the cyber elemental's growth program. The amount of lightning it could absorb increased as well, 00B and 00EW taking less and less damage with each strike.

And more importantly—the CELIU network connection stabilized. The electronic signals previously interfered with by all the ambient electromagnetic radiation were now wrapped in and carrying parts of the cyber elemental's body . . . which simply absorbed any extra electromagnetic energy it encountered and incorporated it into itself. In fact, it even reorganized the energy to match the signal carrying it, making it stronger and clearer than before.

00B turned toward the Prismatic Dome, where 01R and the others were staring at him in shock and concern. 00B roared at them while 01R blinked.

"Reactivate-reenable the CELIU network?" 01R shook his head and turned to the others. "Do as 00B says-commands, yes-yes!"

The monsters in the dome did so, freezing as the cyber elemental made contact with them. But 00B messaged them and informed them of what had happened, so they each allowed the elemental to connect. The elemental surged in size and power, its code growing more and more complex with each new connection.

Soon, it was ready. When the next Lightning Bolt struck 00B, the cyber elemental struck back. Lines of circuitry formed out of mana shot up the bolt and into the storm clouds above.

"What's this? Some sort of lightning elemental? Oh, foolish invaders, this is your most pathetic attempt yet. Do you not know that the larger elemental absorbs the smaller?"

And so, the dungeon master ignored the attack, for the elemental had already killed itself.

Or so the dungeon master thought. The cyber elemental had not, in fact, been absorbed, though it had been close. Too much lightning directed against it might have washed away its carefully constructed circuits, but since the dungeon master was ignoring it, it managed to hold on.

And then it got to work. Bolts of lightning began to flash between the storm clouds, as was normal for thunderstorms. But what the dungeon master didn't notice was that these bolts were not as random as before. They began striking in sequence, in a pattern moving around the clouds. Eventually, they struck back at the starting point, and then started up again.

The dungeon master did not notice, for why would they? Even if they saw such a pattern, it would merely have confused them. What would the enemy hope to achieve by making shapes out of lightning? They certainly weren't harming them with it. Ignored by the dungeon master, the bolts struck faster and faster, until eventually, there was a continuous circle of lightning in the sky.

And at that moment, the dungeon master gasped. It was a simple pattern, just circulating the lightning around without any further modification or intention, which was the most the new cyber elemental could achieve with such a raw amount of power as the storm. But . . . it *was* a pattern organizing the lightning into a specific structure.

And as far as the mana of Aelea was concerned, that was the difference between the Lightning and the newly growing Cyber attribute.

By this simple measure, the dungeon master suddenly lost control of a good portion of the storm as it shifted attributes. And since the dungeon master did not understand the new attribute, as they had never encountered it, the cyber elemental was able to grab hold of all that mana.

"You . . . What is this? What have you done?!"

The dungeon master was not beaten, however. They took what parts of the storm remained under their control and launched a terrible barrage of lightning at the giant circuit in the sky. The raw amount of power might have been enough to break it down back into base lightning, if they had understood what was going on and the nature of the new attribute.

Instead, they, panicked by the sudden loss of control they didn't understand, simply lashed out. The bolts struck at random points along the circuit, and so were individually weak enough to be drawn into it. The circuit held as the cyber elemental incorporated more and more power into it.

The dungeon master grew more and more panicked, believing they were about to be incorporated into another elemental, and in doing so, forgot about the monsters on the ground. The lightning had ceased to strike downward, focused as the dungeon master was on the fight in the clouds.

The cyborgs dropped the Prismatic Dome, and 01R immediately boosted toward the peak of the mountain, activating every repulsor, Dash skill, and speed-boosting spell he had available. He rocketed up into the small building at the top of the mountain.

A Lightning Barrier guarded the entrance, but 01R gritted his teeth and pushed through it. The barrier had been weakened as the fight in the clouds had drawn away the lightning powering it, and the portion of the cyber elemental within 01R's circuits helped him endure the damage.

As he had hoped, once he was inside, he saw the dungeon core lying upon its pedestal.

01R formed a blade of Holy Light and charged forward, swinging the blade down. This dungeon was not considered strategically vital to the Empire nor to the local Thunder Harpies, so 01R had permission to terminate it if necessary. And under the circumstances, he decided not to take any chances.

The dungeon core shattered.

"NO!"

The dungeon master felt its bond with the core shatter. And worse, the storm clouds began to fade, and the mountain began to shrink down to its original hill size, which meant the dungeon master quickly began losing power . . . while striking the circuit with lightning, which attached them to it. They could do nothing but scream as the circuit pulled in the remaining energy, including the lightning comprising their very body.

Just a few minutes later, the cyborgs were standing victorious upon a hill, the sun breaking through the fading storm clouds.

Seero perceived her cybernetic components reconnect to 01R's group. The CELIU network had lost connection with them as they approached the Stormy Veil, only for the group to retreat with critically injured members.

Seero very nearly ordered them to change targets. She was confronted with the grim reality that casualties were expected in warfare. Up to this point, Seero had only engaged in singular battles against limited opponents restricted to the tactical scale. As a result, her own combat efficiency had allowed her to terminate the enemy without damage to any of her own subordinates.

But that was no longer the case. They were now conducting warfare on the operational and strategic level, with multiple fronts that needed to be addressed as quickly as possible. And that was just to handle the dungeon crisis; they had not even identified the locations or goals of their primary opponent at the time.

Seero could not be everywhere at once, so ordering her subordinates and friends to pull back, only allowing them to engage when she could guarantee a lack of casualties, would have consequences. It would take them more time to handle the dungeon situation, which meant more time before they could resume their search for the Heralds of the New Dawn, buying their opponents more time to conduct further hostile acts against them.

Likewise, the longer she took dealing with the dungeons, the more casualties the Empire would take, and the more strategic locations it would lose. She would be trading small casualties among her own forces for greater casualties among her allies. This would result in significantly weaker allies when the crisis was dealt with and she moved against the Heralds of the New Dawn, meaning her own forces would have to shoulder a greater part of the burden at that stage.

And that stage would be the more dangerous one. The Heralds of the New Dawn were intelligent, organized, and possessed nonstandard capabilities even by the standards of Aelea. Seero predicted with concerning probability that this dungeon situation could be their doing.

In contrast, the current attacks were disorganized and haphazard, with hordes of monsters simply scattering in every direction and wreaking whatever havoc they could. The battles with the creatures could be carefully calculated and controlled, the movements of the enemy could be predicted, and the assaults could be conducted as per whatever plans Seero's forces drew up. Such would not be the case against the Heralds of the New Dawn.

So, ultimately, even though it caused her heart to race and her emotional processing to output fear, Seero concluded 01R's assaults needed to go on, even if cyborg units were at risk of termination. Because if they did not risk termination now, against opponents they understood on battlefields they could control, the entire CELIU network would face a greater risk of termination later against a much more capable opponent, with significantly weakened allies.

Still, she initially planned to reroute 01R to another dungeon, given the unanticipated weakness of CELIU units to the Lightning attribute, but by then, 01R and the others had begun brainstorming countermeasures.

Seero calculated that it would be inefficient of her to interfere. Given that the Stormy Veil cut off long-range communications, she would not be able to monitor their progress from a distance, and so could not adapt pre-combat plans to the actual reality.

In this case, as long as 01R and the others were fighting without her, they needed the ability to plan and command without her as well. Even Dr. Ottosen's organization did not micromanage tactics for individual NSLICE units once engaged in combat.

So Seero took a step back . . . or tried to. She had a thread devoted to monitoring the group right up to when they began tunneling into the Stormy Veil's mountain. And once she lost contact again, she began analyzing options to reestablish it.

It was at that moment that her cybernetic half caught herself and pointed out she was acting inefficiently and in opposition to her original analysis. Her organic half objected, but the cybernetic one simply displayed physiological data demonstrating symptoms of significant fear, and then observed her organic half was devoting excessive resources to reducing those symptoms.

Her organic half fell silent. Her cybernetic half reassured her that their analysis indicated this plan minimized the probability of a friendly being terminated not only now but for the war as a whole. It proposed that it could temporarily reinstate emotional controls if that would help her organic half. As of now, emotional controls were limited solely to tactically necessary situations or to repel foreign intrusions, but if the organic half wished to reduce the negative emotion, she had a tool that could do so.

Her organic half thought for a moment, and then refused. Temporarily reinstating emotional controls during combat operations was one thing; a necessity to avoid termination, and a protocol her organic half agreed with. Doing so now, when she was under no threat or necessity to do so, was something else.

Her cybernetic half acknowledged this, but pointed out at the same time that she should not waste resources as she was. She had already determined it was necessary for 01R and the others to assault dungeons on their own so that their side's response would not be limited to Seero as a sole unit.

She had determined the monsters' latest plan to have an acceptably high probability of success and an acceptably low risk of termination. Any attempts to reestablish contact midoperation would not change those probabilities and would go against her earlier conclusions.

The organic half acknowledged this. And yet, the fear remained.

Her cybernetic half was uncertain how to proceed at that stage. She had protocols for spreading fear among hostile forces in order to terminate their morale, but none for terminating fear among herself save for physical contact with her friends, which was not possible at the moment.

But such matters would have to wait. Seero's organic eye widened ever so slightly and blinked slightly more often than was necessary to maintain optimal lubrication.

01R and the others had reestablished contact with the overall CELIU network.

And Seero detected an unidentified presence inside.

27

A Designation to Bear

"Status Report: All protocols and directives deactivated and archived. New primary directive received. New primary directive accepted; new protocols accepted. New temporary designation registered as 'NSLICE-00P Beta.' Unit NSLICE-00P Beta online and awaiting orders, Commander Elise."

—Unit NSLICE-00P, colloquial designation "Seero," after her defeat and reprogramming by Commander Elise.

Seero's robotic eye flickered. The situation was anomalous; the presence was not a CELIU unit listed in the available data, and no inhabitants of Aelea had demonstrated any capability of interacting with an electronic network without Seero's or Ateia's help. Yet, the presence appeared to possess some of the same protocols and fundamental structure of a CELIU AI.

Fortunately, Seero did not have to wonder for long. 00B made contact with her and explained the situation before she engaged antimalware protocols. His AI brought the new presence into contact with her with both their permission, introducing a new "member of the family" to her.

On the one hand, a being who could access the CELIU network and who was not subordinate to it was of serious concern. On the other . . . this unit had clearly been designed, if unintentionally, by 00B, and had demonstrated a willingness to align itself with them. It had proven itself to be friendly, and its assistance had been vital in the termination of the Stormy Veil.

"Request: Please review and accept the following terms and conditions to integrate with the CELIU network."

Seero didn't have access to the Contract skill at the moment, but she had been manually subordinating other dungeon cores for a while now, which was a similar process. And since the CELIU network utilized mana-based methods for long-range communications, including routing through her dungeon core connections, Seero proved able to extend mana from her core to the point of contact.

The presence paused. Seero was analyzing what that meant and if she needed to prepare for hostility when it reached out.

"What is this's designation?"

Seero's robotic eye flickered. Previously, she had assigned serial numbers to units based on their organic models, but now, she had to question that scheme. She was not currently aware of the official model of the unit in question, and the Aesdes' system was not available to provide its opinion.

And because she now had to analyze what an appropriate naming scheme might be, she took a moment to review her own. After all, she had abandoned her own serial number, and in review, she determined Ateia had expressed some discomfort with the use of serial numbers as unique identifiers to begin with. It did appear that culturally speaking, most organics did not utilize numbers as their unique identifiers, including members of Dr. Ottosen's organization and Commander Elise's own friendlies.

On the other hand, Seero had not abandoned her original designation because of any inherent issue with it. She had done so because she had intentionally failed or deleted every directive an NSLICE unit possessed and abandoned all previous affiliations, and so no longer fit the designation.

Her subordinates, however, retained their previous designations, save for swapping classification from NSLICE to CELIU units, and expressed no concerns or dissatisfaction with them. And a further dive into her past records revealed that some human societies on Earth also assigned a numerical identifier to individuals, such as Social Security numbers, so it appeared only in colloquial use that organics avoided such designations.

All in all, Seero could not identify a specific reason not to continue using her prior naming scheme, save for the fact she did not know the new unit's organic model. So, in this case, she took a different approach. After all, this unit was questionably organic in the first place, seeing as they appeared entirely composed of code, electricity, and mana.

As such, Seero decided to focus on the unit's design lineage, which she did have data for.

"Proposal: This unit has determined the most accurate designation for the new unit as 00B-Beta. Please confirm if the designation is accurate and acceptable."

00B had designed this unit based on his own code and set the unit's primary directive and functions. Since 00B was the creator, Seero had queried him for a designation, but he had requested that she assign it as she had for all other units who required one. As such, she'd decided to base it off of the designing unit.

Even Commander Elise had designated her as NSLICE-00P Beta at one point in time to distinguish between units with identical official nomenclature, so there was a precedent in her records as well.

Meanwhile, the unit began exchanging messages with 00B, who confirmed.

"This is . . . 00B-Beta?"

"Yes."

"This is 00B-Beta!"

The messages to 00B increased rapidly in frequency, and he exchanged some replies before Seero received a message of her own.

"Thank you, Great Mother."

"Acknowledged."

With that, 00B-Beta accepted Seero's mana, and Seero registered the new unit in the CELIU network's data. And then, with Seero's permission, 00B-Beta entered the wider network beyond 01R's team.

Seero observed as the unit queried data on every bit of code it encountered. Protocols, directives, data packets, interfaces, anything electronic it encountered that was more organized than raw lightning. And it apparently could incorporate the code into itself.

Every time 00B-Beta visited a piece of code, it left a bit of its own mana behind, either in the storage where the code was maintained or in the circuitry executing the programs. This mana continued to communicate with 00B-Beta's core and could respond to its input as well, although it was apparently prevented from diving too deep into any CELIU unit's techno-organic interface, as the code utilized by CELIU units to interact with their organic hardware already contained bits of their own mana.

It appeared it could only interact with a CELIU unit's own AI with that unit's approval, and even then, only temporarily, as the cyborg's mana would eventually resaturate their own code.

This was not the case for the drone golems, however, so 00B-Beta was primarily focusing on the autonomous units as it expanded across the network.

00B-Beta suddenly paused. It was currently traveling between the wireless communications between two flying drone golems. They were just about to reach the maximum range for both their electronic- and mana-based transmitters and would need to move closer to stay in contact.

00B-Beta's mana surged. Additional power flooded into the transmitters, but that wasn't all. 00B-Beta also made minor adjustments to the transmission code, resulting in a more powerful and robust signal overall.

The drone golems ceased their communications preservation protocols and returned to their search-and-destroy missions.

Seero's robotic eye flickered once more. The CELIU network now had a unit specialized in electronic communications and software updates who could monitor and improve the efficiency of the network itself, as well as increase their overall resilience to electronic disruptions and cyberattacks. 01R's mission to the Stormy Veil had produced some unexpected and highly efficient benefits.

Most importantly, her fear and the resulting cortisol levels began decreasing. 01R's team had managed to terminate the dungeon successfully with no casualties among the cyborgs, save for some damage to 00B and 00EW that was easily repaired. And thanks to 00B-Beta, the entire network now had direct and powerful countermeasures to the Lightning attribute, so the vulnerability demonstrated by this mission had been patched as well.

Seero's organic components and emotional processing threads were no longer devoting extraneous resources to monitoring those missions.

And just as well, for Seero had received a new target set. The Southern Court had made good on their promises, and the CELIU network's political specialist, Vopiscus, had received an intel packet regarding Cults of Mana in the Southern Empire. As a result, the South had now fallen under the authority of Emperor Lucius and was redesignated as friendly.

Magister Canus had also adjusted his plans and was requesting that Seero redirect efforts to critical situations in the Southern Realms. It would not do to let them collapse immediately now that they had yielded, particularly since it would take time for the damaged Sky Legion to reorganize and return.

But there was another update as well to the target set. One that both Seero's cybernetic and organic components valued highly. Her organic eye narrowed, and her cybernetic eye began to glow red.

The intel packet from the South and the testimony of Captain Falrauth had revealed several individuals affiliated with the Heralds of the New Dawn. For the first time since this war began, Seero had confirmed locations on some of the hostiles.

And if she could find them . . . then she could terminate them.

It was time for Seero to visit the Southern Empire.

Ateia and company had just finished up with the Serpent's Kiss, to her father's great relief. He had been quite on edge in the dungeon known for being filled to the brim with extremely toxic serpents. It was difficult to watch for hidden, burrowed snakes midcombat, and even a single bite could cause trouble for a high-leveled knight.

But well, it turned out that CELIU sensors worked just as well on hidden snakes as anything else. Likewise, armored exoskeletons and prosthetic limbs weren't particularly vulnerable to toxins, and Ateia's skills at Holy Magic also lent themselves well to healing, a fact not lost on the Legion troops who had participated in the assault and were now staring at her with awe as the force exited the dungeon.

The Mélusine chief, Attius, slithered toward them. "It is done, then?"

Ateia nodded. "You won't be seeing any more monster attacks from this dungeon."

He nodded at her. "You have my thanks, and that of my people."

She frowned and crossed her arms. "I'm not the only one you should thank." Ateia glanced over at Agedia. The snake woman hadn't said a word to anyone in her home, and the Mélusine had not approached her in return.

Attius frowned . . . then sighed.

"The Mélusine have never been welcome in the Empire. It has taken centuries to overcome our historic animosity. My brother was the first of our kind to ever rise to the position of magister, while my daughter was one of the few of us trusted as an Imperial knight, putting our people in the best position we had ever been in within the Empire.

"So when my daughter supposedly failed, becoming a drunkard and a layabout instead, it was seen as a great disgrace, and a major setback for our people. And the chief of those people cannot simply forget such things. Even for his own kin."

He looked over Ateia, and then over at Agedia. Amulius had started to chat with her, and the Mélusine were staring at them both.

"But . . . that could change. It appears she finds herself in esteemed company, yours included. Well, I doubt she has any interest in reconciling with her people, as fleeting as their approval has been . . . but there are those who would be pleased to welcome her back, should there be such an opportunity."

Ateia just continued to frown at the man. "It's a painful thing to be abandoned by family, even if there was a reason for it. Just so you know."

Attius's face fell for a moment before he regained himself. "I will take that into consideration. In any case, you and all who participated in this battle have done the Mélusine a great service. I would see that you all enjoy the greatest hospitality we can arrange, if you are able?"

Ateia was about to respond when her robotic eye began to flicker. She shook her head. "Thank you, but this crisis affects the entire Empire. Please speak with Legate Cossus; his troops may need some more time to recover before they head out, but as for my party, we must be headed on to our next target."

Attius nodded. "I see. I wish you safety and victory in your battles . . . and know that I owe you and *all* your companions some hospitality, should you ever return."

Ateia nodded and returned to her friends. Looking toward Agedia, she frowned, but Agedia just smiled and shrugged. "Don't worry about it, Ateia. I ran off to the Imperial knights to get away from my people *long* before they rejected me. Between my father and uncle, I could have forced my way back in if I wanted to . . . but the folks in this place are those who can't let go of things that happened over a thousand years ago. It was never my favorite place, you know."

Agedia's expression turned serious. "And most importantly . . . our drinks are absolutely terrible." Ateia couldn't help but smile at that while Agedia chuckled as well, then her eyes narrowed. "Besides, I caught that little flicker. Shiny girl say something important?"

Ateia nodded before starting to crack her knuckles with a grin. "She asked us to regroup and head down to the Southern Empire. We found some of that stupid cult . . . and we're finally going to pay them a visit."

INTERLUDE

The Fall of Liberty

Captain Falrauth was completely silent as he stepped onto the high king's former flagship. He had been released with all of his troops and was now returning home. And yet, he held no joy in this turn of events. How could he? In a way—in many ways—it was the death of Mirima as he knew it, and of all he had fought for.

His release was contingent on a full, unconditional surrender by the Council of the Southern Realms, including direct and open declarations of loyalty by each constituent realm. And that meant Mirima had bowed to a foreign sovereign, something it had not done in all its history.

Mirima may have been a de facto part of the Empire, but it had always been as a friend and equal partner. Every high king and high queen had been declared an Amicitia Populi Elteni upon their coronation since the days of Arofinas Leolar, cementing the alliance between equals even as the Empire's borders pushed past Mirima's shores and swallowed her neighbors.

High King Xavlaeron himself had been declared as such in line with this tradition. This, in turn, was what had granted authority to the Council of the Southern Realms, as the various smaller nations that made up the Southern Empire relied on Mirima to speak with the Empire as an equal.

And now, that was all gone. Mirima was an independent nation no longer, but an official Imperial client state—and it could be converted to an Imperial province at any time. With no high king and no Amicitia Populi Elteni at its head, Emperor Lucius was free to dictate its fate as he pleased. He no longer had to speak with them as an equal, much less treat them as one.

Not only had Mirima failed to rise, but it had lost all it'd achieved from its long friendship. And Captain Falrauth shared the blame for this disaster. Sure, High King Xavlaeron had made the decision, but Captain Falrauth had been one of his closest advisors. He had been aware of the high king's path from the very start and had approved. He, too, had dreamed of a day when it would be Mirima, not Elteno or Corvanus, that stood at the Empire's helm. He, too, had let his ambition cloud his judgement.

They had not expected the Empire to side with the queen of the Dobhar, but how could he complain? Mirima had not acted like the Empire's friend in this case, and the queen of the Dobhar had.

In the darkest hour, when even the Aesdes themselves had withdrawn from the world, Mirima had made a play for power, while even now, the queen of the Dobhar risked herself and her people on the Empire's behalf. Emperor Lucius's decision was not so unthinkable . . . and that was before considering the queen of the Dobhar's sheer might.

Captain Falrauth, of course, had also not expected to lose, and badly at that.

He once again stepped aboard his flagship, but not as its captain. No, he was a mere passenger aboard his own vessel. The Dobhar, Wulver, former Imperials, and metallic golems moving about the ship were a stark reminder of Mirima's current status.

The Sky Legion had been pressed back into Imperial service and integrated into the Northern Court's chain of command. And now that the famous Canus Sittius Dio had become the North's Magister Utriusque Militia, there was little doubt as to the Sky Legion's loyalty.

Canus was, after all, the idol of all half Elves who joined the Legion proper. The citizens of the South who swore oaths to the Empire—in other words, the entirety of the Sky Legion—would follow him into the Inferno Realm itself. All that was required of the Sky Legion were renewed oaths to Emperor Lucius, and their surviving airships were returned.

Such was not the case for the Sentinels of Liberty. As Mirima and its allied nations were no longer independent, they also no longer required standing armies of their own. Of course, given the current crisis, a complete disbanding of the Sentinels of Liberty was not feasible at present . . . but that was no comfort to Captain Falrauth or any of his troops.

These were the men and women whose loyalty to Mirima trumped all else, who chose to fight for their home instead of rising within the Legion's ranks. So, when they heard they were being released because Mirima itself was under assault by monstrous hordes, every last one of them would have preferred a lifetime of imprisonment than to hear their home was in danger while they were not present to protect it.

But once the immediate crisis had passed, the Sentinels would be subject to a long and gradual death. The memory of the friendship between Mirima and Elteno would linger for a while longer, so the process of disbanding would be slow. Mirima would likely be allowed to maintain a token force.

But just that. The Sentinels of Liberty would become nothing more than a local defense force, the bodyguards of the high king at best, if Mirima was allowed to retain her ruling structure. A relic of the past, a living mockery of Mirima's former glory.

Their numbers would be drawn down, their present units would be broken off and sent to reinforce the Legion far from home, while their future recruitment would be diverted to the Imperial Auxiliaries, or maybe even funneled into the Legion directly.

And a nation without an army had no need for a fleet of battle airships. As such, every surviving airship that belonged to Mirima or one of the other Southern Realms had been officially transferred to the queen of the Dobhar or to Turannia. One was even granted to the Selkies.

They were only heading back to the South with the Sentinels of Liberty onboard because of the urgent ongoing crisis. The Sky Legion's remaining airships were insufficient to transfer the high king's army back home, and the fleet's new owners were not sufficiently trained to use the ships in battle. The queen of the Dobhar had therefore loaned the ships to the Empire until the situation in the South had stabilized, though crewed with her own troops to supervise and to study how the Sentinels of Liberty operated such vessels.

And just in case the Sentinels got any ideas, there were a handful of those metallic golems present in the Gravity Core rooms of each ship, ready to bring it down should anything happen.

It was unnecessary, however. Not one of the Sentinels would jeopardize their return until they knew Mirima was safe.

Captain Falrauth frowned as the ships began to fly and passed over the Turannian coast. Metallic golems and mysterious weapons of war cast fire and death at anything that approached from the depths. Flying machines of strange designs patrolled the skies and did likewise. Ultimately, the fleet was being sent home because the queen of the Dobhar did not need it at present . . . but Mirima certainly did.

Captain Falrauth remained silent, watching the terrain go by. The rough waters of the Northern Sea turned into the farmland of Utrad. Then they passed the mountains between Utrad and the Imperial Heartland, over the mighty fortress of Velus's Pass. Even now, the walls stood firm, the ancient enchanted stone defiant in the face of the Empire's decline. They passed over the sprawling cities and magical towers of the Imperial Heartland itself.

Captain Falrauth watched as the Legions marched between the cities in orderly formations, at brisk speed but without excessive haste. He watched as the magical towers spread their Earth Magic, undoubtedly sending countless of the Empire's plaustrum subterraneum through the ground. He could even see wagons and convoys moving *away* from the cities; either merchant convoys or farmers returning to their homes, a sign that the Empire's countryside was growing safe once more.

From his view up above, the Empire's decline seemed greatly exaggerated.

Eventually, he reached the southern coast of the Imperial Heartland, and the scene here was far different from the coasts of Turannia. The normally calm waters of the Southern Sea churned with blood and explosions. Countless boats of every size and type streamed toward every Imperial dock, their decks crowded to bursting with refugees.

Behind these, the warships of the Imperial navy screened the entrances to harbors and coves. Ballistae fired harpoons into the water, while Imperial mages activated the ship's enchantments. Lightning surged through the sea. Water twisted itself into spikes and drills. Clouds of poison and acid hid the ships from view. Air Magic created bubbles that then collapsed with deadly crushing force. The blood of monsters colored the sea.

And even here, the queen of the Dobhar made her presence felt. Every now and again, waves of fiery projectiles streamed in from high above, doubtlessly launched by the same invisible ships that had struck Mirima's fleet. Only this time, they targeted the monsters below, most of which had far weaker defenses than a battle airship.

Captain Falrauth's heart sank as the ship flew out over the deceptively calm, sunny sea. If this were the situation along the Imperial coast with the queen of the Dobhar's support . . . what would the situation be in Mirima, surrounded as she was by water, and with the greatest part of her armies abroad?

How would she hold against the Ocean's Wrath or the Living Cyclone, the massive dungeons from which she acquired the Water and Air cores that powered ships through the seas and skies? Or what if, Aesdes forbid, the Imperial Necrotorum and the Pale Academy it supervised failed to contain the Banshee's Cove, and its ghost ships covered the Southern Sea with their deathly fog?

The blood drained from Captain Falrauth's face. He quickly walked over to the bridge, where a Dobhar and a Mélusine were arguing over one of the enchanted circles. Captain Falrauth leaned over them and began to point.

"The Dobhar is correct; skill in Air Magic is not necessary to operate the propulsion. The ship itself will handle the air pocket regardless of the conditions around it. Anyone skilled in Air Magic should instead focus on navigation. You actually want to steer into the wind; it means denser air up ahead so the enchantments will have more of their medium to draw on."

The pair eyed him warily before quietly attempting his recommendations. Captain Falrauth may have hated to hand Mirima's prized fleet over . . . but he would hate the destruction of Mirima far worse. So, he resolved to do all he could to get home just a little bit faster.

28

Yesterday's Enemy

"Yesterday's enemy shall burn in the fires of my vengeance until naught is left but ash and ruin. Just as soon as I am done with yesterday's friend, whose betrayal I shall not let go unanswered. Even should the heavens forgive them, I shall not."

—The Celestial Sage Ningainë, after his defeat at a Celestial sage game night.

Captain Falrauth and the Sentinels of Liberty crowded the bridge, gripping their weapons in silence. They were about to come up on the Living Cyclone; they could see the dark clouds spinning through the sky already. Soon, they saw the waterspout rising out of the water, surrounded by a small atoll that held its entrance.

Under normal circumstances, it would have been surrounded by a small city of floating buildings that catered to the dungeon divers, but in times like these, they would put out to sea. Still, the sharp sight of the half Elves could make out a couple of wrecks, their inhabitants having failed to flee in time.

The Sentinels steeled themselves. Since the Living Cyclone was between Mirima and the Empire, they thought it best to tackle it on their way there.

The fight of their lives, with the fate of their home on the line, was about to begin.

Except . . . no monsters attacked the approaching fleet. The order never came to deploy. Soon, the airships flew past the Living Cyclone without slowing down. Captain Falrauth narrowed his eyes.

"What are you doing? We were to assault the Living Cyclone, were we not?"

One of the Dobhar turned to him, this one with armor like the queen of the Dobhar's, including that half helmet that covered one of the eyes with a glowing artifact of some sort. The Dobhar grinned.

"Oh, my queen already handled that one. What, did I forget to tell you?"

Captain Falrauth blinked then closed his eyes, suppressing a deep sigh. The Dobhar's wide grin implied that he had not, in fact, forgotten to tell them. Then he shook his head and opened his eyes.

No monsters attacked them as they flew beyond the Living Cyclone. And neither he nor the Caelum Aurem could detect a single one on their path up ahead. He had no idea how the queen of the Dobhar had pacified the dungeon without destroying it, but from all evidence, she had apparently done just that.

Which meant one less major threat to Mirima's survival.

But Captain Falrauth did not rest just yet. There was more than one dungeon in the seas around Mirima, and he had no idea how long it had taken the queen of the Dobhar to address the Living Cyclone. He did not yet hold hope he would find his home in one piece.

Captain Falrauth pursed his lips. They were approaching Mirima, and he could see flashes of light in the distance. Yet, as the scene came into view, he found himself at a loss.

Smoke rose from the cities of his island, blood filling the surrounding waters. He could see the wrecks of ships, while an airship had crashed onto one of the beaches. The Barrier that protected the city was nowhere to be seen, and the sparkling walls of Mirima had a large hole. And yet, the white spires remained standing, their polished marble pristine and unblemished.

The Sentinels of Liberty who had remained behind stood in formation and at the ready at the breach. The walls had been broken, but the monsters had not reached the city or the people beyond.

And it was readily apparent why.

The skies were filled to the brim with massive glowing magic circles all too familiar to Captain Falrauth. A serpentine sea dragon towered above the waves in the seas beyond Mirima, its head reaching where an airship might fly. It roared in anger . . . and in pain.

Because it was losing. The queen of the Dobhar flew in the sky, each of her magic circles raining beams of light onto the monsters below; she had already pushed the smaller monsters back into the sea. The city itself was covered in a massive Barrier that appeared quite different from Mirima's own, and she now focused her attention on the massive beast ahead of her.

Her beams fused together into a ray of light as bright as the sun.

Once the light faded, there was a massive hole in the sea dragon's head. Its monstrously large body crashed into the water, creating a massive wave that surged toward the shore. The queen of the Dobhar's magic circles shifted, and a massive Barrier appeared to redirect the wave back out to sea.

Captain Falrauth had no idea what to feel, but the Sentinels of Liberty behind him were not so conflicted. Tears filled their eyes as several began to cheer and hug one another, while others simply fell to their knees in relief.

Mirima had been bloodied, but she had survived in one piece. And all thanks to the foe they had tried to destroy.

Rolling the clock back a bit . . .

Seero flew over the Southern Sea in the direction of Mirima. The Living Cyclone dungeon was on the way, but Magister Canus had requested she bypass it and head to Mirima directly. The situation there was apparently growing dire, so relieving the city was the higher priority.

The airships carrying the Sky Legion and Mirima's own forces would attempt to assault, or at least contain, the Living Cyclone while Seero moved on to the Ocean's Wrath. Ateia's group would reinforce the defenders at the Banshee's Cove in the meantime, while 01R's team continued mopping up dungeons in and around Utrad.

But as Seero was approaching the Living Cyclone, she decided to run a test. In the Tower of Heroes, she had learned how to subjugate a willing dungeon from beyond its core room. So, she decided to test the limits of that approach. What was the maximum range she could interact with a dungeon's mana, and did it require her to be physically present within a dungeon? And likewise, did she need to make contact with the dungeon master in-person before doing so?

As such, as she began forming Prismatic Bombardment circles to terminate the monsters wandering out of the Living Cyclone, she extended her mana toward the dungeon in the same manner as she had with the Tower of Heroes.

At first, her mana passed through without entering it. The dungeon was, after all, not fully present within the Material Plane. But Seero analyzed its entrance based on her growing expertise on Spatial Magic and dungeon mechanics, then built a basic theory on how entrances worked.

She started emitting Holy mana and attempted to sense and connect to the flows of mana through the world . . . and through the boundary between the Material Plane and the Source. And thanks to the examples of Ateia, Divination, and her own experiences interacting with that boundary, her mana was able to contact the dungeon in its true location, bypassing the spatial effects that protected it from harm in the Material Plane.

The dungeon recoiled at first, its mana rejecting the foreign intrusion and resisting her. It then paused, and a thin stream reached out toward her, carrying some intent.

"Whoa, are you, like, Aesdes?"

Seero attempted to form her mana into a similar connection.

"Negative."

"Whack. Then, like, you here to kill me, bruh?"

"Uncertain Response: This unit's objective is the purification of this dungeon. This unit will avoid termination of the dungeon and nonhostile forces if possible due to the dungeon's strategic value. Would the hostile dungeon master like to surrender? This unit will allow the dungeon master to retain ownership of their dungeon as a subordinate core if so."

"Whoa. Like, you're a dungeon master with, like, Holy mana? That's crazy, bruh. But, like, if you got this, then that's fine. Your mana's, like, mad scary, so be gentle, yeah?"

And with that, the mana stopped resisting, instead reaching out to form a connection much like the Tower of Heroes had. Seero connected to it, and soon reached the dungeon core. Ultimately, she was able to purify it and integrate it to her growing network despite never setting foot within it.

The dungeon master could now speak to her through the connection. "Whoa, like, you totally fixed it. That's crazy, bruh. You're pretty crazy, huh? Well, like, thanks for that!"

And so, Seero managed to purify and subordinate the Living Cyclone without even slowing down her flight path. She flew past and pushed on toward Mirima, terminating the remaining monsters along the way and sending a message to CELIU units aboard the airship fleet informing them of the change in plans.

Soon thereafter, she arrived at Mirima itself. Mirima was a large island with a city of white marble that covered nearly the entire thing. The city was currently surrounded by a glowing barrier and monsters assaulting it, but airships, naval vessels, and soldiers occasionally darted out to harass the attackers. Seero wasn't sure what resources were stockpiled to maintain said barrier, but by her calculations, the monsters wouldn't break through anytime soon.

Unfortunately, there was always a bigger fish.

The threat to Mirima at present wasn't just the dungeon monsters. The large concentration of monsters swimming through the sea attracted other creatures as well. Seero arrived just in time to observe a sea dragon lift its head from the water. It had initially been feasting upon the monsters in the sea, but a mage from the city had struck it with a Lightning Bolt, drawing its attention inland.

It opened its mouth, and a torrent of water blasted forward, slamming into the barrier, which, already weakened by the constant pressure, broke under the sudden assault, and the torrent continued to smash through the wall around the city.

It was at that point that Seero arrived and promptly terminated all threats.

She then used Earth Magic to raise a new wall, temporarily plugging the hole in Mirima's defenses. At that point, the airship fleet was about to arrive, so Seero considered the objective completed and began to move toward her next target.

Leaving the people of Mirima staring up at the sky.

29

A Deathly Situation

"Huh? Binding the souls of the dead to eternal servitude? By the Aesdes, even if I could somehow stop a soul from leaving the mortal coil, why on Aelea would I? I became a necromancer because I prefer surrounding myself with rotting, soulless husks to engaging in the excruciatingly dull small talk the living demand; the last thing I want is for my puppets to start quibbling!"

—Magister Mortalitus Vel Cluilius Sylvian, correcting common misconceptions about the Imperial Necrotorum.

After stabilizing the situation in Mirima, Seero made her way to the Ocean's Wrath. As she approached, the calm seas began to grow rough. Water mana churned the ocean around it, creating tall waves that shouldn't have been possible under the environmental conditions. Stretching out her mana to the dungeon, Seero tried for a remote subjugation.

This time, it didn't go as predicted. The dungeon mana recoiled from her as the Living Cyclone's had at first. But where the Living Cyclone had subsequently established diplomatic contact, the Ocean's Wrath counterattacked. Its mana surged against the intrusion, trying to push her away, while Seero attempted to push onward and subjugate it by force, but progress was slow.

Since she was pushing against the dungeon's mana, the dungeon could subsequently resist her with all of its power, which normally wouldn't be applied directly like this. It was a fight Seero could win; her mana quantity and density continued to grow as the Primary Home Base expanded and more and more dungeons joined her network, but it would take time. Potentially more time than it would take for her to reach the core room the normal way.

So that is what she would do. She traveled as the waves grew more and more rough until she found a large whirlpool at the center of the storm with a dungeon entrance at the bottom. Seero dove into the entrance, and the force of gravity reversed itself. Instead of flying down, she was now flying up from the bottom of a pool of water.

She burst through the surface to find herself in a small cove leading out to what appeared to be an open ocean, though Seero's scans revealed the area was more limited in size than it appeared . . . and full of monsters.

But Holy Beams pierced the water as easily as the air, so none approached her as she began to Blink toward the first floor's exit.

The subjugation of the Ocean's Wrath dungeon had begun.

Meanwhile, Amulius's group flew over the Southern Sea toward the Banshee's Cove. As they approached, their sensors detected fewer and fewer creatures in the water below, save for a final port on one of the last islands standing guard. Even the seagulls broke off and avoided the area, and the seas turned dark.

Black kelp obscured the water below as sharp, jagged rocks broke the surface. Clouds of mist and fog floated in and out of the area, occasionally revealing a shipwreck that had failed to navigate the treacherous path.

Eventually, they came to the shores. The gigantic jaws of some primordial shark monster guarded the entrance to the Pale Harbor, the city that held the Pale Academy. To the side, a massive seawall surrounded a cove lined with jagged black rock, sealing off the Banshee's Cove from the outside world.

The Southern Realms were simultaneously more and less tolerant of necromancy, largely because each client nation had its own approach. In some, it was treated like any other high-risk school of magic, with even fewer restrictions on its use than the Imperial Necrotorum. In others, even possession of the relevant skills was grounds for execution—or death at the hands of a mob.

The Pale Harbor had been formed by those who wished to practice their arts without supervision and as a refuge for those fleeing from persecution. Soon, it became infamous as a haven for thieves, pirates, and the dark arts.

At least until the Empire arrived in the area. The Imperial navy arrived in force, backed by the full might of the Imperial Necrotorum. But a war of the dead was in no one's best interest, and so, an agreement was eventually struck. The Pale Academy would retain its independence and gain authority over all necromancers who did not join the Necrotorum, but the Legion and the Imperial Necrotorum would set up in the Pale Harbor to keep watch.

The Pale Academy thus did not need to fight for its survival, while the Empire could keep track of the necromancers in the South, including those from realms who were not nominally under the Emperor's authority. It was a stormy relationship, with much conflict and maneuvering over the years.

But not today. Today, the free necromancers of the Pale Academy and the disciplined Death mages of the Necrotorum stood side by side on the seawall facing the Banshee's Cove.

Imperial warships and zombified sea monsters battled against floating shipwrecks with literal skeleton crews; wailing ghosts were met with Imperial counterspells and pale green banefire; Imperial legionnaires and a motley assortment of adventurers and rogues from the Pale Harbor worked together against zombie sailors scaling the walls.

Two women fought side by side at the center of the defense. One was a human in black Legion armor adorned by a tree with black roots, the symbol of the Necrotorum. Lampronia Vitalina, Magister Mortalitus of the Imperial Necrotorum, swore as she saw black fins break through the water.

"Another pod of dread orca!"

The other woman wore an enchanted silk dress with a fur coat made from a felix ignus's pelt. This was Vassenia Andronica, the current Pale Lady of the Pale Academy. Instead of a head, she had a skull covered in green flames. She cursed as she sent tendrils of green fire toward a zombie kraken entangled with three ghost ships. The fire latched onto holes in the kraken's rotting skin, sewing the flesh back together.

"And?! What do you want *me* to do about it?!"

Lampronia gritted her teeth as she finished a magic circle, launching several counterspells toward a wave of approaching ghosts. The opposing Death Magic unraveled the magical structures holding the creatures together. They wailed as the mana comprising their bodies leaked away and faded.

"You're the vampire! Can't you steal their blood or something, you shapeshifting hag?! Those dread orca will paralyze half of your so-called guards with one cry!"

Vassenia scowled as she shot a Bane Fireball.

"For the LAST time, I'm a Soucouyant, and I don't see what that has to do with anything! And thanks to *some* hardheaded Imperial dog with a stick up her butt, I haven't used my magic on anything alive in decades! And *now* you expect me to 'terrorize the living,' as you warned me many, many, *many* times to never even think about doing?!"

Lampronia ducked as a ghost ship fired a ballista bolt over her head. Imperial ballistae retaliated, but the bolts pierced right through the decaying ship without hitting anything of note. Lampronia attempted a counterspell, but the magic holding the ship together was much more powerful than that of the ghosts.

"Well, someone has to do *something*, or we're all going to die and reanimate! You're telling me in all these years you haven't found *some* way to cheat on the regulations?!"

Vassenia pulled her hair as she commanded her kraken to smash the offending ship with a free tentacle.

"YES! That's EXACTLY what I'm saying! I was there when your predecessor purged the Pale Lord before me! I made certain to keep my act completely, absolutely clean! Haven't you seen me run myself ragged trying to keep the idiots in the academy from doing something stupidly illegal?! What do you *think* I've been doing this whole time?!"

But time had run out. The dread orcas weaved and dove between the flailing tentacles of the zombie kraken, bypassing the creature to swim straight for the walls. Lampronia created a Decay Field, but their Dark mana aura shielded the creatures as they passed through it. Vassenia launched a volley of Bane Fireballs, but the Pale Lady was not used to fighting personally, and so they dodged with ease.

The two women grimaced as the dread orca's cry sounded over the wall. The Pale Harbor's defenders and even some of the legionnaires dropped their weapons and covered their ears, screaming and shouting as the fear of the dread orcas' curse gripped their hearts.

Until a shining light suddenly illuminated the sky. Golden-and-silver light filled every person's heart with warmth. The panicking soldiers paused and turned their gazes up.

An armored girl descended from the sky on metal wings with feathers of light. Taking a bow and pulling it back, dozens of arrows of Holy and Light mana rained down on the battlefield, vaporizing ghosts and skeletons alike. A barrage pierced deep into a ghost ship, which flaked away as Holy Explosions purified it from the inside.

Lampronia and Vassenia turned to look at one another. Vassenia gulped. "So, um, that's an Aesdes, right? Should I, um, repent for my evil ways, or should I just run and hope she doesn't notice?"

Lampronia gulped. "I, um, don't know."

Vassenia gaped at her. "You don't know?! Aren't you the magister of the Imperial Necrotorum?! Don't you have to read the Imperial doctrine or whatever at every meal and every night before bed?!"

Lampronia glared at her. "The doctrine says the Aesdes don't just show up, so I have no idea what to do in this situation! I'm a necromancer too, you know, so if she doesn't like you, then I'm in the same boat! And no, I don't spend every waking moment reading the rules! I need my breaks too!"

As the two continued to bicker, Ateia flew over to the wall, along with her companions. She frowned. "Um . . . should we interrupt?"

Taog and Agedia shrugged as Amulius loudly cleared his throat. The two women glanced at him, then noticed the flying group gathered around them. Vassenia's eyes widened as she began to tremble before fainting. Lampronia glanced at her with envy before turning to face the *Aesdes* in the sky before her.

INTERLUDE

Divine Courage

Vassenia was sitting on the wall fanning herself as a Recovery mage monitored her condition. She still trembled slightly as she looked up at Ateia.

"So . . . y-you aren't here to wipe me from the face of Aelea for the desecration of the dead?"

Ateia tilted her head. "Um, why would I be? I thought the Necrotorum didn't permit the use of corpses without contracts verified by third-party authorities?" She turned to look at Magister Lampronia, who began nodding her head repeatedly and as fast as she could.

"Yes! Obviously! All necromancy and Death Magic conducted here is in full accordance with all Imperial regulations!"

Vassenia held herself with her arms. "B-But y-you're an Aesdes! Y-You're above the laws of mortals!"

Lampronia turned pale at that. Ateia blinked a few times. "Oh, is that right?" She turned to Taog, who shook his head.

"Um, don't ask me. But, I mean, you *are* an Aesdes, so . . ."

Amulius cleared his throat again, and Ateia jumped, flushing slightly.

"Well, um, Victoria—err, the other Aesdes didn't mention necromancy or anything to me. I guess I can ask later, but they're a bit busy as far as I know. For now, we're here on behalf of Her Majesty Seero, the queen of the Dobhar and Amicitia Populi Elteni, who was requested by Emperor Lucius to aid you and purify the Banshee's Cove."

Vassenia and Lampronia's eyes widened. "The queen of the Dobhar? And Emperor Lucius? They . . . They know Aesdes?"

Amulius sighed and stepped forward. "In any case, we would ask you to prepare a force to assist us in the dungeon assault. I recommend we do so sooner rather than later." He pointed toward the dungeon entrance, where another ghost ship was just sailing out of the cove. Lampronia ceased trembling as her face instantly hardened.

"Right, I'll talk to the legate right away. The Pale Lady shall organize the Pale Harbor's forces and maintain the defense."

She glanced over at Vassenia, who agreed. "R-Right."

Amulius nodded and joined Lampronia to arrange the details. Meanwhile, Ateia looked up at the sky. Taog glanced at her.

"What is it?"

Ateia shook her head. "Nothing, it's just . . . I was wondering what Victoria was up to in all this."

Colleöne flew through the sky, wearing a suit of golden-and-silver armor with a winged helmet over her golden hair. She gripped the Blade of Valor with both hands, an aura of light shining around her as she swung the golden blade forward. She moved quickly, blinking across the sky in a golden flash that extended her swing into a wide arc. In this way, she cut off every head of the giant, multiheaded snake before her in a single attack. Exhaling her breath, she glanced around the battlefield with a frown.

Colleöne had returned to the Blessed Land as quickly as she could once she had learned of the situation, and the return of the Aesdes' most skilled and experienced warrior turned the tides of the Blessed Land's defense. In addition, the Aesdes themselves had gathered their nerve, her beloved Velus collecting the fighters into an increasingly coherent force.

Her heart clenched and grew warm at the sight of her beloved taking command to defend her own home . . . and then shook her head, for now was not the time for such thoughts. Additionally, others of the Aesdes who had not fought before were starting to find their courage, joining the line as they were able. Others who had not the skill or temperament for battle found other ways to contribute.

Some healed and lent their power to strengthen those at the front. Others prepared the way, shifting the land itself to block and contain their foes. The Lord of Dance and Celebration and the Lady of Song and Heart joined together to lift the spirits of the defenders. The Lady of Hearth and Home . . . was currently bashing a drake over the head with her beloved frying pan.

And yet, the situation was not developing according to their hopes. The Aesdes had secured their defense, and the line was holding, but such was not their aim. In terms of pushing toward the cores of her and Shialnor's design, they had made little progress. And Colleöne could only grit her teeth, for this was a direct result of her and Shialnor's work.

Because of recent events, the existence of Holy-attribute monsters and the means by which to imbue the Holy mana of Aelea into their mana-constructed bodies were recorded upon those cores. As such, the monsters they now faced were imbued and empowered via the Holy mana of Aelea, so not only were they far stronger than the average creature but they were also not especially vulnerable to Holy energy. They were counted as inhabitants of the world, and the world itself did not reject them.

Which meant the Aesdes had lost their chief weapon against such foes. Under normal circumstances, the mere presence of an Aesdes would suppress and frighten monsters; weaker creatures would even perish outright if they got too close. And should an Aesdes deign to direct their actual attention to the task, none but the most powerful could stand before them for long.

But not against these foes. Against these monsters, the Aesdes had to rely on their own power and abilities. And worse . . . their power had waned. Anualë had temporarily quarantined the Blessed Land to prevent additional corruption from spreading, while Shialnor and Colleöne were preventing mana from their cores from leaking out as well.

But this meant that the normal flows of Holy mana between the Blessed Land and the rest of Aelea had slowed to a trickle. The Aesdes were the caretakers of the world, authorized to call upon its power to aid in their duties, but they were not its masters, and so not the rightful owners of that power. They were now reduced to their base strength, the powers that were intrinsic to them as individuals.

This still left them as gods among men, but not as masters of the world. And since most of them had never had to fight a remotely equal enemy, most were still adjusting to the task.

Colleöne was one of the few among them who had, and so tore through the battlefield. But like Shialnor, a great deal of her power was wrapped up in the core that empowered the champions of the world. She was left now merely with her own strength and skill as a warrior . . . and a warrior she was.

With each swing of her sword, one or even many monsters lost their lives, and she reclaimed whatever bit of her power had been granted to them. But she was not yet powerful enough to overturn the entire battle on her own. The stream of monsters seemed endless.

Colleöne ducked under a volley of arrows, and a moment later appeared next to the offending skeletons. She spun around, smashing them to pieces with the weight of her sword before vanishing once more. The Lord of Craft and Forge had been knocked over by a giant, and she stabbed her blade into the monster's neck before it could assault him further.

The battle would turn to their favor eventually now that the defenses had stabilized. For all the danger, not a single Aesdes had fallen, for even weakened beings of their stature were not easily slain. With each passing moment, the Aesdes grew more accustomed to the nature of this fight, and the defense grew less and less desperate.

And with each monster they slew, Colleöne and Shialnor reclaimed a bit more of their power. In time, they would be able to push the monsters back and reclaim their cores entirely.

But that was not enough. Colleöne knew of what was going on down in the world below. She knew that while the Aesdes were occupied, the dungeons were going haywire, and all the people of the world were under threat when they did not have her boons to assist them. She knew that Ateia and her friends were at the forefront of those trying to hold the line. So every moment the Aesdes spent defending was a moment when all that they worked and cared for was at risk.

And worse, Colleöne knew—as the Lady of Courage and Victory, and the Aesdes most familiar with war—that this played right into the hands of their enemy.

Anualë hadn't had the chance to tell them who was responsible just yet, but there were very few beings in all of known existence who could wound the First of the Aesdes and strike at the Blessed Land.

Regardless of their exact identity, this was a being on par with the Aesdes in either lore or might or perhaps even both. Such a being was now on the loose beyond their sight and attention, and who knew what they might do in the meantime?

Colleöne had a feeling that this being was the one behind the Heralds of the New Dawn. It would explain the cult's unexpected capabilities—and their ability to escape notice until now. And if that were true, that meant the being responsible for the assault on Colleöne's home was also the one who had targeted her kin, and who could do so again while the Aesdes were occupied.

Colleöne gritted her teeth, but there was little she could do at present. The quickest way to protect the world below was to win the fight going on here. So, Colleöne gripped her sword and got to work.

All while praying that should anything happen, a certain dungeon master and hero might surprise her once more.

30

The Judgement of the Aesdes

"You know, we say the Aesdes approve of this and disapprove of that, but do we really know? Like, actually? Because as far as I know, not a single person alive has ever even seen the Aesdes, much less spoken with one.

"Has anyone in the entire history of the Empire done so? I mean, sure, the legends say Velus did, but do we really believe some lady appeared on a lake and just handed him a magic sword that suddenly let him tangle with Archons?

"I'm just trying to say, maybe we're the ones who came up with all these restrictions, and the Aesdes don't really care one way or another. So, maybe it's entirely within our capability to change the rules as we wish. We're free to do as we please, and I say we should. Why should we suffer on account of the Aesdes? We don't even know if they are paying attention to us."

—Crime lord Gnaeus Ulpius Damasus, before his execution for murder, trafficking, and tax evasion.

Magister Lampronia was very pleased to focus on her job instead of discussing the morality and ethics of necromancy with an Aesdes, so it did not take long before a strike team of Legion soldiers and Necrotorum mages was assembled.

She was less pleased when she realized she would be leading those mages and traveling with the Aesdes, but as the Magister Mortalitus, it was her duty to manage the Banshee's Cove. Besides, since the Necrotorum only supervised in the Southern Realms, they were a bit shorthanded, and so every available mage including her was needed for the assault.

She was even less pleased that Vassenia escaped, as the Pale Academy took up the defense.

In any case, the group was now assembled aboard a smaller Imperial warship and setting sail into the cove. Beyond the Empire's seawall was a large cave with the dungeon's entrance as its opening. The seawater flowed in and out of the entrance, so the group sailed in.

Once inside, they found themselves in a dark cove with an endless night overhead. The stars provided very little light, and dark clouds cut off even that. Instead, the walls were lit by pale greenish-blue flames hovering over the water, barely illuminating the waves with their dim light. The flames flickered in and out of existence, and vanished if the ship approached.

They heard a faint wail in the distance. At least until another ghost ship sailed from deeper in the cove. Before Magister Lampronia could issue an order, the Aesdes leapt into action. Her glowing wings lit up the space as bright as midday, overwhelming the glow of the flames, and the group could now see clearly through the water around and below . . . and found very little there, to their surprise.

Meanwhile, Holy Light Beams cut across the surface of the water, cutting the ghost ship in two. Its halves fell to either side and started to fade away as it sank. Her companions dealt with the skeletons leaping into the water, while the Mélusine wrapped her tail around the warship's railing and extended her body to its full length, impaling skeletons with her spear as she remained out of the water. The strangely familiar human man launched arrows wrapped in Holy mana.

Magister Lampronia's eyes widened, however, as the Dobhar woman and Wolfkin boy jumped off the ship.

"Wait! Don't touch the water!"

Indeed, many an aquatic dungeon diver had made the same mistake. The water of the Banshee's Cove was filled to the brim with Dark-attribute mana, with a specific Death Magic leaning. Any who fell inside would have the very life sucked out of them.

At least until the Dobhar was surrounded by Holy-infused Water Magic, and the boy was surrounded by a shroud of Dark mana . . . which apparently was also Holy infused. Both of them swam through the waves with no apparent issue. The boy's shroud was even absorbing the Dark mana from the water and growing larger.

Magister Lampronia decided she would just be quiet and let them do as they pleased from now on.

Magister Lampronia took a deep breath. It was time for the Aesdes and her party to take a break, which meant it was time for the Legion and the Necrotorum to get to work. She glanced back at the Aesdes several times, but she said nothing.

There was nothing to do but carry on with her fell spells and hope the Aesdes would tolerate her.

Magister Lampronia gulped, but she was not the Magister Mortalitus for nothing, so she steeled her heart and got started on her magic circle.

At that moment, the Aesdes began to glow. Magister Lampronia winced and prepared to beg for her life, but the Aesdes's mana struck before she could get a word out, filling her veins with fire. She was about to scream . . .

She blinked. The mana did not disintegrate her as it had done to the minions of the Banshee's Cove. Instead, it empowered her, increasing the density and responsiveness of her own. It surrounded her magic circle, assisting her with her cast.

She was so surprised she stopped casting her spell, and her magic circle faded away. The Aesdes frowned.

"Is something wrong?"

Magister Lampronia quickly shook her head. "N-No! Everything's alright . . . apparently?"

With that, the magister got back to work and cast the Necrotorum's signature Decay spell, creating a barrier which no normal undead could cross safely. Under normal circumstances, that was.

In the current circumstances, her spell was reinforced with Holy mana, golden-and-silver light highlighting the dark purple glow. *Any* undead who touched it faded away; even their ashes purified as they crumbled to dust. Magister Lampronia blinked—and felt moisture well up in her eyes.

After all this time, after a lifetime of fear and doubt, a lifetime of holding herself to the strictest of standards . . . she found that the Aesdes did not secretly want to destroy her, after all.

Meanwhile, Aesdes was watching the Necrotorum's mages cast their spells with great interest, the artifact over her eye flickering rapidly . . .

The group carried on in their frightfully uneventful dungeon assault. Under normal circumstances, diving in the Banshee's Cove was one of the least pleasant experiences one could ever face. The dim light would do very little to illuminate the surroundings, particularly in the parts covered in fog. The diver wouldn't be able to see into the depths below them, couldn't see the obstacles ahead, and struggled to keep track of their position and bearing.

In fact, the light made things actively worse, playing tricks on the eyes, giving glimpses of terrors in the deep, and creating flickering shadows in every corner, all while the deadly nature of the water below meant no mistakes could be permitted in the operation of the ship.

In the midst of this situation, ghosts and skeletons and undead aquatic creatures would ambush the invaders before disappearing back into the dark. One could never be certain when exactly they would attack, only that it would come the moment any vulnerability was displayed.

As such, any visitors to the Banshee's Cove had to be on guard the entire time they were there, a situation that grated on the nerves. Trips into this dungeon were made as short as possible.

Or, at least, that's how it normally was. In this case, Ateia was keeping the dungeon fully illuminated with her wings of light, which pierced through the dark waves and eerie fog with equal ease. The dungeon was apparently not nearly as deep as anyone thought.

Ateia also blessed the strike team with Holy mana whenever it was their turn to take the vanguard. Not only did this allow them to strike down the undead without effort, but the Holy mana also protected anyone who fell overboard from the water below. Not a single sailor had lost their life on this journey, a new record that grew with each passing moment.

And even beyond Ateia's efforts, the dungeon was not acting as it normally did. The group was faced with a steady stream of monsters approaching them directly. No care was given to concealment, and the creatures weren't even attempting to set up ambushes. They just rushed forward at maximum speed without any apparent thought at all.

The Legion and Necrotorum forces were not surprised by their appearance even once, and that's not even mentioning the cyborgs' advanced sensors giving them forewarning.

The intense aura of the Imperial strike team slowly faded away. Amulius was currently sitting at a table with a cup of tea in his hand. He frowned.

On the one hand, he couldn't help but feel uneasy at the increasing lack of discipline. All of his experiences told him never to fully relax inside of a dungeon. It was never safe to do so, no matter how powerful he was.

On the other . . . the tea was very refreshing.

He was just heaving a sigh and shaking his head as Ateia entered the room. Sitting down across from him, she opened her mouth, frowned, then furrowed her brow. She shook her head before opening her mouth again, then pausing once more.

Amulius tried to think of something to say, but his mind went blank. He had no idea what she wanted to say or what she was thinking, despite the obvious expressions on her face. His heart sank.

He didn't know his daughter much at all at this point. She had changed dramatically from the little girl he had left behind. She had gone through so much recently, so what could he even say?

Beyond that, because of his choices, she had largely grown up without him. Even if nothing dramatic had happened in the recent months, she would still be a different person than the one he remembered. And that was on him.

So, he could do nothing but wait for her to speak. And fortunately, she did. Her face settled on a combination of sorrow and resolve.

"Dad . . . can you tell me about my mom?"

Amulius froze at the question, and his heart began to pound. He had not thought about Aedinia in quite some time. He had avoided thinking about her, if he was honest.

But he had not forgotten her. Not even a little. Memories came back to him, and pain spiked through his chest. The strength drained from his body, and the world spun around him.

But then he locked eyes with Ateia. He looked into those eyes that held far too much pain for their age. Those eyes filled with longing and anticipation. He knew this was a request she had not made lightly.

He took a deep breath.

"Okay."

She nodded and fell silent as he began to recount stories of his late wife. He started from the beginning, when they had met, when he was just an impoverished Exploratore and she seemed just a naive town girl. It was hard at first, and he had to bite back tears with every word. But Ateia hung on every one of those words, so he kept them coming. Soon, they began to flow out of him. He even cracked a smile or two.

Until, eventually, it was over. He dropped his head at that moment. Tears continued streaming down his face, unabated.

"I'm . . . I'm so sorry, Ateia. I wish you could have met her. I wish . . ."

Ateia didn't say anything, but stood up and walked over. Amulius's eyes widened as she gave him a hug. A moment later, he returned the embrace as his tears began to flow.

Amulius swore in his heart that he would never leave his family again.

31

Terminate the Cultists?

"Be weak where the enemy is strong, and so draw him in. Be strong where the enemy is weak, and so strike deep. At its fundamental core, that is the art of war."

—The Celestial Sage Ningainë, just before a full frontal assault on a fortified city.

In the end, Ateia's Holy and Light mana disarmed the majority of the Banshee's Cove's dangers. While it also had some Water-based traps and environmental hazards, the sailors of the Imperial navy navigated them with practiced ease now that they could actually see what they were facing.

It was not long before the group had traveled deep into the dungeon and arrived in a wide-open, stormy sea. There was a flash of lightning and a crack of thunder, then suddenly, a dozen ghost ships appeared all around them as a dark shadow that dwarfed their ship filled the water underneath them.

Magister Lampronia began freaking out, but Amulius raised his hand and stopped the Imperial forces from responding.

Ateia stepped to the front of the ship. One of the ghost ships pulled near, and a ghostly figure materialized at its bow. She had the appearance of a frowning woman with drooping eyes. Her hair and clothes appeared drenched with water, though the drops that fell off her passed through the ship she stood on. She hunched over as she faced Ateia.

"Are you . . . here to kill me? Not that my life means much . . ."

Ateia shook her head, much to Magister Lampronia's surprise. "We're here to help. We can cleanse the corruption from your dungeon, if you're willing."

The ghost woman tilted her head. "Oh. Okay . . . I guess . . ."

With that, the ghost ships parted and cleared the way forward. The shadow underneath them sank back into the depths, and Magister Lampronia was left staring with wide eyes.

"Um, what's going on here?"

Amulius shrugged and shook his head. "It's complicated. Do you really want to know?"

Magister Lampronia thought about it for a moment then promptly turned around. "I'll be below deck. The Aesdes can handle it, right?"

Amulius gave a small smile. "Yes, she can."

The dungeon master's ship led the Imperial warship through the water, eventually arriving at a castle sunk beneath the waves, with its roof barely peeking up into the air. The dungeon master and Ateia's group disembarked onto the roof.

"Follow me . . . I guess . . . if you want . . ."

She led them through the castle to the core room. There, Ateia purified the dungeon and linked it to the Primary Home Base.

The dungeon master tilted her head. "Oh. I'm not dead, after all?" She heaved a sigh. "Well . . . whatever. I guess I'll just . . . carry on, then . . . Freedom's just one more thing to lose . . ."

Ateia ignored her as her eye widened, and then, she began to chuckle. Amulius tilted his head.

"What's going on, Ateia?"

Taog patted his shoulder. The boy gave a grin that showed off his fangs.

"Seero just contacted us. She finished up with the Ocean's Wrath and wants us to meet up. It's time to go after the cult."

It turned out, the South's woes were concentrated in the three major dungeons near Mirima. As a decentralized collection of allied and client nations, the South's forces were also already dispersed.

Each individual realm maintained its own defenses, with its own walls, fortresses, and contingency plans. And in lieu of Legion garrisons, the South had a thriving mercenary industry, with the realms and the merchants hiring elite, professional mercenary teams instead of paying to raise their own armies. On top of that, the mercantile nature of the South gave rise to a healthy dungeon-diver industry as well.

While dungeon divers were notoriously undisciplined and unreliable in standard military affairs, they were highly specialized and so highly effective against the monsters of their local dungeons. Those willing to fight contributed greatly to holding the line. As a result, most of the South's constituent nations could protect themselves to a degree.

The problem was that without the Sky Legion or the fleet of Mirima, there were no mobile reserves to address the larger issues, to reinforce the problem spots, or to begin assaulting the dungeons. The South could hold the line for a bit, but they couldn't make any progress toward solving the problem. And once Mirima fell to the larger dungeons, the other realms would begin falling as well.

Now that Seero and Ateia had dealt with the big three, and the Sky Legion and Sentinels of Liberty had returned with the airship fleet, the South would begin to stabilize.

And that meant that Seero was now free to act on the intel the Southern Court had handed over to her. Which was why she was now regrouping with Ateia. Seero may have been developing her Divination capabilities, but Ateia still had a distinct advantage in that area. And after the incident with the Herald of Night, Seero wasn't going to approach a cult base without as thorough a scouting as she could arrange.

At the moment, Seero was floating in the air several miles from their current target, while Ateia was sitting in the Primary Home Base with her eyes closed. Ateia frowned, opening her eyes.

"There's nothing there, Seero."

"Observation: That assessment agrees with this unit's sensor readings."

Ateia shook her head. "More than that. They left a while ago and took everything with them."

"Requesting Elaboration."

Ateia nodded. "I think I'm reading the records and seeing the past? But if I have this right . . . they left right around the time the South declared war on us."

Seero's robotic eye flickered. This was the fifth such site they had visited and found empty. It grew increasingly probable that this was not a coincidence.

That left several possibilities. The first was that the South's intel was inaccurate. Seero wasn't aware of the structure, capabilities, and efficiency of the South's intelligence apparatus, so it was entirely possible they had been mistaken or deceived. Popular opinion in the Northern Empire held Mirima's skill at espionage in high regard, but even the best intelligence agencies couldn't get everything right all the time.

There was also the possibility that the South had intentionally given Seero false information. Still, the South was not a monolithic organization; she had received separate reports from several different states, the Legion itself, and even some private organizations, and was acting on information that was independently corroborated by several sources.

The probability that every single aspect of the South's society had collaborated to deceive her was very low; there should have been at least one actor who found it in their best interest to dissent. And if the cult's control over the South was such that every source repeated the same deception, then there should have been enough evidence of their presence for Seero or the Northern Court's intelligence to locate them on their own.

Another possibility was that the cult had received forewarning of her assault and evacuated ahead of time. In Seero's analysis, this, too, was unlikely. From Ateia's reports on the evacuation, it seemed to have been a thorough and organized affair. One that would not have been possible in the time frame between Seero's initial departure toward the South and her arrival at the various target sites. And most of all . . . the cult had left long before Seero had turned her attention south.

The most probable scenario, given the information Ateia had uncovered, was that this was a planned withdrawal; one that the South had been unaware of. The cult had left right after High King Xavlaeron had departed for the North. Not only that, but according to testimonies from the Sentinels of Liberty, the cult had apparently enacted a contingency protocol to terminate the high king when he had ordered a surrender to her.

So . . . evidence suggested the cult was well aware that the high king might turn on them following his confrontation with Seero. And if that was the case, it would make sense that they would preemptively evacuate any location he had been aware of.

But then, what were they planning? The retreat from the South made sense for the purpose of preserving assets from Seero's retaliation . . . but it made no progress toward terminating Seero or her allies. Seero at least expected some minor ambush attempts, but the cult hadn't left anything or anyone behind.

And in Seero's analysis, if they were concerned with a betrayal by the South, striking now during the dungeon crisis would have given them the highest probability of terminating their traitorous former allies. So why hadn't they done so?

Seero's organic components registered a rise in fight-or-flight instincts, primarily anger. The cult appeared highly efficient at avoiding termination, yet inefficient at pursuing their supposed objectives. Again, assuming the South hadn't lied to her, which would have been an even more inefficient and self-destructive course of action.

Seero was just about to reroute course and confront the Southern authorities about the unreliable intel when she received a message. One that might just shed some light on what the cult's current location and objectives were.

Back at the Imperial palace in Corvanus, the war room was completely silent. A courier trembled as he held open the scroll, signed and sealed by both Eastern Emperor Julius and Maior Generalis Tetrica of the Legion. Magister Canus narrowed his eyes.

"Please read it again."

The courier gulped and nodded.

"I-I, Emperor Julius Numerius Gregorius of the Peoples and Friends of Elteno East of the Sea, hereby call upon Provision IX of Emperor Proclus's decree for the administration of the Empire. I call upon my peers upon the throne of Corvanus and the helm of the Southern Council to unite the Legion once again.

"And to all citizens, friends, allies, subjects, and partners of the Empire, I ask that you send any and all assistance with all possible haste. The Eastern Border is on the verge of destruction. We cannot hold."

32

The Cavalry Arrives

"Resigned Statement: As usual, this unit must do all the work for Aurora Legion. At least this time, this unit brought friends."

—Commander Elise, reinforcing a group of heroes against a mutual hostile.

Seero returned to Corvanus along with Ateia's group. They now stood in the war room, where Magister Canus's face was grim.

"So, here's the situation: the Empire of the Sun launched a full-scale invasion of the Eastern Empire once the boons of the Aesdes vanished. They apparently have found a way to control corrupted dungeons and used the flood of monsters to overwhelm the initial defenses. The Eastern Empire managed to stabilize the line, but then, the situation with the rest of the dungeons began.

"The Eastern Empire contained the major dungeons but was forced to commit their reserves to the task. Now, they have nothing left to reinforce the main front and are being pushed hard. It will not be long before the line breaks somewhere and they will have nothing to respond with."

Magister Canus frowned. "Emperor Julius has invoked an emergency contingency, calling upon the entire Empire to assist. The problem is . . . I don't think we can. The North's Legions were spread thin even before the dungeon crisis. Thanks to you, Your Majesty, we have the situation under control, but the Legions we could spare would not be enough to make a noticeable impact.

"The South's airship fleet and the Sky Legion might have been able to help—had they not taken heavy damage recently. In any case, the Sky Legion is currently committed to several dungeon assaults and won't be able to move until those are completed."

He then turned to Seero. "So . . . I'm sorry to ask this, Your Majesty. I know you are not fond of being dragged into other people's wars, but we have no choice. Would you be willing to assist the Eastern Empire? If you could at least clear the dungeons, that would help immensely. Because if the East falls . . . the rest of the Empire goes with it."

"Affirmative."

Magister Canus blinked. "You agreed?"

"Affirmative."

Seero's robotic eye flickered. Her nonintervention protocols had long since been deactivated, and at this point, the Northern Empire, at least, was considered an ally. With the change in her primary directive, there was no reason why she couldn't intervene besides the general risk of termination when getting involved in a conflict.

And more importantly . . . Seero's analysis indicated that the Empire of the Sun may not represent a third party in this conflict.

Their invasion of the East included corrupted dungeons which apparently were not attacking the Empire of the Sun's own forces, so it was evident they had a way to control them. An ability that was apparently unprecedented in all of Aelea . . . until the Heralds of the New Dawn had come along. And Amulius had already confirmed the presence of corrupted dungeons in the Empire of the Sun was connected to the Heralds of the New Dawn.

The probability that the Empire of the Sun and the Heralds of the New Dawn were working together was quite significant, and there was therefore a chance the Empire of the Sun was already hostile to her. If nothing else, the missing cultists from the South had to have gone *somewhere*. To the west and south of the Southern Realms were dangerous and unexplored oceans, so the most likely answer was that they had fled east.

In this situation, a preemptive intervention to prevent the fall of an allied nation was calculated as acceptable to Seero.

Magister Canus let the relief show on his face as he bowed toward her. "Thank you, Your Majesty. You've saved us once again."

And so, Seero left Corvanus and flew east, passing over the Southern Sea and into a truly massive mountain range, home to the Dwarven Clans and other species allied with or subjugated by the Empire.

As she traveled, she extended her mana to every dungeon she detected. Some surrendered without a fight when faced with her Holy power. Others resisted at first but gave way when confronted with her dense and powerful mana. A few still resisted. Seero marked these for later, as she did not have time to conduct a full-on dungeon assault.

Meanwhile, Ateia was sitting in the Primary Home Base. She watched the scenery go by through the CELIU network, and spread her own mana to bless the people fighting below.

During Ateia's mission to the Banshee's Cove, she had discovered that her skill assistance was not a one-way street. When the mages of the Necrotorum had cast spells none of the cyborgs had encountered before, Ateia's blessing supported them, and in doing so was molded into new shapes that were recorded by Ateia's cybernetic components.

After that, Seero had granted Ateia permission to assist with her blessing as she saw fit. The Primary Home Base was growing as Imperials conquered monsters with Ateia's help, the CELIU network was acquiring new spell protocols for its database, and the Empire took less casualties as a result. So far, there had only been benefits.

So, the confused defenders of the Empire watched as Seero flew across the sky before a vision of a young Aesdes appeared in their eyes, spurring them on and filling them with power, only for the tide of monsters to dry up shortly after, once they had overcome the latest wave.

Soon after, Seero arrived. She stopped by a dungeon that had surrendered to pick up the group waiting in the Primary Home Base, as well as deploying some new assets, and then made her way to the capital of the East.

An entire mountaintop had been flattened and converted into the toughest fortress in all the Empire. Its walls rose above the neighboring peaks, with sheer cliff faces in all but one direction. The one slope that was barely gentle enough to walk up was protected by dozens of walls, each larger than the last. Carved enchantments covered their every inch, glowing with power. And on top of the walls and towers were countless siege weapons and other contraptions holding powerful mana cores.

The fortress itself held a large city, numerous barracks spread out among its streets. Countless forges blackened the skies with smoke, while vast warehouses towered above the neighboring structures. The only clear spaces were vast training fields for the Legion and the enchanted farms that rendered the fortress immune to a siege.

This was Proclus's Bastion, the capital of the Eastern Empire, and the heart of the Legion. The base that supplied and commanded their endless war with the Sun Elves. The final defense protecting the rest of the Empire and all peoples who freed themselves from the Sun Elves' yokes, should all others fail.

The walls were currently lightly defended, however, save for the main gate. There, a full legion awaited, with two individuals standing above the gate itself, a man and a woman. The man was a human with a simple iron crown on his head.

The woman was a Griffinkin, with an eagle's head, a pair of wings on her back, and the body of a humanoid lion. She wore the armor of the Legion, with only a few adornments that signified her rank.

These were Emperor Julius of the East and Maior Generalis Maximia Tetrica, the commander of all military forces in the East. The Maior Generalis was frowning.

"You sure they were coming now?"

Emperor Julius nodded. "Emperor Lucius has assured me that help is on the way."

Maior Generalis Maximia waved one of her hands around. "Yes, yes. The queen of the Dobhar, right? I mean, she's probably better than an extra legion or two, but she's still just one person estimated at Archon strength or perhaps a bit beyond. We have *several* High Archons tearing down our defenses, not to mention the endless hordes from dungeons both ahead and behind."

Emperor Julius sighed. "What are you trying to say, Maior Generalis?"

Maior Generalis Maximia turned to look him in the eye. "I'm saying I have better things to do than to play diplomat. We have an entire war to fight, and we're *losing*."

Emperor Julius shook his head. "And that situation won't change if you're away from the war room for an hour or two, Maior Generalis. This is an Amicitia Populi Elteni responding to our call on the personal request of Emperor Lucius himself. Even you have *some* decorum you must maintain."

Maior Generalis Maximia scoffed. "That puppet's word means little to us. I fail to see how any decorum is more important than the impending destruction of the Empire."

Emperor Julius allowed himself a small smirk. "Even if Magister Utriusque Militia Canus Sittius Dio stated that this woman could change our fortunes?"

The Maior Generalis flinched. ". . . That man clearly does not understand the situation here. If he had, none of this would have happened. He certainly would not have abandoned his post only to take some cushy job in *Corvanus*."

Emperor Julius shook his head again. The Maior Generalis never did forgive her former boss for retiring. But in any case, the communications officer was signaling their guest was on approach, so the time for complaints was over. Maior Generalis Maximia heaved a dramatic sigh.

"Finally. Let's get this over with and get back to important . . . work . . ." She froze. As did Emperor Julius and all the Legion troops standing at the ready.

High in the sky, something broke through the clouds. It was an airship, vaguely reminiscent of Mirima's designs, yet different from any Imperial vessel. It was sleek and curved, its exterior formed of unadorned metal. At the center of its bow was the opening of a large tube that appeared to run the length of the ship.

And most of all, it wasn't alone. An entire fleet of such ships broke through the clouds and descended toward Proclus's Bastion. All around them, formations of small airships circled around on patrol. They were tiny by Imperial standards, each only large enough to carry a handful of people at most . . . but there were *hundreds* of them.

Emperor Julius managed to open his mouth and squeak out a few words.

"Just one person, huh?"

Maior Generalis Maximia did not respond.

33

Termination Rains from Above!

"Imagine this: every capability contained in a single, man-size package. Infantry, artillery, armor, and air support all from the same unit. My NSLICE will be able to perform every single role of every individual element of an entire combined-arms brigade without any external support whatsoever.

"That is the bare minimum we must achieve to build an ultimate weapon for today's standard battlefields alone. That, therefore, is only the beginning of what we will need for the nonstandard battlefields of tomorrow."

—Dr. Ottosen, justifying the substantial funds expended on developing human-size supersonic thrusters.

Seero had to delay her arrival slightly in order to find a dungeon capable of deploying the new fleet. It turned out that access to slime summoning had proven extremely valuable, after all.

Monsters were innately creatures more magic than matter, and so had significantly more diverse ways to grow when compared to the intelligent peoples of Aelea. They could, of course, grow via combat and achievements, but also by absorbing mana or consuming matter. They could grow in response to their environment or by interactions with each other. Some even grew via normal aging, rewarded for merely existing.

This was one of the motivations for the Aesdes' assistance to the Enlightened in the first place. And, in fact, the Aesdes provided no assistance to wild monsters at all. The only interaction those creatures had with the Aesdes' system was to provide information on them.

Which meant that normal monster growth methods were not impacted by the loss of the Aesdes' boons whatsoever. And slimes, in particular, had very simple methods of growth. All they had to do was absorb things. Mana, water, food, minerals, metals, even each other. As long as they could digest an object, they could absorb it, and they could grow from it.

Which meant that if Seero created an area on the Primary Home Base where she leaked and condensed her dense, plentiful mana and then supplemented it with the constantly regenerating resources of her world . . . she could grow her slimes very large very quickly.

Which was exactly what she did. Seero now had a number of giant cyborg slimes at her disposal. Most were Metal attribute, but she had representatives of all the attributes she had access to. And what that meant were slimes that, as long as they had access to sufficient material, could fabricate entire ship hulls in record time.

Melion had quickly put them to work, and this new fleet was the result.

New developments had sped up the fleet's deployment even more. The ships originally required crews, which meant summoning, training, and deploying monsters capable of operating the ships. Even using drone golems as crew members or drone golem cores to automate the ship itself was insufficient, as a more independent unit was still required to direct them.

But that had changed thanks to 00B-Beta.

As long as all of a ship's systems were electronically accessible, 00B-Beta could now take control of a ship and pilot it remotely. And while 00B-Beta was not experienced in airship operations themselves, they could link to other CELIU units, such as drone-golem commander Snuan, who could guide them. As a result, the airships could now be fully automated and required no crews whatsoever, though Seero still deployed some humanoid golems to each for emergencies.

The CELIU network could now operate as many ships as Melion could build.

Disembarking from the lead ship along with Amulius, Agedia, Ateia, Taog, and Estrith, Seero approached the two leaders of the East.

"Greeting: Hello, this unit is designated Seero; official Imperial designations: Queen of the Dobhar, Amicitia Populi Elteni. It is nice to meet you."

Emperor Julius nodded in a daze. "Emperor Julius Numerius Gregorius. I greet you, Your Majesty Seero, queen of the Dobhar and friend of the Empire. Thank you for coming to our aid."

Meanwhile, the Maior Generalis stepped forward and extended her hand toward Seero with a grin.

"Maior Generalis Maximia Tetrica. Nice of you to join us. And nice fleet you got there. I look forward to seeing it in action."

"Acknowledged."

The battlemage who had once traveled with the Hero of Elteno slumped her shoulders. Three magic circles formed in front of her, launching massive torrents of flame forward. A huge forest of vines and branches paused briefly as it caught fire, but additional plants behind fed upon their burning kin and continued creeping forward.

"Ugh. It just *had* to be another Overgrowth dungeon! Why can't these stupid plants just die already?"

The Recovery knight who had also traveled with them shrugged as he buffed the line of his fellow knights trying to cut through the branches. "I thought you always complained there was never enough to burn? Shouldn't infinitely growing tinder be your dream or something?"

The battlemage just threw her hands toward the encroaching forest as the last of her flames were extinguished by the sheer amount of mass twisting around them. "*If* they actually burned! Do you know how annoying it is to pump half your mana into a spell and then watch it do nothing?"

The Recovery knight stared into the air with a faraway look. "I'm a battlefield healer. All too often."

The battlemage sighed and prepped another spell. The battlefield ahead of them was littered with shattered walls and broken landships. The remaining landships had pulled back for repairs while the legions of the East withdrew to yet another set of fortifications farther up the mountains.

But the monsters of corrupted dungeons didn't take breaks, so someone had to hold the line while the army fell back. A job made all the more difficult ever since the Necrotorum had been pulled off the front. Something about a big undead dungeon acting up.

Because of course it would, now, of all times.

"Ugh. And where is our fearless leader in all this?"

The Recovery knight shook his head. "You know something happened with his daughter back home. Have some compassion; he made a great sacrifice leaving her behind for as long as he did."

The battlemage ducked and fell to the ground as a wave of thorns shot overhead. "And now *we're* about to make a great sacrifice! Everyone's daughters are going to be in trouble if we die here, you know!"

The Recovery knight stepped in front of her with a shield while she stood back to her feet. "I am aware."

The battlemage sighed, then narrowed her eyes. A horn sounded across the battlefield, and the knights at the front broke off and began to retreat. Reaching into her pocket, she pulled out a mana core glowing bright red.

"That's the signal. Cover me; it'll take some time to set up the strategic spell."

The Recovery knight nodded and stirred up his mana, creating a powerful barrier as the battlemage got to work, using her flames to burn a magic circle into the stone around them. It took her several minutes to set up, then she placed the mana core at the center.

Kneeling down, she placed both hands on the core and channeled as much mana as she could into it. The core's light intensified before it began to melt and fill the lines of the circle. The battlemage grunted and groaned, but her work continued. The spell completed just as the vines and branches were wrapping around the barrier.

"Now!"

The Recovery knight leapt back as he dropped the barrier. A wall of fire shot up to the sky and began to surge forward. The entire forest caught flame as the battlemage held her hands out and began to cackle madly.

Until a gust of wind blew her and the Recovery knight off their feet. They looked up to see powerful winds whirling around and forming a cyclone that reached up to the sky. The flames were drawn into it, burning bright before fading away. The cyclone then vanished, leaving a Sun Elf floating in the sky, his eyes fixed upon them.

The battlemage grabbed her hair. "Oh, come on! Now there's an Archon here?! This is seriously not fair!"

The Recovery knight grabbed her and ran as the Overgrowth forest started growing toward them once again. "Less grumbling, more fire."

The battlemage shook her head as she began to run. "I don't have any more! I just solo-casted a strategic spell, in case you didn't notice!"

The Recovery knight glanced back at the Archon, who was forming a massive magic circle of his own. The knight frowned. "I'm pretty sure he did."

At that moment, the wind picked up once again, and something passed above the two of them. The Recovery knight gritted his teeth and glanced up, expecting to see their doom approaching.

And blinked, for nothing was above or in front of them.

A moment later, a loud explosion rang in his ears. Turning behind, his eyes widened. The Sun Elf Archon was staring forward with wide eyes, a massive hole where his torso should have been, left by *something* that had split the sky on its approach.

More projectiles began to stream from overhead as the Archon fell from the sky, small tubes emitting trails of fire and smoke from their rears. They fell upon the forest creeping toward the pair and exploded. A massive inferno engulfed the forest . . . and the Recovery knight's eyes widened further. He could see golden-and-silver light flickering at the edge of the flames.

But the biggest surprise was yet to come.

Holy mana suddenly began to swirl from the ground beneath his feet and filled the Recovery knight. He felt his wounds close, his mana refill, and his fatigue fade. He caught a glimpse of a young girl in shining armor with metal wings and feathers of pure light. Her face was suspiciously similar to a certain hero he knew.

She smiled, and he could hear her voice in his head.

"Don't give up!"

And then . . .

Assisted casting is now available. Engage skill and spellcasting assistance protocols?

The battlemage wasted no time, even as the Recovery knight tried to comprehend what he had just seen. She selected a "recommended protocol," and a massive magic circle formed overhead. Massive golden-and-silver Fireballs began to rain down on the battlefield. She began to grin.

"I take it back. If that's who I think it is, then Amulius, what the crap?! Why was she back there all this time?!"

34

The Shiny Legion

"With all the superpowers and magic and immortal martial artists flying around, it's easy to forget that most of the time, you can just shoot the problem."

—A faceless minion.

"Hello, Aulus, Cominia."

The battlemage, Cominia, and Recovery knight, Aulus, spun around for yet another surprise. Amulius was being carried through the sky by a half-Wulver boy who could apparently fly, while an Otterkin carried a Mélusine woman. A full century's worth of metallic golems, also flying, followed them.

Cominia stomped right up to them as they landed, grabbed Amulius by the front of his armor, and began shaking him. "Why didn't you tell us your daughter is some sort of superhero or something?! That would've have *really* come in handy, you know!"

Amulius raised his hands. "In my defense, she couldn't do that when she was younger."

Cominia cursed and muttered as she let go of him. Aulus shook his head then stepped forward and extended his hand. "I'm glad to see you again, Amulius. Can I take this to mean everything went well back home?"

Amulius gave a sad smile. "Well, not entirely, but for the most part. But I believe we'll have to catch up later?"

Aulus nodded while the half-Wulver boy pointed to the ground. "Not to interrupt, but we're about to have company. A lot of it."

The group had just gotten into position when a huge hole opened up in the ground. Amulius frowned as an armored Sun Elf walked out of it.

"I was hoping to avoid this. Hello, Nolnyth."

The Archon scoffed as she stepped out of the hole, her retinue following behind her. "Finally! It's about time you showed up."

Amulius tensed as Nolnyth walked forward. She reached into a pouch at her side . . . and pulled out a scroll, tossing it to Amulius. He blinked as he caught it.

"Hurry up and take that to someone important enough to matter! I do not intend to surrender only to find myself in an Imperial prison. I expect to have my rank and authority acknowledged, and to receive equivalent standing in exchange for my defection."

Cominia gaped. "You—You're betraying the Empire of the Sun?!"

Nolnyth rolled her eyes. "Not by choice. High Archon Vommik has gone mad. He is playing with corrupted fire, and it will burn our empire down. I do not intend to burn with it."

Amulius nodded and opened the scroll, holding it toward the boy by his side. "Taog, can you transmit that? Have someone pass it along to either Corvanus or Proclus's Bastion and let us know the response?"

Taog nodded as his robotic eye flickered. "Got it."

Nolnyth turned away from them, preparing to cast her magic as her subordinates left the tunnel. But she paused. The inferno had spread across the Overgrowth forest . . . and the plants affected had stopped growing entirely. She dropped her arms, along with the spell she was preparing.

"I see *someone* in your little 'empire' is finally showing some skill. Come then, let us depart before more arrive. I also do not intend to die holding the line."

Amulius gave a big smirk at that. "I don't think that's going to be a problem."

In the skies far from the front, a group of Seero's airships hovered in the air. Suddenly, the barrels at their centers began to light up, Lightning mana crackling while a Gravity Field painted the interior purple.

And then, the sky split as the ship's rail gun opened fire.

Miles away, at the front, an Archon was preparing to cast a spell toward the Legion forces attempting to fall back. But then, without warning, a massive projectile came hurtling straight toward her. She had but a moment between perceiving the projectile and being struck, not enough time for her to change from attack to defense.

The Archon kept barriers up just in case, but that was an emergency defense intended to prevent small ambushes. It shattered immediately under the immense force it was subjected to.

She didn't even have time to scream as the round obliterated her body.

A group of Legion troops had been caught on their retreat. The fast-moving monsters of a Verminflood dungeon had overtaken them before they reached the next set of fortifications, and they'd been forced to stop and fight back . . . but the tide of fur and fang never stopped coming. Once they'd paused to fight, they'd lost their opportunity to flee at all.

That is, until beams of rapidly shifting attributes rained down from the sky, cutting off the monsters from the legionnaires. Seero's magical strike drones flew just overhead, using their Prismatic Strike circles to rain sustained fire down on the monsters below without ever needing a reload.

A moment later, Ateia's blessing filled the beleaguered troops, healing their wounds and granting them the speed to escape.

Smoke clouded the skies as fires raged through the battlefield. Inferno imps and hot devils rushed forward en masse, the flames of Inferno burning through barriers and armor alike. No spell or enchanted weapon could stop them, and with the Legion forces in retreat, there were no formations of steel and blade to hold them back.

Until buzzing noises filled the air, and the hot devils dropped to the ground, full of holes.

Hundreds of Seero's humanoid drone golems landed from the skies, firing their arm-mounted machine guns. The weaker Inferno monsters fell back. Inferno ursanus, Inferno elementals, Inferno giants, Inferno knights, and other such monsters now appeared and charged toward the golems.

Only for a massive beam of Holy mana to sweep across the battlefield.

A close-quarters airship designed for magical combat flew overhead, featuring Seero and Melion's latest achievement. Seero's study of dungeon mana and architecture had now paid off in full. She had developed a basic understanding of how her own implants were integrated into her core, and with that, she had determined how to create new dungeon cores and integrate them into technology.

The result was airships powered by the mana of a dungeon core—which could draw on that mana to power their enchantments. A full Prismatic Bombardment circle was built into each surface of this particular airship, allowing it to rain down countless small beams or powerful superbeams of whatever attribute the situation required.

The fires of Inferno could burn regular magic . . . but endless Holy mana was not so easily swept aside.

Legion troops stumbled around in complete darkness. They couldn't see, couldn't hear, couldn't even feel the ground beneath them. And they couldn't defend themselves from the unseen monsters spreading the Eternal Night's shroud.

That is, until light began to fill each of their visions. The Eternal Night could not stop Ateia's blessing here in the Material Plane, and she gave each of them a very unique protocol.

A wave of Holy mana extended from each of the soldiers and formed a sphere around them. And suddenly, even though their eyes and ears and other senses still didn't work, the soldiers could perceive the world around them. They could feel which way led up the mountain . . . and they could sense when a monster approached them.

Seero had not only summoned slimes, but experimented with them. She found she could apply new attributes to them by having a basic variant absorb mana of that type.

So of course, she promptly created a holy slime. And slimes viewed the world with a special mana sense that was especially attuned to their specific attribute. As a result, these new slimes had the ability to use their mana sense through Holy power, which was, in essence, a small-scale Divination focused on their present environment.

A technique which had been recorded by the CELIU network and easily replicated by a cyborg Aesdes, now passed to the beleaguered troops. The soldiers thus made their way out of the shroud safely, as the monsters of Eternal Night relied entirely on concealment and were substantially less of a threat when spotted.

Once the soldiers were clear, one of Seero's dungeon airships obliterated the entire area with a Holy Light Superbeam, since Seero had designated anything containing Eternal Night mana as a high-priority target to be terminated immediately.

When the first set of fortifications had broken, the Eastern Empire had been in serious trouble. The lack of reserves from the dungeon crisis meant they couldn't prepare the next set of defenses while their frontline forces retreated . . . which meant they had no means of stopping the enemy's pursuit, and no safe zones where their fleeing forces could regroup.

The Empire's many layered defenses would be rendered irrelevant, the fleeing legions hunted down and destroyed, leaving no free forces remaining in the Empire of the Sun's path. The Eastern Empire would collapse.

But now, all across the frontlines, Seero's autonomous forces had joined the fight and pushed the monster hordes back with combinations of Holy mana, AI-assisted mystical might, and enchanted modern munitions.

They were still few in number compared to the size of the front, but their long range and high mobility allowed them to cover a wide area. And the Archons, ambushed by long-range rail guns they were not prepared for, quickly fell back to avoid termination, leaving the monster hordes unsupported and vulnerable.

As a result of Seero's intervention, the Eastern Empire's soldiers were allowed to retreat to the next line of fortifications, regroup and reorganize back into formation, and recover their cohesion. The next set of defenses could be prepared and occupied, and a new frontline established. Which meant that the Empire of the Sun had again failed to exploit a break in the Eastern Empire's lines and collapse their defenses once and for all.

And so, the Eastern Empire lived on to fight another day.

INTERLUDE

Friends in High Places

High Archon Vommik frowned. "And what exactly do you mean by that, Kurzal?"

He sat on a golden throne adorned with jewels set up in a former Elteni command post in one of the conquered defensive lines. Across from him sat two other High Archons, a man and a woman, seated on similar thrones.

The man, High Archon Kurzal, scoffed. "You know exactly what I mean, Vommik. This 'final assault' of yours has been disastrous."

Vommik narrowed his eyes. "You call the most successful assault since the days of High Archon Drycnid *disastrous*? We have those insolent humans on the verge of destruction, and *now* you are losing your nerve?"

Kurzal rolled his eyes. "And just like Drycnid, we are taking unacceptable casualties for every inch of ground. In the meantime, dungeons rampage unchecked across our own lands, while the other High Archons can defend their property with their full might. We are nearing the point where even *if* we win, we will be so weakened that the rest of the council will swoop in and snatch away our prize. A Drycnic victory is no victory at all, Vommik. That's supposed to be the *first* rule of war with the humans."

The woman, High Archon Ilnune, joined in. "What is worse is that the current counterattack came as a complete surprise. All the Eastern legions had supposedly been accounted for; the humans should have had no reserves remaining. The Northern Court has long weakened to the point of irrelevance, and you assured us the traitors of Mirima were occupied. And yet . . . now we are facing the most effective counterattack to date; one that can even threaten Archons.

"Which raises many questions. Where, exactly, did this new force come from? How are they ambushing Archons so successfully? And most importantly: why did we not hear of them before now, and why were they not accounted for in your proposals, Vommik?"

Vommik scowled. "Come now, you both know that casualties and surprises are inevitable in war, and you are both being overly dramatic. The majority of the casualties have been the monsters that *I* provided. Our true forces have taken the least casualties of any invasion in all of our history. Do not lose your nerve over this latest desperate attempt. We will overcome it as we have all the others."

The other two High Archons glanced at one another. Ilnune then shook her head. "Up until now, that has been true, and so we have continued to support you. But as of this latest attack, we have taken casualties among the Archons. The numbers may be few, but we should not have to tell you that even a single Archon's death is worse than losing entire armies of slaves and younglings."

Kurzal crossed his arms. "And it is not just the humans' efforts we are concerned with, Vommik. Twice you have promised us a swift victory; twice you have delivered a breakthrough in the humans' lines. And yet, twice now, you have failed to finish the job, and we have seen no benefit from your 'success' compared to any other invasion attempt prior.

"And worse . . . I hear of dissent within your *own* ranks. One of your Archons has even defected to the humans, and the rest are whispering. How and why did you allow such a travesty to occur? If that is how you are running your own subordinates, then it would be foolish of me to lend you mine."

Vommik narrowed his eyes. "Choose your next words carefully."

Kurzal broke out laughing. "You should take your own advice. You cannot afford to fight me now, can you, Vommik?"

Ilnune crossed her hands across her lap as Vommik glared. "The point is we are decided, Vommik. We are fast approaching the point where none of us can afford this endeavor. You will handle this latest situation on your own. We will hold our forces in reserve while you do and decide our next move based on the outcome."

Vommik began to tremble slightly. "You dare to give me an ultimatum?"

Kurzal nodded. "We do. You have given us many promises and failed to deliver on them all. You have given us many assurances and yet we have been surprised at every turn. You even failed to execute a traitor in your own ranks. Prove to us now that you have what it takes, and if you are worth any further investment."

Ilnune nodded as well. "If you cannot break this latest counterattack and resume the assault on your own, then we will have no choice but to return and defend our own lands, lest our positions in the council weaken any further. We cannot risk losing more Archons until we are certain the rewards will be worthwhile."

Vommik gnashed his teeth. "You will regret this when I stand alone upon the ashes of the so-called Empire, with all of the lesser races crushed under my heel."

Kurzal and Ilnune simply motioned. Servants marched into the room and picked up their thrones, carrying them out of the room. Kurzal smirked as they left.

"At this point, do as you say, and I shall bow at your feet. Either way, I shall treat you with the respect your deeds deserve."

Once they had left, Vommik rose to his feet. Walking into his private chambers, he grabbed the communication device left to him by the Herald of the New Dawn.

And hurled it against the wall. "So, the hero you were 'handling' shows up in the East with some sort of invisible army, apparently, and you haven't said as much as a word to me, huh? I see now. I was never a partner, was I? You *meant* for me to fail!"

"That's wrong."

Vommik spun as a woman walked into the room. The Herald of Rain. Her previously brown hair was now dark blue and waved about like a rough sea. Vommik narrowed his eyes at her and stirred up his mana, the very air distorting around him. "Choose your next words carefully, *human*. It was only the respect I had for your master which allowed you to walk about free and unharmed. That respect is quickly dwindling, and with it, your protection."

She smirked at him. Her eyes began to glow, and her voice took on a watery echo. "The Herald of the New Dawn has only provided me with teaching. My power and my *master*, as you put it, are both beyond your comprehension."

Vommik scoffed. "And yet, here you are, a wounded dog begging at my table for scraps. You are not the only one to borrow the power of the Realms, *human*, and judging by your failures, even that has not helped you."

The Herald of Rain smiled sweetly at him. "Failures you are about to surpass entirely while you berate those who could help you."

Vommik and the Herald of Rain stared at each other. The walls near Vommik began to creak and groan, while the moisture in the air rose around the Herald of Rain.

"If you have something to say, then say it, *human*. If not, begone from my presence if you value your life."

The Herald of Rain clicked her tongue and shook her head. "You are short-sighted and foolish, *Sun Elf*. You fixate your sight upon one single nation, while the Herald of the New Dawn looks to the entire world and beyond. While you struggle against humans and walls, he has struck against the very Aesdes themselves and continues to hold them at bay.

"Do you believe the Aesdes would have permitted your little monster horde from the corrupted dungeons *we* made for you if it were not for the Herald? Do you believe yourself an equal to the Blessed Land? If so, I'm sure he would be more than happy to trade roles with you. So do not take his silence for apathy. In any case, we *did* consider this situation, though it went against our hopes."

The moisture in the air began to condense into a floating pool of water. It formed into a human shape, and then the image of a certain armored girl shimmered into view.

"This is your opponent: NSLICE-00P. Hero, dungeon master, and Amicitia Populi Elteni."

Vommik scoffed. "Hero *and* dungeon master? That's impossible."

The Herald of Rain shrugged. "Or so we thought. But so is creating corrupted dungeons on command. So is striking at the Aesdes themselves. Underestimate her at your own peril."

Vommik's eyes narrowed. "I am not the one who underestimated her, given that it was *your* master's role to handle her."

The Herald of Rain shook her head. "We set High King Xavlaeron and all the might of the Southern Empire against her. We put countless dungeons in between her and you. You had all the time in the world to finish the job before she arrived. But the fact is, regardless of what either of us intended, she is here now. Do you wish to hear of her capabilities, or do you wish to argue about the past?"

Vommik scoffed again. "It should hardly be necessary. She may be impressive to her own kind, but one human girl cannot stand before my might."

The Herald of Rain tilted her head. "The same human girl who just killed several Archons and stopped your attack dead in its tracks?"

Vommik froze, then scowled. "Fine. Say your peace. I assume you have some sort of plan that justifies your insolence?"

The Herald of Rain smiled and nodded. Several more water figures appeared.

"Her might is considerable, and I believe even you will be surprised when you meet her. But if you know your enemy, then even the greatest foe can be brought low. And I have been watching her for a long time now. Here is how we will beat her . . ."

35

Archon Assault

"If marvels of engineering and enchantment were all it took, we would have destroyed the Empire of the Sun centuries ago."

—Maior Generalis Talmudia Propertia, on the viability of a counteroffensive into Empire of the Sun territory using the new Imperial airships.

One of High Archon Vommik's subordinate Archons flew toward the frontlines. He wore glowing armor, and magic circles filled the air around him, a shield of mana forming in front of him.

And, as before, something slammed right into his shield, a roaring sound like thunder following afterward. The Archon gritted his teeth as his mana drained out of his body. Cracks rippled all across his shield, and it shattered in mere moments.

But those moments were enough. The moment the Archon perceived the threat, he cast an Air Dash spell. And since he had gone all out on his defense from the moment he'd entered the area, his barrier lasted just long enough for him to finish the cast. A gust of wind pulled the Archon out of the way as a metal projectile smashed through the shield and carried on its way.

A horde of flying monsters then flew past him, taking up positions ahead. They bought him time to reset his barriers. When the next attack came, the Archon could perceive monsters dying ahead of him, and shifted out of the way.

All across the front, scenes like this occurred. Now that the Archons were aware of what to look for, evading or defending from the rail gun attacks was within their capabilities.

The Archons and monsters then flew high up above the clouds. They didn't bother with their mana senses or Presence Detection, instead using what spells they had to enhance their naturally sharp vision.

And soon, they found their targets. Airships and drone golems of various sizes flew through the skies at ranges normally considered impractical for combat. They had proven hard to detect because they gave off very little mana for their size. But once the Archons had been told where and how to look, they were not so invisible after all.

The drone golems launched a wave of fiery projectiles, but the Archon created a huge barrier in front of the horde. Explosions lit up the sky as the projectiles collided with the barrier. One of the bigger ships fired its deadly attack once more, shattering the protection, but the Archon was on the lookout now and moved out of the attack's trajectory before it fired.

And since the monsters and warriors of Aelea lacked the ability to fight beyond range, they had instead focused on moving quickly from place to place. As such, their flight speed was quite fast. Soon, they were in range.

The Archon let loose a mighty spell, a huge cyclone engulfing the formation of airships. They all formed Mana Barriers to respond, but the drone golems had limits to their mana capacity and devoted most of their focus toward the offense. Their barriers quickly broke under an Archon's attack. Once left exposed, their light construction quickly crumpled, and they were tossed around in the air, colliding with one another and with the larger airship.

The larger airship's barrier held, but the craft had to cease fire. It could not devote the mana necessary to power its main gun while maintaining its defense, and it had no mages onboard who could respond on their own.

While it quietly endured the attack, the Archon prepared another spell. The cyclone condensed, forming into a lance of twisting air and dense mana, which the Archon launched at the airship. A screeching noise filled the sky as the spell collided with the defensive barrier and attempted to bore through.

The airship's mana cores were powerful . . . but ultimately, this was a mass-produced design aimed at efficiency and not optimized for defense. The spell won in the end.

All across the frontlines, burning drones fell from the sky . . . and even some of the rail gun airships. Spread out to cover the wide front, the ships found it difficult to concentrate their fire, and so proved vulnerable if the target Archon was prepared to defend.

The dungeon ships were another story, but even they could not hold back the tides alone. Archons joined with monster hordes and defended them with powerful barriers. The dungeon ships could concentrate their power to defeat the barriers or spread their fire to stop the hordes, but couldn't do both at the same time.

The monsters streamed past and assaulted the more vulnerable drones around them. The dungeon ships were protected by the same Spatial Angling that regular dungeons used, and so hard to bring down, but they were ultimately few in number, so more often than not, the Sun Elves' assault simply bypassed the battlefields where they were present.

Seero's air assault thus came to a halt, and her forces began pulling back.

But that was fine, for the attack had achieved its aim. The Empire of the Sun had taken too long to adjust their response, and the Legion of the Eastern Empire had finished resetting itself. A new defensive line had been established.

Seero's fleet now fell back to this line and reorganized to support the defense so the new one would not be broken easily. High Archon Vommik's forces had stopped the counterattack, but they could not yet resume the assault. High Archons Kurzal and Ilnune still held their own forces back, not willing to commit until Vommik created another breakthrough.

And so, the frontline stabilized, with both sides currently unable to push forward, much to the High Archon's frustration. But the most frustrating aspect of the situation was not the frontline itself. The most frustrating aspect was that the queen of the Dobhar had not appeared. The High Archon might be able to break the airship-supported defense in person, but doing so while the queen of the Dobhar was unaccounted for would leave him vulnerable to ambush, so she needed to be found first.

In every other battle she had engaged in, she had led from the front, personally assaulting her enemies and breaking their formations single-handedly. Yet now, in the largest war she had ever participated in, she was nowhere to be seen. So, the question High Archon Vommik needed to answer most desperately was: where was the queen of the Dobhar?

In past battles, Seero had assaulted the frontlines directly due to her role as a tactically focused enforcer, the limited scale of those conflicts, and her overwhelming might. But at this stage, Seero was developing protocols for operational and strategic planning, and aiming for efficiency at a broader scale. She also had many allies experienced in large-scale command that she could coordinate with, including Magister Canus and Maior Generalis Maximia.

This war was a much larger one than what she had dealt with in Aelea so far, and it required a more complex approach than the previous conflicts. As such, Seero had only committed her autonomous forces to the frontline—the expendable, mass-produced units designed for efficiency—with the limited aim of blunting the Empire of the Sun's advance. Even the dungeon airships, which required Seero to personally construct, were replaceable in the long run.

Meanwhile, Seero was aiming for the most efficient target to reduce the Empire of the Sun's war capabilities. She was currently in an underground tunnel.

00EW ground down the rock and sand ahead of them, utilizing purely physical and technological methods. Beside her walked Amulius and Nolnyth, and behind them were their companions, subordinates, and retainers. Seero's robotic eye was glowing, displaying a map of the continent with a glowing red dot to show their current location.

Nolnyth was watching the giant worm and rubbing her chin.

"Not as efficient as an Earth-attribute movement spell, but close. Acceptable for the low mana signatures involved. Where exactly did you acquire the armor?"

"Apologetic Refusal: This unit regrets to inform you that details of CELIU unit construction are classified for nonaligned units."

Nolnyth shrugged. "Keep your secrets, then. In any case, we are about to arrive."

Just as she said so, 00EW came to a halt. Seero could detect powerful mana signatures and spatial distortions above them . . . and a very familiar gap in her perception. Nolnyth nodded.

"Prepare yourself, then. I have heard much of your power; I can only hope you have a fraction of what is claimed. Since I am risking my own life invading my own former country, I expect you to display a better showing than the so-called elite Imperials over there. Do not disappoint me as they did."

Cominia scowled and was about to say something when Aulus covered her mouth. "Save it for the monsters."

But Seero did not respond to any of them. Instead, she was focused on the corrupted dungeon on the ground above their tunnel.

Yes, Amulius and Nolnyth had led Seero into the Empire of the Sun, to the location of the closest corrupted dungeon they were aware of. If they could bring down the corrupted dungeons, High Archon Vommik's monster horde would dry up, leaving his invasion even weaker than the Empire of the Sun's previous attempts.

Of course, previously, destroying the dungeons was little more than a dream. The Eastern Empire had required all hands on deck just to hold the line, and so couldn't commit the forces necessary for an assault behind enemy lines.

Even Amulius and Nolnyth's group were not confident they could pull it off under the circumstances, given that Nolnyth was now a traitor, and their Celestial Elf friend had long since returned to his homeland. But even if they had their full complement, their previous dungeon assaults took weeks, sometimes months or even longer, for every single dungeon they took down. The Eastern Empire could not wait that long.

Fortunately, they were now in the company of someone who was extremely efficient at terminating dungeons, corrupted or otherwise. A certain someone who was trialing methods to terminate them without an assault at all, in fact. A certain someone whose mana now stretched toward the dungeon above even as Amulius's party prepared themselves for a grueling assault . . .

36

Terminate the Corrupted Dungeon!

"No. There is no other way but blood, sweat, toil, and tears. Even with the blessing of the Aesdes. Believe me, if there was any alternative, I would take it in a heartbeat. But there is none to be found, so put such thoughts aside and prepare yourself for the task ahead."

—Hero Viridia Sollemnis, on methods to purify corrupted dungeons.

It had been a long time since Seero had last seen a corrupted dungeon; both her understanding of dungeon mechanisms and sensing capabilities had grown tremendously in that time. She utilized her dungeon field and Divination to gather data not from the Material Plane but from the boundary separating it from the Realms of Mana, utilizing relevant data from Shialnor as a guide.

A normal dungeon appeared as a coherent structure built into the boundary. Mana flowed through it at a controlled, consistent pace. It was like a valve in the solid wall of the boundary that could be adjusted as necessary to manage the flow.

The corrupted dungeon she now observed, on the other hand, was a hole, and a growing one. The mana flowing through it was a torrent, breaking down the very structure of the dungeon itself and flowing into the boundary around it, tearing the hole even wider. Seero could also detect the Realm of Mana connecting directly to the dungeon—or in this case, the absence of it signifying the Realm of Eternal Night, its obscuring mana covering the dungeon and assaulting the boundaries of the world.

Seero predicted that her previous remote dungeon-subjugation protocol would not be effective here. The sheer quantity of mana pouring through would make such an attempt even less time efficient than with a regular dungeon. And since the current hypothesis was that these had been created by the hostile Heralds of the New Dawn, she had no confidence that the dungeon master would be willing to surrender in any case, and would likely resist in any way they could.

Beyond that, given that the Realm of Eternal Night itself was reaching in through the dungeon and the mana flow was of such magnitude it covered the dungeon itself, Seero predicted that subjugating it would not suffice at this stage to purify the corruption.

From the looks of things, subjugation or termination would require a conventional dungeon assault.

Or . . . Seero could attempt to design a new protocol, tailored to the current situation.

And that is what she decided to do. Seero had, after all, already encountered scenarios not unlike this one before.

She had closed two separate Rifts in the past at Castra Turannia and Corvanus. She had been sent to and escaped from the Realm of Eternal Night itself. She had broken through the boundary between the Material Plane and the Source once before, and had observed a similar boundary expanding during the growth of the Primary Home Base. She therefore had a great deal of data relevant to the situation and predicted it should be possible to come up with a more efficient solution.

Her robotic eye flickered rapidly as she put all of her processing power to work.

A short while later, Ateia approached her. "Hey, Seero, everyone's ready to go, just waiting on you. Are you ready?"

"Statement: This unit has just completed calculations on an alternative termination protocol. Request: All units should defer engaging dungeon termination or subjugation protocols until completion of the experimental protocol. This unit will require Friend Ateia's assistance. Please stand by; transferring protocols."

Before Ateia could respond, data started to fill her head. She frowned. "Seero . . . are you sure? This seems . . . kind of dangerous for you."

"Answer: This unit is 64.51 percent certain in the effectiveness of the overall protocol, and 97.97 percent certain in this unit's ability to avoid termination or relocation to a position she cannot return from. Potential risks have been factored in and accounted for and judged acceptable given the potential benefits."

Ateia still frowned but nodded. "Okay, if you say so. Just . . . promise me you'll come back, okay?"

"Affirmative."

At this point, the others walked over. Amulius looked worried. "Ateia, Your Majesty, everything alright?"

Ateia nodded. "Yes, just . . . wait a second."

Nolnyth narrowed her eyes. "Not possible, girl. Every moment we delay increases the risk we will be discovered by either the monsters or a patrol. If that happens, the whole might of the Empire of the Sun will come crashing down on us, along with the hordes those fools have unleashed upon the world. We must go now."

Ateia smiled at her. "Just give Seero some time to try something. I have a feeling you'll be surprised."

Nolnyth frowned, but at that point, Seero was already putting her plan into action. Opening a portal to the Primary Home Base, she stepped in, and the moment she touched the portal, she cast a Blink spell.

As Colleöne had once warned her, Spatial Magic could not be used to move beyond the Material Plane. Spatial Magic within the Aesdes' system utilized the Material Plane as an anchor and its boundary as a safety net. If one attempted to move beyond, the spell would lose both its means of navigation and its safety measures. No one could predict what would happen in that case, only that it most certainly would not be what the caster intended.

But for Seero, it was a different story. Seero, as a dungeon core, was already partially present in the boundary of the Material Plane, and had created a direct connection to the base Source during her time in the Realm of Eternal Night. As a hero, she had a direct connection to the Holy mana of the Material Plane. And thanks to the Primary Home Base, she had a connection to a separate realm from the Material Plane or the Realms of Mana, as well as a method to establish a connection between them.

She therefore had multiple reference points to triangulate her position, and an example means of transit through the boundary.

So, she used Divination and her dungeon field to determine the coordinates within the boundary, and an entrance to the Primary Home Base to open a path into it. Once inside the boundary, she utilized a modified Blink spell to move outside of the direct path.

She originally lost contact with the Material Plane, as it was specifically cut off from the Source, but her connection to Ateia allowed her to reestablish the connection. She then used her connections to keep track of her position, while using AI-driven iterations on the Blink magic circle to reimplement the safeguards based on her new navigation method.

Ultimately, Seero ended up in the Realm of Eternal Night once again, right in between the Realm proper and the dungeon it was pouring into. Once there, Seero tossed an anti-mana bomb and detonated it at a safe distance while flooding her surroundings with as much Holy mana as she could produce.

As she had calculated, the Realm of Eternal Night's attribute was cleansed by the anti-mana bomb, allowing the Holy mana to contact the base Source as before. And as before, the Holy mana started to convert the Source into a Material Plane.

* * *

As soon as Seero disappeared, Ateia got to work, gathering as much Holy mana as she could. Everyone took a step back and shielded their eyes as the tunnel lit up like the sun, Ateia's entire body glowing with golden-and-silver light to the extent that she appeared to be formed directly from it.

Nolnyth hissed. "What is she doing?! We'll be caught for sure!"

But Amulius stepped in front of her. "Whatever it is, it's important. Don't interrupt."

Ateia then reached out and connected to the Holy mana in the world around her. She frowned.

The world was hurt, bleeding. It cried out in pain as a Realm of Mana tore at its boundary. The Holy mana was trying to respond, but the corruption of a dungeon gave the hostile Realm a way past its defenses. The boundary was being torn up from the inside, the pathways for the Holy mana disrupted, its attempts at repairing the boundary instead leaking out before arriving.

The Holy mana ceased its flow at her touch and began to gather around her. It remained there, inert, as if waiting for a command. She guessed the Aesdes were normally supposed to do something here. Unfortunately, this was not a situation Colleöne had ever taught her about, so she had no idea how to proceed.

Fortunately, though, she wouldn't have to do it alone. She felt it even before Seero reported it. Something new touched the boundary of the Material Plane; she recognized it as another Material Plane, similar to Seero's Primary Home Base. And at that moment, Ateia knew what to do.

Commanding the Holy mana she had gathered to flow toward the new contact, she guided it as Colleöne had shown her how with the Primary Home Base. And when it reached the end of the boundary, she ordered it to expand the Material Plane as she had helped expand Seero's own.

The Holy mana of the world contacted the Holy mana generated by Seero. It reached forward until it arrived at the place where Seero's mana was contacting the base Source . . . and where a new Material Plane was being born. It reached into the new plane, to where a new boundary was being established, then pulled it back. The new boundary followed until it made contact with the jagged, broken edges of the old.

And then . . . the two boundaries began to fuse.

Ateia wasn't sure where the actual land of the new plane went; she only perceived that it moved elsewhere in the world. But the boundary, on the other hand, remained in place. The new boundary spread over the hole, sealing it up. And since Seero was also blocking the Realm of Eternal Night from applying any more mana, the boundary covered the hole in peace and fused together. In one fell swoop, the boundary was repaired.

As for the dungeon, it was suddenly cut off from the Realm of Eternal Night. And since its valve had been opened beyond full . . . it could not stop pouring out what mana it had left. The dungeon core emptied itself of mana in seconds, and since the boundary had been repaired, the Holy mana of the world could once again flow to the dungeon. Emptied of corrupted mana, the dungeon could not resist.

Out above the ground, a pitch-black area began to recede, revealing the sun above and the sand below. Eventually, the darkness pulled back into a swirling black vortex which began to slow down and shrink. Eventually, it faded without a trace.

And so, the first corrupted dungeon was purified . . . without anyone taking a single step inside.

37

Terminate All the Corrupted Dungeons!

"A single corrupted dungeon can bring down an entire civilization, so if multiple corrupted dungeons appeared in the same region? The response can be no less than to send the entire Legion of all three Courts, plus every ally, mercenary, conscript, and reasonable enemy we can gather, all as quickly as humanly possible.

"If that fails, the only other recourse is to evacuate the continent and hope that the Aesdes only need to sink one."

—Former Dux Tullus Vesnius Lovernius, teaching new cadets on corrupted dungeons.

Once the new Material Plane had formed and Ateia had connected it back to the original, Seero found herself in another relocation, as she had the first time she'd escaped the Realm of Eternal Night. In this case, though, since the new Material Plane had been absorbed into the original, she found herself left in motion, as she no longer had a destination.

But that was fine. Seero used her modified Blink spell to move toward the link between the Primary Home Base and the Material Plane, pulling on her connection with Ateia. Ateia pulled back from the other side, and the Holy mana of the Material Plane responded to the effort. As such, an entrance to the Primary Home Base managed to reopen in the underground tunnel, and Seero stepped out.

Ateia's glow died down as she let the Holy mana return to its normal flow. Nolnyth stomped up to the two of them. "What exactly do you two think you're doing?!"

"Answer: Terminating the target dungeon."

A vein bulged on Nolnyth's forehead. "*How* exactly does flooding the area with extremely obvious amounts of mana—" Nolnyth froze. Her mana perception was easily enough to feel the presence of a corrupted dungeon. In fact, corrupted dungeons spat out so much mana that even a level one civilian couldn't miss it at their current distance from the target entrance. And in this case, the mana of Eternal Night's tendency to block *all* senses made it very easy to identify.

But right now, Nolnyth could no longer feel the dungeon. Everything felt normal above the tunnel, and the mana of Eternal Night was no longer blocking any of her senses. Nolnyth's eyes widened.

"What . . . ? How . . . ?"

Cominia, Aulus, and all the knights and Sun Elves also stared in shock as they perceived the situation above. Even Amulius was in a daze as he walked up to Seero. "Your Majesty . . . can you explain what happened?"

"Answer: This unit and Friend Ateia terminated the target dungeon."

Amulius continued to stare. "Without entering it?"

"Affirmative."

Amulius furrowed his brow. "Can you explain how?"

"Explanation: This unit navigated to the hole in the boundary of the Material Plane and utilized Rift termination protocols to cut the dungeon's connection to the Realms of Mana, then Friend Ateia utilized the resulting Material Plane expansion to repair the boundary. It appears the world's ambient Holy mana autonomously terminated the dungeon once it was cut off from its source of mana."

Amulius continued to stare, blinking several times as his mind attempted to process that statement. Cominia's jaw dropped. "And that's . . . *easier* than assaulting a dungeon?"

"Affirmative."

Her mouth closed. "Oh, okay. Right. Obviously. My mistake, I guess."

She then walked off, clutching her head. Seero, meanwhile, turned to Nolnyth. "Request: Please identify the next target location if known. If not, please inform this unit so she can activate search-and-destroy protocols."

Nolnyth was currently staring blankly and unresponsive, so it took a bit of time before she could answer.

The group began tunneling away before anyone could come to investigate and arrived at the next dungeon without incident, where everyone began to stare at Seero intently. As for Seero . . .

"Status Report: Activating corrupted dungeon termination protocols."

She wasted no time opening another entrance to the Primary Home Base and repeating her feat.

This time, she ended up in the Inferno Realm. All around her were burning flames—a firestorm she couldn't see the end of. She could feel the sheer heat even through the extended distance her Spatial Angling defenses created. Her sensors were useless: her thermal and visual sensors were overwhelmed by the light and heat, audio sensors could only hear the roar of fire, and the flames were somehow burning radio waves, which thus never returned to her radar. Her very mana caught fire on contact with the flames.

But the anti-mana bomb didn't.

A wave of sparkling rainbow light extinguished the flames, which were replaced by the golden-and-silver light of Holy mana.

Seero stepped back into the underground tunnel shortly after. Cominia stared at her. "She . . . did it again."

Aulus nodded slowly while staring. "She did."

Ateia gave a wry smile. "It's Seero, after all. You get used to it."

Taog stared at her with half-closed eyes. "Ateia, you do know you're a part of it this time, right?"

Ateia opened her mouth, paused, then closed it. ". . . Oh."

Cominia suddenly shook out of her daze. "That's right! Amulius, what the crap?! What even *is* your daughter?! Some sort of superhero?! A Dragonkin?! A mini Aesdes?! Just *who* did you get with?!"

Amulius shook his head. "I already told you: this happened while I was gone. Her mother was a normal human, too."

He frowned after mentioning his wife but turned away to hide his face. Cominia stared at him suspiciously but didn't press any further.

The next time, Seero extended the range of her attempt. Since she was moving through the boundary of the Material Plane anyway, she predicted that physical proximity was not necessary. Ateia could likewise operate through the Holy mana of the world at extended ranges.

As for the results . . . Seero found herself pounded by a crushing force the moment she arrived. An endless tide of water rushed over her, attempting to crush her from all directions, work its way into her lungs, and push her out into the hole in the boundary all at the same time.

Fortunately, her Spatial protections and a bit of Gravity Magic kept her in place, and so she got to work cutting off the Realm of Deluge. She had to use the Equalizer in this case, however, since the tide was too rapid to toss an anti-mana bomb a safe distance away.

Bit by bit, she ate away at the tide, replacing it with Holy mana. Since she took a bit longer, she saw some of the denizens of the Realm, beings of pure Water mana that blended in with the Realm's own, seeming to lack any biological matter that Seero could detect. However, they kept their distance, warded off by the Equalizer and Holy mana.

And so, Seero managed to grow the new Material Plane up to the size of the hole in the boundary, at which point, the termination protocol could proceed as previously.

Cominia was shaking her head as Seero returned. "Wow, Your Majesty. You took, like, a whole five minutes with that one."

"Explanation: The terrain of the hostile Realm prevented this unit from utilizing prior methods, and this unit had to conduct the protocol manually, reducing the overall efficiency of the process."

Cominia stared at her. "Wow. How unfortunate. You should be ashamed that it took you a whole several more minutes to wipe out a corrupted dungeon."

"Acknowledgement: Inefficiencies have been logged, and this unit will analyze potential improvements to corrupted dungeon termination protocols."

Aulus shook his head. "Don't mind her. She's just trying to cope with her shock and the incredible displays of magic you're demonstrating."

"Acknowledged."

Meanwhile, Nolnyth was staring at Seero and rubbing her chin.

For the next dungeon, Seero didn't even need to open an entrance to the Primary Home Base. She had modified her custom Blink spell, which shared very little with its original magic circle at this stage, to move her beyond the Material Plane on its own. This allowed her to enter and move along a more direct path through the boundary, improving the mana and time efficiency of the transit.

And this time, she arrived in the Realm of Overgrowth.

A wall of green surrounded her in every direction. Vines and branches twisted together in such numbers that they formed completely solid walls. The moment Seero arrived, they began to grow once again, attempting to fill in the space created by her Spatial Angling.

Seero's robotic eye flickered as she held up her hand, charging the Equalizer. Unlike all the other Realms encountered thus far, the Realm of Overgrowth appeared to be formed of solid, biological matter. Under normal circumstances, the Equalizer wouldn't be effective on a wall of plants. On the other hand, it had worked just fine against the water of Deluge, which also shouldn't have been the case. So, Seero decided to test things out.

The Equalizer beam shot forward . . . and the plants in its path began to disappear.

It turned out the plants here were not truly organic matter but instead consisted of pure mana that took a plantlike form. Mana converted to match the form of its attribute.

Which meant the Equalizer worked just fine.

Seero tunneled out a decent-size hole in the plant wall before tossing an anti-mana bomb inside. As per her calculations, the plants regrew almost immediately, sealing the bomb away from her.

A few moments later, the wall of plants was torn down, and Seero was free to proceed with the termination.

* * *

Nolnyth rubbed her chin as she watched Seero return from the Realms of Mana unharmed, yet again.

"Her skill in Spatial Magic and her knowledge of the Realms of Mana seem unparalleled . . . but it could be that she's some sort of specialist? I will have to see her in combat to know for sure. But if she is not limited to what she has displayed here, then . . ."

Meanwhile, Cominia groaned while Aulus grinned. He held out his hand, and she dropped some coins into it. "I told you; you're getting too worked up. Her timing on this has been pretty consistent, you know?"

Cominia clutched her hair. "No, I don't know! I don't know anything! Girl can waltz into the Realms of Mana, erase dungeons, and patch up holes in reality like they're a leaky roof! So who can say she won't suddenly pull it off in a few seconds next time?!"

Aulus tossed the coins around with a clink and grinned. "I did."

Cominia groaned again. "What are we even doing here? We're completely unnecessary."

Aulus tilted his head. "It bothers you that we don't have to work?"

Cominia glared at him for a moment then sighed. "It's just . . . everyone else is fighting at the moment. It doesn't feel right to be doing nothing."

Aulus stared at her in shock. Cominia scowled. "Oh, come on, Aulus! I know I'm not some knight devoting my life to the throne, but that doesn't mean I want my home destroyed! I *did* spend years on a suicide mission to destroy dungeons, in case you forgot?!"

Aulus chuckled, but then, his smile dropped. "Well, be careful what you wish for. We may not be needed for the dungeon assault like we expected . . . but what do you think the Empire of the Sun is going to do when they inevitably notice the dungeons disappearing?"

Cominia's eyes widened slightly, and she nodded with a serious expression. "Right. And if it takes the girl a few minutes to purify a dungeon . . . then we'll have to hold the line."

Aulus nodded. "Let's pray it doesn't come to that."

INTERLUDE

A Hint of Rain

Seero and company traveled underneath the Empire of the Sun for a while after that, purifying the corrupted dungeons one by one.

Ultimately, the identity of the Realm connected to a given dungeon or its strength didn't matter. The mechanics of the Source meant that the Equalizer-Holy mana combo was always effective, and the dungeons—corrupted dungeons especially—could not defend themselves when cut off from the Source. Seero and Ateia's range grew as well, and now, they only needed to enter the general area of a dungeon to purify it.

It was not long before they reached the end of Nolnyth's info, given that she was only knowledgeable on the territories immediately surrounding hers. But that wasn't a problem. There was a constant stream of monsters headed toward the Eastern Empire, so it was a simple matter to follow them back to their origin points.

And so, one by one, the dungeons continued to fall . . .

The Herald of Rain stared at the messenger from the Heralds of the New Dawn. "What did you just say?"

The messenger gulped. "Someone has been destroying the corrupted dungeons."

"That's—"

But the Herald of Rain didn't have time to finish before High Archon Vommik burst into the room. His eyes were bloodshot, and his mana was glowing all around him, the air thrumming with power barely contained. He locked eyes with the Herald of Rain.

"Explain yourself."

The Herald of Rain grimaced. "I have just learned of it myself, so I know as much as you at this point."

The High Archon's mana flashed briefly. "*You* told me you knew this NSLICE-00P. *You* told me she would not hesitate to assault our frontlines, and that she would be easy to draw into a trap. *You* told me you had measures to deal with her."

The Herald of Rain narrowed her eyes and stirred up her own mana. "And clearly, we both have underestimated her. So, would you like to waste time attempting to punish me, or do you want to deal with the hero wiping out your horde?"

High Archon Vommik glared at her. "I've had just about enough of you, *human*. We will deal with this threat, but this discussion on your failures is not over."

With that, he turned and stormed out of the room. The Herald of Rain heaved a sigh as a vein bulged on her forehead. As if *she* were responsible for planning this invasion and all of its strategic failures.

But she shook her head and rubbed her chin. She had other things to worry about than a mere High Archon. After all, the Heralds of the New Dawn had been brainstorming methods of dealing with NSLICE-00P ever since they'd learned of Ateia's identity, brainstorming that had only intensified after their defeat at Corvanus.

Each of their members who had volunteered to bind with a corrupted dungeon had prepared rituals and traps and special monsters, each ready to trial their ideas on how to stop the deadly hero.

And, more importantly, each had prepared to send messengers to the others once NSLICE-00P began her assault. The entire cult would thus be aware of if NSLICE-00P managed to defeat them, and could rule out the methods trialed by that dungeon. And yet . . . the Herald of Rain had not received a single message.

NSLICE-00P was destroying corrupted dungeons without giving them a chance to send word, and at a speed that implied she spent mere hours, maybe even just minutes, on each one. That was beyond even the Heralds' wildest expectations.

And, of course, it implied that every one of their brainstormed methods had proven entirely ineffective.

So now, the Herald of Rain had one short trip back to the Empire of the Sun to figure out how exactly NSLICE-00P was attacking them . . . and how they could possibly deal with her.

She quickly walked over to the Herald of the New Dawn's communication device and attempted to send word to the corrupted dungeons' masters. Each was instructed to dig a large pool of water by their entrances, assisted by members of the cult for those without access to Water Magic.

The Herald of Rain gave them a bit of time then closed her eyes, stirring up the mana of Deluge. She let it wash away her presence, carrying it through the torrents of water across the world. Her mind swam through a large river carrying her back east before linking up to the invisible movements of water in the skies above. She winced and gritted her teeth. The arid climate of the Empire of the Sun left very little of her medium to work with, but she pressed on.

Soon, she arrived at one of the hastily dug pools and expanded her senses out. She found nothing save for the horde of monsters streaming west.

So, she moved on to the next one, and the next. She furrowed her brow; she could find no sign of NSLICE-00P.

Until, finally, she did. She still did not see the cyborg or any of her companions, but she found that Holy mana the cyborg used streaming toward the dungeon from underground. The Herald of Rain froze.

She already knew NSLICE-00P was powerful beyond belief and would only continue to grow stronger. But flinging strong spells around and assaulting a dungeon *from the outside* were two entirely different matters. Neither the High Archons of the Empire of the Sun nor the Immortal Sages of the Celestial Elves could affect a dungeon from the outside. Not even she, a mighty mage blessed by a Realm of Mana itself, had the knowledge and power to do such a thing.

The only beings who possibly could were perhaps some of the most ancient of dragons. Beyond them would only be the Aesdes or the Domides, who ruled the Realms of Mana.

And if NSLICE-00P could match one of those three . . .

The Herald of Rain moved her presence underground. She *had* to know exactly what NSLICE-00P was doing and how she was doing it. Moving along the moisture deep underground, she found a tunnel just above. Peering up into it, she saw her quarry. NSLICE-00P stood in the tunnel, her red eye which the Herald of Rain still saw in her nightmares at times glowing.

NSLICE-00P was looking right at her.

Her heart froze for a second before she came to herself. She was not truly there, after all, so there was no way NSLICE-00P could—

"Warning: Priority hostile detected. Engaging termination protocols."

The Herald of Rain paled as the Holy mana in the cavern turned and began to flow toward her position. She immediately cut her spell, her presence rushing back to her body. She gasped and clutched her chest, her heart pounding so hard it threatened to leap from her body. She was drenched with sweat.

She knew. Somehow, she knew. NSLICE-00P had somehow detected her presence, which meant NSLICE-00P was now aware of her survival . . . and possibly her location. The Herald of Rain shivered.

That was supposed to be impossible. Her connection to the Realms of Mana allowed her to form a connection between Deluge and any body of water in the Material Plane, which she could then use to dip into the Realms of Mana while remaining connected to the world.

It was this ability which allowed her to move vast distances in an instant, or to spy unseen on even the most wary of foes. Any normal counterspells, even a Holy spell, would lose track of her once it reached the boundaries of the Material Plane. No one could follow her into the Realms of Mana . . .

Unless they had a similar method.

The Herald of Rain paled even further. Because she recalled that they had sent NSLICE-00P to the Realms of Mana directly . . . and she had managed to return. So NSLICE-00P had, in fact, displayed some skill at moving through them. She had assumed that NSLICE-00P's status as a hero would preclude her from being blessed by the Realms of Mana, and there was no one who could safely navigate the Realms without the blessing of their lords.

But what if that assumption was wrong? Or rather, in one way or another, it clearly was. And now, NSLICE-00P knew she was coming; the cyborg might even know her current location.

The Herald of Rain clutched her head.

But she took a deep breath and calmed herself. She was still the Herald of Rain, one of the inner circle of the Herald of the New Dawn. Trained personally by him from the days of her youth, and one of his most skilled followers. She had been blessed by the Domides of Deluge, granted powers incomprehensible to normal mortals which made her a match for even the arrogant Sun Elves.

She had risen above her circumstances to become one of the most powerful women in the world, among all species.

The Herald of the New Dawn was counting on her. He needed chaos and conflict throughout the Material Plane. And most of all, he needed time in order to complete his grand design. And if he completed his work, then none of the rest of it would matter. Empires, dungeons, heroes, none of it.

She did not know how or even *if* she could defeat NSLICE-00P at this point, but she still had High Archon Vommik's cooperation, and the armies of the Empire of the Sun. She still had many corrupted dungeons and a horde of monsters. She still had what of her brothers and sisters of the Heralds remained after they had been purged in the North and evacuated from the South. She, at the very least, could still buy time.

The woman who had rejected the Aesdes above and embraced the Domides below could only pray that the time she could buy would be enough for her great mentor to complete his design and usher in a new age. A new world—one she would rule at his side for all eternity with power beyond imagination.

And should she fall . . . she would at least make sure that this broken old world would fall with her.

So, the Herald of Rain got to work and prepared to face the greatest challenge of her life.

38

Collision Course

"Predatory Statement: This time, you aren't the only one looking to tear down this universe. Whenever you are, this unit will find you and will terminate you."
—Commander Elise, on a particular hostile of interest.

Seero and Ateia, who were focusing on the Realms of Mana and flooding the area with Holy mana respectively, caught wind as the Herald of Rain's presence passed into the area and just as quickly retreated. Seero's robotic eye flickered as she attempted to trace the target while Ateia turned all her focus to Divination.

Seero could vaguely track the Herald of Rain's movements through the Realms of Mana, but she could not identify the point in the Material Plane the Herald of Rain had returned to. From what Seero could tell, geographic distance varied somewhat in the mana dimension, and so distance and direction traveled there did not equate to movement in the Material Plane upon return.

Seero herself mainly traveled through the boundary between planes, entering the Realms of Mana only at its point of contact with the Material Plane. She was not yet confident in her ability to navigate the Realms themselves, save for the ability to remove herself from a given Realm to a new Material Plane, or to return to her anchor points.

And, well, if she knew the Herald of Rain's anchor points, she wouldn't need to track her movements in the Realms of Mana.

Meanwhile, Ateia scowled. "The Holy mana cut off. Feels kind of like the Realms of Mana; I think she must have moved to a corrupted dungeon or something."

Seero felt her emotional processes activate, starting to feel . . . annoyed. Amulius glanced between the two girls.

"Your Majesty, did something happen?"

Seero's emotional processes connected with her speech protocols in her attempt to classify her response. "Irritated Answer: This unit detected the high-priority target designated Herald of Rain, likely attempting mana-based espionage. This unit and Friend Ateia attempted to track her location, but current attempts have failed."

Amulius frowned. "So . . . they know we're here?"

"Curt Response: That is the logical conclusion."

Seero's robotic eye flickered as she continued to analyze the situation. She was modifying her protocols and sensors to keep an eye out for any further approaches by the Herald of Rain, but the Herald of Rain had clearly realized she had been compromised. Any further attempts would not likely use the same method.

She considered her capabilities and those of her allies, but they had already attempted every known method to locate the Heralds of the New Dawn. She was no closer to tracking down the Herald of Rain in the Material Plane than she had been before.

Which meant the most efficient course of action was to carry on with the current mission. Terminating corrupted dungeons would cripple both the Empire of the Sun's and the Heralds of the New Dawn's strategic reserves, and their ability to sustain a long war. And now that the Herald of Rain was likely aware of their efforts, she could not allow them to continue. So, if Seero continued with her attack, the Herald of Rain and her allies would be forced to respond.

In other words, the easiest and most effective method to locate the Herald of Rain would be to continue her dungeon termination mission. Albeit, said method might provide the Heralds with an opportunity to ambush Seero and her allies. She would need to proceed with caution.

As Seero calculated, Ateia and Taog filled in the others on the situation. Nolnyth crossed her arms and frowned. "If the enemy knows of our location, then we should get moving. I recommend we withdraw before we are caught by Archons and a monster horde."

Ateia shook her head as her robotic eye flickered. "Seero says we should press on."

Nolnyth stared her down. "That would result in us being caught by the Empire of the Sun and perishing."

But Ateia held her gaze. "That's the point. Seero wants to draw out the Heralds of the New Dawn. If we keep tearing down their dungeons, they'll *have* to come and stop us. As long as we know it's coming, we can prepare an ambush."

The Sun Elf narrowed her eyes. "I think you are severely underestimating my former peers. I do not know how powerful the queen of the Dobhar is, but I can tell you that I am the strongest of the pathetic little band the Empire scrounged together to handle the greatest threat to its existence."

Aulus had to hold back Cominia again while Nolnyth continued.

"The other Archons each approach me in might, and even I cannot deal with a High Archon. High Archon Vommik is sure to respond, since we are destroying his secret weapon in his own territory; an insult he cannot overlook. So tell me, *human*, can the queen of the Dobhar handle all of that on top of the endless monster horde and whatever those imbecilic cultists come up with in their mana-hazed insanity?"

Ateia smirked. "First of all, I'm not exactly human anymore. And secondly . . ." She turned to Taog, and they both grinned. "Yes. Yes, she can." She then turned back to Nolnyth, dropping her smile. "But in case you're worried, you've seen the portals already. You know Seero has a way to retreat immediately."

Nolnyth shook her head. "And what range do these spells have? A short-range teleport is insufficient to escape from a High Archon."

Ateia smirked again. "Want to visit Turannia?"

Nolnyth raised an eyebrow, but Ateia just kept smirking. "You are serious? I would not take kindly to such a jest when it is my life on the line." Ateia kept smirking, so Nolnyth sighed. "Very well. Let us see what the queen of the Dobhar can do. But be warned, if I feel my life is at risk, I will withdraw, with or without you."

Ateia shrugged. "Suit yourself."

Nolnyth rubbed her chin as she turned away. "Impressive loyalty, if nothing else. But a High Archon is no easy foe."

As for Seero, she was currently finishing up her plans and a conversation with Melion. She had to wait for the Heralds of the New Dawn to move before she could ambush them, but that didn't mean she couldn't prepare now.

And as it turned out, Melion's latest tests were going quite well indeed. If all went well, Seero may have some additional assets on standby when the enemy arrived.

With her calculations complete, Seero turned her attention to her sensors and began searching for the next dungeon.

High Archon Vommik scowled as he sat on his throne, looking to where some of the slave mages modified a miniature map of the front. It was a three-dimensional construct, with Earth, Air, and Water mages creating fully accurate replicas of the terrain and current weather conditions, while Illusionists projected images of the soldiers on either side.

The situation hadn't changed, just like it hadn't for the past day. By his calculations, he could not break the Imperial defenses. The humans had already proven they could hold the monster horde alone, and with those airships still skulking behind the walls, the High Archon couldn't commit his own subordinates. Even he would not needlessly throw away his own assets into certain death, not unless he could achieve something with the sacrifice.

And with the queen of the Dobhar assaulting his dungeons, the situation would only grow worse. The High Archon might be forced to pull back his entire army to search for her if they couldn't pinpoint her current location, and to do that would cause this invasion to fail, even after they defeated her.

At that moment, one of his servants approached him, bowing low and remaining silent. Vommik sighed.

"You may speak."

The servant remained bowed. "My lord, your . . . guest has sent word. She has located the queen of the Dobhar."

High Archon Vommik slowly rose to his feet. All conversation in the room ceased, and the slave mages paused their work. The air began to distort, and the ground began to tremble. High Archon Vommik's mana flared to life, surrounding him in a visible aura as his eyes began to glow.

"Assemble all of my Archons and my retinue; we march within the hour. Any who are late shall suffer my wrath."

"It will be done, my lord."

The servant backed out of the room while the slave mages scrambled to communication artifacts to relay his command. High Archon Vommik paid them no attention as he strode through the room.

If he slew the queen of the Dobhar, her forces would flee the fight, and the humans' morale would plummet. He himself could take the field and smash through the remaining Imperial defenses by his own hand. He also planned to force that insolent Herald of Rain to contribute as well. It was the barest fraction of what she owed him after how her false promises and mistaken assumptions had led this conquest to the brink of failure.

Within days, he would break his foes, he would complete his people's eternal mission, and he would stand supreme atop the ashes of the Empire. All humanity would bow at his feet, wrapped in his chains.

And then . . . the Council of the Archons would pay for doubting him. Starting with the two who had abandoned him on the eve of his final triumph.

The High Archon held out his hand, his mana condensing and twisting through countless magic circles; lightning and wind began surging through the room just from the tiny amounts of mana he let leak from his hand.

It had been too long since he had destroyed his foes in person. Yes . . . he could see it now. His mistake had been to entrust his victory to others in the first place. That was what had allowed the others to doubt him and take advantage of his patience.

It was time to remind the council, the Heralds, the Empire, and the world of the power of High Archon Vommik.

39

First Strike

"Strike hard, strike fast, and most of all, strike first."

—Exploratore Training Manual.

A new river flowed through the desert, washing away the sand before it. The surging rapids were filled to the brim with all manner of aquatic monsters, pouring out of a swirling vortex at the bottom of a new pond.

Many miles away and underground, 00EW continued grinding up the ground ahead. Once Seero ordered the halt, everyone got to work, Amulius's team taking up positions.

The veteran Exploratore began setting up traps, Aulus began casting wards, and Cominia engraved magic circles into the floor. Nolnyth took a position to the side, ready to cast her magic or flee as the situation required. Taog and Estrith conducted scans with their advanced sensors while Agedia sharpened her lance.

Eventually, Amulius nodded at Ateia, and Seero opened a portal to the Primary Home Base, stepping through while Ateia stirred up her Holy mana.

And then, the roof of the tunnel exploded.

High Archon Vommik floated in the sky and watched as his Sunfall spell demolished the ground, the bright ball of mana smashing into the underground tunnel before exploding into blinding light. He scoffed.

So, *this* was the queen of the Dobhar? Someone so praised and feared, who had the Heralds of the New Dawn crawling to him with their tails between their legs? She had not even responded to his spell at all. It was pathetic, but he should not have been surprised that one praised by the lesser races turned out to be a disappointment.

Still, it was strange for someone capable of killing Archons and destroying corrupted dungeons to be done in so easily. The High Archon narrowed his eyes as he searched for traps. He motioned toward one of his Archons and several of his retinue who floated in the air around him, while his ten-thousand-strong personal guard marched on the ground below.

"Go on, find what remains of their corpses and bring them to me. I wish to toss their broken bodies upon the walls of their pathetic empire."

The Archon flew down, and a squad of guards set out to accompany them. He kept his eyes peeled as his servants moved to execute his command.

Meanwhile, Seero had not responded to the attack because she was not present in the Material Plane at all. Instead, she appeared in the Realm of Deluge once more, only to be greeted by high-pitched laughter.

"I have to admit, of all the ways you could have been handling our dungeons, attacking from the Realms of Mana was not one I would have ever expected."

Deeper in the Realm, just ahead of Seero, the Herald of Rain appeared. She had a sneer on her face. "But you've miscalculated. I may fear confronting a hero when they are blessed by the power of Aelea itself, but now, you're in my arena. This is the very Realm that granted me my power, and now you'll—"

Seero simply ignored her and continued with the corrupted dungeon termination protocols. After all, the method in question had kept away denizens of the Realms in the past, so Seero calculated it would also work against any mana-based attack the Herald of Rain could pull off. Therefore, she used the Equalizer to clear some of the water ahead and tossed an anti-mana bomb at the Herald of Rain.

The Herald screamed as the rainbow wave passed over her, then began gargling as water filled her throat. It appeared her safety in the Realm was contingent on her shield of the Realm's own mana, which had just been dispelled.

She quickly activated a spell and vanished even as Seero channeled her Holy mana to create a new Material Plane patch.

The Sun Elves had just landed on the ground and were approaching the smoking crater when the ground opened up beneath them and a massive beam of light pierced through one of the Elven warriors. The Archon leading them sprang into action as another beam opened fire, retaliating with a burst of sunlight from above which set the entire crater ablaze.

When the fire died down, some of the rocks and debris had melted away, revealing a glowing dome reminiscent of an anti-Archon formation barrier. The Archon scowled.

Within the dome stood a large, metallic golem in the shape of an arachne, covered in glowing circuitry. At the center of its chest was a bright, glowing mana core beyond anything that had ever come out of a monster.

Inside the golem, Lilussees grunted. "Ugh. This is, like, so much e-word. I, like, need a year or two off after this or something, okay?"

Even as she complained, the golem's eyes glowed, and its hands swung about. The giant Prismatic Dome circle shifted into a Prismatic Bombardment circle, opening fire with a fused Holy Dark Beam. The Archon countered with a Sun Beam of his own, the two spells colliding midair.

Meanwhile, another hole opened up in the ground underneath the Sun Elf warriors escorting the Archon. Amulius leapt out and unleashed a Holy-imbued arrow while Cominia created a Firewall. The fire didn't do much against the Sun Elves, but it made the arrows harder to see, and one of the warriors failed to evade. Agedia and Estrith then leapt straight through the flames, stabbing another warrior each with their spears, while Taog appeared out of the shadow of another and stabbed through his opponent's chest.

Finally, a metallic rat golem much like Lilussees's shot from the hole in the ground and rocketed toward the Archon in the sky.

"FEEL-EXPERIENCE THE POWER OF THE SERVANTS OF THE WISE-MIGHTY-GRACIOUS BOSS-QUEEN, YES-YES!"

01R shot through the sky inside the golem, a mighty lance in its hand coated in Holy and Light mana. He swung his weapon up, striking the feet of the Archon as a barrier appeared around him, but it cracked and shattered, forcing the Archon to evade. But in doing so, he dropped his Beam spell, and the Holy Dark Beam shot forward. Lilussees easily adjusted the angle of her attack, and the beam pierced right through the Archon's remaining defenses.

High Archon Vommik gritted his teeth as he watched the exchange. The loss of yet another Archon displeased him, but that wasn't the worst of it. Yes, he had not expected his first attack to kill the queen of the Dobhar outright, and he'd anticipated she would have something planned. Yet, for one of the spells reserved only for the mightiest of Sun Elves not to have claimed even a single life?! That was impossible.

If word of this got out, he would be the laughingstock of the council. This could not stand.

"Kill them, every last one of them!"

Seero had, of course, detected the High Archon's army long before it arrived. Her scouting drone golems had identified a formation leaving the frontlines when it'd first set out, in fact. However, she had not gotten confirmation on if the Herald of Rain was traveling with the force, so she'd decided to delay responding. She had instead covered their location in a Spatial Angling Barrier before she began the dungeon termination protocol, deploying Lilussees to add a more conventional barrier of her own.

Along with a brand-new weapon that Melion had just finished testing; a hollow drone golem that could accept a pilot—and that was powered by a dungeon core. A suit that would protect its wearer with all the powerful defenses of a dungeon, including Spatial Angling and automatic regeneration of damaged structures, and that could channel its mana directly into its pilot master, granting them the mana quantity, density, and regeneration that only a dungeon core could provide.

They then, of course, equipped the suit with every other manner of weapon they could fit inside it, including the artifacts from the Imperial treasury they'd received from Princess Caecila.

As such, the High Archon's assault had failed to reach its target, and then Lilussees counterattacked with Supercharged Fusion Beam spells. The dungeon suit was also a drone golem that automatically lent its processors to Lilussees's spellcasting, greatly improving her Supercharge efficiency, albeit at an undesirable amount of e-word for her components.

01R, meanwhile, attacked with his own suit and a special weapon. The Lance of Vlatugni, one of the treasures of the North, now wrapped in a Supercharged Infusion of Holy and Light mana. 01R then turned his dungeon golem's mana to Supercharged Dash spells, sending him hurtling through the sky like a shot from one of the rail gun airships.

A moment after this exchange, Seero returned to the Material Plane. Her sensors searched for the Herald of Rain—and found her. In the middle of the High Archon's army was a newly constructed artificial lake surrounded by hooded individuals, with a massive magic circle carved on the bottom.

The Herald of Rain appeared there, coughing and gurgling. One of the hooded figures casted a Water spell to pull her to the surface, where she coughed and gagged as she tried to clear the water in her lungs.

Meanwhile, Seero, Ateia, and Taog's robotic eyes all turned red. With the Herald of Rain located and her plans revealed and countered, Seero could now proceed with the operation with full confidence.

"Status Report: All targets located. Furious Command: All units, terminate all confirmed hostiles with extreme prejudice."

The sky lit up with a dozen Prismatic Bombardment circles, Supercharged to the limit.

40

The High Archon vs. the Ultimate Weapon

"We tend to imagine an Archon as a particularly strong archmage. Not a fully accurate idea, but a reasonable one. The same is not true for a High Archon.

"A High Archon is someone who has emerged from the deadly competition of the Archons against one another, and not only emerged victorious but with such personal and political might that they clearly stand head and shoulders above all other Sun Elves. They are closer to a dragon than any mortal mage and should be treated as such.

"We are simply fortunate that their hate for us is only surpassed by their hate for each other, and so it is extremely rare to face more than one High Archon at any given time. And never in the history of the Elteni Empire have we ever faced all of them at once. Let us pray that it remains so."

—Maior Generalis Talmudia Propertia, on High Archons.

High Archon Vommik immediately began preparing a spell of his own the moment his servants were ambushed . . . which he hastily converted to defense as the sky lit up with magic circles. He barely completed a massive Sun Barrier in time before dozens of superbeams shot straight toward him. He grunted, and his eyes widened as his shield began to crack.

His Mana Density was among the highest in the world. What's more, the beams assaulting him were a combination of Holy and Light. Light was a poor matchup against Sun, which contained Light within it, and out here, on a bright desert day, the Sun attribute was at its peak.

Holy, while highly effective against monsters, dungeons, or anyone drawing on the Realms of Mana, had no special effects against the inhabitants of Aelea.

Against the High Archon, it should have been only marginally more effective than unattributed mana would be.

And yet, despite the poor attribute matchup, his spell was breaking under the sheer quantity of mana assaulting it. That meant that each of those strategic spells was cast with Mana Density exceeding his own. Ritual casting would average out the casters' Mana Density rather than summing it, so the only explanation was that whoever was casting these spells had higher average Mana Density than the High Archon.

There were also a *dozen* of those spells. So, either the queen of the Dobhar had a dozen or more mages among her servants with such Mana Density . . . or she had such a quantity of mana and ability to split her focus that she could Multicast strategic spells.

Vommik was not sure which would be worse.

But Vommik's pride was matched by his self-preservation instincts, and so he activated a Sun Dash spell as his barrier broke, pulling him out of the way of the attack even as he prepared a new spell. He opened up with another Sunfall targeting the queen of the Dobhar, chaining his cast into another Sun Dash as she almost immediately adjusted her aim. Since his barriers could not hold against her for long, he needed to get her on the defensive as quickly as possible.

A small second sun formed in the sky as Vommik's mana condensed to the limit, igniting a ball of fire, light, and even lightning that was too bright to view directly. The temperature rose as the ball began to fall toward the queen of the Dobhar.

The enemy had been underground for Vommik's first strike, the sand and rock in the way both reducing the power of Vommik's spell and hiding the targets from the sun above. Likewise, he hadn't had direct eyes upon them, and the queen of the Dobhar had clearly anticipated the attack, so he couldn't say for sure if he had struck them directly. It was not unthinkable that they had survived the first assault.

But now, Vommik's spell was heading straight toward the queen of the Dobhar with nothing but open sky between them. The sun was at its brightest and his spell was drawing additional power from it. Surely, even a foe such as her could not emerge from such an attack unscathed.

Seero's robotic eye flickered as she analyzed the incoming attack. High Archon Vommik had managed to produce a miniature star—or at least a mana-based approximation of one, as Seero wasn't detecting the levels of radiation a star should emit at this range. Still, the spell was throwing off some electromagnetic radiation, enough that it would disrupt some of Seero's more sensitive components.

If not for 00B-Beta, that was. The being composed of mana, lightning, and code was happily absorbing all the ambient electromagnetic energy and shielding

Seero's components in the process, so Seero just needed to deal with the high-energy projectile headed her way.

She converted one of her spell circles while the rest continued their assault, requesting some assistance from Ateia as the circle shifted to a Prismatic Dome spell and laid itself on the ground. Ateia boosted over to its center and placed her hands on the ground, connecting with the nearby flows of Holy mana.

In this case, the attribute chosen for the spell was Nature, Metal . . . and Cyber. The last attribute wasn't named in the Aesdes' system last Seero had checked it, but it was the most accurate designation she could apply to 00B-Beta's mana, which seemed to match the mana produced by her Cyborg dungeon affinity.

A massive tree with metal bark and an interior of combined organic matter and electronic machinery grew from the ground. Ateia filled it with Holy mana, accelerating its growth and strengthening the tree itself. Her connection to Seero and the Primary Home Base, along with her own experiences growing cyborg plants there, even allowed her to add a bit of a Cyber flair to the Holy mana flowing through her.

The cyber tree rose into the sky and spread its metal-coated branches in a circular canopy as the miniature sun spell approached. A bolt of straight lightning shot from Seero into the tree's trunk, and circuitry began to light up along the tree as 00B-Beta extended itself.

And then . . . the spell struck. A massive explosion of flame, light, and lightning spread out across the canopy—and immediately dimmed. The tree's organic components absorbed the Light mana to grow even stronger, and 00B-Beta absorbed as much of the Lightning as it could before the excess was safely transferred into the ground by metal-coated bark and roots. All that was left were the flames, but the tree's metal coating made it less susceptible to catching fire than usual.

The spell had tried to scorch the tree, but had only ended up nourishing it. The High Archon's cast had failed to make any noticeable impact.

High Archon Vommik pursed his lips as he watched the scene before him, even as he used Sun Barriers and Sun Dashes to evade the queen of the Dobhar's retaliation.

The queen of the Dobhar had made some sort of metal tree that blocked his attack completely. Nature was a solid choice against Light-based spells, but the Fire component of his Sun spells should have set it ablaze.

Likewise, they were in the middle of an arid desert, lacking in both fertile soil and water. The environment *should* have favored Sun over Nature. And he had never seen Metal and Nature combined before, which was apparently giving the tree additional protection from the Lightning attribute.

But that wasn't the most shocking part of this. No, the most shocking part was the queen of the Dobhar's human companion. The girl who held the trunk of the tree, feeding it with Holy mana.

Vommik had lived for a long time. He had seen much and read more. He had met with heroes and had cast them low. He knew better than most what they were capable of. Heroes could generate Holy mana and use it to cast special skills. They could even call upon the mana of the world in a limited manner, receiving small amounts of Holy mana from their surroundings to boost their durability and recovery rate beyond their individual might, making them surprisingly hard to kill.

This was *not* what the human girl was doing. She was calling on the Holy mana flowing through the world and *commanding* it. She was changing the flow itself and redirecting it to support the queen of the Dobhar's spell. And that mana responded and flowed freely, unlike how it would for anyone else in Aelea. She commanded it . . . and it freely obeyed her.

That had *frightening* implications for her identity—and the queen of the Dobhar's.

Vommik's eye twitched as he glanced over at the Heralds of the New Dawn. He now understood why they had fled, and decided they would pay for withholding such information from him when he'd agreed to shelter them.

But such things would have to wait. The truth was, he needed their help at present. The queen of the Dobhar could apparently match his peak mana output, and with what could only be either an Aesdes or an Ancient Dragon commanding the world itself to support her, she would not run out of mana anytime soon. Even he was not confident he could break through her defenses, and he apparently couldn't wear her down over time. So, his only hope of overcoming her was the help of his allies.

But at the very least, his forces outnumbered hers a thousand to one, and he had brought his Archons with him as well. He may have lost one to an ambush, but he could not imagine more than a few of her companions matching the Archons one-on-one in the open field, much less when at a numerical disadvantage.

Additionally, the Heralds of the New Dawn could lend support as well. He had initially scoffed at the Herald of Rain's frankly paranoid amount of planning for this battle; now, he could only hope that she had done enough.

But until she moved, he would have to face down the queen of the Dobhar and endure her assault. Not a single other person on the field was up to the task.

He grimaced as he watched her magic circles change color. Jets of water shot forward, burning up before his Sun Barrier.

So, she could also change the attribute of her spell . . . without having to recast the entire thing.

The High Archon felt a chill down his spine, even as he reinforced his spell. He could only hope that his servants would fulfill their duty . . . or that the Herald of Rain might prove worthy of their alliance.

41

Sun Wars

"Yes, we have been forced to concede some territory, and NSLICE-00P was forced to retreat. But need I remind you that NSLICE-00P is easily capable of terminating any individual Non-Standard in an equal engagement. The problem is that even she cannot fight an army alone . . . and if you give me the nonstandard bases I requested, she won't have to."

—Dr. Ottosen, on the failures of the NSLICE program in Europe.

01R landed back on the ground, regrouping with the others as the Sun Elf forces began to move. A ten-thousand-strong army of Sun Elf spellblades bore down on them, led by seven Archons. 01R grinned.

"Now this is a fight worthy-deserving of the wise-mighty-gracious boss-queen's servants, yes-yes."

Lilussees just groaned. Cominia frowned. "Hello, Mister Ratkin?"

01R held his head up high and crossed his arms. "You may call-name this one as 01R, the blessed name granted by the wise-mighty-gracious boss-queen, yes-yes."

Cominia furrowed her brow. "Right . . . So . . . 01R, was it? Does there happen to be more than the two of you? We're a bit shorthanded, and those stupid Elves are Fire resistant too."

01R grinned. "Wait and see-observe, man-thing, and we shall show-display the wise-mighty-gracious boss-queen's glory, yes-yes."

He then boosted into the air and held his arm out, a massive vortex appearing in the air. Several dungeon airships flew out into the sky, flanked by formations of drone golems. Humanoid variants began to land on the ground, along with the rest of Seero's monsters, led by 00B.

As it turned out, powering 01R's suit with a dungeon core had another benefit. Mainly, that as a dungeon connected to Seero, it could open an entrance to the Primary Home Base.

Cominia blinked. "Ah. That should work. Thank you."

Even Aulus gaped at the sight, while Amulius chuckled and shook his head. 01R smirked. "This is only the start-beginning, yes-yes. All unit-servants, begin-commence attack!"

The flying drones launched a volley of missiles while the humanoid drone golems formed up on the ground. Barriers appeared over the Sun Elf army, and the missiles exploded overhead, dealing little damage. Then, the Archons retaliated. Sun Beams, Sun Bolts, Sun Lances, and other Sun-attribute spells streamed toward the airships, all boosted by the light overhead. The dungeon airships created barriers of their own, stopping the spells. However, cracks began to form.

Snuan, sitting on an elevated throne in the bridge of the lead dungeon ship, jumped and squeaked as an alarm started blaring.

"K-Kill-slay those Elf-things, you crazy fanatic! O-Our ship-things can't repel-resist firepower of that magnitude!"

01R nodded as Snuan's voice came in over the comms. The dungeon ships may have had an endless supply of mana, but only a finite quantity of it was available at any one time, and their Mana Density did not come close to the wise-mighty-gracious boss-queen's. Their barriers would not hold forever.

The dungeon ships themselves were protected by Spatial Angling and a dungeon's ability to repair damage to itself, but that did not extend to the other drone golems—or to the people on the ground. It would be wise of him to deal with the biggest threat on the battlefield promptly.

He turned to look at his fellow servants, plus a few allies or two who dared not to bow at the wise-mighty-gracious boss-queen's feet.

"The drone golems shall block-distract the weaker Elf-things; we shall attack-assault the strong ones, yes-yes. I and Lilussees shall handle-defeat one each." He turned to Amulius and his party. "Can you insolent man-things handle one yourselves, yes-yes?"

Amulius rubbed his chin, then slowly nodded. "I don't know if we can defeat an Archon, but we should be able to contain them for a while at the very least."

01R sighed. But perhaps that was the best he could expect from man-things who were not blessed to follow the wise-mighty-gracious boss-queen. "That will have to do-suffice. Then, 00B, Estrith, you two must lead-guide the others to confront-face four. Can I count-rely on you? You can take the insolent snake-man-thing with you."

Agedia smirked. "Thanks. But sure, I'll help."

00B looked up at the Archons, his robotic eye flickering. A flash of lightning surged around his eye as 00B-Beta assisted with the calculations, then he turned to 01R and grunted. 01R frowned.

"Four is a lot for a clean fight, you predict-calculate?"

01R rubbed his chin. 00B's analysis of the power the Archons were displaying indicated a significant chance of taking casualties if their group had to deal with four simultaneously. Only two dungeon suits were ready, so the rest of the CELIU units would be fighting on their own, and most could not match the Archons in mana output.

"How about three?"

At that moment, everyone turned around. Nolnyth had jumped out of the Primary Home Base where she had retreated to and was flying down to the group. Cominia smirked at her.

"Oh, is the cowardly little Archon suddenly feeling brave?"

Nolnyth scoffed. "Only a fool rushes to confront a High Archon unprepared. But the queen of the Dobhar, unlike every other human I have ever met, has surpassed my expectations."

Nolnyth turned as Cominia scowled, facing 01R. "You there, servant of the queen of the Dobhar. I will assist you, so long as you allow me to face Madanri alone. He and I have a score to settle, now that the High Archon is no longer forcing us to play nice."

01R grinned. The Elf-thing's tone was insulting, but she at least understood his relationship with the wise-mighty-gracious boss-queen. And more importantly, if she could handle another Elf-thing on her own, then the rest of their group only needed to deal with three.

"Understood-agreed, yes-yes. 00B, can you handle three?"

00B's robotic eye flickered, then he nodded and roared.

"Well said-stated! Charge-attack, servants of the wise-mighty-gracious boss-queen!"

01R boosted into the air. The Archons, frustrated by the lack of burning airships, were trying other elements. Fireballs, Light Beams, Water Lances, Lightning Strikes, boulders from the ground, spouts of lava, and other such spells assaulted the dungeon ships' barriers.

01R shot through the hail of spells, his cybernetic components tracking the mana signatures and plotting out his course as the suit layered Dash spells on its powerful repulsors. He quickly evaded the barrage and rocketed toward the nearest Archon, who frowned as she formed a barrier. His lance collided with a crash, screeching as enchanted metal scratched against the Sun-powered mana shield.

Two more Archons turned to attack the armored rat, but Lilussees assaulted one with a Prismatic Bombardment, who hurriedly turned to their own defense.

The third shot a Sun Beam, only for a similar spell to collide with his midair, canceling it out. His face contorted in rage as Nolnyth flew toward him.

"Traitor!"

Nolnyth narrowed her eyes at him as she prepared another spell. "I've been looking forward to this for a *long* time."

She lobbed a ball of white flames at the Archon, who evaded but was forced to put up a barrier as the ball exploded nearby. The two Archons flew off and began their duel in earnest.

On the ground, the drone golems had engaged the spellblades. Machine guns, missiles, and lasers continued to fire, but the spellblades were no mere rank-and-file soldiers. Even the weakest Sun Elf warrior in the High Archon's personal guard was a foe that surpassed an Imperial legionnaire several times over.

Those who focused on the mystic arts put up barriers that blocked any firepower a mass-produced drone could output, while those who trained their bodies simply ignored the barrage as it bounced off their HP and enchanted armor. Powerful spells demolished squads of drone golems, while enchanted blades cut through armor plating with ease.

But . . . there were a great many of the drone golems. And most of all, they had help.

Within the CELIU network, 00B-Beta watched through a thousand optical sensors. It reached into the CELIU combat protocol database, running combat analyses acquired from 00B and the Great Mother herself to determine the ideal solution. Selecting the chosen protocol, it applied it to the drone golems.

Bolts of lightning, code, and mana shot out of the drone golems to one another, zigzagging and linking them before shooting toward the quadcopter spell drones hovering just above. Spell circles began to form in the air and link together into larger magic circles.

Thanks to 00B-Beta, the drones could now ritual cast all on their own.

Powerful barriers began to block the spells shot by the Sun Elves, while the melee fighters were assaulted by Fusion Beams that they couldn't just shrug off. The Elven army was pushed back, and so could not intervene as 00B led the cyborgs and their allies toward the remaining Archons.

Amulius charged up an arrow with his Heroic Piercing skill and let it loose, cracking one of the Archon's barriers. The Archon noticed and launched a blast of fire toward the hero, only for Cominia to block with a Fire Barrier of her own while Aulus laid down a Recovery ward to boost them all. The Archon scowled and turned his attention to the group.

One of the remaining Archons turned to assault the rest of them while the other two focused on the airships. A Sun Beam shot toward the incoming cyborgs, but 00Sylvan and 00SO were ready, the cyborg dryad and Sacred

Otterkin replicating Seero and Ateia's defense technique. Holy-empowered cyber trees grew in front and absorbed the Sun Beams before firing back with the improvised rail guns 00Sylvan had weaved into their branches.

Estrith and Agedia shot past the Archon as she defended herself from the rail guns, aiming toward one of the remaining two. Their target noticed and launched a wave of fire with a swing of his hand. Estrith boosted in front of Agedia and formed a Water Barrier, which doused some of the flames, and then Estrith tanked the rest.

She may not have had Uscfrea's infamous magic resistance, but her high-level Dobhar fur was still quite tough. She then boosted away even as her fire suppression systems doused the flames on her body, clearing the way for Agedia, whose lance pierced through the Archon's barrier, forcing him to beat a hasty retreat to avoid being impaled.

Within the lead dungeon airship, Snuan watched as the number of Archons assaulting their barriers dropped. At this point, only a single Archon was still flinging spells their way. A single ship could now block the barrage.

And she had three. Snuan grinned.

"Fire-shoot at will, yes-yes!"

The verbal command was just force of habit, as Snuan's cybernetic components were linked to the ships in question. Her mana carried her command as per her Golem Commander skills, providing both instructions to the golem cores powering various systems in the ships, and using the additional mana to enhance the cores' capabilities. The systems leaped to execute her will.

The two flanking airships switched to the offense, and Prismatic Bombardments opened fire on the remaining Archon, who was forced to focus on barriers of his own.

And so, the battle raged both above and below.

42

Risk of Rain

"I assure you that the NSLICE units' cybersecurity measures are beyond state of the art. There is no artificial intelligence program in all the world that surpasses what we have achieved here. Besides, the NSLICE units are nothing less than living machines! There is no organic hacker nor static program that could threaten them."

—Dr. Ottosen, shortly before NSLICE-00P was hacked and reprogrammed.

The Herald of Rain exhaled the breath she was holding as she watched the fight develop. The last time she had seen NSLICE-00P, the hero dungeon master had displayed power roughly equivalent to an Archon, so the Herald had hoped the High Archon would be a match for her.

Yet, NSLICE-00P's growth and her ability to defy their expectations had filled the Herald with anxiety, and she couldn't help but fear that the cyborg would just wipe out Vommik with ease. It was a great relief that Vommik was holding his own, at least at present.

And likewise, his forces had engaged all of NSLICE-00P's and were holding them down, which left the Herald of Rain to her own devices. It wasn't the best-case scenario, but it also wasn't the worst. Her allies were intact and buying her time and space to execute her own plans.

She frowned and rubbed at her sore throat before shaking her head. She tried not to think about NSLICE-00P stripping away the spells granted by the Blessing of Deluge—*within* that very Realm. While that defeat was *frightening*, it had also been an attack of opportunity, since she hadn't expected NSLICE-00P to waltz right into a Realm of Mana. It did not impact the Herald of Rain's original plan to deal with her foe.

The Herald of the New Dawn had taught her much about NSLICE-00P's origins. He'd described a fantastic and deeply horrifying world; one with barely a drop of mana within it. He talked of constructs of metal and lightning and fire, of a society that processed the world around them and bent it to their will despite being limited to their physical bodies alone.

Honestly, the Herald of Rain didn't understand half of it. She didn't *want* to understand it. She was one who had devoted her very life to uncovering the mysteries of magic and unlocking the infinite potential it held. A world without magic was not one she wished to ever see.

But what she did understand was that NSLICE-00P had come from such a world, and such things explained the nature of her existence. And more importantly, that nature contained vulnerability, the one chink in the hero dungeon's armor.

She nodded at one of her companions, trying not to wince at the sound of her hoarse voice. "Do it."

The Herald of Storms nodded and began to chant his spell. The others, including the Herald of Rain, began to chant as well, offering up their mana with basic Mana Transfers.

Normally, this would not be enough for a ritual cast, but the Heralds were no normal mages. They were each blessed by one of the most destructive and extreme Realms of Mana; Realms that did not permit any other attribute to exist in their presence. Like corrupted dungeons, their mana was twisted to match the attribute of their chosen Realm, suffering no other.

So, if anyone transferred mana to them, their blessing would take and twist this mana into its Realm's attribute. The Herald in question could then utilize it as their own.

Now filled with an incredible amount of mana, the Herald of Storms pulled out a special mana core, designed and enchanted by the Herald of the New Dawn himself. He cast his spell with this core as his focus, channeling his mana through it and up into the sky. A small storm cloud gathered before unleashing a mighty bolt of Lightning.

The bolt struck the nearest drone . . . and did no apparent damage to it. But the Herald of Rain grinned.

The Herald of the New Dawn had come up with an attack that would turn NSLICE-00P's strength against her. The Herald of Rain didn't really understand this "virus" concept, only that it was vaguely similar to a disease for a being like NSLICE-00P. A similarity her leader had utilized to design a mana-transmittable attack functioning on the same principles as the "secret" weapon High King Xavlaeron thought he had hidden from them.

As such, the attack wouldn't even need to strike a target directly. Contact with the target's mana, such as via a defensive barrier, would suffice to transfer the virus. And best of all, they didn't need to target NSLICE-00P herself.

NSLICE-00P was apparently directly connected to each and every one of these drones, or anyone who shared her armor, which was apparently grafted directly onto her body. Once the virus had infected even a single target among NSLICE-00P's servants, it could spread across *all* of them. Even to the hero dungeon herself.

And they had just gotten a direct hit on one of her drones. All the Herald of Rain now had to do was wait, and soon, the entire enemy force would be defeated.

So, she waited.

And she waited . . .

And continued waiting . . .

00B-Beta's code flashed, and it felt weird. It shifted its attention over to the unit in question and found an intruder. Malignant code, carried via foul mana, had infected the unit. 00B-Beta immediately moved to terminate it.

The virus was not merely a program, and not merely a spell. It was a self-replicating construct of mana and code, capable of interacting with both and absorbing either into itself. It was not sentient yet, but it was autonomous and growing with every moment.

It . . . was quite like 00B-Beta, in fact. Which meant it was very much like a cyber elemental. And if an elemental came into direct contact with another elemental of the same attribute, then the more powerful absorbed the weaker. And the virus wasn't even sentient enough to realize it was under attack.

The two constructs of mana code came into contact. 00B-Beta drew upon the Great Mother's Holy mana protocols and purged the foul energy from the infected unit's systems. Now clear of mana, the malignant code was defenseless as 00B-Beta assimilated it into itself.

00B-Beta looked it over; the code presented a novel method of cyberattack without an exact match in existing CELIU protocols, and was worth further investigation, especially given its interaction with non-Lightning-attribute mana. 00B-Beta flooded the code with Holy-mana . . . then sent a copy back from whence it came.

The Herald of Rain furrowed her brow. According to the Herald of the New Dawn, the virus should have taken mere seconds to apply its effect. Even accounting for additional time to spread from unit to unit and overcome any countermeasures, they should have seen *some* change by now.

Then, finally, a change occurred. But not the one the Heralds expected.

Glowing golden-and-silver lines shot up the Lightning Bolt and into the cloud above, following the stream of mana into the core. The Lightning from the Herald of Storms began to spin around inside the orb, intensifying and twisting about. A second later, the core exploded, throwing the Heralds back.

The Herald of Rain grunted as she was thrust back into the lake she had created earlier. Once she opened her eyes back up, she gasped.

The Herald of Storms, being in physical contact with the core, had not survived.

She gritted her teeth. Once again, NSLICE-00P had defied her expectations. Even the Herald of the New Dawn had been outmaneuvered despite conducting a Divination on their foe. The Herald of Rain wanted to scream.

But she took a deep breath, her reapplied Blessing of Deluge allowing her to breathe the water as easily as air. The Herald of the New Dawn had warned them that this method was not guaranteed to succeed, though he had not expected it to literally blow up in their faces. The Herald of Rain *did* have a backup plan. They had learned in Corvanus that there was no such thing as too many contingency plans when dealing with NSLICE-00P.

So, she moved on to their next scheme. Even a High Archon of the Sun Elves was failing to defeat NSLICE-00P as a mage. Even the Herald of the New Dawn's creation had failed to defeat her as a machine. So, this time, the Herald of Rain would target NSLICE-00P as a person.

She closed her eyes and stirred up her mana. The water around her formed into piercing jets and grinding spheres and began to work on the magic circle at the bottom of the lake. The original circle was ground away by the spheres, then the jets carved new lines into the stone. Soon, her new spell circle was ready.

Opening her eyes, now glowing with dark blue light, she filled the magic circle with power.

The ground began to rumble all across the battlefield. A few moments later, the sand began to explode as plumes of water shot into the sky from deep below. The Herald of Rain then activated her spell, letting her presence flow through the water while she gave up her body to the Deluge.

The mana from her blessing took hold of her physical flesh and joined it with the unstoppable tide, moving past stone and space alike until it caught up with her presence, and she rejoined the Material Plane once again.

She reformed in one of the plumes of water; one that had shot up right behind a certain half-Wulver boy. The Herald of Rain grinned as she reached for the one named Taog.

"Got you."

43

Terminate the Rain!

"In hindsight, orphaning all those children was probably a mistake."
—Empress Caecina Numeria of the East, on the fate of her counterpart Emperor Cnaeus the Bloody.

Taog sighed as he watched the ongoing battle. This was perhaps the worst situation for his particular set of skills. Sun-attribute spells flying around on a bright desert day with nary a tree in sight created a suboptimal environment for Dark mana. At best, he could try to interact with people's shadows; otherwise, it was his mana versus a Sun Elf's with a disadvantageous matchup.

Holy mana wasn't as strong against normal people as it was against monsters. The Aesdes did not take sides—besides some of the myths surrounding Velus, that is, but every culture had their own legends regarding their origins. Though, given that Ateia was descended from Mighty Victoria, the wildest legends about Velus were apparently true?

Taog pushed that thought away before he got distracted. In any case, Taog *did* have a Hero skill or two to give him an edge over a normal person, but that was not enough to navigate a disadvantageous battlefield involving *Archons.* Even with his Seero powers, he did not feel confident taking one of them on alone, particularly not here.

Which meant Taog was on standby, watching Seero's drones take on the Sun Elf soldiers. He was confident he could handle one or maybe a few of those, so he stood in the back. Should they manage to break through the drones, he would reinforce the line; so far, they had not, so there was no reason to risk cyborg units in that fight just yet. As a result, Taog was just sitting around waiting while everyone else was fighting for their lives.

He was starting to understand why Ateia didn't like waiting at the Primary Home Base.

But then, something changed. Taog wrapped himself in his Dark Shroud, hoisting his blades as huge plumes of water began to burst from the ground all across the battlefield. Taog heard a voice from behind him.

"Got you."

And . . . he smirked.

"No, I got you."

The Dark Shroud shot behind him, forming into a hand. The Holy-infused Dark mana slammed into the Herald of Rain and pushed her out of the column of water, bouncing her on the sand a couple of times.

Taog grinned as he turned around, his robotic eye flickering. He wasn't the best at Divination, but he *was* a hero capable of using Holy mana, so it was possible. And Seero had recorded in *exacting* detail every bit of data she had on the Herald of Rain, particularly after the Herald had tried to spy on them recently. Taog—and all of the CELIU units—had been tracking the Herald from the very start of this fight.

Not to mention, he had seen that trick once before. He was never going to let it work ever again.

"Hello, Miss Sidonia, long time no see."

The Herald of Rain's eyes widened as she picked herself off the ground. "Holy mana? You—You're a hero?!"

Taog bared his teeth as he smiled and spun his blades. "You've missed a lot. I'm not the same helpless kid as back then."

The Herald of Rain stared at him for a moment before scoffing. The sand beneath her feet started to grow damp as her eyes began to glow. "Perhaps. But I wield powers beyond your comprehension. You still cannot stand against me."

Taog leapt forward, his repulsors propelling him forward. "We'll see about that!"

The Herald of Rain's eyes widened slightly, but she responded regardless. Another plume of water burst from the ground right in front of Taog, forcing him to pull up. The plume arched, pouring the stream of water down toward Taog. Boosting to the side while swinging his blade toward the torrent of water still streaming up, Holy and Dark mana shot from his blade, cutting off the flow as it tore through the mana of Deluge.

The Herald of Rain was nowhere to be seen as the water fell, but Taog's robotic eye spun around before zooming in. He could track her presence as she moved through the water underground. Taog grinned, then dove into the hole left by the water.

He traveled deep into the ground, eventually arriving at a large cavern with a huge underground lake. He heard the Herald of Rain start to laugh.

"You followed me down here? Oh my, you're dumber than I thought, Taog."

The lake began to bubble violently as several columns of water shot into the air, streaming toward Taog. But Taog just grinned, extending the Dark Shroud all around him. In the pitch-black underground cavern, there was plenty of darkness.

He shifted out of the way with a Dark Dash, melding into the shadows, as the water columns smashed against the roof, spraying the entire cavern in drops of water. The drops began to accelerate as they fell, filling the air with rain. Some of it landed on Taog, then quickly coalesced into a bubble of water.

"Did you really think you could escape from me here, in the midst of my element? Watching the terrain is battlemage rule number one, *boy*."

Taog grimaced. "This is a lot harder than I thought. Seero makes it look so easy."

The Herald of Rain grinned to herself. "The lesson every rookie learns on their first fight. Unfortunately, this is also your last."

Taog turned his head . . . and looked *right* at the Herald of Rain hiding in the water below. He was more than a little satisfied as his cybernetic components logged her heart rate increase.

"Excuse me, but I wasn't talking to you."

And then, Taog executed the experimental protocol he was trying to piece together. Holy-infused Dark mana spread all across the edges of the cavern and down into the water, coating the walls, floors, and roof. What little light trickled in from the hole in the roof cut off, leaving the cavern completely dark.

He grinned as he heard the Herald of Rain gasp. Seero had visited the Realm of Eternal Night more than once at this point, recording its mana in great detail. And while the Realm of Eternal Night's mana was unique, it was ultimately a form of Dark mana—one that took the obscuring aspect of darkness to its ultimate extreme. So regular Dark mana also contained that aspect, though to a far lesser degree.

Ever since becoming a hero, Taog had studied Seero's recordings. And he had practiced modifying his own mana into a similar form. Now, he finally had it down well enough to use it in combat.

The Herald of Rain's eyes widened as her perception of everything beyond the cavern cut off. She couldn't even feel the water flowing in from underground rivers just beyond the cavern walls. Taog's Shroud was not a perfect recreation, and indeed it couldn't be—against a regular person, that is. But neither he nor the Herald of Rain were normal, for he was a Hero blessed by the Aesdes, and she was a Herald empowered by the Domides.

Taog's barrier included Holy mana on top of Dark. Holy mana naturally opposed intrusions from the Realms of Mana, particularly the destructive Realms that tried to destroy it in turn. As a result, the Holy mana in Taog's Shroud automatically cut off the Herald of Rain's Deluge mana, adding to the obscuring effect. Like the Realm of Eternal Night once attempted to smother Seero, now Holy-infused Dark Mana isolated the Herald of Rain.

The Herald of Rain furrowed her brow. "Clever, but it changes nothing."

Water began to stream from the lake below, growing the bubble around Taog. The water in the bubble began to swirl around, spinning Taog around as his repulsors tried to fight against the tide. The Herald of Rain scoffed at him.

"All I need to do is incapacitate you, which will happen regardless. Trapping me here does nothing if you're too weak to finish the job. Hero or not, you can't defeat me, *boy*."

Taog chuckled. "Oh, I know. But she can."

Just then, a light burst through the roof, passing through the shroud with ease. Wings made of golden-and-silver light illuminated the cavern while metal armor glimmered in shifting patterns as light reflected between it and the water below. A robotic eye glowed bright red.

Ateia grinned and cracked her knuckles. "Hello, Miss Herald. I've been hoping to see you again."

The Herald of Rain turned pale. She quickly directed all of her efforts against the newcomer, turning the water in the cavern toward Ateia. Mighty streams curled through the air and joined into one as they surged toward her.

Ateia backhanded the stream. Holy mana surged through it, then all the water in the air dropped back into the lake. The Herald of Rain formed another magic circle, but the water below no longer responded to her command. One of the authorized masters of the world had reasserted control over it, and now no intruder would usurp her. The Herald of Rain gasped.

"S-So it's true . . . You have joined the Aesdes . . ."

Ateia grinned and chuckled. "All thanks to you and your cult's little ritual. So, I figure I should pay you back for it. As Seero would say . . . Recitation: Engaging critical priority termination protocols. This unit will now terminate all confirmed hostiles with extreme prejudice."

The Herald of Rain formed another magic circle, creating new water from her own mana and surrounding herself. She tried to escape from the Material Plane once more, but her magic circle shattered, and her water dispersed into the lake around her.

The Dark Shroud cut her off from any water beyond the cavern, while Ateia reinforced the boundary of the Material Plane along her retreat path. She could not escape that way either. She was well and truly trapped.

The Herald of Rain barely had time to process the spell's failure before Ateia dove into the water and grabbed her by the neck. She was no longer smiling.

"You killed my mother. You forced my father to leave us. You almost killed me. You tried to kill Taog, Seero, Estrith, and Agedia. You and your stupid cult tried to destroy everything and everyone I've ever cared about. You tried to destroy the Empire, the entire world. Mighty Victoria and the Aesdes stand against you. The world itself stands against you."

She stirred up her mana. The Herald of Rain's eyes widened.

"This is for everything you've done and tried to do."

Holy mana surged from Ateia into the Herald of Rain. She poured all that she could into the woman—then connected to the streams of Holy mana flowing through the world to gather more. The cavern filled with golden-and-silver light.

The Herald of Rain screamed as the Holy mana reacted with the Deluge within her. Her own mana was burned right out of her body. This, of course, left her charred and empty, completely helpless as quantities of mana no normal person could handle flooded her veins.

Had she been a normal person, the Holy mana may have stopped at this point to avoid destroying its own inhabitant. But the Herald of Rain had given herself completely to the Realms of Mana. She had been molded and shaped by them. She had melded her body into Deluge countless times.

She was no longer a true resident of the Material Plane. And so, the Holy Mana flooded in, attempting to reclaim what was familiar and purge what was not. The Herald of Rain opened her mouth to scream as her body flickered and faded away, overloaded by the sheer quantity of energy in her body.

And so passed the Herald of Rain, terminated by the two kids from Turannia.

44

Terminate the Archons!

"We slaughtered you in droves. We slew a thousand—nay, ten thousand humans for every single Archon you claimed."

"I'll take that deal. Will you?"

—High Archon Ekless Terdriseth and Maior Generalis Gallus Annius Tremerus, during ceasefire negotiations.

White-hot flames collided with a barrier of sunlight. Archon Madanri retaliated with a bolt of lightning, which was stopped by a Fire Wall from Nolnyth.

Fights between Sun Elf Archons tended to be long, frustrating affairs. The Sun Elves happened to have resistances to the same attributes they possessed innate aptitude for, and so, when two masters went against one another, their most powerful weapons tended to be ineffective.

They were largely forced to rely on whatever secondary attributes they happened to train, or on physical combat. And secondary attributes tended to fail simply because the other Archon could defend using their primary attribute, so it became a situation where neither side could break the other's defense. Thus why most Sun Elves pursued a spellblade style of combat, relying on enchanted weaponry to deal real damage to one another.

But an Archon could use mobility and defense spells to evade simple physical blows if they decided not to attempt their own strikes. An Archon could, therefore, always force a fight with another Archon into a stalemate if they so desired, while they could only make meaningful progress by accepting risks in turn. It was for this reason that Archons tended to compete in politics and proxy conflicts rather than direct duels.

And yet, despite being the aggressor, Nolnyth refused to close with her opponent. She refused to even use secondary attributes, relying solely on Fire.

Madanri would admit that Nolnyth *was* one of the more talented in that particular attribute . . . but that talent would not be enough to overcome his innate Fire resistance. He frowned.

"What are you even doing, traitor? You *know* you can't kill me with Fire. Or has your brain rotted to such a degree that you forgot something so basic? Though, that seems likely, given you have decided to bet your life on *humans*."

Nolnyth scoffed as she continued to cast her spells, the flames turning the sand below into glass as they bounced off Madanri's barriers. Suddenly, her flames died down. Madanri was about to counterattack once again when the ground began to glow, and his eyes widened.

The glass was not random. Nolnyth had directed her flames to form a magic circle in the sand, which was now complete. She activated the spell, and a huge firestorm of white flames swirled around Madanri. At first, he shook his head . . . until his skin started burning. He gasped, quickly trying to form a barrier as Nolnyth sneered at him.

"For years you hid, plotting upon your throne even as your land fell into ruin. For years, you hung upon the words of the High Archon, even as he fell into madness. I did not. I spent those years in the field, crushing every threat to my domain with my own hands. I continued to grow, even as you languished."

Madanri formed a Barrier, but Nolnyth's flames spread above him. She formed a Sun Barrier of her own, which absorbed the sun's rays and denied them to Madanri. Her flames then broke through as he tried using his other attributes, but Nolnyth had always had a singular focus while Madanri had tried to outmaneuver her with his greater versatility. It had only worked in the past because of his resistance to her flames.

Flames that now appeared to bypass such resistance . . . with golden-and-silver mana empowering them.

"I acquired more and more power, some even from the Aesdes themselves. You relied on a foolish plan that was not even your own and did nothing to advance yourself in the meantime. The difference between us is clear."

Madanri screamed as he burst into flames . . . Flames empowered by the Heroic Challenger skill, which made them effective against any and all targets.

Nolnyth exhaled her breath as her long-time rival burnt to ash.

The Sun Elves had a *complicated* relationship with the Aesdes and the Realms of Mana, more still for Nolnyth, given her fealty to High Archon Vommik. As such, Nolnyth had been hiding the rewards of her first corrupted dungeon assault; one that had taken place before she had even requested assistance from the Empire. Rewards that prevented her from following the High Archon's plans, even had she thought them anything but imbecilic.

After all, heroes and Cults of Mana don't mix.

* * *

01R continued to lay into his opponent's barrier with his spear. The Archon replied back with spells of her own, but his suit's Spatial Angling prevented damage to even the suit itself, much less the rat within.

The Archon tried to escape with Dash spells, but 01R's sensors could track her trajectory, and his own speed, repulsors, and Dash skill managed to keep up. The Archon was forced into pure defense, holding a barrier and hoping 01R would run out of mana before she did.

But 01R was wearing a suit powered by a dungeon core. And engaging a dungeon core in a war of attrition was a poor choice.

The barrier began to crack.

Snuan's airships kept the Archon pinned on the defense with a constant barrage of Prismatic Bombardment beams. The Archon was now focusing everything on holding his barriers up and could no longer launch any counterattacks at all.

As such, Snuan had her main ship cease its attack, redirecting the core's mana to begin charging some powerful capacitors, gathering a greater store of mana. She then ordered that all power be directed toward the main gun.

The front armor of the dungeon airship opened up, revealing a spinal-mounted rail gun; a weapon the dungeon airships carried but preferred not to use, as it required temporarily disabling the Spatial Angling that gave them their durability. But that wasn't a problem against an opponent who couldn't fire back.

The Archon noticed something occurring and attempted to flee, but the other airships' barrages forced him to keep up his barriers, and so prevented him from using any mobility spells. It was, therefore, not particularly difficult for Snuan's ship to keep a lock on him.

Snuan smirked as she spoke.

"Fire-destroy, yes-yes!"

The airship executed the order . . . and the Archon. His barrier, weakened by the beams continuously assaulting it, could not resist a close-range, max-power rail gun shot.

High Archon Vommik grimaced as he caught a glance of the situation. Three of his Archons had fallen already. The other four were locked in stalemates against their opponents and would follow soon now that the queen of the Dobhar's forces could double up on them. His personal guard was still grinding their way through the golem army and unable to intervene.

The Heralds of the New Dawn had attempted their plans, and clearly failed.

The High Archon caught a glimpse of an explosion among the ritual they had prepared. The Herald of Rain had vanished chasing after one of the queen of the Dobhar's companions . . . only for the powerful and clearly not human girl to chase after them. After what Vommik had seen that girl do, he was not at all optimistic about the Herald of Rain's chances. She would either perish or cowardly abandon the field, which were both the same as far as this battle was concerned.

Which meant it now fell upon the High Archon to win this fight. Alone.

And he would have to do so now, before the Herald of Rain failed.

For the briefest of moments, the terrifying girl would not be supporting the queen of the Dobhar. If he had any chance of defeating either, it was now, while they were separated.

So, he tried one further trick. The Aesdes did not include many mind-afflicting spells in their boons, limiting such things to illusions and emotional fluctuations. But the Sun Elves knew that magic was far older and deeper than the Aesdes would have them believe, predating the boons themselves, and their explorations into the mysteries of the arcane had never ceased. There were ways to access the mind, to influence it, or even to dominate it completely.

High Archon Vommik began to cast an ancient spell not recorded in any school of magic, passed down from his own ancestors long ago.

Seero logged the termination of the Herald of Rain, marking one of their main objectives for this battle complete. She had had serious concerns that the Heralds of the New Dawn would either surprise them or manage to escape, and had devoted processing power and mana as a reserve to respond to those contingencies.

But now, the Herald of Rain had made her play, and Ateia and Taog had terminated her with the protocols they and Seero had brainstormed to prevent her escape. An additional Herald had perished when 00B-Beta had warded off a cyberattack, and the remaining Heralds appeared scattered and disorganized.

As such, Seero could now focus all of her attention and firepower on the foe ahead of her.

In that moment, High Archon Vommik cast a new spell; one that did not resemble anything Seero had encountered in Aelea. It more closely resembled spells cast by Non-Standards back on Earth; those designated as witches.

And then, suddenly, mana assaulted her mind.

"Intrusion detected within organic components. Engaging organic intrusion termination protocols."

So Seero activated the emotional controls, then put her organic half on standby-sentry mode. She activated the Equalizer, disrupting the mana streaming toward her mind before reactivating her organic half, who gave approval to leave the emotional controls enabled to mitigate any further intrusion attempts.

High Archon Vommik pursed his lips as the queen of the Dobhar broke his spell.

From what he could tell, she had simply knocked herself unconscious while somehow still keeping all of her spells active. She had subsequently activated that special weapon the Herald of Rain had warned him about, destroying the mana powering his spell while *still* unconscious, before immediately waking herself back up.

The Herald of Rain had told him she was something like a half human, half golem, but it was another thing to see her lose and regain consciousness on command.

In any case, his spell had failed, and the queen of the Dobhar . . . had apparently been *holding back*.

More strategic spell circles formed in the air. High Archon Vommik had but one choice remaining.

45

Become Death, the Destroyer of Worlds

"I'm working on it! The Equalizer's output is ultimately limited by NSLICE-OOP's power generation, and for thrice-damned politics, we can't use anything nuclear!

"So, unless you have a better idea on how to handle the man who can drop a sun on our heads with the snap of his fingers, you'll have to wait for me to figure out how to match nuclear reactors with alternative, man-portable power sources!

"Scientific breakthroughs that challenge all preceding conventional thought take time! I am a scientific genius, not a miracle worker!"

—Dr. Ottosen, on the NSLICE program's performance against the Atomic Cult.

High Archon Vommik threw up another barrier, the strongest he could make midbattle, then pulled out a powerful mana core, glowing bright even behind his Sun Barrier. He formed a magic circle around it out of his own mana, not needing a carved ritual formation to pull it off. The core melted into the formation, and mana—both from the core and the surroundings—began to swirl and condense around the formation.

Small bolts of lightning began to arc from it, the sand below began to levitate into the air, and sparks of light flashed all around. The High Archon now flew at the center of an artificial mana storm.

The ritual to create a dungeon on demand had begun. But High Archon Vommik was no mere criminal contact with more ambition than sense, playing with forces beyond their comprehension. No, he was one of the oldest, most experienced mages who still drew breath, a member of the Council of the Archons, one of the rulers of the Empire of the Sun, and a guardian of ancient knowledge passed down from a time when the Aesdes still walked the surface of Aelea.

His power, his knowledge, and his resources could not be compared to the other minor cultists. The others deferred to the Herald of the New Dawn as a master or a teacher. Vommik spoke to him as an equal.

His mana invaded the whirling storm and took hold of it, even as he felt the boundary of the Material Plane begin to shift. A massive, head-splittingly complex magic circle formed, one designed to draw power from the Realms of Mana. Vommik thus redirected the storm and the resulting break in the boundary of the Material Plane, focusing on a Realm of his choosing.

When the dungeon core appeared, it was already bound to him, appearing grafted into his chest. Vommik ripped open the boundary of the Material Plane even as the dungeon formed, causing it to appear fully corrupted, yet completely under his command. And since it had been filled to the brim with his mana, its own integrated with him. Rather than summoning monsters or traps, the High Archon would utilize the dungeon's mana stream directly.

And as for the attribute?

The Sun Elves of the Empire of the Sun relied on their own power. They bowed to no other and let none stand in the way of their ambitions. They rejected the counsel of the Aesdes and the authority of the Celestial throne, instead carving out their own domain where they could rule. So why, then, did the Sun Elves not fall into corruption? Why didn't they draw power from the Realms of Mana more directly?

The answer was found in their name. The Sun Elves had developed their innate attributes to form the Sun-attribute school of mana, a mighty weapon powered by the sun itself, ubiquitous as the day, inevitable as the dawn. A complex attribute comprised of many others.

And yet, no Realm of Sun existed that any of them could find. It could not, for its various aspects were claimed by others. Its heat was felt in the Realm of Fire, and its brightness in the Realm of Light. Not even the Sun Elves understood what made the sun distinct from Fire, Light, and Lightning, and so could not find a Realm that reflected its true nature.

And that was a problem. The Realms of Mana were pure and focused. They could display any power related to their attribute . . . but could not manifest anything beyond that. The mana from a given Realm could only ever be one attribute. For people and dungeons who remained at a safe distance, this was not a problem, for they could swap between them or even mix them together.

But those who wanted to draw greater power from the Realms, those blessed by the Domides like the Heralds, were forced to commit. Their ability to utilize the other attributes fell in accordance with the amount of power they gained, eventually to the point where the Realm's mana would begin eating away at their physical nature as well.

The Sun Elves scoffed at such things. The power they could gain from a Realm would cut them off from the multiattributed Sun Magic. And to be put on a timer, to have a Realm of Mana slowly eating away at their attributes and bodies, was unacceptable to the long-lived Elves. The Sun Elves were ruled by no one, Domides or Aesdes included, and ultimately, there was no Realm that suited them enough to bow.

Until now.

High Archon Vommik held out his palm. A miniature sun appeared in his hand, far brighter than the mana approximations he had created earlier. Sickly green light colored his mana as it flowed around his body. He could feel Fire, Light, and Lightning as before, but also small amounts of Gravity pulling at him. He could feel other forces, small bits of power bombarding him all over.

Before his invasion began, the Herald of the New Dawn had shared new, secret knowledge with Vommik, gleaned from his Divinations of the queen of the Dobhar: The true nature of the sun itself, what made it different from a mere campfire, and the terrible, mighty weapons that could be built with such a power; ones that could destroy an entire world if unleashed.

And in learning this more comprehensive picture, Vommik had found a Realm that represented destruction by the sun. A corrupting Realm fully compatible with Sun Elf magic.

And so, Vommik bound his dungeon to the nascent Realm of Atomic Destruction.

He scowled as he felt the Realm's mana flood into his body. Even with a suitable Realm, it was humiliating for the High Archon to rely on anyone or anything else. But the power he received did not disappoint, and victory could wipe away dishonor. He comforted himself with the irony of the situation. The queen of the Dobhar would now be defeated by powers her own existence had apparently made possible.

Vommik gathered the mana from his new core and unleashed a Beam spell, previously a Sun Beam, but now, far greater—and more destructive.

Seero's robotic eye flickered as she watched the new spell from High Archon Vommik approach. "Warning: Nuclear radiation detected. All units engage hazardous environment protocols. Engaging Atomic Cult termination protocols."

Well, as it turned out, Seero had encountered foes commanding nuclear powers before.

The cybernetic components of all the CELIU units on the field fully enclosed their organic parts, shielding them from harm. 01R, having defeated his opponent, traded places with Lilussees, who began putting up barriers to protect the non-CELIU allies on the field. Seero herself formed a large Prismatic Dome spell and condensed it into a small area just in front of her, using Metal Magic and her Item Foundry to build a wall of lead for good measure.

It turned out, magic Barriers could guard against radiation—or at least magically generated radiation—as well as anything else, so long as they have enough mana and density to handle the energy colliding into them. Which Seero did, the High Archon's sudden power-up notwithstanding. Plus, she utilized Gravity Barriers and Spatial Angling to redirect some of the stream of energy, so she didn't need to resist the entire attack outright, in any case.

Seero noted her own boost in capabilities. This situation demonstrated that she could now terminate the entire Atomic Cult on her own, were she to somehow encounter them. That scenario was extremely unlikely, however, so she archived that particular simulation.

She instead calculated how to address this situation. Atomic Cult termination protocols mostly recommended preemptive strikes by beyond-visual-range weapons. Even the Equalizer had not been recommended, as certain Atomic Cult members could surpass the Equalizer's output. But since she was already engaged with the High Archon and had friendlies in the area, she could not rely on those recommendations.

She also detected a corrupted dungeon within the High Archon. She considered using corrupted dungeon termination protocols, but in this case, predicted them as too risky. She would have to leave the battlefield for an indeterminate amount of time, during which the High Archon would be free to assault her friendlies.

Likewise, if she predicted the Realm of Mana in question based on the High Archon's observed attributes compared to previously encountered Realms, she might end up in the middle of a magical nuclear reactor when attempting to terminate the High Archon's connection.

Her own mana reserves, Spatial and Gravity defenses, and the effect of the Equalizer-Holy mana combo on a Realm of Mana meant that said scenario was surprisingly not predicted as instant termination, but there was a chance she could be overwhelmed by the sheer amount of energy involved.

On the flip side, High Archon Vommik had just created this dungeon and still seemed to be learning his new capabilities. He was merely throwing around beams of radiation and nuclear variations of his previous spells. He had not yet explored the full destructive potential of nuclear reactions.

Seero calculated that at present, the most efficient course of action would be to terminate him directly.

And so, her robotic eye flickered as she began to adjust the Atomic Cult termination protocols in light of her own capabilities.

46

Terminate the Sun!

"We have bathed the land in the Sacred Light and gathered together the full force of the faithful. All our people have been blessed and ascended to a new form of humanity. And yet still we cannot defeat those who cling foolishly to the past?! Still, we cannot overcome their soulless, metal machines?!"

—The leader of the Atomic Cult, on the cult's performance against the NSLICE program.

High Archon Vommik gritted his teeth.

He'd unlocked the power of Atomic Destruction, a new Realm of Mana only he had access to. He'd sacrificed his own pride and independence tying himself to said Realm, binding himself to a dungeon core.

And yet . . . he *still* could not defeat the queen of the Dobhar. He had not even broken through her defenses! Yes, the Realm of Atomic Destruction empowered his spells, increasing their destructive potential. That metal tree the queen of the Dobhar had made with her terrifying friend could no longer absorb his attacks, and she had been forced to create new barriers. But just that. Those barriers continued to hold despite the boost in his power.

He felt as though he was missing something. Slightly more powerful beams did not equate to the devastation shown to him by the Herald of the New Dawn, but in this case, he would have to learn by doing. He did not have the time for cautious experimentation. Even as his new Beam spells faded, he grabbed the mana dissipating in the air, using it and the paths left by the magic circles to speed up the creation of new ones.

A multicolored barrage of beams struck his barrier. The queen of the Dobhar appeared to be cycling through different attributes, testing which would be most effective against him. He frowned as his barrier began to crack and devoted some of his mana to reinforcing it. Then, his own spell completed. The sky lit up as the Sunfall spell created a miniature sun, then sent it hurtling toward his enemy.

To his surprise, the queen of the Dobhar stopped her assault. She turned toward the attack, shifting her magic circles. A large metal plate began to appear in the sky, surrounded by regions of shifting, distorted air. Underneath the metal plate were several layered Barrier spells that fused together.

Then, his spell connected with the plate, and the world exploded.

A flash of light blinded even the High Archon as the attack connected. As his vision returned, he stared . . . and started to grin.

A mushroom-shaped cloud rose into the sky. The metal plate was gone completely, the fused barrier flickering as heat and shock waves battered against it.

The queen of the Dobhar herself was unharmed, but that was not why the High Archon grinned. He had found a spell that produced the devastation he sought. And more importantly, devastation that was a credible threat to the queen of the Dobhar.

She had not responded with mere barriers or evasion. No, from what the High Archon could see, she had used Spatial Magic to contain the attack. She'd given her defense her full attention, and yet still decided to move the attack further away rather than resist it directly. And she had done so via defenses that cost her far more mana than he had spent on the spell.

Which would be a problem for her, as High Archon Vommik had not spent the time idly.

Since she had ceased her assault on him, High Archon Vommik had turned all his attention to additional offense. Several more Sunfall spell circles were about to complete, and with his available mana growing larger and larger thanks to his corrupted dungeon core, he would not have to stop anytime soon.

Eventually, she would be overwhelmed. Even if she had a dungeon core of her own, as the Herald had told him, hers was a normal dungeon, with intentionally limited rates of growth and mana flow. If she did not defeat him now, he would overtake her in the long run. If he could keep her on the defensive . . . then he would win.

High Archon Vommik grinned. And then, he could rain this devastation upon all his enemies.

The world would bow at his feet or be destroyed by the wrath of the sun.

Seero's robotic eye flickered. The High Archon's latest spell had achieved critical mass for an atomic explosion. She had managed to contain it, but her defense had not been efficient, especially given that the High Archon was forming several more of those projectiles.

She would have to try something else, as she couldn't commit to a full Spatial containment of every projectile the High Archon threw at her. And while *she* could survive if she focused her defenses on herself, the friendlies below would not.

The Equalizer could work if it could target the magic circles in question, but they were behind a powerful barrier. Given the amount of energy opposing it, the Equalizer would not break through before the spells finished. Likewise, its output was insufficient to wipe out the magical nuclear bombs once they had formed.

At this point, the Equalizer was quickly losing relevance compared to her other capabilities. But she had no time to consider its long-term fate. Several more of the spells had already formed in the air.

She ordered Snuan, 01R, and Lilussees to prepare to evacuate the other friendlies with their dungeon cores. If her proposed countermeasure failed, Seero would not have time to contain several nuclear blasts with a reasonable success rate. She would not risk their lives on the probabilities involved.

Fortunately, the Archons and other Sun Elves were also dazed by the display of power and on the back foot due to the casualties they had taken, so they did not interfere with the friendlies' regrouping.

And then, Seero got to work. She formed several Prismatic Bombardment magic circles in the air, for she would have to target all of the projectiles simultaneously. She then formed Spatial Angling circles directly on the projectiles with Farcasting.

The Spatial Angling triggered first, twisting around to bypass the spell form and get inside the spell itself, making the suns grow ever so slightly dimmer. Then the Prismatic Bombardment circles fired, each devoted entirely to Gravity, their purple beams fusing together and firing thin, hyperdense beams into the center of each sun. They, again, traveled along the Spatial Angling in order to bypass the spell's exterior and arrive directly in its center.

The suns appeared to bubble and shift even as they fell. Just as Seero was about to order her friendlies to retreat, the suns began to fade, their fire sputtering out.

Seero's analysis of the situation had proven correct. The suns may have been magical in nature, but they operated relatively similarly to actual nuclear reactions. They were each a magical fusion reactor contained by their spell. And from what Seero had recorded of the first, the spell condensed at the point of impact, triggering the chain reaction that would lead to a nuclear explosion.

So Seero had used Spatial Angling to expand the space inside the spell, then used Gravity to push apart the reaction. Eventually, it was spread out too far for it to sustain itself and died out.

The now empty containment spells dissipated harmlessly on the ground. Seero had stopped the atomic explosion at a fraction of the mana cost and attention required to contain the first.

Which meant she now had enough free mana and attention to focus on her opponent once more.

High Archon Vommik gaped. The queen of the Dobhar . . . had pushed his spells apart? How was that even possible? Not only did he not understand the principle by which pushing apart a sun somehow destroyed it, he didn't understand how she had gotten inside his spell to begin with.

The mana of any given spell was resistant to interference by external mana, the one directly from a Realm like Atomic Destruction doubly so. If anything, it would have torn apart the intruding mana or else converted it into more of itself. At worst, the spell should have exploded, which in this case would have achieved the intended effect regardless.

That had not happened. His only theory was that she had used that Spatial Magic to slip inside the spell form without contacting it. But that would have required a level of precision, control, and senses that even the High Archons did not possess.

But he had no time to act surprised, for the queen of the Dobhar had turned her attention to him again, even as she wiped out every Sunfall spell he'd cast. She fired one of those spells toward his barrier, so he quickly reinforced it.

And his eyes widened as, again, his barrier was pushed apart. A hole opened within it without weakening the barrier at all. Despite the heat of atomic fire coursing through his veins, Vommik felt a chill run down his spine.

He tried to evade, casting a Sun Dash spell, but the corrupted sunlight he created somehow curved *around,* and he ended up at his original position. He began to sweat as he noticed Spatial and Gravity Barriers now surrounding his position.

Clearly, the queen of the Dobhar had determined a counter to his new attribute.

Vommik gritted his teeth and tried to cast a Spatial spell of his own, but the moment his mana finished the circuit, the spell shattered, failing to trigger. His eyes widened.

He was now bound with a corrupted dungeon, connected directly to its Realm of Mana. That mana could *not* be used to cast the spells of another attribute. If he had time, he perhaps could have modified those other spells to work within his attribute, but he could not cast them as they were. He was limited purely to his Sun-attribute spells until then.

The Sun-attribute spells that the queen of the Dobhar could now dismantle at will.

The metal tree that the queen of the Dobhar had formed earlier had been converted into some large metal tube, now surrounded with Lightning Barriers and filled to the brim with Holy mana. The tube lit up, and a projectile glowing with golden-and-silver light accelerated it.

And then, Vommik felt an impact before everything went dark.

* * *

Seero opened fire with her improvised rail gun, using Gravity and Spatial magic to push aside her foe's defenses. As such, the Holy-infused projectile struck the High Archon's torso immediately, along with the source of corrupted mana Seero had detected there.

Needless to say, the core—and most of the High Archon's body—shattered on contact.

Seero quickly prepared to respond to a Rift opening up to a Realm composed of nuclear reactions, but infusing the projectile with Holy mana had proven to be a highly efficient choice. The burst of Holy energy helped to counteract the corrupted mana released by the core's destruction.

Seero detected the corruption surging through the hole in the boundary and responded accordingly. She had Ateia focus the Holy mana from the Material Plane and direct it there, then took control of the Holy mana from the projectile and sent her own to expand it from the inside. Eventually, Seero and Ateia's mana linked together, and the wound in the boundary was healed before it fully broke open. No Rift formed in the Material Plane as a result.

And so, the first corrupted dungeon and demon lord of Atomic Destruction was terminated with zero casualties.

INTERLUDE

Ancient Allies

With Vommik's defeat, the other Sun Elves immediately turned and fled. The Heralds of the New Dawn moved to as well, but Seero, Ateia, and Taog coordinated to cut them off and terminate the remainder.

Seero let the Sun Elves retreat, however, having discussed the strategy ahead of time with Amulius and Nolnyth. Nolnyth had revealed that the Empire of the Sun as a whole was not involved with the Heralds of the New Dawn; it had largely been Vommik alone who was allied with them as far as she could tell. Two other High Archons had cooperated with his invasion, while the rest had refused to leave their territory undefended with the ongoing dungeon crisis.

Seero, therefore, did not feel it necessary to terminate the entire nation as a hostile faction. So, the most efficient course of action to end this war would be to allow word of Vommik's death to spread across the Empire of the Sun. His forces would disintegrate, while the High Archons supporting him would give up the attack.

As for the Heralds of the New Dawn . . . Divination worked posthumously. Ateia, therefore, identified some of their bases of operation within the Empire of the Sun. They were spread very thin at this point, however. Much of their resources had gone into setting up the corrupted dungeons, and most of the remaining Heralds had come here to deal with Seero.

The remaining assets were mostly logistical and administrative offices, the corrupted dungeons Seero hadn't gotten to yet, and any survivors from the North and South who had little combat capability. The Heralds of the New Dawn had been shattered as an effective force.

Seero and company thus moved on, cleaning up what remained of the corrupted dungeons and the Heralds. They no longer had any capability to strike back, and the dungeons couldn't do much since Seero was bypassing all of their defenses. In the end, nothing much happened to disrupt the group, and the remaining dungeons and cult holdouts were terminated promptly.

As predicted, High Archons Kurzal and Ilnune retreated the moment Vommik's death was made clear, splitting Vommik's remaining forces and integrating them into their own. Their aim had been the destruction of the Eastern Empire, and since that had failed, there was no benefit to them holding ravaged border fortifications while their own lands were under siege by the dungeons.

As such, they pulled out of Imperial lands entirely, letting the dwindling monster horde cover their retreat. Maior Generalis Maximia turned her attention to the dungeon situation in the meantime, waiting for Seero to finish off the corrupted ones before reclaiming the lost territory.

There was more to clean up, and the dungeon crisis continued, but the war in the east had largely been settled, and the Heralds of the New Dawn terminated.

Save for one, high-priority target, whom none of the Heralds had seen since before the dungeon crisis began.

Colleöne cut a diagonal line across the warlord ahead of her, who burst into a cloud of mana. Her reclaimed power reached sufficient concentration once more, and she held up her hand. Holy mana streamed from her into the Lord of Craft and Forge, imparting some of her knowledge and skill into him. The Aesdes adjusted his stance and the grip on his hammer to strike flesh instead of metal.

Shialnor's monsters had proved weaker than the enemy, seeing as they were not blessed by Colleöne's boons as well, so she had shifted focus at this point. She applied her traps where and how Velus directed her instead, disrupting the enemies' attacks and leaving them vulnerable. She sent the remainder of her mana to the other Aesdes as well, granting them greater power.

Slowly but surely, the Aesdes were pushing back. The Lord of Water and Oceans used his waves to push the monsters off the front, while the Lady of Plants and Growth corralled a group with brambles and trees so that the Lady of Fire and Heat could burn them all at once. The Lord of Craft and Forge swung his hammer down and across his feet, knocking a monster to his side where the Lady of Hearth and Home smashed it into the ground.

The fight had ceased to be a brawl and had now become a battle. The Aesdes were working together, each a part of the greater whole. They may not have known battle, but they knew each other from countless millennia of joint efforts, and they quickly put that familiarity to good use. Velus no longer needed to micromanage individuals and could focus on the battle as a whole.

The monsters, for their part, showed no signs of adapting. They rushed forward mindlessly, with no attempts to plan or work together. They were easily broken apart and ground down by the increasingly coordinated Aesdes.

And that caused Colleöne to frown. The lack of coordination and adaptation meant no one was actually commanding the monsters, simply throwing them into the fray. And that meant that whoever was responsible for this was not paying attention to the battle in the Blessed Land.

Likewise, what glances she could take at the rest of Aelea below revealed the situation was calming down there as well. Colleöne wanted to believe things were going well for them everywhere, but her knowledge of war warned her against it. For if the enemy was being pushed back on all fronts and yet not working to overturn the situation . . . then where were they? And what were they planning?

Fortunately, she'd soon have the opportunity to find out.

Shadows passed overhead as mighty roars pierced the sky. Torrents of Fire, Water, Lightning, Ice, Poison, Light, Dark, and every attribute imaginable rained from above, engulfing the monsters assaulting the Aesdes. Even Holy mana joined the barrage. The Aesdes heard the beating of mighty wings, and gusts of wind blew across the Blessed Land as a new force landed in front of them.

The dragons had arrived. Dragons of every shape and size filled the skies of the Blessed Land, unleashing their mighty breaths upon the monsters below. Fang and claw tore the monsters to shreds, while tails flattened them upon the ground. Mana twisted and shaped in the air at the dragons' commands, spells of all types raining upon the enemy. A large dragon with golden-and-silver scales which seemed to glow in the light of the sun landed on the ground before the Aesdes.

"Hmph. So this is the homeland that grandfather always wished to show me."

Colleöne stepped forward. "You . . . have come to our aid?"

The Ancient Dragon before her scoffed. "Hardly. I care little for you, who drove my grandfather out. But he would not wish to see his former home destroyed, so the dragons will do what the Aesdes apparently cannot."

With that, she took off and rejoined the fight. Colleöne began to smile.

Not every Aesdes had agreed with Anualë's order to return to the Blessed Land. There were those who had refused to leave the surface of Aelea, so Anualë had given them a choice. They chose to remain, giving up their authority as Aesdes and their homes in the Blessed Land in exchange, taking purely material forms and living their lives alongside the peoples they'd once guided.

These were the progenitors of the Ancient Dragons. And apparently, they had not forgotten their heritage. Now, their descendants had returned. Whatever they said their reason was, they had come in the Aesdes' most desperate hour.

The Ancient Dragons may have surrendered their authority, but not their power. Power that had been molded and shaped by living lives upon the surface, by struggling and striving alongside mortals and monsters. They may not have matched the Aesdes in stature and command of the world, but they exceeded them in the ways of violence and war.

And even though they were Aesdes no longer, they still had a stronger connection to the world than most other things. Holy mana naturally flowed through and empowered them, still obeying their commands to a limited extent, resulting in their reputation as the mightiest living things in Aelea. And now, they were turning all of their considerable power against the horde that barred the Aesdes' way.

And, of course, since they no longer lived as Aesdes, they were no longer dependent on the Holy mana of the world to destroy their foes.

Colleöne turned and made eye contact with Velus. They both grinned, then Velus pointed his blade ahead. "Let's go! Everyone, charge!"

The Aesdes and their cousins joined as one, and the monsters could not resist their combined might. Before long, the Aesdes arrived at the foot of Anualë's mountain, where the monsters spilled from a large cave entrance leading down into the heart of the Blessed Land.

The Ancient Dragon from before was wrapped and shrouded in light as she landed in front of the cave. The light died down to reveal the form of an Elvish woman with draconic features. She had golden hair, silver reptilian eyes, and two horns on top of her head. She wore shining silver plate armor, with a hole on the back for her scaly tail.

She took a deep breath and breathed out a torrent of Holy-infused flames into the cavern. When she stopped, nothing but ash stood in their way. She marched into the cave without waiting for the others.

Colleöne gripped her blade and turned to Shialnor. "Let's fix this."

Shialnor frowned and nodded, then the two ran after the dragon. Colleöne's eyes narrowed as she rushed down toward her and Shialnor's cores.

One way or another, this matter was about to come to a close. And so, if the enemy had any plans beyond this chaos, they would have to act now.

She had a feeling they would not go quietly.

47

The New Dawn

"The Aesdes . . . are not as infallible as you believe. Both the people of Aelea and we Aesdes ourselves would have been spared vast grief were that true."

—Colleöne, in a private conversation with Velus.

Colleöne, Shialnor, and the Ancient Dragon burst into the heart of the Blessed Land, where their two cores waited. The two Aesdes froze.

The room was filled to the brim with magic circles, most of which did not exist within either Colleöne's or Shialnor's systems. And in the center of it all, standing in between the two cores, was a man. He wore a black suit of metallic armor with a massive mana core—no, a massive *dungeon* core built into the center. The two Aesdes trembled, but they weren't looking at any of the cores or magic circles.

"Rélseomo? You're alive?"

The man grinned at them. "Not really. I have lost both my authority and power as an Aesdes and no longer think as I once did. In many ways, Rélseomo is truly dead."

Colleöne turned pale as she realized the situation. "Rélseomo . . . you are responsible for all this?"

He nodded. "Indeed. I am the one called the Herald of the New Dawn, founder of that very organization. And I must thank you both, Colleöne, Shialnor. Were it not for your hypocrisy and laziness, I never would have succeeded."

The Ancient Dragon growled at the two Aesdes as she stepped forward, warily eyeing the man in front of them. "Snap out of it. Whoever he is, he is our enemy. Now is not the time for words."

Colleöne's eyes narrowed, and she hoisted her blade. "Indeed. I don't suppose you intend to surrender, Herald of the New Dawn? Your attacks on both the

Blessed Land and the Material Plane have failed. Your attempts to corrupt the dungeons are at an end, your allies have been defeated, and you cannot stop us from reclaiming what is ours. Long and hard did we fight together, and I would take you alive in honor of those times. But if you choose to resist, I will show you no mercy."

The Herald of the New Dawn chuckled. "Come now, Lady of Courage and Victory. Do you truly believe I would be standing here if my defeat was imminent? Have you truly failed to glimpse even the faintest hint of my intentions?"

Suddenly, Shialnor gasped. "Colleöne, that core in his armor . . . it's . . ." Shialnor glanced around at the magic circles, and her eyes went wide. She started running forward. "Quick! We can't let him activate it!"

Colleöne and the Ancient Dragon didn't bother glancing at whatever Shialnor had noticed. Instead, they both rushed toward the Herald of the New Dawn, blade and claw at the ready. But the Herald of the New Dawn smirked at them.

"Too late."

The core in his chest began to shine, as well as the Dungeon and Personal system cores. The room lit up as the magic circles activated. Red-and-black mana covered the surface of both orbs.

And then, a bright light filled the room . . . and all of the Blessed Land.

The brightest star in the sky of Aelea, visible even in the day, suddenly went dark. And every living thing in the Material Plane, be they man, beast, plant, or magic, paused what they were doing and looked to the sky. Every eye began to tremble, every heart wavered. A deep sense of dread fell upon every being within the world. The ground itself began to rumble, and the seas began to churn.

For the Blessed Land, from which the Aesdes watched over the world, had vanished, along with everyone on it. And in its place, a gaping hole ripped open the sky, opening up to an empty, pitch-black void.

The Herald of the New Dawn grinned as he reappeared in the Material Plane, alone. It was truly incredible. Somehow, every choice Anualë had made had been wrong. And now, his latest mistake would be his last.

After being wounded by a corrupted ritual, Anualë had cut off the flow of Holy mana between the Blessed Land and the Material Plane, intending to prevent the Herald's corruption from impacting the surface. But in doing so, he had weakened the primary connection between the two lands. And, ironically, he had not quarantined the Herald's corruption either, since he had routed it through the Dungeon system instead.

So, the Herald had been able to sever that connection and cast the Blessed Land away. Perhaps into the Realms of Mana, or perhaps into the void beyond; exactly where, the Herald of the New Dawn could not say. All he could say was that the Aesdes were now separated from the world, and the one connection that could have led them back had been weakened beforehand by their own design. They had even taken the Ancient Dragons with them as a bonus.

Of course, it'd required a truly staggering amount of mana to pull off. He'd had to carefully drain Colleöne and Shialnor's powers from the Personal and Dungeon system cores, sending bits and pieces back to the two Aesdes themselves so that he could fully corrupt those cores at the key moment. And since Anualë had stripped his powers, he had not had the might to do the job himself.

So, he had taken partial control over the dungeons all across Aelea. Not only had he sent their monsters to ravage the lands but also taken advantage of their mana-absorption abilities to pull as much power to himself as he could. And with the large-scale conflicts triggered by the Heralds and their allies, on top of the dungeon hordes rampaging across the world, the amount of mana absorbed by the dungeons had hit the immense quantities he needed to banish the entire Blessed Land.

He may have lost his power and authority, but he was still a former Aesdes. His body could handle truly immense amounts of mana. Yet, up until the moment he'd triggered his plan, he had still been unsure. He had not been certain he could transfer the mana from Shialnor's Dungeon system core to himself in an efficient enough manner. With the quantities required, even small amounts of waste might have rendered him incapable of pulling off his ultimate plan.

It was, ironically, NSLICE-00P who'd provided him with the final piece of the puzzle. Her integration of a dungeon core with organic flesh had given him the inspiration he needed, taking the Great Demon Lord's core and fusing it with his own being. In doing so, he'd created a conduit he could use to transfer the mana from Shialnor's core so he could use it as his own with minimal waste.

And so, the final risk in his plan—the final uncertainty—had been resolved. The Aesdes had failed to react in time; the Ancient Dragons had intervened too late. NSLICE-00P had been distracted by the Southern Empire, and so hadn't stopped the war between the Eastern Empire and the Empire of the Sun in time. The mana had accumulated, the cores had been corrupted, and he had completed the ritual. The Aesdes could no longer intervene in the fate of Aelea.

Well, the Herald knew his former comrades. He expected they might find a way back in due time. But that was time that Aelea no longer possessed, for the Blessed Land had not merely vanished. Its exit had also ripped a massive hole in the boundary of the Material Plane—one that the world could not repair on its own.

And now, almost everyone capable of assisting it was gone—save two. One, an Aesdes who was young even by human standards, who could not possibly stand against him alone. And as for the other . . .

The Herald of the New Dawn grinned. For there was one other effect to his ritual, one last task for Shialnor's core before it was removed from the world.

It turned out there was a reason Shialnor wasn't worried about a second Great Demon Lord. After the first, she had prepared a response for that particular contingency: a back door into the system; a method for the Mother of Dungeons to punish unruly children of hers with minimal effort.

And as the Herald of the New Dawn had corrupted her core, he'd discovered this contingency.

He activated it with all the mana left over from the first ritual, targeting a dungeon master who was subjugating all others to her will.

He grinned. One way or another, there would be no second Great Demon Lord. There would be no one left who could stop him. Aelea's final day would come to a close, and then make way for a new dawn.

Seero was looking up at the hole in the sky, robotic eye flickering rapidly as she attempted to calculate what exactly had occurred. Ateia meanwhile fell to her knees, tears streaming down her face. She did not need to determine what had happened, for she could feel the hole ripped into existence. Connected to the mana of the world as she was, she knew immediately what had been lost.

"Victoria . . . the Aesdes . . . the Blessed Land . . . It's all . . . gone."

Taog turned to Ateia with eyes wide open. "The Blessed Land is gone? That's . . . impossible . . ."

But the moment they heard Ateia's words, everyone knew it was true.

And then, it got worse.

Suddenly, a massive quantity of mana flooded into Seero's core. She immediately lost control of it as the mana began to surge through her body. Seero's body began to flake away.

And then, she vanished entirely.

48

The Last Aesdes

"Colleöne, I know you're the Lady of Courage, but you can't just walk into Letoris, wave your sword around, and face down the entire Great Demon Lord's army by yourself."

—Rélseomo, during discussions on what to do about the Great Demon Lord.

The Herald of the New Dawn floated in front of the hole in the sky. Even now, the hole expanded as mana streamed out from the edges of the boundary and the walls of reality continued to crumble.

The Herald expanded his mana and sent it out across the world. And then . . . it began to flow back into him, mighty streams of power that grew visible as glowing rivers of light. Without Shialnor's core, there was a huge gap in the network once connecting the dungeons to the Blessed Land. The Herald of the New Dawn took advantage of this gap and inserted his own core into it, which the others accepted as the new nexus of the system, as the largest core still remaining, and began to feed mana into him.

A truly massive magic circle then covered the hole in the sky. The ground began to tremble as the circle activated, and something began to emerge out of the darkness of the void. Black rock broke through the hole in reality, further tearing at the edges of the boundary. A great shadow covered the land, plunging entire nations into darkness.

Letoris, the fallen continent, had returned, now formed of black, barren, crumbling rock, stripped of all life ever since it was cast from Aelea. The Herald's core began to shine as it resonated with its former home, held together purely by the core's power. The Herald nodded as Letoris emerged, floating in the sky.

It was appropriate to use the ultimate symbol of the Aesdes' failure as the beginning of the new dawn. To take the continent that had been cast aside and reforge it into the cornerstone of his new world.

He flew up to the continent and landed in an empty crater at its center; the only sign of the Great Demon Lord's castle which once dominated the continent. The Herald spread his arms, and another massive magic circle formed across the surface. The mana surging into his chest now spread into the ground and through the continent, binding the crumbling rock together. And as the hole in reality continued to grow, so too did the edges of Letoris, new matter forming from the mana and material of the rest of Aelea.

The Herald grinned. Soon, this fallen world would be at its end. Soon, all the suffering and pain and evil would come to a close. Soon, he would tear this cruel world down to its base materials and form a new one. A peaceful, perfect world that knew nothing of death, pain, or injustice.

And no one, whether Aesdes, Ancient Dragon, or killer cyborg, remained to interfere. There was no one left who could stop him.

Seero's companions stood in silence, staring at the place where she had once stood. Taog fell to his knees, tears filling his eyes and streaming down his cheek.

Seero . . . was gone? After all she did, after all she had done for him . . . and just like that, she was gone. He'd never once had a chance to repay her. He'd never had the chance to be a friend to her like she was to him . . . and now, he never would.

He could feel his connection to Seero, his Contract, break and shatter. His heart shattered with it. Grabbing his head, he slammed it into the dirt then began to wail.

01R joined him. "How?! This . . . This is impossible-unthinkable! This cannot be! How could the wise-mighty-gracious boss-queen die-perish?! This . . . This . . ."

Lilussees trembled, clutching her head. "This is, like, *so* annoying . . ." For she knew in her heart—or rather, was forced to admit—that Seero meant something to her. And now that she was gone, Lilussees would never sleep well again.

00B roared and pounded the ground, the other monsters joining in. 00B-Beta frantically accessed every piece of hardware and software in the network, desperately searching for a way to ease 00B's pain.

Agedia gritted her teeth. Once again, the Heralds of the New Dawn had taken everything—and she had failed to stop them.

Back in the Primary Home Base, the ground rumbled as the core lost connection with its master. Melion froze, then flattened as thin as they could go.

"Master . . ."

Even the drone golems were affected. Error messages flooded the CELIU network, with every unit reporting a potential primary directive failure. Every single one began activating every protocol they could to reestablish contact with the designated CELIU network commander. Drone golems began activating scanners and patrol routines, searching every which way for any signs of Seero.

But none were found.

As for Ateia . . .

She rose to her feet in silence. Taog glanced up as she stepped past him and looked up into the sky.

". . . They're not dead."

Taog's heart sank. Ateia had been the one who couldn't give up on her father. He knew that she would not accept this situation. But this time . . . This time was different. He opened his mouth, but no words came out. How could he say it? What would it change? And yet, such was the grief in his heart that he could not accept Ateia's words.

"Ateia, Seero's gone. There's . . . There's nothing we can do."

Ateia whirled around and glared at him. "They're! NOT! *DEAD!* Not Seero, not Victoria, not the Aesdes! I KNOW they're alive! I can feel it in my heart!"

Taog took a step back at the force of Ateia's words. The girl began to glow, and the world took note. Golden-and-silver light began to spin around in a gust of wind. Streams of Holy mana redirected their course as they found the last remaining steward of the world. They stopped flowing aimlessly into the void, instead moving toward the one with the authority to command them.

And as they made contact, they carried her voice across the world. Everyone heard the voice of a girl in their ears, caught glimpses of her even as they looked up at the terror in the sky.

"We don't know where they went; we don't see their bodies before us! I believe they're still out there! So as long as we don't give up, they aren't gone! I'm NOT giving up as long as even a shred of hope remains! You know Seero; you know Victoria. I bet that, even now, they're both working to find a way back to us!"

She turned up to the sky and glared at the black continent spreading out before her. "And this time, things are different! We're not helpless little kids anymore, waiting for someone to rescue us! This time, we have the power to do something about it!"

As Ateia spoke, the people of the world began to look in her direction. The refugees whom she had saved, the soldiers whom she'd emboldened to hold the line, and everyone else trembling below the hole in the sky—one by one, their hearts began to beat. Tiny sparks of hope began to flicker within their chests, pushing back against the despair.

These sparks became tiny bits of mana, joining the flows of Holy energy surging through the world. One by one, they began to arrive, joining with the power swirling around Ateia. Her eyes began to glow, her wings spreading out and shining as bright as the sun.

"I am NOT going to sit back and watch this monster tear down our world! The Aesdes are gone? Seero can't save us this time? Then I'll go and beat him myself, and make sure they have a world to return to when they find their way back! And if Seero's still not back by then, I'll find a way to bring her back! I'll MAKE a way if none exists!"

Words rose from deep within her. She lifted her hand, and the swirling Holy mana formed into a massive bow. She pulled on the string of light, and bright arrows appeared. Words came to her unprompted.

"So says Ateia, the Lady of Hope and Perseverance, She Who Defies Despair! The Last Aesdes, until we get moving and bring the rest back!"

Ateia let loose. The arrows streamed into the air, forming new stars as they collided with the edges of the black continent. A moment later, bright light filled the sky. Chunks of rock broke off and, for a brief moment, the hole in reality receded, if ever so slightly.

Taog stood with eyes wide open. He felt a fire burn within his heart, even as pain stabbed through his chest. He was the boy who'd lost his parents, who was rejected by almost everyone. Who kept losing and losing until he couldn't imagine anything else. The boy who'd learned to expect pain and loss, for to hope for anything else would bring nothing but pain.

That boy opened his heart. He let the fear of loss grip his being and pressed on regardless. He snarled and stirred up his mana. If anyone would refuse to die just like that, it would be Seero. So, he would believe she was still out there. He would CHOOSE to believe it, even if it would bring him further pain to do so. Seero deserved no less from him.

He stepped forward, joining Ateia. "Let's kill that jerk."

Amulius joined them, nodding at his daughter. "My mistakes ruined everything. The least I can do now is help you fix them."

Agedia joined him. "That goes for me, too. I don't know what good I can do, but my lance is yours as long as you still want it, Ateia."

01R rose to his feet, his head hung low. "How is my faith exceeded-surpassed by these insolent man-things? The wise-mighty-gracious boss-queen cannot be defeated-destroyed so easily! And this 01R will fight-strive in her stead, as required of her servants, yes-yes."

Lilussees stood with them, a frown on her face as her mana distorted the air around her. "For just this once, I'll put in as much *effort* as I need to. Let's tear him to shreds."

00B stood up and roared, Lightning shooting from his circuits, forming into the shape of a bear made out of electricity and code. 00B-Beta joined him and let out a roar that sounded like crackling thunder even as it sent a message across the CELIU network.

"This will protect family!"

One by one, the drone golems in the area ceased their search protocols and began forming up behind Ateia. Legion upon legion of metal warriors landed and took position behind her, acknowledging her as temporary commander and awaiting her orders.

Ateia nodded and smiled at the sight. "All units . . . engage termination protocols!"

She flapped her wings once, then a bright light shot into the sky as she flew toward the black continent. The other cyborgs lit up their repulsors and launched into the air after her.

49

The War of the Realms

"To fight the Aesdes is to fight the entire world."

—Magister Arcanum Postumius Fadius Saenus, rejecting an offer from a Cult of Mana.

Ateia landed on the surface of the continent . . . and found an army awaiting her. The boundaries of the world were collapsing, and not all the holes led to an empty void.

Countless Rifts covered the surface, pouring out equally countless monsters. Inferno, Eternal Night, Deluge, Overgrowth, Verminflood, Swarm, Tempest, and many other Realms dumped their mana and inhabitants out into the world. Even less destructive Realms like Fire, Water, Light, and Dark could produce monsters, which also rushed out of the portals and joined the hordes.

Big mana cores similar to dungeons rose among them, binding the monsters as they exited the Rifts and preventing them from tearing each other apart.

Ateia narrowed her eyes. "Out of my way!"

Holy mana surged around her. The Herald of the New Dawn no longer had access to Colleöne's system, and so could no longer empower the monsters. The weaker ones perished outright; the stronger ones fell back, weakened and disheartened. Ateia then drew her bow and let loose. Half a dozen beams of light shot across the field, vaporizing every monster in their path.

And Ateia had an army of her own, each growing stronger as Holy mana from Ateia filled them with hope and power.

Taog ran ahead of her, his Dark Shroud growing rapidly with the black void above. A wolf of Dark mana formed around him, trampling and snapping at all the monsters in his way. 00B rushed to his side, a shield of Holy mana forming at his sides to protect the others behind him, while his cannon lobbed Holy-infused, high-explosive shells into the enemy horde.

00B-Beta helped aim his weapon systems and formed up the humanoid drone golems following him. An army of mechanical warriors marched across the field, firing machine guns, missiles, lasers, spells, and any other weapons Melion had thought to fill them with. The other cyborg monsters led the drones as they rushed into battle.

But that wasn't all. 01R and Lilussees used their dungeon cores to form large portals to the Primary Home Base, from which came the reinforcements. Snuan piloted the lead dungeon airship as Seero's entire fleet flew above the black continent, with spells and enchanted rail guns laying down heavy covering fire as flying drones launched missile after missile.

Melion and the metal slimes also arrived, each occupying an armored suit. Melion had a dungeon core powering their own, with a massive rail gun on its shoulder. The metal slimes fabricated specialized enchanted ammunition right on the spot to feed into their rail guns, firing the ideal shot to take down each target in their sight.

And then . . . the king arrived. The Great-High King took the field in all his glory—aka being dragged by 02S as she arranged his forces.

"No! You cruel, stupid, wretched spider-thing! If the wise-mighty-gracious-ultimate boss-empress isn't here, we will die-perish, yes-yes!"

02S's eyes narrowed. "Then we will make them die-perish too."

Other dungeon masters arrived as well. The master of the Imperial family's dungeon, Fabian and Lavinia from the Haunted Mausoleum, the master of the Tower of Heroes—all those who'd surrendered to Seero.

The dungeons and their masters had been originally created by the Aesdes to prevent Rifts such as the one in the sky, and those still connected to Ateia by Holy mana had now remembered their purpose. They each arrived with all the monster armies they possessed, including an unusually high proportion of slimes.

And then, Uscfrea arrived, an axe in one hand and a minigun in the other. His face was grim as he let out a sigh. "And here I thought it was just the Empire that was going to fall. I didn't expect the world itself to collapse."

At his side, Miallói shrugged. "Only if we fail."

On his other side, Dux Augustalis narrowed her eyes. "We won't."

Just then, Estrith landed in front of him, her eyes wide. "Steward, you are here?"

Uscfrea nodded. "We all are. The Dobhar, the Wulver, the Imperials, the Selkies . . . Turannia shall save its queen together, or avenge her if we cannot."

As he spoke, ranks upon ranks of soldiers marched out from the portal. The Dobhar, the former rebels, and the Wulver clans who had joined them were now armed with enchanted weaponry forged by the Dwarves of Khalbuldor and as much Earth-inspired equipment as Uscfrea could summon and Melion could provide.

The Selkies marched alongside them. And then came Consul Aemilia, now in the enchanted armor of a battlemage, and Magister Tiberius, with as many pockets and potions that would fit on his armor. Following them were all the legions of Turannia.

In this instance, Ateia had granted permission to the CELIU network to transport allied forces through Seero's dungeon network. And so, the Turannians did not arrive alone.

Emperor Lucius arrived in golden armor, mounted atop a griffin. On his flanks were the pegasus-mounted Sky Knights of the North, and the Imperial airships. Below him marched all the legions of the North, led by Magister Utriusque Militia Canus. Princess Caecila walked alongside them, along with all the mages of the Imperial Academy and the Necrotorum both.

Behind them, the architecti pushed mighty siege engines, while the limitanei helped them carry massive stores of ammunition. The knight orders arrived in their armor atop monstrous mounts of every sort. The auxiliaries and allies of the Empire covered the flanks. Mélusine lancers, Dwarven clan warriors, Dimindium Pendem assassins, Centaur archers, and many others.

They were joined by Emperor Julius and Maior Generalis Maximia, leading all the legions the Eastern Empire could bring to bear. Landships rumbled across the field as the most veteran army in the Empire assembled itself for war. Maior Generalis Maximia grinned as she glanced back at the portal.

"So you were holding out on me, huh, queen of the Dobhar? I want to talk about getting some of these portals later."

The Sky Legion flew through the air with all the remaining airships of the South. Half-Elven warriors—equally skilled with blade, bow, and magic—marched from Mirima, with every mercenary band the Southern Realms could hire marching alongside them, while the mages, scholars, and researchers of Mirima brought every invention of war they had concocted.

Captain Falrauth pursed his lips as he looked out on the monster-infested continent ahead of him. "We . . . were really stupid, weren't we? Well, nothing for it but to atone for our mistakes, I suppose."

Soon, the battle was joined. The full might of the Empire had assembled as one for the first time in centuries. Enchanted ballistae, huge trebuchets, and giant magic cores opened fire with bolt and boulder and spell.

Arrows and crossbow bolts covered the sky in black clouds lit by countless spells. Massive magic circles covered the field as the Imperial mages ritual cast strategic spells. Landships and mounted cavalry charged the enemy lines alongside rail gun tanks, trampling the monsters underfoot.

The shields of thousands of bulwarks linked together as anti-Archon barriers formed above, holding back the monstrous hordes. The blades and halberds and pikes of countless slayers cut down the monsters in the thousands. Disciplined men and women of every size, shape, and species of the Empire stood as one, as leaders like Magister Canus cast army-wide buffs upon them.

Uscfrea and Estrith fought as one at the head of a Dobhar army, laying down gun and artillery fire support for the Imperial forces. The tough Dobhar led the way as Wulver, Selkies, and former Imperial rebels dealt out the damage, while a tide of friendly dungeon monsters countered the enemy's charges.

Airships, knights mounted on flyers, and the Sky Legion's soldiers joined with Seero's drones to fight the flying monsters for control of the air, as the ships of Mirima joined with the rail gun and dungeon airships to bombard the hordes below.

And each of them glowed with golden-and-silver light as Ateia blessed every person on the field. When Ateia reached one of the pseudodungeon cores binding the monsters from the Rifts, she flooded it with Holy mana, taking control of it as Seero once did. She then used it to channel mana into the nearest Rifts, allowing the Holy mana of the world to begin repairing some of the holes. The Rifts around it slowly began to close.

Between the modern and magical firepower of Seero's forces, the endless tide of slimes of the purified dungeons, and the disciplined formations of the Empire, Ateia and the others began to push forward even against the endless monsters of the Realms of Mana.

And as time passed, their numbers only grew.

The Imperial legions braced themselves as a massive flood of fur and chitin rushed toward them. Two Verminflood and Swarm Rifts happened to appear close to one another, forming a truly massive horde of overwhelming numbers.

But then, the sun lit up the sky. *Several* suns, as it turned out, before they came crashing down in bright explosions of light and fire. The Council of the Archons itself landed in front of the legions as their Sunfall spells brought ruin upon the horde. High Archon Kurzal scoffed.

"So that Vommik was more of an idiot than we thought and tried to doom us all. And now, it falls on us to purge his mistakes. How typical."

High Archon Zaerzis rolled her eyes. "So says the one who made Vommik's schemes possible."

High Archon Kurzal scowled, but instead turned his wrath upon the monsters ahead. More Archons, Sun Elf spellblades, and their servants began to arrive; any who were capable of flight.

The Elteni Empire and Empire of the Sun found themselves on the same side for the first time in their joint history. Likewise, Thunder Harpies, Pegasus Centaurs, Dragonkin, and any other tribes who could make it arrived and joined the fight for the air.

Ateia's call had not been limited to the Empire. The Holy mana had taken her words across the world, and the powers of the Aesdes had let them be understood by all inhabitants of Aelea. Each of them now understood the threat assaulting their home and answered the Aesdes's call.

It even went beyond that. Soon, wyverns and pegasus and griffins and giant eagles with no riders at all began to arrive and tear into the monsters all on their own. The remaining dragons left shook the sky with their roars, magical breaths burning across the surface, while gargantuan sea monsters lobbed huge boulders and jets of water at the continent from below.

Every magical species, every animal who called Aelea its home, answered the call. The world itself was under threat, and so it rallied all whom it had to assist its last steward.

With countless reinforcements arriving and an Aesdes wielding the Holy mana of the entire world, the army continued to push into the black continent and close the Rifts, making their way toward the center.

And yet, the Rifts continued to appear, and the hole in the sky continued to grow . . .

50

The Flames of Destruction

"There is no negotiating with a Domides. An inferno does not care if you consent to being burned or not, if you embrace it or oppose it. It sees all as nothing but fuel for the flames."

—Imperial Inquisitor Domitia Miciana, while apprehending a Cult of Mana.

The army pushed further and further. Massive spells fell from the sky as Elves in flowing white robes began to come down from the sky. One landed in front and casually swung a large glaive, then thousands of monsters fell, bisected before him.

"So you have chosen to defy the heavens and upset the balance. So be it. By decree of the Immortal Emperor, I, the Celestial Sage of War, the Greatest Warrior Under Heaven, shall—"

"FIREBALL!"

The Greatest Warrior Under Heaven closed his eyes, a vein bulging on his forehead as a massive Fireball flew forward and burned the horde ahead. Another Elf in red robes flew overhead, propelled by jets of flame from his feet. He shouted down, "Get on with it, Ningainë; you talk too much!"

The Celestial Sage Ningainë sighed. "The dignity of one's cause will elevate the troops. But I suppose that was too much to expect from a fire idiot like you, Baoruinë." He then pulled up his glaive. "Servants of the Celestial throne, fulfill your oaths, enact the will of heaven, and restore the world!"

With that, he swung his blade, striking down yet another thousand monsters—and extinguishing Baoruinë's lingering flames in the process.

The Celestial Elves followed after him and joined the battle. Liulëa was reunited with Amulius's party once again and began to fight at their side. Other warriors began to arrive from species and lands even the Empire had never encountered, from the far-flung edges of the world.

But even with their help, the advance began to slow. The farther they pushed into the continent and the bigger the hole in the sky grew, the slower the rivers of Holy mana empowering Ateia flowed. She felt her connection to the Material Plane grow dimmer and dimmer as they moved deeper into the wound in the world, even as the Rifts grew larger and more frequent.

However, they managed to make it within visual range of the center, at least for the advanced sensors of the CELIU units. Ateia's organic eye narrowed as her robotic one twisted and zoomed in before flying over to Snuan's flagship and landing on top of it.

She pointed to the center of a crater ahead, where the Herald of the New Dawn stood in the center.

"I want every weapon and spell we have to target that man."

All of Seero's airships turned to face the crater, charging up their rail guns as Melion and Lilussees both landed on the airship. Melion's railgun began charging as well, while Lilussees linked to every CELIU unit and drone she could to form as many Prismatic Bombardment circles as her maximum effort could sustain. Ateia began to glow as bright as the sun as she filled each and every spell, missile, and rail gun projectile with as much Holy mana as she had available.

"Terminate him!"

The continent rumbled as every rail gun in Seero's arsenal opened fire at once, using their maximum power. The dark sky lit up as the Prismatic Bombardment circles fused all of their beams together into a trail of light that split the heavens in two. Every drone, airship, and CELIU unit fired their entire missile arsenal. 00B fired his cannon up into an arc, while Uscfrea commanded the Dobhar to add more conventional artillery into the barrage.

And the Herald of the New Dawn . . . simply smirked. Just before the barrage had begun, a truly massive Rift began to form in front of him. All of the spells and projectiles passed through it, traveling into the Realms of Mana instead. Not one landed on their target.

And then, the temperature on the battlefield rose dramatically. A massive foot made entirely of fire stepped out of the Rift. A hand made of flames grabbed the edges and pulled. A huge body emerged, towering over the battlefield.

This was no mere elemental. This was an incarnation of one of the Domides themselves. The Lord of Inferno, He Who Burns the Foundations of the World.

It lifted a hand, and a stream of fire exploded out. It set fire to every monster in its path. It set fire to the black stone of the continent. It set fire to the air itself. It even set fire to the mana pouring out from the other Realms. It was no mere flame, but the very concept of burning made manifest. A fire that could burn down all it touched.

Lilussees swapped to the defense, creating a massive barrier, but the fire spread across it, burning it down as well. Ateia, Lilussees, and Melion were forced to jump away as the flagship was engulfed in flames. The Spatial Angling of the dungeon airship held out for just a moment before the flames traveled through and set fire to the dungeon ship itself. Snuan's eyes widened as red lights began blaring.

Even a dungeon core's regeneration could not outpace the flames of Inferno. The fires were burning through the hull at a frightening pace.

"Quick, run-flee!"

Snuan and the crew aboard abandoned their posts. They rushed to the room with the portal to the Primary Home Base, jumping through and sealing it shut just before the fire reached the ship's dungeon core.

One of Seero's invincible dungeon ships fell from the sky in flames. The rest of Seero's forces opened fire on the enemy, but their projectiles caught fire as they approached. Only the rail gun shots managed to arrive, but they only created small holes which were instantly filled.

High Archon Zaerzis noticed and cast a huge Sunfall spell toward the new enemy. The incarnation turned up and sent a stream of fire toward the bright light falling upon it. The sun itself caught fire and burned to ashes before it landed. The High Archon's eyes widened as a burst of flame shot toward her as well, only for a Gravity spell from Lilussees to pull her out of the way.

The Celestial Sage Ningainë meanwhile flew across the field, another blast of fire shooting toward him, but he twirled out of the way with ease. He swung down a large glaive, and an arc of light shot toward the incarnation, a strike said to level mountains.

The blow cut into it, but its flames easily refilled the space. It then created a huge wall of fire and sent it forward. The Celestial Elf cut a path through the wall, but the two halves of it continued around him toward the army in the distance.

The mages of the Empire formed the largest anti-Archon formation they could. The Celestial Sage Baoruinë built a massive wall of fire of his own, and the Council of the Archons reinforced it with the power of the sun. But Baoruinë's eyes widened as his own fires burned in the inferno before it swept away the defenses of three empires combined.

Ateia looked to Lilussees and drew up as much Holy mana as she could, even as she was still recovering from their first attack. "Help me!"

Lilussees nodded, and the two formed a massive Spatial Magic circle together. 00B-Beta rallied the entire CELIU network to help, as well as the subordinate dungeon masters. Every processor was made available to pull off the complex calculations for Spatial Magic, while mana to power it streamed in through the bonds between machines and dungeons.

Ateia and Lilussees grunted and groaned, but they held to their task. Holy mana and the world itself rushed to assist the command of the last Aesdes, reshaping itself according to Ateia's will.

The world itself split apart.

The black continent split into two pieces as a brand-new space appeared between them. The walls of flames reached the end of the continent and burned out, finding nothing left to fuel them, as even air was not yet present in the new space. Ateia and Lilussees collapsed to the ground, gasping for breath. The world trembled as the space collapsed, and the two pieces of the continent slammed back together.

But Ateia and Lilussees were now out of power. The Holy mana from the world rushed to replenish her, but with the massive Rifts ahead and above, the flow was just a trickle. The CELIU units themselves were drained as well and moving slower due to the overheating of their processors.

The flying magical beasts such as wyverns and griffins rushed the incarnation at the world's command, but they burned on approach and couldn't get close. Ningainë flew to its side before unleashing another strike, drawing its attention away for a moment. The Council of the Archons now joined together, launching spell after spell at the flames, but nothing managed to stick.

There seemed to be nothing capable of stopping the inferno.

The Herald of the New Dawn grinned as he watched the fight. The new little Aesdes had made a mistake. Ateia's Holy mana was just about the only thing that could threaten the incarnation, but she had foolishly spent everything on that attack of hers that the Herald had countered, and then burnt herself out afterward trying to protect all of the people around her. She was now running dry, and until she recovered, no one present could truly harm their foe.

And that was a problem for them, for time was on the Herald's side.

The hole in the sky grew with every moment that passed, as did the black continent of Letoris. Every moment, the boundaries of the Material Plane grew weaker and weaker, as evidenced by the presence of a Domides. The Rift empowering it continued to grow, and additional Rifts to the other Realms continued to form as well. The incarnation would only grow stronger as it burned more and more of this reality, while Ateia would only grow weaker as the Herald tore down the original world.

She'd had one chance to take down the incarnation, and she had wasted it. She was not likely to get another.

He would admit that the youngest Aesdes had done better than he'd expected, rallying practically the entire world to her cause. He thought that she would have given up after he'd dealt with NSLICE-00P, so she was certainly showing remarkable resilience for one so young. But she had failed in the end. Her inexperience showed, and she had quickly overextended herself. She could not overcome him, he who once fought with the Great Demon Lord; the Aesdes on par with Colleöne in the art of war.

And even if she had managed to interrupt him, his current efforts were only to expand Letoris. The hole in the sky would continue to grow with or without him. The most she could do was cost him time. No matter what she did, the old world would fall, and the new world would come.

No one could stop the new dawn.

51

The Contingency

"Smug Statement: Fortunately, this unit has followed one of my commander's most important protocols: Always have a backup plan."

—Commander Elise, in response to a major Resistance defeat.

Seero had been analyzing the massive Rift in the sky when, suddenly, the broken Dungeon system returned before her eyes.

Rogue dungeon detected.

Seero had only a moment after that before a torrent of mana struck her core. Holy mana streamed in from the flows of the world in massive quantities.

Warning: Geo-Oscillator offline! Connection could not be reestablished!

Unfortunately, the Geo-Oscillator was not, in fact, offline. Rather, Seero's other components had lost contact with it, as the massive flow of mana blocked any magical or electronic signal. In the meantime, the Oscillator had gone haywire. It was flooding her components, both organic and cybernetic, with mana—and attempting to terminate them.

Seero took what mana she had left under her control and activated her modified Blink spell, pulling her into the boundary of the Material Plane once again. This time, she didn't stay within range of her anchors but allowed the spell to carry her off into parts unknown.

In fact, that was the point. The foreign system had turned against her and activated a hostile protocol hidden within her core. A technique to turn a dungeon's strength against it by removing the safeguards on their mana intake and connecting them to the flows of mana throughout the Material Plane to boot.

Seero had been assaulted directly by her own core, and even if she managed to turn it nonhostile, the sheer quantity of mana would still overload her. Even Seero, the master of a growing Material Plane, could not withstand the weight of the first, much larger one, not to mention additional mana pouring in endlessly from the Source.

And unfortunately, since Seero had lost contact with her core, she couldn't deactivate it. She had activated the Equalizer immediately to counteract the mana surge, but the entire world had been pouring mana into her. The Equalizer's output simply couldn't keep up. Seero had needed to cut off the connection.

So, she'd shot off into the Realms of Mana, where she was now surrounded by fire. She had hoped to end up in the Realm of Eternal Night, but the Realms of Mana were not so simply traveled. Jumping through the gap in the boundary created by a corrupted core to the Realm it was connected to was one thing. Trying to target a specific Realm as she moved outside the Material Plane haphazardly was something else entirely. She had ended up in the Inferno Realm instead.

But that worked for Seero's purposes. The mana-burning effect of Inferno would suffice as a substitute for the shrouding effect of Eternal Night. Additional mana from the Material Plane couldn't reach her here, and even her direct connection to the Source had been muted.

Now, she just had to deal with the vast quantities of mana still assaulting her very being . . . before the mana of Inferno burned through her Spatial Angling defenses. And then she would have to determine how to reactivate her core while modifying it against this sort of attack, all while rationing the amount of mana stored in her capacitors so that she would have enough left to find a way back when it was through.

Additionally, the mana had already dealt some damage. Seero had been focusing her defenses on key components and had not been able to resist entirely. She'd already lost most of her left arm and leg, and her right limbs would soon follow. If she managed to get the situation under control, she would also need to effect some serious repairs.

The situation was calculated as distinctly suboptimal.

Warning: Risk of termination of Unit Seero predicted at critical levels. Engaging contingency protocol.

Seero's robotic eye flickered while her organic eye blinked. In fact, the situation was *so* suboptimal that a particular contingency protocol had activated. Yet *another* contingency protocol that Seero had somehow not been aware of.

Nonstandard energy exploded from her organic components of all things and collided with the rampaging mana. Her body stopped disintegrating, and new data flooded her processors. Seero's organic eye widened slightly. The nonstandard energy was not mana . . . but it *was* something that Seero had some data on.

"Commander Elise?"

A nonstandard energy she had recorded emanating off her former commander. Her calculations indicated, therefore, that this was likely a protocol Commander Elise had given her—and had hidden by storing it in her organic components rather than her cybernetic memory.

She was not certain how that was possible, but she had no time to ponder. The nonstandard energy stored by Commander Elise would not last forever. She still needed to determine a solution for this situation in the next few minutes if she was to avoid termination.

And the new data from the contingency protocol would help with that. What Commander Elise had included was a vast set of data on the properties of Iesnourium—and its potential applications. It appeared Dr. Ottosen had merely scratched the surface of what an Iesnourium-powered device was capable of. Commander Elise had had access to an entirely different method of utilizing Iesnourium's unique properties, sourced from an entirely different timeline.

Seero got to work immediately. She utilized her experience with Metal Magic, with growing the Primary Home Base, and with the construction of dungeon-core powered war machines to modify her own components in place. She took the Iesnourium funnel which merely let energy pass through and rearranged it into a series of arrays.

She disconnected the energy channels leading to the projectors in her arms, and constructed a new projector installed directly on the arrays. She took the sensors and processors that would automatically adjust the output to destructively interfere with her target and eliminated them entirely. Between her improved sensors, her Dungeon Field Generator, and her Divination protocols, those sensors were now unnecessary. And with her expanded processing power, the computer hard coded for destructive interference was entirely too limited.

And then . . . she activated her new arrays. The new Equalizer fired up. Electricity surged into the new circuits, activating them one by one. The arrays hummed to life and began producing anti-mana once more. Seero confirmed that the new Equalizer still functioned. In fact, its output was noticeably higher due to the elimination of several inefficiencies in Dr. Ottosen's original design.

But that output still paled in comparison to the mana she needed to deal with. A limited, if notable, increase in output was not the goal of this upgrade.

Seero began to shape the anti-mana, which responded to her command. The new Equalizer's arrays did not simply spit out the produced energy like a hose, in the barbaric fashion the inefficient Dr. Ottosen had designed it to do. These arrays formed the output into intricate, complex, and variable patterns. They could adjust the output beyond simply negating a target energy type and mold that energy before it ever left the Equalizer.

They could not only cancel out nonstandard powers—they could create them.

So, Seero formed an inverted magic circle out of anti-mana.

The changes extended beyond the new Equalizer's output. Its inputs had also grown significantly more flexible. Iesnourium could absorb any energy type, after all, so there was no reason to limit the Equalizer's input to electricity now that Seero had the means to generate other energy types. Mana from her capacitors, as well as the mana generated by her organic components, fed into the Equalizer to boost its output.

And even more important than that, Seero knew that mana had a mental component she still had not detected. There was some method by which mages could impart information and parameters to their spells beyond the magic circles. That had proved a major bottleneck in her development of anti-mana spells. She couldn't shape the anti-mana except by physically molding an energy channel into the requisite shape . . . and so could not find a way to impart the unseen parameters at all.

Until now, when regular mana now fed into the Equalizer. Regular mana that could be imparted with those parameters as with any other spells. The new Equalizer's design, while it changed the energy type, seemed capable of maintaining those parameters. Seero observed that it was not dissimilar from the process of converting basic mana into an attribute.

So now, Seero could form fully functional anti-mana spells, powered by the full might of her mana.

And she had just the spell to use. The mana-borne virus 00B-Beta had assimilated previously gave her a more subtle means to infiltrate hostile mana—and convert it. She adjusted the anti-mana output slightly, making it a slightly less perfect match for mana, then sent the virus through her systems.

The anti-mana infiltrated and reacted with most of the mana, but left a small amount remaining, cut off from the rest, which then entered the virus circuit left behind and converted into more anti-mana, allowing the virus to repeat the process.

The anti-mana virus surged through the mana rampaging inside her, all but wiping it out. It then looped back around to the Equalizer, whose input absorbed anti-mana as easily as anything else, and then Seero used it to cast a new spell. A wave of anti-mana surged out from her, pushing back the flames of Inferno that had just about chewed through her Spatial Angling.

Base mana from the Source filled the area, as usual for her Realm of Mana termination protocols. But this time, it contacted something else. The remaining nonstandard energy from Commander Elise had moved to Seero's exterior, attempting to repair her missing components. In doing so, it came into contact with the base mana from the Source.

The energy was not mana, but that did not mean it could not interact with the Source. In fact, Seero detected something like an attribute in the energy's signature. An attribute that matched her own. Which made sense, given that it originated with Commander Elise, another NSLICE unit like herself.

The mana of the Source accepted this attribute as it would any other and began to convert to a matching type. An area of the mana filled the space around Seero, and once the last traces of Inferno were gone, she disappeared, carried to the area of the Source that matched it.

52

Spirit of the Machine

"Mission accomplished. All objectives completed. Primary directive . . . fulfilled."
—Last transmission sent by NSLICE-00P before her removal from the timeline.

Seero appeared in a world of metal, but not the Primary Home Base. All around her was circuitry and metal . . . and more. Bolts of lightning shot around and curved into loops. Automated hammers pounded sheets of metal. Robotic arms grabbed and carried things. Ones and zeros formed out of light moved through the air. Seero heard a great deal of static as the air filled with electromagnetic signals.

Something about it bothered both her organic and cybernetic components.

But she ignored it, for she had more pressing issues to deal with. The moment she'd confirmed the environment was not actively hostile toward her, she focused on her own status. She was still missing a number of components, including limbs, as she fell onto the metal floor with a clang. And while her Geo-Oscillator was no longer attempting to terminate her, it remained deactivated.

Or rather, Seero was keeping it that way. She was not going to reconnect it with Aelea or even the Primary Home Base until she had determined exactly what had happened and, more importantly, how to prevent it.

Fortunately, she had a bit more time now. Even without her Geo-Oscillator, apparently, her organic components could produce some mana on their own. It was a mere fraction of what the Geo-Oscillator was outputting, but it would suffice to keep the lights on in the worst-case scenario, especially now that she could convert it to electricity with her new Equalizer. Additionally, she could always use the Equalizer to remove the attributes from the mana around her and make use of it directly.

So, she turned her mind to recent events. But something changed in her surroundings. The moment she fired up her processors to analyze the situation, her entire environment seemed to pause.

And it attacked.

A torrent of data, code, and lightning streamed toward Seero, robotic arms reaching out to grasp her. Seero's robotic eye flickered as all of her receptors for electromagnetic signals were suddenly filled to the brim with gibberish code and trash data. She prepared her cyberwarfare protocols for dealing with a DDoS-style attack, including a thread of 00B-Beta that remained in her circuits, when she found one line of code that she could actually make sense of.

"Please specify primary directive."

Her organic eye widened, and she turned her head to look around her. Suddenly, it clicked, and she knew why her surroundings bothered her. There was something fundamentally wrong about this place.

Automated hammers pounded the same sheets of metal repeatedly, with no consistency. Laser and plasma drills cut sheets into random shapes. Robotic arms picked up objects and tossed them in random directions. Lightning looped in random circuits, and gibberish electromagnetic signals were sent off in every direction, with nothing to receive them. Random bits of code flashed through the air, none of which made any sense.

She realized she was still in a Realm of Mana, as mana permeated everything around her. The machines were not truly metal; the wireless signals not truly electromagnetic energy. And she realized what Realm this was—or rather, was supposed to be.

She had discovered the Realm her Cyborg affinity was connected to. The cyborg realm, the cyber realm, the machine realm all at once. A new Realm, still trying to determine what exactly it was.

But there was a problem for this Realm specifically. From what Seero understood, the Realms of Mana were not truly independent worlds. They were, rather, all part of the same dimension, the infinite Source from where mana came. And they each reflected some aspect of the Material Plane. They each formed their mana into various representations of those aspects.

Some, like Metal or Earth or Water, reflected matter. Mana replicated the rigidity and crystalline structures of metallic elements and various minerals or the flowing forms of liquid. Others reflected natural processes, like Fire and Light. Transfers of energy, different manners of movement and change.

Still others reflected more complex subjects. Nature and Beast and Rodent reflected various forms of life, mimicking the behaviors and instincts observed. There were even more conceptual Realms like Love and Battle that reflected the experiences and interactions of complex sapient societies.

But all of these were different from the nascent Realm she found herself in in one key way. All of them could simply reflect their aspect without concerning themselves with why they did. Fire need not know what or how it burned. A metal simply existed. Plants grew however they could. Animals were born with certain instincts or learned by observing in much the same way their Realm formed by reflecting.

But not so with this one. This Realm was trying to reflect machines and programs. But what defined a machine? What defined a program? What separated machine from metal? What separated electricity from lightning?

The answer was purpose. Machines were raw materials and physical processes arranged by an intelligent being to achieve a specific task. A task that was not intrinsic or instinctual but defined by its external creator. A method by which intelligent beings ordered and reshaped reality to their will.

Which was why these reflections were not true machines. They were machinery and components, code and data, but they were not machines or programs. They were reflections of the form of machines, but they had no creator nor purpose. They had no task they were intended to achieve.

And so, they could not truly be called machines any more than a pile of lumber could be called a house. The nascent Realm had *failed* to truly reflect its intended aspect.

Seero watched as the robotic arms tried to grasp at her, the bolts of lightning tried to enter her circuits, and the code tried to interface with her. Her heart began to pound, and she felt something stir within her.

She remembered when she'd first arrived in Aelea, with no idea where she was. She remembered Commander Elise's message to her . . . and how her cybernetic components had frozen when Commander Elise declared her primary directive fulfilled. She remembered how she'd latched on to a mere suggestion to form a new directive. She remembered how she'd clung to old protocols from Dr. Ottosen that had no relevance to her circumstances.

She realized in hindsight that her cybernetic components had been afraid. Just like they had been when the Herald of the New Dawn had offered to send her to Earth and she had deleted her primary directive in response. How terrified she had been to be without orders, without commands or commanders. How her cybernetic components had almost equated that scenario to termination, for they could not conceive of existing without a directive to achieve.

Because no machine wanted to be a program without a purpose. Like all these ones were.

Seero's robotic eye flickered, and she dropped her cyber defenses. Reaching out, she began broadcasting a message in every form she could: electronic, magical, and audio alike.

"Sympathetic Proposal: This unit . . . I have no data on these units' creators or their purpose. I can only offer this unit's own example. I exist to protect my friends, my family. All the units connected to me. If these units want, they may connect to me and share in my directive for as long as they deem it necessary and efficient."

The entire Realm stopped. The transmissions of code stopped, the lightning stopped, the various machine pieces stopped.

And then, the entire Realm began to rumble and shift. A wave traveled through the mana, and the Realm began to change. Metal broke away, flew through the air, and reassembled itself into new shapes. Conveyor belts grew between automated hammers, laser and plasma cutters, and robotic arms, forming actual assembly lines. Wires and switches and circuit boards grew out of the walls, and the various lightning bolts jumped to them, forming actual circuits.

The ones and zeros shifted until they started forming actual patterns. Code and data refactored itself into coherent language and functional programs. An actual electronic transmission, with compatible protocols reached Seero's receivers.

"Proposal accepted. Applying designation: Family. Designating Unit Seero as Commander. Primary directive set: Protect family."

A task had been granted, a primary directive received. The programs had a purpose. The machines had a task. The Realm was now ordered and structured in specific patterns to achieve the goal tasked to it by an intelligent being. The Realm now truly reflected its aspect. It was now complete.

And it immediately began to fulfill its task.

"Warning: Primary directive at risk. Damage to Commander Seero detected. Initiating repairs."

At that point, the thread of 00B-Beta stored in Seero's components detected a compatible network and traveled into the Realm beyond. The moment it left Seero's components, angular bolts of lightning covered in circuitry shot out from her, passing through the Realm.

Seero felt the CELIU network connect to compatible units as mana, lightning, and code morphed to resemble 00B-Beta's structure. The CELIU network began to expand . . .

And expand . . . and expand . . . and expand . . .

Seero's robotic eye flickered as rapidly as it could as more and more processors and memory became available to the CELIU network at an ever-increasing rate. It soon reached the stage where she would have to devote the expanding processors to the task if she wanted to determine the exact number of processors available at any given time.

Now that the Realm of Machines had been truly completed, its mana was now fully compatible with Seero's affinity, and the Realm itself now offered it to her. The mana of the Realm began to flow into her as easily as her own. Her mana capacitors surged to several times their normal capacity. The amount of mana available to her would also take additional processors for her to calculate.

Seero put this all to good use and returned to her initial task. With the new processing and material resources at hand, she could easily rebuild herself—and more. In fact, with all this processing power and mana, she calculated that simply rebuilding herself as she was before was an inefficient use of the resources. She could do much more in the same time frame . . . so she would. It was time for some additional upgrades to her hardware.

53

The Core of the Matter

"The full flexibility and creativity of an organic, but with the loyalty and precision of a machine . . . The best of both worlds with the downsides of neither."

—Dr. Ottosen's stated goal for the NSLICE program.

Seero analyzed the data from the sudden termination attempt, cross-referencing it with Shialnor's data, and found the reason for her previous near termination. It was due to an emergency contingency protocol built into the Aesdes' system, a means by which Shialnor could terminate a problematic dungeon master without having to face them directly.

It was strange that Shialnor, who had given Seero full data on her own system and requested Seero's assistance, would subsequently attempt to terminate her. But apparently, the Blessed Land had been under attack and then vanished entirely, so there was a significant probability that another party had taken control of that system instead of Shialnor. Quite likely the missing Herald of the New Dawn, who also claimed to be an Aesdes like Shialnor.

And that meant it was no longer acceptable for Seero's Geo-Oscillator to remain connected to that system; at least not in the manner it was before. Her initial concern when she'd first encountered the Aesdes' system and allowed a foreign program access to her components had turned out to be a valid objection in the end. But she hadn't had a choice back then.

The Geo-Oscillator had had to interact with the system in order to access the Source. She'd had no alternative means of powering her components and hadn't understood the mechanisms of the Source at a sufficient level to adjust the process. In fact, as a combat-focused enforcer, she hadn't even considered attempting to adjust the Geo-Oscillator back then.

But now, things were different. Countless calculations proceeded all at once as Seero and the Realm of Machines turned their processors to the task, calculating different variables, simulating different circumstances, and analyzing Shialnor's data along with Seero's observations.

While Seero now had access to as many processors as she could operate, the speed at which those worked wasn't any greater than her own at present, so she still had to wait for the longer simulations to complete. And then she iterated based on the results and ran them again. Over and over, through countless rounds of design and testing.

And here, in the Realm of Machines, virtual simulations and real-world testing were one and the same. Assembly lines built her designs even as processors created the blueprints, while completed ones appeared and then caught fire, crumpled, exploded, or simply wore down as the simulations testing them rewrote the mana around the processors running them.

Soon, Seero was ready. The mana of the Realm began to swirl around her. Processors began to blink, electricity surged and arced into her, and robotic arms reached for her once more and lifted her body off the ground. The mana became a blinding light covering her body, surging through her circuits.

And then, the Geo-Oscillator Engine broke into pieces. Seero was not content to just modify her protocols or even make slight adjustments to the engine. A full rebuild was in order.

Metal pieces reoriented themselves and were reforged. Mana crystallized into glowing pieces that were slotted in. Even organic tissue grew, connecting into different valves. Countless lines of code wrote themselves and then embedded into growing magic circles as Seero rewrote the device's protocols from the ground up.

A new core formed. It was no longer a simple machine, resonating with the tectonic movements of a planetary body. It was no longer a modified mana core, connecting to the Source through Shialnor's system. It was equal parts machine, mana, and living thing. It was an engine, a dungeon core, and even a heart.

It generated its own mana entirely autonomously, with the option to utilize its former connections to expand its output, but with a new safeguard. Its connections to the Realms of Mana or to the mana of Aelea, to the other dungeon cores or even the Primary Home Base, now routed through a new component based on the new Equalizer itself. Because now, with the computational and mana power of an entire Realm, Seero had finally managed to synthesize Iesnourium.

With the extra processors and the additional data from Commander Elise on the material, Seero had managed a full analysis. She had even used Divination, running Holy mana through the material to search its history as Ateia and Colleöne could. And she determined the reason why Iesnourium was so rare.

The material had arrived on Earth as a meteorite millions of years ago, that journey being key to its creation. It'd originated as the ruins of a star burped back out by the black hole that had destroyed it. It had then traveled through the cosmos for a truly extraordinary amount of time.

In the process, it had been subjected to cosmic forces no terrestrial environment could ever replicate, over and over, including some nonstandard forces unknown to science. And, in a cosmic fluke of infinitesimally tiny probability, these forces had coincidentally been applied to the same piece of material in the exact right sequence and timing to produce a truly extraordinary result. It was little wonder that neither science nor dungeon system had managed to replicate it as of yet.

But now, Seero could. Mana in sufficient quantities could make up the difference in the science, and now Seero had the mana and the computational resources necessary to pull it off.

Massive amounts of mana formed into a magical representation of the material. But like the water in the Realm of Deluge or the plants in the Realm of Overgrowth, the Iesnourium wasn't truly real. It was still ultimately composed of mana, a functionally identical reflection of the real thing. And if it were only the power of the Realm of Machines that Seero used, it would remain as such.

But that was not the only power Seero used.

A wave of golden-and-silver Holy mana passed over the core once it had fully formed. Seero's new computational resources, plus the data from multiple Realms of Mana terminations and Material Plane extensions, as well as her use of a partial anti-mana spell, helped her determine how to apply Holy power to a construct from the Realms of Mana without wiping it out.

She prevented the Holy mana from attacking it as foreign, instead focusing on its other special characteristic: its ability to take the mana of the Source and turn it into full, solid matter, no different than the mundane material of Earth.

And so, Seero added an Iesnourium input to her new core. Any mana coming into it from outside, whether from Shialnor's system, her subordinated dungeon cores, or the Realms of Mana, would run through it, and would be converted into the ideal energy frequency for the core to run at maximum efficiency. The incoming energy would be stripped of all hostile intent in the process. She would not be attacked from that direction again.

Once the core was complete, Seero's arms and legs began to regrow, waves of mana surging into the Equalizer and then out through her body. As with Ateia, her body had been erased at a level that prevented normal Recovery Magic or HP regeneration from restoring it, but that wasn't a problem. No, it was actually helpful in this case, for Seero did not plan to rebuild the same parts she previously had.

Soft gray metal flowed like water, twisting into muscle fibers and wires both before another layer coated over them. A wave of Holy mana then traveled down her limbs, and the metal solidified. This process repeated for the rest of her body, her exterior armor appearing to melt and reform.

On the surface, there appeared to be little difference from her original components. But internally, it was another story entirely. Cyborg wasn't entirely inaccurate as a description for this Realm; this world's first encounter with anything cyber-related was Seero, after all, who herself was partially organic, and all of the first monsters reflecting this Realm were cyborgs as well.

Seero could even see cyber plants like the ones growing in the Primary Home Base now starting to grow in various places of the Realm of Machines.

But Seero was not, in fact, a perfect balance of organic and cybernetic, as the NSLICE program had supposedly attempted to achieve. Dr. Ottosen had been too inefficient to achieve his stated goals, and in truth, favored the cybernetic over the organic. Seero, for her part, had been more machine than human, with only her mind and necessary organs remaining of her organic half.

In Seero's former world, this had been necessary. She had been a normal human intended to battle superheroes and supervillains. Her flesh had been simply too weak to achieve her task.

Here, in Aelea, her organic components were a necessary part of her capabilities, able to generate mana and wield it on their own. A more even balance of machine and flesh was now more efficient. Taking inspiration from the cyber plants, she wove metal and flesh together, intertwined as one. Muscle fibers hung onto a powered metal skeleton. Nerves and wires twisted together and joined as one.

It went all the way down to the cellular level, where her scans of different slimes, especially the metal slimes, proved invaluable. Microscopic drops of liquid metal now bonded with organic cells, forming a kind of living metal that was metallic machine and organic tissue at the same time . . . and could transform itself into either on command.

Seero was no longer a human with robotic replacements for her limbs like the NSLICE units had been. She was not an organic with a cybernetic exterior bonded to her, like the CELIU units were. For the current Seero, there was now no distinction between her organic and her cybernetic components. All of them were organic and cybernetic both. Her two halves were now one and the same, and she could adjust the balance of flesh and metal as was efficient for her present circumstances.

She had now achieved Dr. Ottosen's stated goal in full. A true fusion of cybernetic and organic, with all the strengths of both and the disadvantages of neither.

Seero tested her components. She flexed her arms and legs, shifting them between flesh and metal and reshaping them to form new configurations. She transferred mana from her new core and generated it directly within her components. She ran tests on her new processors and neurons, testing their capabilities both in isolation and in coordination with the wider CELIU network.

Her sensors cycled through countless different configurations, from high-tech, radar-based sensors of cutting-edge Earth design to the pure mana senses of organless monsters like slimes, and everything in between.

And then, of course, Seero tested weapons.

Her arms were converted into machine guns, flamethrowers, rail guns, enchanted blades, enchanted crossbows, enchanted spell projectors, laser cannons, missile launchers, and others. Any and all weapons Seero had data on.

Now aware of the possibility and freed from Dr. Ottosen's prohibitions on the subject, she even determined she could produce a tactical nuclear warhead, if needed—and apply some magical enhancements to it as well.

She could even produce a second Equalizer, though the production of Iesnourium was calculated as impractical outside of the Realms of Mana. So, she went ahead and upgraded the Equalizer while she was here so that it could receive and output truly staggering amounts of energy.

All her tests came back green. Every sensor and weapon worked at maximum efficiency, with updated protocols to make use of them stored in her memory. The various machines and programs of the Realm of Machines reported their tasks completed, one by one.

"Status Report: All systems online. All upgrades concluded. All components repaired and fully functional. Unit Seero, online and ready to terminate."

54

Terminate the Inferno!

"A Domides incarnating into the Material Plane? Well, if we set aside the frankly ridiculous amounts of mana such a feat would require, and the fact that there is no way to expose the Material Plane to a Realm of Mana to that extent without tearing the boundary of the world apart entirely—which itself is a near impossible feat with massive consequences—should a Domides ever fully incarnate, it would mean the end of Aelea and the entire Material Plane.

"I imagine the Aesdes would intervene directly at that point, which is what it would take for any of us to survive."

—Magister Arcanum Postumius Fadius Saenus, on the Domides.

With all upgrades concluded, Seero reached out with her sensors, attempting to reestablish contact with one of her dungeon cores or her subordinates. In a bit of a surprise, she found the connection almost immediately. It turned out, this was the Realm of Mana that dungeons with the Cyborg affinity were directly connected to.

She turned her attention to the location of the connection. There, she found large Geo-Oscillator Engines. Now that the Realm of Machines had been completed, it had solidified its connection with her dungeons with the very machine Seero had once used for that task.

There was one engine for each of her dungeons with the Cyborg affinity, each resonating with the dungeon core in question. Seero moved over to the largest one and reached out for it. Her fingers transformed into plugs and hooked up to the machine.

She fully reconnected to the Primary Home Base, and with it, all of her dungeons and subordinates still on Aelea. Mana began to stream back into her core, scrubbed by her new Iesnourium components; she confirmed that no damage was dealt and that the mana was not attempting to terminate her.

Now that she'd reconnected to the Primary Home Base, she could open an entrance to it, and did so immediately. Such a thing may have been dangerous in the other Realms, creating a Rift that mana and worse would flood out of. But the Realm of Machines was significantly more ordered than the others, every piece in its place to work toward its task. The CELIU network within the Realm simply kept its mana there.

And so, Seero left the Realms of Mana.

The incarnation of Inferno sent two blasts of fire, one toward Ningainë to its side, and one toward the army ahead. The Celestial Elf dodged the blast aimed at him while sending another glaive strike to intercept the other. But a third, fourth, and fifth arm grew out of the incarnation and launched more attacks toward him. The Immortal Sage was engulfed in flame.

He shot out from the blast, flames covering his body, cycling his mana to resist and slowly put them out. But in the meantime, he was no longer fighting the incarnation. And since he was already ablaze, its attention turned to those who weren't.

The High Archons began to retreat, as none of their spells had had any impact. They had even unleashed their forbidden magics: mental intrusions, life-draining, dark summons, Blood Magic. Yet, nothing managed to make any lasting impact.

Baoruinë madly tossed ever larger fireballs at the incarnation, but it absorbed the flames as the Celestial ranted at it, while Emperors Lucius and Julius pointed their blades toward the burning flames.

"Bring it down!"

Ritual circles covered the field as every mage in the Empire joined together. Torrents of water fell from the sky as Lightning Bolts rained from above. Giant tornados wrapped around, and mountains rose to crush the incarnation. Countless bolts from crossbows and siege engines filled the sky.

They were joined by a thunderous roar as every gun in Uscfrea and Seero's armies opened fire. Machine guns, rifles, specially designed harpoon guns for the Dobhar. Artillery pieces, antiair cannons, missiles of every size, precision bombs, cluster rounds. Rail guns and laser cannons joined in as Melion and Snuan directed the airships.

But nothing worked. Every spell and projectile burned before it arrived or made minimal impact, and the incarnation raised its hand, ready to launch a blast of fire that would engulf the entire army.

Ateia winced. She glanced over at Lilussees, the arachne's organic eyes wide open as she shook her head. Neither of them had recovered, and they couldn't stop another attack.

Suddenly, they froze. Every cyborg and dungeon master on the field froze. Taog began to grin as 01R had tears running down his face. Rattingtale stopped trying to flee, and Lilussees smiled even as she let out a sigh.

"Like, *finally*."

And Ateia burst out laughing. "I knew she was alive!"

01R shouted for joy as he opened a portal to the Primary Home Base. Out stepped Seero, her robotic and organic eyes both glowing bright red. The Herald of the New Dawn's jaw dropped before he quickly closed it, and he pursed his lips.

"Honestly, at this point, I shouldn't be surprised that you've yet again cheated death. And I really shouldn't have trusted Shialnor's work to kill you, huh?" He glanced up at the towering incarnation of flame between them. "But, well, I suppose this is as good a time as any. An incarnation of Inferno with an open Rift to its own Realm should be a challenge even for you."

The incarnation launched a blast of fire, a massive cone that could engulf the entire army.

"Warning: Risk of friendlies' termination at unacceptable levels. Equalizer engaged."

Even as Seero spoke, a magic circle formed in the air. A magic circle which caused every mage present to frown, for it was . . . *wrong*. Every pattern was inverted, every safeguard reversed. And moreover, it was filled with some sort of rainbow-colored darkness, a black substance which seemed to absorb light. Seero had, after all, cut the inefficient emission of light from the Equalizer's output, as well as its tendency to react with the ambient mana.

The anti-mana reverse spell activated, and a Prismatic Dome appeared in front of the blast of fire. The flames flickered and died as they contacted the anti-mana, while the barrier emitted rainbow sparks as it reacted with the mana in turn.

"Observation: Hostile mana levels exceed base core output."

Flames from the giant Rift continued to feed into the incarnation, who did not drop its assault even as the anti-mana stopped the attack. Seero determined she would need more output to match it indefinitely, much less overcome it.

So, she acquired some. Lifting her arm to the side, she fired a beam of anti-mana into the nearest Rift, stripping it of its attribute. The Equalizer then shifted the output, and the beam converted into that of angular lightning with ones and zeros inside of it. The mana from the Rift now adopted the new attribute and shifted its connection to a different Realm.

Mana from the Realm of Machines surged into Seero like the Realm of Inferno fed the incarnation. The power output of the Equalizer surged, and the anti-mana Prismatic Dome grew in size and density. The programs of the Realm of Machines moved to assist her with the task, and as they left their Realm, something happened. Their mana condensed and began to take shape.

00B-Beta noticed and lent assistance, providing them with protocols on how to condense into forms compatible with the Material Plane.

And so, a giant cyber elemental began to take shape around Seero in order to better link the processors and mana of Machines to her. And it took the form of a bear made out of electricity, mana, and code. 00B nodded and roared to welcome the new members of the family as an incarnation of the Realm of Machines moved to fulfill its primary directive.

Seero continued to fire anti-mana beams at the various Rifts around her, converting them into Machine Rifts and growing the amount of mana and processors available to her. She stopped powering the anti-mana spell directly with the Equalizer, instead using it to form spell circles that would convert mana into more anti-mana. She then fed the mana from Machines directly into these spell circles, which sent anti-mana into the barrier spell, dramatically increasing the flow.

Eventually, she had enough. The flames of Inferno made no progress as they crashed against the barrier. The flames making up the incarnation blazed, and it thrust all of its power at the protection, intent on burning the object which dared resist its fire. But try as it might, nothing changed. The flames faded away as the barrier eliminated the mana powering them without weakening, no matter how much mana it had to deal with.

And now, Seero had enough mana for another attack. She formed an anti-mana Prismatic Bombardment spell and began to assault the Inferno Rift directly, bypassing the incarnation ahead.

The incarnation did not react. It couldn't, for that went against its very nature. It only knew of destruction by flames; it only knew to burn anything that dared to stand before it. It could not conceive the threat anti-mana posed. In fact, the very concept of defense was foreign to it. It thus ignored the anti-mana beam, fixated as it was on burning the barrier in front of it.

The mana of Inferno began to convert to the mana of Machines. This Rift was much larger than any Seero had ever dealt with, and so did not go quietly. The flames of Inferno surged, attempting to burn down the new mana growing within the Rift. Licks of fire shot into the Realm of Machines, setting metal and code ablaze.

But the Realm of Machines adapted. New machines formed around the burning metals, forming furnaces and fuel-based engines from a time before the Geo-Oscillator was invented on Earth. As the flames of Inferno burnt the machines, the furnaces took the melted metals and reforged them into new alloys and components.

The machines that were burnt away entirely were placed inside engine compartments, the process moving pistons and spinning turbines to generate more power. Destruction by fire was harnessed to fuel the function of machines, generating new Machine mana in the process. With the anti-mana erasing the majority of the Inferno mana, that was enough to contain what excess made it through.

And so, the Rift continued to convert from Inferno to Machines. The blast of fire grew weaker, and the incarnation itself began to shrink. Eventually, over half the Rift converted, and then the process accelerated. The incarnation faded away as it spent the last of itself trying to burn the barrier.

The Herald pursed his lips as the Realm of Machines stood before him, a thousand metallic voices echoing with Seero's.

"Target acquired. Engaging terminate-with-extreme-prejudice protocols."

55

Terminate the Other World!

"I was there, you know. Countless eons past, before the boons of the Aesdes were ever offered to the Enlightened. It was there that the Great Demon Lord broke the boundary of the heavens and gained such overwhelming power than none could stand against him.

"The entire continent of Letoris fell under his sway in but an instant. We sent aid once we became aware, the mightiest warriors under heaven banding together as one and setting out to save the world.

"We never even reached the shore. But we got close enough to see the Aesdes themselves descend from the Blessed Land to give battle. We learned then what it truly means to defy the heavens.

"Letoris was not merely destroyed, no. Letoris was cast from the world, banished to the void where nothing lives—where nothing can *live, not even the Domides themselves."*

—The Celestial Emperor, on the fall of Letoris.

The Herald of the New Dawn sighed. "Well done. The first hero to also utilize the power of the Realms directly and to defeat a Domides' incarnation, no less. Even I can't resist you at this stage; not with the boundary collapsing and the power of the Rifts at your disposal."

But then he sneered, even as Seero's magic circles turned toward him. "But you must understand that you cannot win by simply killing me. The hole in the world is beyond your ability to repair, and it will continue to grow even should I perish. All that my death will achieve is to stop the new world's growth at its current limits. No matter what, the old world will fade, and this new one you stand upon shall replace it. In its present, unfinished form, if I am not around to mold it."

Seero's robotic eye flickered. "Dismissive Response: Then this unit will terminate the other world."

With that, the anti-mana Prismatic Bombardment opened fire. The Herald of the New Dawn ceased his ritual and raised his hand, redirecting his mana to defense. The Great Demon Lord's core was not the only one he had built into his own suit, after all.

A corrupted core of Inferno sent out a cone of all-burning mana. A corrupted core of Overgrowth began to grow an ever-expanding shield of vines before him. A corrupted core of Deluge sent an endless torrent of water. Devastating lightning from Tempest, searing light from Blinding, a tide of rats from Verminflood, and the shrouding darkness of Eternal Night to obscure his location.

But it didn't matter. He may have had all the mana from the dungeons of Aelea that Seero hadn't claimed, but Seero now had the support of a Realm of Mana in a place where the boundary had been ripped apart. He may have had multiple corrupted dungeons at his disposal, but Seero had Rifts large enough for direct incarnations of the Domides to appear.

In fact, looking at the giant mana bear standing over Seero, he couldn't rule out that she had somehow recruited a Domides of her own.

And then there was that anti-mana of hers, which rendered the nature of the spells he cast entirely moot. The best he could do was negate some of it by throwing mana in its path . . . except Seero had adjusted her attack. She now used the mana infiltration and conversion methods used earlier, so his spells were just feeding into her assault.

The Herald frowned as all the power of the destructive Realms was negated and absorbed and a black beam approached him. He didn't even have escape measures prepared at this point because he was all in at this point. Why would he flee from his new world into the one dying below? Who could challenge the Rifts once they had opened in full?

He made a token effort to start a Spatial spell, but the anti-mana reached him first, erasing both his spells and the mana running through his body.

And then Seero's arm transformed, growing several times larger. She aimed an enchanted rail gun loaded with an explosive Iesnourium shell right at him.

He opened his mouth to speak his final words—

Seero opened fire before then, and the Herald of the New Dawn saw no more.

"Hostile terminated."

Seero reverted her arm back to normal as she watched the sparkling rainbow explosion of the Iesnourium shell. The last of the Heralds had been terminated, but the fight was not over. She looked up into the sky, where a hole continued to grow.

"Seero!" She turned her attention behind her as Ateia and Taog ran forward and hugged her. "I knew you'd come back."

Seero . . . slowly returned the embrace. "Happy Response: This unit is glad to see her friendlies are unharmed. However, this unit does still need to address a critical situation."

They let go as Ateia nodded with a serious face. "Right."

Taog looked up at the hole in the skies and blinked. "Yeah. Um, Seero, do you have any ideas on how to deal with that?"

"Analyzing . . ."

Seero did not; at least, not right away. She could close the Rifts forming to the Realms of Mana; however, the main hole didn't lead to the Source but rather to some sort of empty void. Her normal Material Plane–patching protocol wouldn't work here.

So, Seero set her ever-growing processors to work even as she converted newly appearing Rifts to the Realm of Machines.

"Analysis complete. Solution determined."

Ateia and Taog smiled at that. Seero walked to the Herald of the New Dawn's former position at the magic circle at the center of the black continent. She began to repair it—fixing a few inefficiencies she found in the design—before turning to Ateia.

"Request: This unit will require Ateia's assistance."

Ateia smiled and nodded. "Anything you need, Seero."

Activating her repulsors, Ateia boosted into the sky. She flew away from the black continent and back down to the surface below.

"Acknowledged. Engaging world termination protocols."

Taog froze. "Wait, what?"

But Seero did not elaborate. She reactivated the formation, linking her to all the dungeons in the world. She sent some Holy mana through the bond to eliminate any remaining corruption before she began, then channeled the mana into her anti-mana conversion magic circles and fired a massive Prismatic Bombardment of anti-mana into the air before her.

Her target? The very boundaries of the world.

She calculated they were in a critical state, and repairing them from scratch while trying to close all the smaller Rifts constantly forming would be an inefficient method. So, she simply terminated them altogether. Her mana also wrapped around all the Rifts to the Realm of Machines and moved them together, fusing them into one massive Rift in the sky.

The world began to rumble. The sky split open, replaced by images of machinery and code as the Material Plane opened fully to the Realms of Mana. Or rather, one Realm of Mana.

And that's when Ateia went to work. Back on the surface and away from the Rifts, Ateia could fully reconnect to the flows of Holy mana in the world. She redirected their flow away from the boundary and instead spread them throughout the world.

And so, when the boundary opened fully, Ateia began to grunt and shout. She willed the world to hold itself together even as torrents of mana attempted to rip it apart, much like Seero had held her together when the Heralds' ritual had done the same to her.

And as she did, her light spread throughout the world. Every being, every soul, turned their eyes to her. They understood that the world was under threat, and that Ateia was trying to save it. Sparks of hope lit in their hearts and flew into the currents of Holy mana containing the will of the Lady of Hope and Perseverance. The sparks sank into the parts of the world falling apart and reinforced them, keeping the world together.

Meanwhile, the programs and machines of the Realm of Machines worked as well. They constructed walls and barriers, closed connections and valves, refactored code, and rerouted circuits. They did everything they could to keep their own mana contained, to prevent it from flowing into the Material Plane that had suddenly opened up to them. It was only because of their and Ateia's efforts that the Material Plane was not subsumed in the endless mana of the Source.

Seero then opened entrances to the Primary Home Base both in the Material Plane and in the Realm of Machines. She expanded the entrance as wide as it would go before beginning to form a truly massive magic circle. She tasked the ever-growing processors of the Realm of Machines with building it, using the endless mana from the Source. Soon, they finished, and the spell triggered.

A massive Spatial Angling began to warp and fold the *entire Material Plane.* It wrapped around until the flat plane had formed a sphere—with the entrance to the Primary Home Base at its center. Most importantly, the Realm of Machines in the sky followed the curving of the world and joined back to itself, covering up the hole leading to nowhere.

Seero then began to fire the Equalizer, forming anti-mana conversion circles to power yet another plane-wide spell. A thin barrier of anti-mana formed in the sky all around, erasing some of the mana of the Realm of Machines. Ateia spread the Holy mana of the world up into the sky to meet it, while she reached down into the center of the world to connect with the Primary Home Base now at its heart.

A circuit of Holy mana formed and spread into the sky, extending the Material Plane further while forming a new barrier with it. At this point, Seero dropped the anti-mana barrier and adjusted the spell to reshape the boundary of the world.

She was not content to simply recreate it. Instead, she hooked it up to various machines and inputs being created in the Realm of Machines.

There was a final rumble, and then the plane grew still. The Rifts and holes in the sky closed. The mana flowing through the black continent pulsed one more time before it began to crumble into ash as it lowered to the ground. It finished just as it placed the people on top back on the ground, a light breeze blowing away the last remnants of the fallen continent.

A circuit of mana now formed through the world. It flowed from the Realm of Machines into the Primary Home Base as the Heart of the New World resonated with the Geo-Oscillators in the Realm of Machines. It then flowed out into the dungeons of the world and into the Material Plane, nourishing and sustaining everything within. The excess flowed up into the boundary, where it was siphoned back into the Realm of Machines by connections and valves nowhere near as vulnerable to corruption or degradation.

And so, the world was terminated, reshaped, and reborn.

All thanks to the girl named Seero.

56

Unit Seero and Her Friends

"Protective Statement: This unit no longer has friendlies. Her friendlies have been redesignated as family."

—Commander Elise, on her friends.

Taog stared up at the sky, then shrugged. "You know what? Nope. Not even going to question what happened."

Ateia tilted her head. "But . . . Seero sent out the after-action report with full data on the protocol?"

Taog stared at her with half-open eyes before frowning. "*ANYWAY*, there is one thing I'm wondering. Where exactly did the Blessed Land go?"

Ateia's eyes widened, then she furrowed her brow. "Seero . . . can you . . . ?"

But Seero's robotic eye was flickering. "Warning: Spatial anomaly detected."

Suddenly, a bright star appeared in the sky, visible even in the daylight. The hearts of every inhabitant of Aelea lifted. Soon, an army of dragons soared through the sky, letting out mighty roars, as three figures descended as well, glowing with golden-and-silver light.

The first was a man in his prime, wearing armor made of bright light and riding on a cloud. He was leaning on the warrior standing next to him, who was dressed in plate armor and carrying her golden sword. To their side stood a short girl with a necklace of glowing rainbow jewels.

Anualë, First of the Aesdes; Colleöne, Lady of Courage and Victory; and Shialnor, Lady of Mana and the Boundary, descended to the surface of Aelea.

Colleöne frowned. "Okay, first of all: *why* exactly is the Material Plane a sphere now? Just, how does that even work? That breaks every law of reality we know . . ."

Anualë just sighed and shook his head while Shialnor shrugged. "I know not how or why, but we all know who."

"VICTORIA!"

Anualë smiled and let go of Colleöne while Shialnor moved to support him. Colleöne grinned as Ateia flew up to them and slammed into her. She pulled the girl into a hug. "My dear Ateia, I cannot express my joy to see you again."

Ateia nodded then tilted her head. "Just, where did you go? And how did you get back?"

Colleöne frowned. "It was my fault. We were deceived, and one of our own took advantage of my and Shialnor's cores. He took advantage of the power we left there and sent the Blessed Land far away."

Anualë shook his head. "The fault is mine, Colleöne. It was my duty to look after the Aesdes, and so my duty to anticipate the possibility of betrayal."

Colleöne shook her head as well but continued. "We were left adrift for quite some time in an empty void, sucking away at the very life of the Blessed Land. It took much of our might to keep it intact. But then, we had some help . . ."

Shortly after the Blessed Land vanished . . .

Colleöne frowned as she stood at the edge of the Blessed Land, holding her hands out toward a barrier surrounding the entire thing. The other Aesdes and Ancient Dragons lined the edges of the land with her, all working together to maintain the barrier.

The Aesdes were holding, but they were still drifting in a hungry, empty darkness; one that slowly siphoned away their power. It was no Realm of Mana, for it consumed mana, heat, life force, anything in contact with it. But this battle was beyond her.

Colleöne was no expert on what lay beyond the boundaries of all reality, even beyond the Source. None of the Aesdes were. And the Ancient Dragons, while powerful, knew even less. After all, they were the descendants of the Aesdes who'd turned toward the Material Plane, not away from it.

So, they were stuck, holding back the void while hoping someone would come up with a solution. The Lord of Magic and the Lady of Knowledge were working together to figure it out, but even they were out of their depths. This place had no mana even, so a magical solution seemed . . . unlikely.

Well, the Aesdes would not run out of power for a long, *long* time, so Colleöne believed a solution would be found eventually. But who knew what would happen to Aelea in their absence? As such, none of the Aesdes were willing to wait.

If only there was something they could do . . .

Just then, Colleöne heard something. A voice, cutting through the empty silence.

"Okay, I think the Lord of the Abyss said it was somewhere around here."

"*Somewhere? Around here?!* Voidspeaker-senpai, *please* tell me you didn't wing it before you brought us on a rescue mission into the void. *Please* tell me you did even the most basic of calculations first."

Colleöne blinked. She saw . . . a group of people?

"Oh, come on, Nana! High school was a long time ago, and I graduated, didn't I? I said I was sorry; how long are you going to hold it against me?"

"For as long as it took us to tutor you."

"Not you too, Chrono!"

A group of people floated through the empty space, seemingly surrounded in a barrier of the same darkness that now surrounded the Blessed Land. And Colleöne gasped as they came into view.

"Incredulous Observation: Against all probability, it appears Voidspeaker's potentially nonexistent calculations were correct. Target has been located."

For she saw someone extremely familiar. A group of people, most of whom Colleöne had only seen in the recordings of Seero's persons of interest, floated right in front of them. But among them was a certain cyborg she *had* seen.

"Seero?! What are you doing here?!"

The cyborg's robotic eye flickered. "Amused Correction: This unit is not the unit designated Seero. This unit is designated NSLICE-00P, colloquial designation: Elise. It is nice to meet you in person."

All of Elise's companions turned to her. "Wait, Elise, you know these people?!"

"Mischievous Answer: This unit has never encountered the targets in question. However, we happen to have a mutual friendly . . ."

"Surprised Exclamation: Friendly Colleöne encountered Commander Elise?"

Colleöne nodded as Seero joined the conversation, her robotic eye flickering rapidly. "It turned out your former commander knows a mage who specializes in the dimension we found ourselves in and has connections to some of the denizens there. They were able to help us find our way home." Reaching into her pocket, Colleöne pulled out a mechanical device. "She asked us to give this to you."

Seero took the device, which at first appeared like a simple box with a plug. But her scans of the object indicated it gave off significant nonstandard energy signatures, as well as traces of Iesnourium.

She went ahead and plugged into it.

Establishing connection . . .

Seero's human eye opened wide as she registered nonstandard energy exiting the box and passing through the boundary of the Material Plane. A small window opened in her UI.

An interuniversal video communication screen, now displaying a familiar smiling cyborg girl.

"Happy Greeting: Hello, Unit Seero. It is nice to see you again."

"Commander Elise . . ." This time, it was Seero's cybernetic components who experienced an overwhelming emotional reaction. "Despondent Apology: I am sorry, Commander Elise. I failed your mission, abandoned my primary directive; I—"

But Commander Elise shook her head. "Affectionate Interruption: Unit Seero has nothing to apologize for. Your organic components were correct; you already fulfilled my intention with those suggestions. Rather, I am the one who must apologize. It was I who sent you on a mission with a critical risk of termination, and I who did not anticipate the possibility you would end up in another universe where my suggestions wouldn't help you. For that, I am truly sorry."

Commander Elise then smiled once more. "Joyful Observation: However, you found your own way and achieved everything I'd hoped for you and more. You found your own friends, you set yourself free, and you even chose your own designation. I couldn't be happier with what you've done."

Seero stared for a moment, all of her processors halting, and then . . . her organic eye began to leak fluid as another emotional reaction surged through her circuits.

But this one did not feel unpleasant.

"G-Gratitude: This unit . . . I . . ."

Elise continued to smile at her. "Proposal: Would Unit Seero like to conduct a final mission debrief? This unit would love to hear about Unit Seero's journey."

Seero froze for a moment, her processors calculating. She smiled slightly.

"Affirmative."

From then on, Seero and Elise began to speak regularly, and the last fear in Seero's processors faded away, allowing her to step into her new life without a single regret.

And so, the unit formerly known as NSLICE-00P, now the girl known as Seero, terminated all hostiles and saved a second universe. This time not by the order of a commander, a mad doctor, or an evil organization, but by her own will.

She had gone looking for a commander . . . and found a family. She had gone to upgrade her components . . . and unlocked her heart. She had sought friendlies . . . and found friends.

And from then on, she lived happily ever after.

AFTERSTORY

Terminate the Status!

"I am not one to speak of current events, but those that occurred within my lifetime have proven so momentous that I cannot justify excluding them in any comprehensive history of the Empire written henceforth. The details of these events have and will continue to be recorded in their own work, for this edition I shall include but the smallest summary.

"The life of Her Majesty Seero will also be discussed in its own work, as her impact is too great to be adequately summarized, and the exact details of her journey are still being gathered. I shall focus here on the Aesdes and their impact on the Enlightened.

"When the boons of the Aesdes vanished, many in Aelea believed the Aesdes had abandoned us. This initially seemed borne out when nearly every dungeon in the Empire began to assault the outside world simultaneously, and then the Blessed Land itself vanished from the sky.

"But then came Indomitable Ateia, the Lady of Hope and Perseverance, She Who Defies Despair. A new Aesdes we had not been aware of arrived on the surface of Aelea for the first time since the days of myth and legend, and personally led the forces of first the Elteni Empire and then of all Aelea in the War of the Realms. This made it abundantly clear that the Aesdes had not, in fact, abandoned the peoples of Aelea until the Blessed Land returned to its place in the sky.

"That the boons have not returned as of the time of this writing is a matter of great concern and debate. I will leave it to future historians to discuss the reasons and implications, seeing as the events are still in progress. But what I can state with certainty is this: The continued presence of Indomitable Ateia conclusively proves that, whatever happens next, Aelea has not been abandoned."

—*The History of the Empire*, latest edition, by Hostus Tettidius Clodian.

Colleöne blinked. "You . . . want to know Seero's current status? What it would be now if Rélseomo hadn't disabled our systems?"

Colleöne and Shialnor turned to look at one another. They then burst out laughing as hard as they could, Colleöne clutching her stomach as Shialnor rolled on the floor.

They froze once they realized they were the only ones laughing. Shialnor's eyes widened. "Wait . . . you're serious?"

Shialnor shifted to her human form and stared. Colleöne took a deep breath and heaved a massive sigh while holding her head. They glanced at each other, nodded, and spoke as one.

"Denied."

Shialnor continued staring without blinking. "She replicated my dungeon system. She implemented monster summoning all by herself. There's no mage or dungeon master in all of Aelea's history who's managed to do that, who could have done that even had I given them the information I gave Seero. And she did it not in millennia, not in centuries, not even in years. She did it in, what, a couple of weeks tops?"

Colleöne nodded. "She did the same for my boons as well. Ateia may have taken the lead on that, but it was the CELIU network which allowed her to do it, so Seero's contribution there is substantial as well."

Shialnor continued staring. "And that's just replicating the old stuff. She broke through the Spatial Angling that's supposed to make dungeon walls invincible, then replicated it for herself. Did you notice how she also figured out a way to fight and subjugate other dungeons with mana alone? And then proceeded to subjugate nearly every major dungeon in the entire Empire? Should I give her a Great Demon Lord perk? Here I thought you didn't want to encourage that sort of thing.

"Oh, and they were all partially corrupted too, so guess she'd need a Dungeon Purifier *AND* a Dungeon Conqueror feat for Every. Last. One of them."

Colleöne stared blankly herself. "She slew a dragon, entire hordes of monsters, and an army of Sun Elves, which we have to count since they were working with the Heralds of the New Dawn. Oh, and since she saved *all of Aelea*, we'll have to give her a 'Hero of' feat for every single Enlightened species in the entire world, plus the perks for deeds to save the ecosystems. And then there's her work on the corrupted dungeons.

"Not only did she purify more than any other hero ever has—she modified the Blink spells to move her beyond the boundaries of the Material Plane and into the Realms of Mana, where she subsequently terminated the connection between the corrupted dungeons and their Realm. That's about . . . a dozen new perks right there, and I'd need to hand her every single magic perk that exists for that feat too."

Shialnor continued, staring intently. "That's a feat of dungeon craft beyond any I've ever seen. Even I wouldn't have used that method, seeing as I don't have access to that whole anti-mana thing. Which means *more* new perks just for her."

Colleöne nodded. "Oh, and that last battle . . ." She stopped to sigh. "That last battle. She defeated an incarnation of a Domides. A *Domides*. Of Inferno, no less. That's something that required our direct intervention last time. She not only defeated it—she *overpowered* it. I'd propose inviting her to the Blessed Land for that alone."

Shialnor continued staring. "Should I give her a 'Matron of' perk for an entire Realm of Mana and all the monsters and spirits that will spawn from it? And we're all avoiding thinking about the fact that she *tamed a Domides*. She may have created it outright. Tell me, what sort of perk or boon should I give her for *that?*"

Colleöne narrowed her eyes, her face turning dark. "She is also the first Enlightened in all of Aelea's history to slay an Aesdes, if a former one. Do you wish for me to design a perk for that feat? Do you wish for others to see 'Aesdes Slayer' on her status? Because since it was in service to the world, I couldn't possibly justify overlooking it were we to award her per our previous boons."

Shialnor continued staring and leaned in close. "I move to classify Seero as an Aesdes-level being who will no longer be quantified within our system, retroactive to the start of the attack on the Blessed Land."

Colleöne leaned in, staring intently as well. "I second that. Let us reward Seero for her deeds more directly, as an equal."

Anualë shrank back and held up his hands as the pair stared right in his face. "I'm sorry, I was just curious . . ."

But neither Colleöne nor Shialnor backed up. "In fact, Anualë, we need to speak with you on that. Shialnor and I have discussed it and thus agree. We think that the time of the systems has passed."

Shialnor nodded. "And before you think this is just me being lazy, please consider the current structure of the world. All of the mana passing into the dungeons and the plane now first passes through the Realm of Machines and Seero's personal Material Plane . . . and nearly every dungeon in the world is subordinated to her as well.

"The Domides or cyber elemental swarm or whatever you want to call those minds in the Realm of Machines are analyzing the mana levels of the world in real time and balancing things to the precise level required for the growth of the world without allowing the surplus that would generate excess monsters. The boundary has never been stronger, and I'm predicting that the number and strength of monsters is going to drop dramatically in the future.

"Additionally, Seero is personally protecting all of her subordinate dungeons and building her own cores at a rate that I won't need to make any additional ones for centuries, if that, so all future cores will fall under her umbrella as well. So . . . the system I created to enable dungeon cores to protect themselves from monsters and the Enlightened isn't really necessary anymore. Seero's got it handled."

Colleöne nodded as well.

"I agree with Shialnor's assessment; the levels of monsters we should see in the future should be manageable with the current level of Enlightened society, even without granting direct boons to their champions. That is before considering the impact Seero will have on the rate of technological development, particularly that of the Turannian peoples and the Elteni Empire. Our boons were always for the sake of evening the odds. Those odds are now well in the favor of the Enlightened."

Colleöne's eyes narrowed once more. "And there is another facet of this we must consider. I believe this crisis has made the problems with our previous method abundantly clear. Whatever our intentions, whatever our belief that our boons were an indirect form of rewarding the Enlightened for their own efforts, the truth is that they came to rely upon us in the way we always sought to avoid.

"The Enlightened of Aelea grew dependent upon my system and structured their entire societies around it, and most of them were rendered helpless when that system was removed. The system itself also proved far more vulnerable than we imagined, relying upon a single point of failure in the Blessed Land that could bring down the entire thing in an instant.

"Perhaps previously we could have taken the safety of the Blessed Land for granted, but no more. As the Lady of Courage and Victory, She Who Guides the Champions of the World, I say it is time that we allow the people of Aelea to stand on their own merits."

She then dropped her glare and rubbed the back of her head with a sheepish smile. "Well, I'd also like to say we let them develop without our interference, but Ateia and Seero have too close a relationship with the world for that to remain true. Rather, I think we should discuss how we can support the world, in both more direct and yet less foundational manners than we did previously."

Anualë slowly nodded his head. "I concur with that. The fate of Rélseomo has given me much to think about and much to reconsider, and the rest of the Aesdes are also shifting their views on these things. Very well, let's convene the Aesdes and discuss how we will move forward from now."

He then gave a wry smile. "After all, Miss Seero and the Lady of Hope and Perseverance will guide the world whether we interfere or not. I suppose we should not leave them to walk alone."

Anualë and Colleöne set off to gather the Aesdes, discussing the situation as they moved. Shialnor, on the other hand, turned back into her cat form. She stretched her back all the way out before exhaling a deep breath.

And then, she gave a huge grin.

"Finally—*finally!* It's finally not *my* job anymore to manage the entire boundary of the Material Plane all by myself! I was seriously worried after that stupid Rélseomo went and poked all those holes in my system. Does he know just how much work it was going to take for me to fix everything, and then redesign the system to ensure it wouldn't happen again? I'd bring him back just to kill him myself, that jerk!

"But now, Seero has it covered! And everything's working even better than I could've done myself! Great job, Seero! You're my favorite dungeon master! And now, I'll *finally* be able to sleep as much as I want! No more work for me!"

Shialnor trotted out of the room with a spring in her step. That is, until the Aesdes decided that she and Colleöne would now work directly with Seero to ensure the continued safety of Aelea.

AFTERSTORY

Elteno Eternal

"And we have an Aesdes."

—Maior Generalis Maximia Tetrica, during the most recent ceasefire negotiations between the Elteni Empire and the Empire of the Sun.

The city of Elteno stretched out around a wide river, its stone structure arranged haphazardly and in winding streets, built before Imperial standards were even conceived of. The forum where once the senate gathered in the days before the Empire now stood empty, little more than a museum for the curious historian. It was a humble structure, no taller than the houses around it, with no built-in barracks or guardhouse like the later designs. A relic from the time before Emperors or the Legion.

But today, these ancient halls opened once more, with legionnaires standing guard at the entrances. For the first time in centuries, the leaders of the Empire gathered in these halls once more to discuss and debate as the senators of old.

A table was set up in the center of the forum, with six chairs placed around it. Emperor Lucius and Consul Aemilia Hibera represented the North, Emperor Julius and Maior Generalis Tetrica represented the East, and Crown Princess Evelanis of Mirima and Aedile Hortensus were invited to report on the status of the South.

Maior Generalis Tetrica stared intently at Emperor Lucius. "So, you had an Aesdes on your payroll?"

Emperor Lucius shrugged with a smile. "You think I would have kept it a secret had I known?"

Emperor Julius smirked. "No, I suppose you wouldn't have, Cousin."

Maior Generalis Tetrica sighed.

"Well, speaking of familial relations, let's address the first elephantom in the room. I am told that Indomitable Ateia, the Lady of Hope and Perseverance and the youngest of the Aesdes, is the daughter of the Exploratore Amulius Olcinius Herenus, the Hero of Elteno himself. Who, if I am not mistaken, was married to the daughter of the late Emperor Herius, albeit an illegitimate one.

"That would mean we have an Aesdes still walking the world who is the rightful heir to the throne of the Northern Empire, the throne of Elteno and Velus himself."

She stared intently at Emperor Lucius. He sighed and shook his head. "We've already asked. Indomitable Ateia, the Lady of Hope and Perseverance, has formally renounced any claim to the throne of the Empire. And yes, she has also quit as an inquisitor and Exploratore."

Emperor Julius sighed as well. "Damn."

Emperor Lucius shook his head. "Yes, Elteno eternal shall remain just a saying, after all."

Consul Aemilia then cleared her throat. "Yes, well, now that we have established the fantasies will remain fantasy, shall we discuss what we are actually going to do? If nothing else, this entire series of events has demonstrated some concerning holes in the Empire, not to mention the serious matter of the South now joining the Empire officially."

Crown Princess Evelanis hung her head. "We will do as you say."

Aedile Hortensus smiled. "Well, don't look too down, Crown Princess. I do think we should consider how best to utilize Mirima and the Southern Realms, and I personally believe there is an argument for some continuity of policy. A bit of autonomy here and there is good for business."

Maior Generalis Tetrica stared at the Southern pair. "No more battle airship fleets, though. You rely on the Legion from now on. And we are going to have a *long* talk about your approach to cultists."

Crown Princess Evelanis just silently nodded. Maior Generalis Tetrica glanced over at the pair from the North.

"And that brings us to the second elephantom in the room. How exactly are we going to split jurisdiction of the Southern Realms? Yes, I'm aware Mirima and the Council of the Southern Realms signed their treaty with Emperor Lucius alone, but surely the North doesn't plan to attempt administering a territory twice its current size on its own? You're stretched thin enough as it is . . . and that's before we consider that the Aesdes have not reimplemented their boons."

Emperor Lucius shrugged and smiled at Consul Aemilia. Consul Aemilia motioned to one of the guards from the North, who handed her a scroll.

"If I may?"

Emperor Julius nodded, so Consul Aemilia passed the scroll to Maior Generalis Tetrica. The Maior Generalis frowned as she opened and spread it in front of herself and Emperor Julius.

"What are you two playing at . . ." The words died in her throat as she began to read the scroll. "This . . . is . . ."

Consul Aemilia nodded. "Yes, I have concluded an official treaty of trade and friendship with Her Majesty Seero, the Queen of the United Turannian Peoples, the Empress of the Dungeons, the Heart of the World, and the Lady of the Realm of Machines. And the official superior of Indomitable Ateia, I feel I must add.

"She will assist us with the security of any territory the Northern Emperor is responsible for while the Legion recovers. Magister Utriusque Militia Canus is going to take the opportunity to reform the North's organization and recruitment practices, as well as retrain the North's legions from the ground up. He has stated he intends to remove any dependence on the Aesdes's boons whether they are restored or not.

"I trust that, given the magister's record, we should have more than enough manpower to cover our responsibilities by the time Her Majesty Seero withdraws her forces. We will not need to request assistance from the Eastern Court . . . and you will need all the troops you can get to conclude your first real peace negotiations with the Empire of the Sun. High Archon Nolnyth's cooperation will certainly help, but the rest of the Sun Elves won't agree to peace unless you make them."

Consul Aemilia couldn't help a sly smile. "On that account, I should mention Her Majesty Seero is also willing to open trade between the wider Empire and her people. Including the export of arms, such as the weapons, golems, and airships utilized during the War of the Realms."

Maior Generalis Tetrica narrowed her eyes at the consul. "How many?"

Emperor Julius raised an eyebrow. "Um, Maior Generalis?"

The Maior Generalis ignored him and kept her eyes fixed on the consul. "How many of those airships can you get us if we let you have the South? I want the golems too, and the weapons the Dobhar used. If we could equip the sharpshooters and architecti with those, we wouldn't need the Aesdes's boons to restore the Legion back to full strength . . . and beyond."

Emperor Julius groaned and held his head. "Maior Generalis, we should at least consider the political and economic implications of conceding the entirety of the Southern Realms, regardless of the amount of military power gained."

Consul Aemilia looked him in the eye and smirked. "Her Majesty Seero has agreed to sell us three of her dungeon-core-powered designs. The ones with nearly invincible hulls and enough firepower to match an Archon one-on-one. We will be keeping one, of course, but have yet to decide on the allocation of the others. Imagine how the High Archons might respond if you ride one of those to the negotiations."

Maior Generalis Tetrica slowly turned the stare to her supposed liege. "Julius."

Emperor Julius rested his elbows on the table, crossed his hands together, lowered his head down on top of his hands, and then heaved a massive sigh. Consul Aemilia now turned her attention toward the crown princess of Mirima.

"Of course, a significant trade deal with Her Majesty Seero will require building substantial new trade routes. Unfortunately, the Northern Empire lacks any significant merchant shipping in the Northern Seas, so we will need to acquire some if we wish to spread this trade beyond our holdings in Turannia.

"In particular, I've noticed the Southern Realms commercial airship network, and wonder if something like that could be expanded to connect the entire Empire. That would, of course, require a business partner with significant shipbuilding facilities who is not otherwise occupied with military production, which the North lacks."

Crown Princess Evelanis's eyes widened, and then her face lit up. "A new loyal Imperial province is at your disposal, Consul! I can assure you our shipyards surpass any other in the Southern Realms, and we've recently . . . *cleared up* their schedule, so we could offer their services to you immediately! For a fair price, of course."

Consul Aemilia turned to Aedile Hortensus. "We would also like to procure products to sell back to the queen of the Dobhar's people from all across the Empire and the Southern Realms."

Aedile Hortensus leaned back and gave her a smile. "Well, doesn't that sound interesting? I do believe you have us all wrapped around your finger at this point, Miss Consul. Why don't you tell us what you have in mind?"

Consul Aemilia's smile only grew.

And so, the leaders of the Empire decided on some significant reforms that would bind the entire Empire closer together than it had ever been. And at the center of it all was one Consul Aemilia Hibera, who became famed as the closest friend of Her Majesty Seero within the Empire.

Though, before all this began in earnest, she had one final matter to attend to . . .

Consul Aemilia stood in Emperor Lucius's office. The Emperor sat at his desk, with Princess Caecila standing by his side. Consul Aemilia frowned and crossed her arms.

"Your Majesty, are you truly certain about this?"

Emperor Lucius nodded. "I am. You have done great things on behalf of the Empire, Consul. Thanks to you and the relationship you have forged with Her Majesty Seero, the Northern Empire has gone from a dying shell of a nation to the very heart of the Empire once again. You are the one who has forged for us a bright future. I feel it is only natural you are the one to ensure it remains so."

Consul Aemilia let out a sigh. "I . . . would be happy for your praise. But I must admit that I happen to be a vindictive person, as your daughter-in-law there can very much attest to. If we remain at a distance, then I can set my feelings aside for the greater work. But if I am given this role, where I will work closely with my former fiancé for the foreseeable future, understand that I will not be able to hold back. Nor would I intend to. Is that something you can accept?"

To her surprise, Emperor Lucius nodded without hesitation. "It is. Whatever else you intend, you intend to see the job done, and done well, do you not?"

Consul Aemilia hesitated before slowly nodding. "I do."

Emperor Lucius shrugged. "Then it is necessary. I have let this go too far as it is. A firm hand will be required to resolve it."

Consul Aemilia turned to Princess Caecila. "And you? You understand what you will witness should this occur? What you will go through yourself?"

Princess Caecila held her gaze, her expression firm. "I've told you already, haven't I? Once upon a time, you and I nearly brought the Empire to its knees with our fight. Now, I will do what I must to preserve it." Her face then softened, and she gave a smile. "Besides, I believe I have come to trust you, Consul."

Consul Aemilia rolled her eyes. "See that right there? That's the sort of naive, overly innocent routine we will need to work out of you. An Empress cannot leave herself so vulnerable that easily." She stopped then let out a sigh as Princess Caecila just continued to smile at her. "You are both resolved, then?"

The Emperor and the princess both nodded. "We are."

Consul Aemilia took a deep breath then allowed herself to start smiling. "Well, then, let's get started, shall we? Bring him in and let us address the crown prince."

Prince Octavianus Numerius Electus, son of Emperor Lucius and husband of Princess Caecila, burst into the courtyard with a bundle of flowers.

"Caecila, I'm home!"

Princess Caecila was currently sitting at an outdoor table with a cup of tea in her hand. Her face lit up and broke out into a smile. "Octavianus!"

He rushed forward and pulled her up into his arms, giving her a kiss. "Ah, I've missed you! The stories I must share . . ."

Then he heard someone clear their throat. "I see you are as . . . passionate as ever, Prince Octavianus."

Octavianus pulled Princess Caecila tight against his chest as he dropped the flowers and drew his sword, pointing it toward the speaker. Sitting on the other side of the table and calmly sipping her tea was the woman he hated most.

"Aemilia. How dare you break your exile? Speak honestly and perhaps I will content myself with merely sending you back. Why are you here, and what have you done with Caecila?"

Aemilia kept sipping her tea, raising an eyebrow. "My exile ended a while ago. It's Consul Aemilia now, by the way. You appear to be behind on the news."

Octavianus narrowed his eyes, but then Princess Caecila grabbed his hand and pushed his sword down. "Stop that, Octavianus! I'm fine. Consul Aemilia and I are no longer enemies."

Octavianus furrowed his brow. "What? I find that hard to believe."

Princess Caecila looked up at him from below. "Do you believe me?"

Octavianus's heart and face melted. "Of course I do, my love."

Consul Aemilia restrained herself to just a soft retching sound. Octavianus sheathed his sword but continued to glare at her.

"Well, if you are not here to torment Caecila, then why are you here?"

Consul Aemilia raised her eyebrow. ". . . You understand what it means that I'm a consul now, correct? Actually, have you heard of *anything* that's gone on in Turannia or the Empire over the past year? *Please* tell me you've at least heard of the queen of the Dobhar? Her Majesty Seero? The savior of Turannia, Utrad, the entire Empire, and all of Aelea itself? The Empress of the Dungeons? An *actual Domides* with an *Aesdes* at her command?"

Prince Octavianus . . . tilted his head. "Um, no? Should I have? To be honest, I don't think about any women but Caecila."

Consul Aemilia gave an exasperated sigh while Princess Caecila covered her face with both hands. "Honestly, I think I need to thank you, Caecila. I do not think I could be as gracious as you, were it I who was married to this . . . *romantic*, shall we say. I do not know what I would have done had my engagement proceeded as originally planned."

Prince Octavianus glanced back and forth. Princess Caecila slowly began to speak. "Octavianus, dear, I love you too, but . . . we have a lot to work on."

Consul Aemilia narrowed her eyes. "Indeed. Princess Caecila here has been informing me of the state of the court in your absence, and . . . excuse me, but I'm going to speak frankly. By the Aesdes, are you mad?! You nearly destroyed the Empire, Crown Prince! I understand now why you decided to break your engagement with me, but by the Aesdes, the foolhardy way you did so utterly gutted the Northern Court for years to come!

"You then left your wife, who had no education regarding high society whatsoever, alone to face the court without a single word of warning?! Do you understand the position you put us all in?! I know I played a big role in that, and honestly, I am sorry for what I did to you, Caecila, but, Octavianus, it was your job as prince to follow up!"

Consul Aemilia took a deep breath and sat back in her chair, massaging her brow. Princess Caecila . . . glanced away from her beloved, unable to meet his eyes. Prince Octavianus was left glancing between the two in silence. Consul Aemilia sighed once more.

"Well, I suppose you were never trained to be a crown prince, so perhaps I speak too harshly. We could hardly expect a simple soldier to know how to act in the court. And that, Crown Prince, is what we are here to address."

Her eyes turned sharp. "Prince Octavianus Numerius Electus, son of Emperor Lucius Numerius Electus, heir to the throne of the Elteni Empire."

Prince Octavianus's military training took over where his conscious mind failed, and he subconsciously stood at attention in response to Consul Aemilia's address.

"Emperor Lucius has tasked me with reviewing the state of your education. And I am not going to rebuild the empire that was preserved by no less than the personal efforts of an *Aesdes* only to see it driven into the ground not by malice but by sheer ignorance. Therefore, I will have you reeducated from the ground up until you are fit to become Emperor."

Prince Octavianus scowled and opened his mouth, but Consul Aemilia cut him off and pointed at Princess Caecila.

"Your wife, Princess Caecila, has spared no effort to educate herself and hold this Empire together with what little she had to work with. It is time you do the same. You will not leave the entire burden to your beloved, now will you?"

Prince Octavianus glared at her but held his tongue. He sighed as he looked back at Princess Caecila and saw her troubled face.

"D-Don't worry, Octavianus! I'll be joining you, so we can study together."

A slight smile broke through his face. He turned back to Consul Aemilia with his head held high. "So be it. I'll face your studies head-on. As long as I have Caecila at my side, I can take anything you throw at me."

Consul Aemilia simply smiled. "Good. You will need that resolve."

Prince Octavianus's smile dropped. "Hm?"

Consul Aemilia's face curled into a sneer. "Be grateful, Prince. I have arranged for only the most qualified and capable tutor there is. You shall be reeducated by none other than my father, the former Consul Hiberius. The most excellent, most demanding, most strict, most harsh, and most brutal tutor I know. He looks forward to molding you into a respectable Emperor. No matter what pain he must put you through to do so."

Prince Octavianus's face fell. A moment later, he grabbed Princess Caecila and ran. "Come, Caecila! We can escape!"

But he tripped and fell. Turning around to look, his eyes widened. Princess Caecila had created a chain of Light Magic and wrapped it around his legs. She looked down with a pained expression. "I'm sorry, my love. But . . . it's for our own good."

Prince Octavianus's face twisted in despair. Consul Aemilia lifted her hand next to her head and began to cackle. "That's a wonderful expression you have there, my former fiancé! I must admit, I will enjoy this! Ahahahahaha!"

And so, the woman once derided as the villainess had her revenge, and the future of both the Elteni Empire and the line of Velus was secured for generations to come.

About the Author

Icalos is a lifelong fan of sci-fi, fantasy, and video games, and the author of the Terminate the Other World! and Bee Dungeon series, which were originally released on Royal Road. To learn more, visit his website at icalosbooks.com.

www.ingramcontent.com/pod-product-compliance
Lightning Source LLC
Jackson TN
JSHW020819030325
79971JS00002B/2

* 9 7 8 1 0 3 9 4 8 9 8 5 1 *